THE FIRE

CONCERTO

THE FIRE

CONCERTO

SARAH

LANDENWICH

**UNION
SQUARE
& CO.**

NEW YORK

UNION
SQUARE
& CO.

NEW YORK

ISBN 978-1-4549-5682-2
ISBN 978-1-4549-5684-6 (paperback)
ISBN 978-1-4549-5683-9 (e-book)

For information about custom editions, special sales, and premium purchases,
please contact specialsales@unionsquareandco.com.

Printed in the United States of America

2 4 6 8 10 9 7 5 3 1

unionsquareandco.com

Cover design by Jared Oriel
Cover art: Arcangel Images: © Natalia Ganelin (piano), © Victoria Hunter
(matches); Shutterstock.com: Remigiusz Góra (back cover)
Interior design by Rich Hazelton

For JSW, who made it possible, in so many ways.
And for CLW, who made me brave.

Principal Characters

Clara Bishop
Julián Sanchez, manager of The Andromeda Club
Ruth and Phillip Bishop, Clara's parents
Madame (Zofia Mikorska), Clara's piano teacher
Jozef Zamoyski, Madame's teacher at the Warsaw Conservatory and Starza's former pupil
Anthony (Tony) Park, Clara's childhood rival
Eleonora Konopnicka, music historian and expert on Constantia Pleyel
Tomasz Górski, director of the Starza Museum

Starza Family and Associates

Aleksander Starza, the composer
Marianna Starza, Aleksander's sister, business manager, and amanuensis
Christoph Windscheid, Starza's publisher
Marek Poldowski, Starza's butler
Piotr Biliński, artist who painted Starza's portrait

Pleyel Family and Associates

Constantia Baranowska Pleyel, the pianist
Olivier Pleyel, an opera singer, Constantia's husband
    Stanisław "Stani" Pleyel, the couple's son
    Helene Pleyel, the couple's daughter
Valeska Holland, Warsaw socialite and Constantia's friend
Nadia Baranowska Brzezińska, Constantia's sister
Amelia Jankowska, Nadia's granddaughter
Mr. Narbut, Nadia's lawyer
Mrs. Andrysiak, Helene Pleyel's paternal great-aunt

PART I

Chapter 1

Austin, Texas
1997

THE INVITATION ARRIVED ON A FRIDAY, care of The Andromeda Club. Concealed as it was inside a plain No. 10 envelope with a stamp of Benjamin Franklin squarely affixed to the right-hand corner, it did not immediately cause alarm. The manager of The Andromeda held it out to Clara Bishop, who was mixing a Manhattan behind the bar.

"Your mom sent you something," Julián said.

Clara glanced at the proffered envelope, registering her mother's looping script, the broad *C* of Clara's name written in a hurried flourish. In the light shining down on the bar she could see the outline of a smaller envelope inside, the muted pink of a magenta Post-it stuck to its front.

"Put it in the back, will you? I'll get it later." It was 4:55. In ten minutes every table would be full with the happy hour rush. Clara enjoyed the Friday shift, when the patrons of the bar were buoyant with the prospect of the weekend. She did not want to dampen the night with mail from her mother.

Julián frowned. Short and stocky, with an endearing layer of pudge around his middle, he had a movie-star smile that lent his boyish looks a dashing quality. Just now, however, he regarded her with a look of patient disapproval that made her think he would have made an excellent elementary school teacher.

"Your mom knows Texas provides home mail delivery, right?"

Clara tipped a bottle of vermouth into a mixing glass. "She thinks it's more reliable to send things here."

"I wonder who led her to believe that."

Two years ago, Clara told her mother that a package Ruth mailed to Clara's house—a book entitled *You Can Be Happy No Matter What*—never arrived. She used the same excuse later that year for a newspaper article about a tennis star who recovered from third-degree burns and went on to win the Illinois state championship. Ruth had declared the postal system of Texas "primitive." Now all mail from Chicago was diverted through The Andromeda Club.

"You would understand if you met her," Clara said, and plucked the envelope from Julián's outstretched hand. She folded it in half, shaking the smaller envelope down to one side so she could shove it in her back pocket. It was probably an invitation to a cousin's wedding or baby shower, one of the endless family events Clara always declined to attend. She twisted a curl of orange peel onto the rim of a coupe glass and walked the Manhattan to a woman at the end of the bar.

"Up, light on the vermouth."

"Thanks." The woman looked up from a pager, her eyes skimming the scars on Clara's cheek. Clara noticed the look but smiled anyway.

"Let me know if you'd like anything else," she said, and turned away.

The door to the bar opened. A dozen serious-faced young people walked in, trailed by a cherubic man in his sixties wearing a *Dark Side of the Moon* T-shirt—Art Druckerman's graduate Nietzsche seminar from the university. They were followed by Barb and Lisa, who lived in the apartment over the bar, and a group of front-desk workers from the Driskill Hotel still in their slacks and starched shirts. Soon the bar hummed with the energy of Friday night.

The Andromeda Club was not a fashionable place. It was old but not historic; dated but not yet vintage. It possessed nonetheless a kind of timeless class that had kept it steadily beloved for over twenty years.

It was cool and dim and faultlessly clean. The cocktails were classic and strong. Smoking was not permitted, as the owner was asthmatic. The brick walls were lined with photos of Austin from the 1800s—the Driskill Hotel, the Millett Opera House, Congress Avenue when it was still a broad drag of rutted dirt. In the afternoons when Clara arrived for her shift and sunlight filtered through the picture windows that faced Fourth Street, the black leather of the booths appeared faded, the blond planks of the floor dull and scuffed. But at night, the room glowed. The ceiling was painted like the night sky, with the blush disc of Andromeda swirling above the bar. Parlor lamps with emerald tassel shades cast each table in tranquil luminescence. Blue pendant lights hung from the ceiling at staggered lengths like stars dripping from the sky. Clara liked the shabby elegance of it, which was comforting and reliable in the way of a very old, very finely made wool sweater. She liked the owner, Dave, a former astronomy professor at UT who ran the club at a loss and gave every employee five hundred dollars at Christmas. And she liked the regulars, mostly artist types and academics who preferred a smaller, quieter place to the college bars and honky-tonks down the street. Saturdays, the stage in the back of the room hosted live bands. Sundays, Dave showed classic films on a reel-to-reel projector. A piano player, Jerry, performed live from the baby grand in the corner three nights a week, mainly jazz standards and arrangements of pop songs, though every now and then Clara heard something less familiar that she guessed were Jerry's own compositions. She never asked. She didn't want him to know how closely she listened.

"Look who's back for another chance at your heart." Julián inclined his head toward the entrance, where a man in black pants and a Ramones T-shirt was holding the door for a group of white-haired women leaving the bar. The man caught Clara's eye and smiled. She smiled back, careful to make it friendly and nothing more.

"Tonight's the night." Julián waved over Clara's head. "I'm gonna ply him with drinks and convince him to do it."

"Don't." Clara mixed gin and tonics for Barb and Lisa as the man made his way through the room and took his usual seat beside the server window.

"You go," Julián said, nudging her in the ribs.

"He's on your side," Clara whispered.

"Not anymore." Julián slid a martini onto a tray and breezed past her. "Who am I to stand in the way of a budding romance?"

Clara jabbed him in the love handle as he went by. On the piano, Jerry had launched into a Ray Charles set. She heard him fumble a few notes of "Come Back, Baby," searching for the right melody. It's an F, Clara thought. Then a G-flat.

"Hey, Luke." She turned to the man and flipped a coaster onto the bar. "What can I get for you?"

He was around thirty, like Clara, and golden and athletic in a wholesome sort of way that contrasted pleasantly with his band T-shirts and black Dickies. They met two months ago when he came to The Andromeda for a jazz guitar performance that was so poorly attended, Clara and Luke were the only audience. Since then, he'd shown up at the bar twice a week. She knew from the small talk they'd exchanged that he ran five miles every morning and was a sound tech at The Continental Club. She also knew that the Jim Beams he ordered were half the price anywhere down Fourth Street.

"The usual," Luke said. He smiled, the faint lines around his eyes creasing, and she noticed for the first time that one of his front teeth was slightly chipped. It was the kind of face you could imagine smiling at you in the morning when you woke up. The thought made something in her chest ache.

She pulled the bottle of Beam from the shelf. Her own standard uniform was a black T-shirt, black Levi's, and black Chuck Taylors. If she wanted to dress up, she wore black Ariat boots. Apart from her scars, which distinguished her in a different kind of way, her appearance was unremarkable. She was pale and tall (gangly, her mother liked to say), with long legs and bony arms. Her eyes were brown and wide, and her hair was a nondescript ash blonde she wore in a high ponytail, with blunt bangs she cut herself. Sometimes she wondered if it was this plainness that interested Luke—something about her simple clothes and makeup-less face that announced that she was like him: alternative, underground, into music. In fact, none of this was true. She had spent her childhood in satin and patent leather. T-shirts and jeans were a repudiation of a stilted youth that had been no real youth at all. But she knew the ensemble would not suit her much longer before she became the oldest cliché—the middle-aged woman who couldn't grow up.

Next to Luke, an older man in a tweed jacket eyed her while he sipped his scotch, trying to decide what was wrong with her face.

"How's business?" Luke asked. He didn't notice the man, or pretended not to. The fact that he never noticed is what convinced Clara it was an act.

"Pretty busy. Friday night, you know. You?"

"A pipe burst at the venue this morning. All tonight's shows got canceled. I haven't been off on a Friday in a year." He scratched the side of his neck, and Clara tensed, sensing what was coming.

"I'm headed to the Elephant Room later on," he said. "There's a local trio playing that'll blow you away. You should come when you get off."

This was the moment she could nudge things along—tell him she'd love to but couldn't, or suggest they get a drink some other time. She was saved by a crowd of twenty-somethings, who burst through the door in a cloud of noise that made everyone in the room look up.

"Sounds fun," she said. "But I'm closing tonight. Have a good time."

The twenty-somethings swarmed the bar and ordered beers and whiskey-Cokes, then stood around the tables waiting for a rockabilly show to start at a bar down the block. While Clara poured a round of pints from the tap, she saw a pretty brunette in a plaid miniskirt and Radiohead T-shirt slide onto the stool next to Luke and stick out her hand. By the time Clara went over to take her order, the woman was touching Luke's elbow. He glanced up, an apology in his eyes that Clara pretended not to see.

"Could be you." Julián leaned against the bar while Clara mixed the woman's Jack and Coke.

"Could be."

"He's a nice guy."

"There are a lot of nice guys."

"Please." Julián made a face. "Throw him a bone or stop leading him on."

"I *work* here. I don't make him come and talk to me."

"No, you're just turning him into an alcoholic. Think of all the extra push-ups he has to do to burn that off."

"He's not my type."

Julian shot her a look of disdain. "Right. You two would look so weird together in your matching black pants. Just say yes!"

"Too late." Clara set the drink before the woman, then went out into the bar to gather empty glasses.

Julián groaned. "You're going to die alone, you know," he called after her.

The Nietzsche students had pushed two tables together and were circled around Druckerman arguing hotly about the existence of free will. "What does it mean to be *good*, anyway?" she heard one of them say. "Look at the last hundred years. Look at the last *thousand* years. Brutality is our nature." Clara observed the young man without turning her eyes toward him. He was thin and attractive, with intense eyes and a voice aggressively set on being right. Had anything bad happened to him to convince him of humanity's evil, or was it simply fashionable, as with so many of the graduate students she overheard at The Andromeda, to assert the obvious as if it were a thunderous revelation? Of course brutality was human nature. It was kindness that was hard. Wasn't that the whole struggle of civilization?

She picked up his empty pint glass and wiped the ring of water beneath it. She was already walking away when someone behind her called out.

"Hey! You dropped something!"

A young woman at the end of the table was holding the envelope.

"Thanks." Clara balanced her tray on one forearm and reached out her other hand, then stopped short. In the glow of the table lamp, she saw for the first time the outline of a small, dark circle through the white sleeve of the envelope—slightly textured, like a coin. A wax seal. Her chest went cold as if she had drunk a glass of ice water too fast on a hot day.

The young woman blinked at Clara through red-framed glasses. "Do you want me to put it on your tray for you?" Her eyes darted over Clara's scarred hand and up the ropey tissue of her arm.

"I've got it, thanks." Clara took the envelope and crumpled it once more into her pocket.

Back at the bar, she put the empties in the sink and filled the tub and tossed in the disinfecting tablets that made the water run blue and frothy, glad Luke and the woman in the Radiohead T-shirt were behind her so she wouldn't have to look at them. She dunked the glasses in the blue water and let her hands sink in the water too, her scars distorted and dissolving beneath the blue liquid. Barb and Lisa asked if she had seen the cartoon of Governor Bush with a Pinocchio nose that had been graffitied in the alley, and the older couple next to them ordered a second round of vodka gimlets. Clara laughed with Barb and poured the drinks, all the while thinking of the envelope that now seemed to rasp so audibly against her jeans. Though she could not comprehend what it might contain, she knew that whatever was inside would resuscitate a thousand withered memories that she did not want here in The Andromeda Club, where she could pretend that the person who sent it had never existed at all.

"Another whiskey!"

Clara looked up. One of the rockabilly guys was waving a twenty at her from down the bar. She took her time placing the clean glasses in the drying rack before pouring him another Jameson. He downed it in a single gulp, then walked unsteadily down the hall toward the restrooms. When he left, Clara noticed his date wobble on her barstool. She filled a glass of water from the tap and walked it over.

"Drink this," she said, nudging aside the young woman's half-finished whiskey. "You want some pretzels? We have some. On the house."

"No, thanks," the young woman slurred. She had bright red curls and wore a black lace dress that looked too small around the shoulders and had chafed one side of her neck. She couldn't have been more than twenty-two.

"How about a cab, then?" Clara asked.

"I'm good." The young woman pulled a pack of Marlboro Lights from her purse and put one in her mouth.

"No smoking in here." Clara pointed to a sign on the wall. "There's a patio out back."

The young woman's bottom lip stuck out in a pout. With the cigarette still clamped in her mouth, she raised her sleepy eyes and looked at Clara as if noticing her for the first time. "What happened to your face?"

In an instant, Barb reached across the woman to push the whiskey glass away. "You've had too much, missy," Barb said gruffly. "Time to go home."

Clara didn't even flinch. She was not the type of person to be cowed by thoughtless criticisms. She had a lifetime of performance to thank for that.

"No more drinks for people who insult the bartender," she said lightly, and tore the couple's tab from a notepad and set it on the bar. But she could feel everyone watching. Mostly she could feel Luke. In her peripheral vision, she had seen him become totally still.

Unembarrassed, the drunk woman swiped her Marlboros from the bar and stumbled off her stool toward the patio.

Julián returned with a tray of empty glasses, having missed the spectacle. "The paper towels are out in the women's room," he said. "Can you go fill the dispenser?"

"Gladly." Clara tipped a smile of gratitude in Barb's direction, then removed her apron and headed down the hall. The sound of the bar dampened as she pushed into the empty bathroom. The tension in her chest loosened in the quiet. She changed the paper towel roll and refilled the Dial soap, then wiped up the droplets of water that speckled the sink. In her own bathroom at home, she used only the overhead light, having unscrewed the three glaring bulbs above the vanity mirror the day she moved in. Under the forensic glow of The Andromeda's fluorescents, every peak and valley of her scars was visible, like the topography of the moon had shrunk to the map of her face. She turned her cheek to the side to examine it, then turned her face in the other direction, where the skin was smooth and perfect, an erasure of the past. A familiar, burning regret welled within her. Banishing the feeling before it could take root, she turned her back on her reflection and pulled the envelope from her pocket. She was debating whether to open it or bury it in the garbage when the door to the bathroom flung wide.

A streak of red curls blurred past, followed by the banging of the stall door. Soon Clara heard quiet retching in the toilet. She was walking toward the exit when she heard a stifled sob. Beneath the stall wall, she saw the hem of the black lace dress as the girl sank to the floor. Clara looked up at the ceiling, annoyed that she was the only one here to comfort the crying girl who had insulted her. Still, she walked back to the sink and ran water over a paper towel, then crouched down to pass it beneath the stall.

"Here you go," she said gently. "You want me to get somebody for you?"

A hand with chewed hangnails reached out and took the paper towel. "No. He doesn't care about me." The girl exhaled a ragged breath. "I'm such an idiot."

"You'll feel better tomorrow," Clara said, then regretted it, remembering how many times people had said that to her, all of them knowing it wasn't true. Sometimes you felt worse tomorrow, and the day after, and the day after that.

"You'll be okay," she corrected, and stood. "Now—how about that cab?"

At two o'clock, Clara herded the last straggling graduate students out the door, and she and Julián closed up for the night. Julián offered to give her a ride, but Clara declined. She liked to bike at night. Back at the beginning, after the fire, she thought about moving to Alaska or Finland, somewhere cold and dark. But that winter, holed away in her parents' house in Chicago, she discovered that cold could penetrate her scars. It bore into the bones of her burned arm and hand, the dead tissue expanding like a river freezing against its banks. By February, the entire right side of her body was frozen. The doctors told her it was just the nerves adjusting and the pain would eventually subside. Her mother used the mysterious symptoms as an excuse to suggest that Clara spend some time away. In the reverse act of her entire childhood, during which all Clara wanted was to get away from her parents, Ruth rustled up the idea of Austin, where the Bishops' neighbor kept a second home, and where the coldest it usually got was a film of frost on a windshield. It was a city of music, but nothing like the music Clara had devoted her life to. Guitars twanged from every bar, but never once did she hear Chopin or Rachmaninoff or even tinny Mozart in a department store elevator. Three months in, she decided to stay.

She saw the rockabilly crowd smoking cigarettes in front of a dive bar down the street, their drunken laughter audible even from a half mile away. Clara mounted her bike and headed in the opposite direction.

Luke and the woman in the Radiohead T-shirt left the bar around eleven. Clara tried not to watch as they walked out the door together, just as she'd tried not to look at the woman's flawless skin for the rest of the night while the two of them talked about the state of prog rock and their shared love of the Replacements. What was the point? She had spent years obsessing about other women's beauty. It hadn't changed anything about her own face and wouldn't ever. Years ago, when her mother was still taking her to plastic surgeons and they had both allowed themselves to believe medicine could reverse what had been done, Clara had rubbed oils and creams into her skin each night and counseled herself that in a year—then two—three—five—she would be good as new. But the oils and creams couldn't change the mottled look of her cheekbone, where the skin had been grafted from her thigh, or regrow the part of her eyebrow that had been forever singed away. Nor had they eased the stiffness in her knuckles or the hot shocks of pain that flickered across the palm of her hand. Forever into the future, her scars would be the first thing anyone saw. Luke would be no different. She could tell by the askance way he looked at her, his eye contact slightly off-center as if he were trying to prove he didn't see them. Clara had dated enough people to know that they wouldn't make it past the second date. He was the type who would want to open the baggage, talk things out, plumb her past. This was why she poured his whiskeys light.

She biked over the Congress Avenue Bridge, where the tall buildings of downtown reflected off the choppy glint of the Colorado River. Across the water it was darker, the glow of the city receding behind her. She passed The Austin Motel and Allen's Boots before turning at St. Mary's United Methodist, where the yard sign said *Come as you are.* Someone had spray-painted *K. Cobain* beneath the words. Clara pedaled past the sign into the leafy neighborhood, coasting by a row of tidy bungalows before dismounting at a chain-link gate.

Bingo, her elderly St. Bernard, was waiting at the door, tail thumping against the screen. He raised up on his stout haunches to greet her.

"Hey, big guy," Clara said, ruffling the thick fur behind his ears.

He waited at the top of the steps while she retrieved his ball from the corner of the porch swing, then bounded after it into the yard.

The house was a little bungalow with vinyl siding painted the color of a daffodil. It sat back from the road so that the shotgun yard stretched before it to the sidewalk. With its unruly landscaping and rusty porch swing, it was the type of house her parents would frown at if Clara ever allowed them to visit. She bought it seven years ago with the last money left from the sale of her Chicago condo. Despite her own initial snobbery, she had grown to like it. The yard especially. Never a gardener in her former life, she had discovered that damp earth soothed the smoldering nerves of her fingers. Loamy soil was a balm no cream or ointment had ever been. Now the yard was a wild zigzag of succulents and flowers. A bed of moss rose flowed from the porch to the front gate, and six giant blue agave plants erupted from the dirt. Like so much else in her life, she had bent around the circumstances and grown into someone different.

She sank onto the porch swing, removing the envelope from her pocket. The paper was creased and abused by now, the blue ink of her name smeared like a setting watercolor. Her parents had known she would be named Clara from the moment she was conceived. Not for Clara Schumann, as Clara used to tell the reporters who came to her concerts and competitions, but Clara from *The Nutcracker*. Her mother had been a ballet dancer, slim and strong and vain, with an artist's devotion to beauty and a lawyer's abhorrence of mistakes.

Clara tore open the envelope and withdrew the smaller one inside. The pink Post-it affixed to the front offered only the simplest of explanations. *This came for you.*

The maroon seal was loose, either from the Texas humidity or because her mother had tried to steam it open over her silver teapot. Clara slid a long, slender finger beneath the wax. It separated from the paper with a soft *cluck*.

The piece of cardstock she withdrew was thick as fabric, heavy as a quarter in her palm. There was no specific address to her as a person. No "dear." No "hello." Not even her name at the top of the invitation. Just three typed lines, after ten years of silence:

```
Final Concert of Zofia Mikorska.
Saturday, the 24th of May, at the residence.
Private. Show your invitation at the door.
```

At the bottom, scratched with the nib of one of the antique pens that had scarred the scores of Clara's Bach and Rachmaninoff and beloved Starza was a single handwritten word: *Come.*

Out in the yard, Bingo barked. He stood at the base of the oak tree, watching a pair of bats flit between the branches.

"Bingo!" Clara called. "Come!" The dog trotted toward her, his eyes yellow in the darkness.

Come. Clara knew the voice, the scrape of the pen. It was not an entreaty. It was a command.

Chapter 2

It was raining in Chicago—a cold, drenching rain that curled the petals of the flowers and bullied spring back into the ground. Clara stood on the sidewalk before Madame's giant house, glad she had remembered to bring an umbrella. The taxi ride to Hyde Park from the airport had been long, impeded by the slick streets and the steady throb of weekend dinner traffic. Clara spent the drive looking out the window at the familiar thrum of Chicago, the Alka-Seltzer she had gulped on the plane sloshing around in her empty stomach. Now, she pulled her jacket more tightly around her shoulders. Eleven years had passed since she last stood before the iron gate that surrounded this house. A lifetime had elapsed, and yet everything looked just the same.

A dark mansion in the Tudor style with a severely sloped roof and heavy brown timbering, it had always seemed to Clara like the misty manor out of a ghost story. The iron gate creaked on its hinges. Ivy smothered half the house. Most memorable to Clara, the long walkway to the broad red door was menaced on both sides by a thicket of towering rose bushes. Every Tuesday when Clara was a child, she had walked close to her mother's slacks in the very center of the brick path, terrified a thorn might prick and poison her like in *Sleeping Beauty*. Once when she was nine, she tripped over her Mary Janes and fell hands-first into their thorny arms. She left blood on the piano keys that day—a tiny, clandestine smear on the underlip of middle C. As she played, Madame's furious breath on the top of her head, she imagined some other unhappy child finding it and seeing in the dried little drop the message *Clara was here.*

Hurrying up the brick path twenty years later, Clara found the house was no less daunting. The rose bushes had grown taller. The bricks of the walkway were surrendering to moss. Upstairs, the diamond-paned windows of the second floor were dark, but from the east wing of the house where the gallery was, light blazed onto the lawn. The sight of it made her want to flee. But she did not want Madame to think she had come all this way and still been afraid. She mounted the porch steps.

A man answered the door before the bell's reverberations had finished echoing. Clara had expected him, though this particular man she had never met. There had always been a man like this, obsequious and urbane, at every performance Madame hosted. This one was about Clara's age, tall and slim, wearing a navy blazer and a starched white shirt.

"Good evening, miss." She saw his gaze dart over her scars before returning to her eyes.

"I'm here for the concert." Clara pulled the invitation from the pocket of her coat. The black polyester jacket with its chic silver belt, like the black dress she wore beneath it and the black ankle boots below, were new. It shamed her that she had bought a new outfit for the occasion, the old urge to please ticking up the back of her throat. At the mall in Austin the day before she left, she had selected a sleeveless blue shift, sapphire-colored, one that would spare no one—and most especially Madame—the damage to her burned arm and hand. She was all the way to the register when her courage failed. The one she actually bought was plain black wool, the sleeves all the way to the wrist.

The man glanced at the invitation, his eyes lingering on Madame's scrawled note at the bottom. When he handed it back to her, he smiled in a way Clara recognized—an expression friendlier now that Madame had deemed her among the chosen. "I'm Stephen," he said, and asked to take her coat.

The floor was the same black-and-white chessboard tile. The same bronze umbrella stand stood in the corner, the same red and gold tapestry on the wall behind it. A high-backed chair with green and blue peacocks embroidered on the upholstery was the sole piece of furniture. Every week when Clara was small, her mother would rise anxiously from the chair when Clara made the long trek back from the gallery. "How did it go?" she would ask, which even then Clara knew really meant "How did you *do*?" Ruth never observed the pink skin on the back of Clara's neck ("Head up! You look like a turtle!") or the pinch marks on her arms ("You move like an automaton! Loosen your limbs!") or the hot tops of her ears, stinging from the blindfold Madame cinched around her eyes while she played. Ruth never noticed, and Clara, for reasons she did not quite understand, never volunteered.

Stephen emerged from the coat closet and clasped his hands behind his back. "I'll escort you to the gallery."

Clara followed him down the long hallway, where voices were audible from the end of the corridor. Here, the marble floor was covered with a red Persian rug embroidered with animals of the hunt. Gold stags leapt over oak leaves in an endless race to death. Oil paintings lined both walls, each one familiar in its triangle of light: a portrait of a woman in a black Victorian gown; a still life of Baroque instruments in a firelit room; a mythic landscape of a dark forest, centaurs galloping into blue dusk. But for every piece of art Clara knew by heart, there were a dozen rooms of Madame's house she had never entered. Her path here had always been fixed and circumscribed: foyer, hallway, gallery, and, on the rare occasions she could not hold it, the east wing powder room. She had never seen any of the private parts of the home—not a kitchen or a bedroom or anything a hundred years close to a television. The house might as well have been a museum, filled with captured beauty but no real life.

At the end of the corridor a final portrait hung alone opposite a plain wooden chair. The composer Aleksander Starza glared from the heavy gilt frame. Seated at the piano in his Warsaw parlor, he scowled at the viewer with vehemence, chin lifted at an imperious angle. Clara had spent many hours in the chair while she waited for Madame to call

her in, contemplating the malice in Starza's hooded eyes and the smugness of his thin lips, baffled as to how such a malevolent-looking man
had composed the music that alone seemed to capture the longing of
her young life. Madame had studied under Starza's most famous pupil,
the renowned Jozef Zamoyski, at the Warsaw Conservatory before
the war. Starza was also what had yoked her to Clara, and Clara to
Madame. Clara's great-grandfather had been the composer's cousin.
Through her tutelage under Jozef Zamoyski, Madame was Starza's
pedagogical descendant; Clara held within her the composer's musical
blood. The combination was to have made her great. But there was no
time for contemplating her lineage now. Stephen was reaching for the
glass knob. With a flourish, he threw open the door as if he were ushering Clara on stage. And then she stood in the doorway to all the sorrow
and joy of her life.

The tremolo that had been building in her chest abruptly stopped
when she realized Madame was not in the room. The voices that had
seemed so loud from down the hall had come from only two people, a
man and a woman who stood around the open lid of Madame's Steinway (Clifford, Clara had named it when she was a child. The red finish on the rosewood reminded her of the big red dog in the picture
books). The pair fell silent as Clara entered the room. Her palms began
to sweat. She had been expecting a gallery full of people. This had foretold plenty of awkward interactions, but she had counted on being able
to blend into the crowd. Instead, a row of only five white folding chairs
stretched in a diagonal line in the center of the room.

"A glass of champagne, Miss Bishop?" Stephen had walked to a
gold-leafed bar cart, his hand stretched toward a bottle cooling in a
leather ice bucket.

"Please," Clara said, and tried to smile.

The gallery was exactly as she remembered. Empty of furniture,
with cloudy skylights in the vaulted ceiling and a herringbone floor that
shone in the lights of the chandeliers, it had the feel of an abandoned

ballroom. On the far wall, Madame's instrument collection was encased behind glass, backlit and humidity-controlled, a mausoleum of muted sound. The two pianos stood in front by the giant bay window, the black Bösendorfer facing the Steinway, keys bared at one another like the teeth of fighting animals. At the sight of them, a memory crowded in on her with pummeling swiftness. She saw herself at the red Steinway playing Starza's *Liberty* Polonaise, feverishly trying to keep up while Madame tromped around the parquet in her wooden-soled mules, shouting at Clara over the revolution of music. *His homeland is gone, his father is dead. I WANT to FEEL his RAGE!*

"Veuve Clicquot," Stephen said, handing her a bubbling flute.

Clara took the glass, wishing it were something stronger, and headed for the instrument case so she would not have to talk to the pair around the pianos. One of them could have been the violinist Alan Feldman, though the last she had seen him was backstage at the Berlin Philharmonic the year she was nineteen. The other, a stately woman of about fifty in an emerald evening gown, was unfamiliar.

The first item in the display case was a photograph of Madame—the only photo ever to grace an album cover or concert advertisement. Madame was famously private. No photos. No interviews. Only music. *Your performance should be your voice!* she would snipe every time Clara sat for an interview with the press. *Only the weak need the crutch of flattery!* The picture was from the 1948 Starza Competition, hosted that year in London while Warsaw reconstituted itself after the War. Madame was an unknown Polish refugee who had been in the United States barely two years, but nothing in the photo belied a life upended. She had played Starza's Concerto No. 3 in E Minor, the so-called *Fire Concerto*, named after the tempo marking of its explosive first movement, *Allegro con fuoco*. At the time of the photo, Madame had not yet been announced the winner of the competition, but it was clear in the glow of her pale cheeks that she knew she had won. Her hand rested on the edge of the piano, eyes flown open in triumph like a huntress throttling her killed dinner. Her red silk gown rippled in the light, the cap sleeve of her right arm turned up from one of her wild flourishes at the piano—the ones Clara imagined as she lay in her bedroom as a child and listened to the recording of that very performance: Starza's *Fire Concerto* hurtling toward a great, wondrous roar. As Madame told her, it was a sound that came not from strength of hand but from a fearless soul. A type of soul Clara did not have.

She stepped past the photo, anxious not to be caught staring when Madame entered the room, and walked by a case of stringed instruments, where a glossy violin with a scratch across its lower bout stood prominently in front, its wood gleaming like the flank of a chestnut horse. Next were the gems of Madame's manuscript collection: an unpublished exercise for the fourth finger by Chopin and an early draft of a sonata by Fanny Mendelssohn Hensel. Clara paused before a new addition—a yellowed score propped on a wooden music stand. Unlike the others, it was not an original manuscript but a print edition, though clearly very old. So engrossed was she in straining to recall the piece that she did not notice the door to the gallery open once again. She registered the long strides echoing across the wood only when the footfalls were right behind her.

"Clara Bishop," a voice said. "At long last."

Startled, she turned from the case and saw a face from childhood grown into a man's. He was taller than she remembered, and broad-shouldered where once he had been thin. His jaw had squared; his slouch was gone. A silver Rolex gleamed beneath the tailored sleeve of his black jacket. Only his hands were the same: lithe and large—so much larger, unfairly so, than Clara's.

"Tony Park." She forced her mouth to smile, acutely aware of the brightness of the chandeliers on her scarred cheek.

"I was wondering if you would be here," he said. She noticed that his eyes refused to cross the midline of her body to take in the right side of her face or her burned hand. "Where have you been hiding?"

She realized she was clasping her hand into a fist and released it. "I live in Austin now."

"Texas?" He laughed, a mixture of sarcasm and amusement that caused an old animosity to rise in Clara's chest. "The last time I saw you, you were complaining about your five-hundred-dollar stilettos," he said. "It's hard to imagine you in cowboy boots."

A memory of those stilettos on the floor of a hotel room in Brussels cost her a momentary blush, but Tony did not appear to notice.

"Imagine it," she said, with a levity she did not feel.

"Are you teaching at UT, then?" he asked.

The prospect of admitting to Tony Park that she was not a pianist or a professor but a bartender barely scraping by made her posture soften. To deflect from the pain of the truth, she reached for a deeper one that she knew would end the conversation. "No. I don't play anymore."

Tony's smile faltered. For an excruciating moment she felt his gaze roam into the past, over the person she had once been and would never be again. Then he settled back on her eyes. "I'm sorry to hear that."

Clara stood up straighter. "My mom told me you were teaching at Juilliard," she said to change the subject.

"Northwestern, now." He crossed his arms over his pressed shirt, the Rolex glinting in the light of the chandeliers. "My mom died. I decided to move back for my dad."

Clara recalled the Parks—a worried-looking Korean woman with severe black bangs; a kindly father whose square glasses reflected the stage light shining into the front row, where they always sat. Unlike Tony, they had made a point to compliment her playing after every performance.

"I'm sorry. Please tell your father I said hello."

They both looked up as the gallery door swung open. Stephen walked in, followed by a boy of no more than ten who wore a white tuxedo that made him look like he was going to a First Communion.

The boy's eyes settled dully on each person in the room, then he slouched to the wooden chairs and dropped into the farthest seat.

"That's Jean-Luc Girard," Tony said. "Madame's latest prodigy. I saw him play in Aspen last summer. He's phenomenal."

Clara didn't know who Jean-Luc Girard was, and she also did not care. "What do you think this is all about?" She gestured to the single row of chairs. "I assumed it would be a larger crowd."

Tony looked over his shoulder at the man and woman standing around the pianos. "Maybe Madame finally burned bridges with everyone she knew," he said. "I came mostly out of curiosity, to tell you the truth. Aside from a letter she sent me last year, I haven't heard from her since she fired me."

Clara recalled clearly the night in reference. Madame had always entered Clara and Tony in the same competitions, sometimes with the same repertoire. Backstage after each performance, she would critique them in front of each other. Clara's Prokofiev was too timid compared to Tony's daring; Tony's Debussy too aggressive beside Clara's whimsy. One could not triumph except at the other's expense. The year Clara was sixteen, she won the Chicago Concerto Competition after years of placing runner-up to Tony. When Madame lined them up for their usual assessment, she berated Tony's performance. *Your fingers moved, and your heart was dead. No one in this theater could bring themselves to listen, it was so dull to behold.* Normally he and Clara stared straight ahead like sentries at a door. This time Tony lifted his eyes. His cheeks were still soft like a boy's though he was nineteen, his black hair parted severely to one side and swooped back like Ronald Reagan's. *How would you know what would move anybody?* he said. *You've never felt anything in your life.*

"Anyway," Tony shrugged. "That looks like Alan Feldman over there." He nodded toward the man by the Steinway. "He studied with Madame in the sixties before switching to violin. The woman is Gretchen Vendermeer, the music historian. She was a student back when Madame taught at Juilliard. I guess it's all former students."

The door to the gallery opened again. This time, instead of ushering the guest through, Stephen seemed to lean on the doorknob for balance. A man in a soaked gray trench coat strode in, rolling a suitcase across the glossy parquet. One of the wheels was broken, and the bag limped after him like a wounded animal as he walked to the front of the room, wet shoes squeaking. The man did not acknowledge the couple around the pianos as he stopped before the red Steinway, picked up the dripping bag, and laid it on the piano bench. The entire room drew in a horrified gasp.

Stephen rushed forward, hand out. "No! No, no, no, no, no, no!" He lunged for the bag.

"Careful!" The man snatched the suitcase from Stephen's grasp and set it gently on the floor.

Stephen clasped his hands together as if in fervent prayer. "Allow me to get you a towel." He hurried from the room. Clara peered after him, wondering what secret chamber of this house held anything as quotidian as a towel.

The man removed his raincoat in a cascade of droplets, then draped it over the handle of the suitcase. Beneath it he wore a gray suit the same dun color as the coat, with a cheerless pink bowtie that emphasized his pallor.

"Good evening." He looked over the rims of his steaming glasses. "Why don't you take your seats," he said to no one in particular.

"Are you the first act?" Feldman asked, chuckling.

The man in gray did not smile. "Please just take a seat so we can begin."

Clara took some pleasure in the peevish look on Feldman's face. She imagined he had not been spoken to that way since the last time he saw Madame.

Clara and Tony followed the rest of the group to the row of wooden chairs. Presently, Stephen rushed through the door with two thick white bath towels and began blotting the piano bench, a look of dismay on his face. The man in gray turned to look at him.

"I'm afraid this is confidential."

Stephen's mouth opened as if to object, then, with a final glance at the dripping suitcase, he stalked from the room.

The man removed a leather portfolio from the side compartment of the suitcase and held it to his chest with both palms like a chorister would hold his music. "Let me see who's here," he said. "Gretchen Vendermeer."

"That's me." The woman in the green dress lifted a finger.

"Jean-Luc Girard?"

"Here." The boy raised his hand, then slouched back in his seat.

"Alan Feldman?"

"Present."

"Anthony Park?

"Here."

"Clara Bishop?"

Clara raised her hand.

The man marked something on the page with a silver pen, then closed the portfolio, a vanishing vacuum of air.

"My name is Vincent Borthram," he said. "I'm an attorney representing Ms. Mikorska. She asked me to come here tonight to talk to you about the bequests she has left to you in her will and your responsibilities forthwith. However—" He looked up with the first sign of strain he'd shown since walking through the door, a micro flinch that revealed in its hesitation a man of great dignity, if not great feeling. "It has come to my attention that perhaps the room is unaware . . ." He trailed off briefly, then, leaning forward as if with the effort of the words, plunged on.

"I regret to inform you that Ms. Mikorska has passed away."

Chapter 3

EVERYONE IN THE ROOM TURNED to look at one another except for Clara, who felt immobilized in her chair. The overhead lights seemed suddenly bright, the rain on the skylights distractingly loud. Madame was dead.

"Was she sick?" Tony turned to Clara.

"I don't know," Clara said. Her voice was hoarse, and she cleared her throat. "I thought we were coming to watch her perform."

"When did this happen?" Feldman demanded. "No one's reported it in the papers."

Mr. Borthram blinked. "I'm unaware of the details. I was only informed yesterday myself."

Another murmur swept down the row.

"What about him?" Feldman flung his arm toward the closed door from which Stephen had exited. "Does he know anything?"

"Evidently not." Mr. Borthram removed his glasses. Without them, he looked tired. "I told him when I arrived."

Clara's eyes went from the open Steinway to the champagne bottle on the bar cart. The room was prepped for a concert.

"How did she die?" Clara asked.

"And when?" Tony added.

Mr. Borthram spoke patiently. "I was informed of Ms. Mikorska's death by a hospital in Vienna. They won't provide specifics until they receive a formal request for a death certificate, which I faxed this afternoon. All they would tell me was that she had instructed the staff to call me upon her death."

"But don't you see?" Vendermeer exclaimed. "We were told to come here weeks ago. And now you're telling us she was in Vienna. Dying!"

Borthram pinched his lips together. On a less severe face, it might have passed for a look of apology. "As I said, I received the call yesterday. I was told the beneficiaries were gathering here this evening. Until I arrived, I assumed you had already been informed."

"Beneficiaries?" Vendermeer leaned forward in her chair. "You mean she left us something?"

"Yes." Borthram held eyes with the group as he donned his glasses and picked up the leather portfolio once again. Everyone shifted in their seats.

"'I, Zofia Helena Mikorska,'" he read, "'being of sound mind and memory, do hereby make, publish, and declare this to be my last will and testament. To Jean-Luc Girard—'" Borthram glanced at the boy. "You are bequeathed the Steinway Model B piano, dated 1972."

The boy's face lit up. For the first time since walking in the room, he looked like a child. Clara glanced at the suitcase, dread ticking inside her. She wanted to run now more than she had while standing at the gate outside the house. Whatever Madame had decided to give her, Clara did not want it.

"To Alan Feldman," Borthram continued, "Ms. Mikorska would like you to have her collection of stringed instruments, including a Mittenwald viola circa 1820, a Paul Bailly violin circa 1875, a Jacques-Pierre Thibout violin dated 1825, and a Gaurneri del Gesù violin dated 1736."

Gretchen Vendermeer emitted a cry. Mr. Borthram looked up, his woolly eyebrows lifting in alarm.

"Madame had a *Guarneri*?" Vendermeer looked around the room incredulously. "That's worth over a million dollars!"

No one replied. They were all staring at the instrument case on the wall, where the chestnut violin gleamed behind the glass.

"That's been there forever," Tony said, looking at Clara for affirmation. "I remember it from when I was a kid. I never knew it was a Guarneri."

Clara nodded. The violin had stood in that exact case, in that exact position, from the first time she had come to Madame's house. Clara had always noticed it, standing as it did in front of all the others. She had never imagined it was one of the finest violins ever made.

Vendermeer had fixed her gaze on Feldman, who had walked over to the instrument case and was now peering at the violin with his forehead pressed against the glass. "Alan, did you know about this?"

Feldman stood awestruck before the instrument, the smugness on his face replaced with the light of reverence. "Not a clue," he said faintly.

Borthram waited for him to return to his seat before continuing.

"To Gretchen Vendermeer—" Borthram looked up. "Ms. Mikorska has left you the remaining items in her collection of historical instruments."

Vendermeer's mouth, previously in a scowl, dropped into an astounded *O*. She turned to the glass case, delight dawning across her face.

"To Mr. Anthony Park, Ms. Mikorska bequeaths to you the contents of her personal library, including all musical scores in her possession; the rights to her own written scholarly works, both published and unpublished; as well as her collection of musical manuscripts."

Tony looked bewildered. He turned to Clara with a look that said, *Great, I guess?*

"And finally, to Ms. Clara Bishop." Borthram unzipped the suitcase and withdrew a wooden box like the kind that might hold a high-end bottle of scotch. The wood was dark and dull, like the hull of an old boat. Plain but expensive looking, with no adornments, it conveyed a quality of tired luxury.

Borthram's dress shoes slurped the floor as he walked it forward and stopped before Clara's chair. "An antique metronome, in its accompanying case." Mr. Borthram bent at the waist, passing her the box. Its heaviness as she accepted it into her hands made Clara sink back against her chair. It was made of mahogany or some other dark wood, with a reddish stain that had worn to a matte finish. The sides were still warm from Borthram's hands, but the weight of it filled her with cold dread.

"Now!" Mr. Borthram turned briskly on his heel, causing everyone to look up. "Ms. Mikorska's will is explicit in regard to your steward-ship of these bequests. She outlines how she wishes them to be treated and has added a note in her own words detailing their use and care."

Borthram pulled a cream-colored envelope from the pocket of the portfolio.

"'Dear pupils,'" he began.

> "'As an orphan who was also the child of an orphan, I have lived my life without the bonds of family. One finds oneself nonetheless surrounded by a nexus of individuals who become, by necessity or chance, the natural offshoots of one's life. I have no flesh and blood descendants, but you gathered here are yet a kind of legacy, my pedagogical and artistic progeny. I have chosen you particularly to care for the most valued objects in my possession. Each of you should understand why you were selected for the bequest you received. If you do not, then I was wrong about you, and I have only to trust that you will not violate the terms of your limited custody of this object before finding a better trustee. Note that I say "limited custody," as this bequest is not a gift or an inheritance, and it certainly does not belong to you. You are its temporary caretaker, charged with shepherding it to the next generation in the same condition in which it has found you. Instruments have a soul unto themselves, and if you do not know or

understand what I mean by this you are not who I thought you to be. I entrust you with the safeguarding of these treasures, which you must keep and maintain until such time as you find another worthy soul to give them to.

Yours,

Mme.'"

Borthram slid the note back into the envelope, a sibilant sound like a breath. It seemed to Clara to signal the dying exhalation of Madame expiring in Vienna.

"A copy of the will and this note will be furnished to you, and additional copies will be provided to your attorneys upon request. Once again, I offer my condolences. I only had the pleasure of meeting Ms. Mikorska once, but I found her to be—" Borthram paused. "She made a distinct impression," he finally said. He nodded as if to indicate his duty had been satisfactorily discharged, then slung his raincoat over his arm and walked toward the door, the broken suitcase lurching behind him.

"What about the other piano?" Vendermeer called after him. "And the paintings? The house? Who gets all of those?"

Borthram turned, the suitcase scuttling to a stop. "Ms. Mikorska requested that the bulk of her estate be liquidated. The proceeds will be donated to orphanages throughout the United States and Poland." He nodded again, then walked out into the dim hallway, closing the door behind him.

Tony raised an eyebrow. "I wouldn't have taken her for the philanthropic sort."

Clara shook her head. "I always assumed she hated children."

They turned to each other, and, seeing their stunned feelings reflected in the other's face, laughed. It was a real laugh, devoid of artifice and pretension, and Clara suddenly remembered him wading after her into the fountain at the Parc du Cinquantenaire in Brussels, both of them drenched and laughing as they tried to retrieve her shoes from the spumes of frothing water. Her face warmed for the second time that evening.

"At least no one got the tuning wrench," Tony said.

"Ugh." Clara clutched the back of her wrist, remembering the sting of the metal socket every time she missed a note. "You too?"

Tony gave her a side-eyed look. "One time she got me on the side of the head with it."

Across the room, the others were beginning to talk as well. Feldman had regained his self-importance and was once again standing before the Guarneri, rocking on his heels with his hands in his pockets like a jolly Santa Claus.

"Does anyone know where the phone is around here?" he asked of no one in particular. He turned and walked eagerly toward the door.

Jean-Luc Girard hadn't spoken since raising his hand during the roll call, but as soon as Borthram left he had risen from his chair and headed straight for the red Steinway. Now he sat at the bench playing a Clementi sonata, the toes of his white patent leather shoes barely brushing the pedals.

Gretchen Vendermeer had also risen and now walked along the instrument case admiring a display of Renaissance flutes. Only Tony and Clara remained seated.

"Aren't you going to open the box?" Tony asked.

Clara looked down at it. What was she going to do with a metronome? She hadn't played an instrument in nearly a decade.

"I don't remember her having an antique metronome," she said. "Do you?"

"Nope. She always just shouted the beat at me."

Clara laughed, relaxing. "All right," she said. "Let's see what I've got."

The box offered no discernible opening, no hinge or clasp. Clara ran her fingers along the top and sides until she found an almost imperceptible groove where the lid fit without a seam. When she pushed, it glided open with a *shhirrp*. She set the lid aside and stared down at the pointed top of a metronome.

Made of a warm, pale wood lighter and finer than that of its case, it stood nestled in the velvet lining of the box like a piece of fine jewelry. Clara picked it up and was again surprised by its heft. Larger and heavier than the Wittner metronome that had sat on her own piano, she had to hold it in both hands to keep it from slipping from her grip. She set it on the empty chair next to Tony.

It stood on three bun feet, beads of pale rose gold. The faceplate was covered with elaborate bronze casting that had darkened with age. Two angels in long gowns lifted an hourglass toward the peak of the pyramid, their feet resting on a vine of oak leaves. Clara undid the gold hook-and-eye clasp that latched the faceplate closed, feeling as she lifted it away as if she were disturbing a long-closed coffin. The brass pendulum inside was dull, but the sliding weight gleamed. Made of the same rose gold as the feet, it was engraved with the face of a roaring lion. The wooden scale behind it was carved with tempo markings from 40 to 208 beats per minute.

"Look at this." Tony reached a perfect finger to the winding key on the side of the metronome, an elliptical ring of rose gold made to look like a lion's curled tail. In the lowest curve of the ellipse were the engraved Roman numerals *LXXII*.

Clara paused, doing the math. "Seventy-two?"

"Sounds right to me," Tony said. "What do you think it means?"

"What's any of this supposed to mean?" She looked down at the metronome, which was at once beautiful and hideous. "Let's see if it works."

Gently, she released the pendulum from its notch at the top of the pyramid, then wound the lion's tail key. The beam began to clock back and forth.

Jean-Luc Girard halted the Clementi and began a Bach fugue to the new beat.

"Why'd she give it to you, do you think?" Tony asked.

Clara stilled the pendulum and looked up at him, utterly confused. "I don't know," she said. "I've never seen this before in my life."

It was almost midnight when she returned to her hotel, a Holiday Inn near Midway Airport. Staying in the city would have been expensive, and would also have necessitated a visit to her parents in Oak Park. Not that she had told them she was coming.

Clara bought two miniature bottles of Maker's Mark from the front desk and took them to her room. She placed the metronome box on the desk, the mahogany looking out of place beside the cheap veneer and grainy Holiday Inn notepad. She removed the lid, then took the metronome out and set it to seventy-two. She half expected something remarkable to happen, like a magic key had been inserted into a magical box. But the pendulum just ticked back and forth, predictable as ever.

She twisted the cap off the first bottle of bourbon and sat on the bed, watching the lion's head swing from side to side. From what she had gathered after Borthram departed, it was clear why the others had been chosen for their particular inheritance. Jean-Luc Girard, she learned from Tony, was considered to be the most technically gifted of all Madame's storied students. He was also, at the age of nine, a published composer, having written three sonatas to wide acclaim. The Steinway was a natural complement to his talents. The Guarneri violin seemed similarly destined for its future custodian. For all his off-putting egoism, Feldman was a violinist of renowned talent. As a former student of Madame's, it made sense that he would inherit the stringed instruments. Gretchen Vendermeer had left the performance circuit at the age of twenty-five to become a music historian. She was now one of the world's foremost experts on instruments of the Baroque and Renaissance periods. Even Tony's bequest made sense. Despite his falling-out with Madame all those years ago, he had gone on to become a specialist in music of the Romantic period, just like her. Whatever animosity Madame might have had over the way they had parted, he'd fulfilled his promise as one of her musical progeny.

Only Clara was out of place. As the metronome ticked on the desk, she could not help but wonder if it was some kind of joke Madame was playing to have included Clara in the will at all. A cruel joke. Her only kind.

The metronome clocked to a stop, the pendulum pointing out the window to the starless sky. Clara rose and wound the key again, then finished the bourbon and turned off the lights. The sound tocked on into her sleep, footsteps following into her dreams.

Chapter 4

CLARA PULLED HER SUITCASE FROM the dripping trunk of the taxi and ran across the street in the pouring rain. The electric sign of The Andromeda Club glowed in the bleary light. She reached the door just as a bolt of lightning veined the black sky.

"Where have you been?" Julián was coming out from behind the bar. "I was beginning to think you were dead!"

The room was nearly empty. Barb and Lisa sat at the bar. Two men in their sixties were in the back booth playing chess. Everyone turned to look at Clara.

"Not dead." Clara squeezed water from her ponytail, lamenting once again that she had forgotten her umbrella at Madame's house. It irked her that she had left something else of herself behind there, however small.

"I called you when I landed," she said. "The line was busy."

"That's because I've been calling your house every five minutes!" Julián said.

"He thought maybe your plane had crashed," Lisa added cheerfully.

"My flight was diverted." Clara removed the soaked polyester jacket and hung it on the coat rack, where it immediately began to drip. "Sorry. I thought the phone line was out because of the storm." She pulled a wilted paper bag from her backpack and held it out to him. "But I got you something."

Julián gave her an exasperated look but swiped the bag from her outstretched hand. He withdrew a box of Sour Patch Kids and a pair of red sunglasses that looked like they'd belonged to a fifties starlet. Clara bought them in the terminal from a Russian woman who passed Clara her change with the advice to rub Vitamin E oil into her skin every night: *It will work wonders for those scars.*

Julián slid on the glasses and regarded her sternly over the rims. "I can tell you bought these in the airport."

Clara knew from the way he tried not to smile that he liked them. Pleased, she picked up her suitcase. "I'll be right back."

She wheeled her bag down the hall to the office in the back of the bar. It was a small room, wood-paneled and windowless, with a single laminate desk and a rolling chair covered in faded green upholstery. A framed photograph of Janis Joplin on stage at Threadgill's hung on the wall. Clara parked her suitcase beside a metal shelf laden with boxes of liquor. The luggage had waited thirty minutes on the tarmac for a crew to unload it. Half her clothes were wet. She dug a pair of limp socks and her Chuck Taylors from where they were smashed into the bottom of the bag. The blue cardigan she'd swaddled around the metronome was damp beside them. The wood had the clammy feel of moisture but appeared unscathed. She set it on the desk, where its presence in the familiar room made her uneasy, solid evidence that the weekend in Chicago could not be left behind as cleanly as she wanted it to be. Avoiding looking at it, she changed into the driest clothes she had and walked out into the bar.

"How's Bingo?" She pulled an apron from a shelf beneath the register and tied it around her waist.

Julián made a face. "He's a beast. You need to train him. He hogs the bed and farts in his sleep."

"Did you feed him ice cream again?"

Julián looked indignant. "Just, like, *one* spoonful. He was slobbering on my thigh!"

"We can watch him next time, Clara," Barb interjected. "Chummy would love the company."

"Where'd you go, Clara?" Lisa asked. She was in her forties, with graying hair cropped in a pixie cut. Next to Barb, who was heavyset and blonde, with wary eyes and a yearlong tan, she appeared small and elfin, like an aged Tinkerbell.

"Chicago," Clara said.

"To see your family?"

"A retirement party. Or, it was supposed to be one." She hesitated, debating how much truth she could reveal without having to lie about her entire life. On the plane, she had dreaded this conversation more than anything: how to explain to Julián what had transpired in Chicago. News of Madame's death had hit the newspapers that morning. Clara read the obituary in the airport bookstore. It called Madame "a behemoth of the stage" and "a celebrated teacher responsible for some of the brightest talents of the age." According to *The New York Times*, she died from stomach cancer the week prior at a hospital in Vienna. Clara had placed the newspaper back on the shelf without buying it. Apparently, Madame never intended to perform at her final concert; Borthram had always been the real featured artist. Fortunately, no one in Austin would be talking about how the great Zofia Mikorska had been lost to the world.

Clara wiped a ring of water from the bar, then looked up at Lisa. "We all showed up, and it turned out the guest of honor had died."

"*What?*" Julián leaned forward at the waist. "Why didn't you say anything?"

"She just walked in the door!" Barb exclaimed. "You've been harassing her about her dog!"

"I haven't been *harassing* her!" Julián sniped back. He turned to Clara. "Are you okay?"

The sympathy on his face made her stomach twist. How could she explain to him that her feelings about Madame's death, still only partially excavated, lay somewhere between relief that a nightmare was over and shame that she had missed her opportunity to face it?

She held up both hands. "I'm fine. I hadn't seen her in ten years, actually. I honestly don't even know why I was invited. We all showed up at her house, then a lawyer came and said she had died. Then he read the will and told us what we all got."

"So she knew she was going to die?" Lisa asked.

"I guess so."

"This sounds like the start to a movie where everybody gets killed in the end," Julián said. Then, to Barb's look of admonishment, lowered his head. "Sorry." He turned to Clara. "Well, what'd you get?"

Clara filled a glass of water at the sink. "A metronome."

"Like, tick-tock?" Julián swayed his index finger back and forth.

"Yes."

"Are you a musician?" Lisa asked.

"I played piano when I was younger." The words felt hollow and clumsy on her tongue, and she chastised herself for being so sensitive. Who cared if the whole city of Austin knew that Clara, like half the children of America, had played piano?

"You never told me you played piano!" Julián said. "You should play for us sometime." He gestured toward the scuffed Yamaha in the back of the room.

"It's been a long time," Clara said. "I think I'll spare you."

The two men in the back booth were rising to leave. Seeing an opportunity to stall the momentum of the conversation, Clara went over to collect their empty glasses. When she'd brought them back to the bar, Julián stood next to her while she washed them in the sink.

"Are you really okay?" he asked.

"I really am," Clara said, though every time she said it anew it sounded less true. Boarding the plane that morning, she had experienced the exhilarating rush of relief and pride she once felt after performing—the sense that she had achieved what she set out to do and had done it well, and whatever worries she may have harbored about her abilities could be forgotten. But since walking in the bar, she had felt that confidence wobble. Seeing Tony had jarred something loose in her. For a while after the fire, she had missed being someone remarkable. That faded over time, like the redness of her scars, and now it was gone and rarely hurt anymore. But being back at Madame's house, back near Tony and his beautiful, healthy, agile hands, she had felt like an amputee, and had walked away feeling that it was not just her hand that was damaged, but her past and her future, too.

Julián was watching her closely. "You haven't been to Chicago in years, then suddenly you get a letter in the mail and you're taking off work at the last minute to go to the retirement party of a teacher you've never mentioned. Then she ends up dead. If you're really okay with all that, there's something you're not telling me."

Barb asked for another gin and tonic, and Clara was relieved when he walked away from her to mix it. How could she begin to describe all she had not told him? Her life prior to Austin had been an anomaly of storybook proportion. There was no way to explain music without explaining her scars; no way to explain her scars without explaining Madame. She didn't want to withhold from him, but she also didn't want things between them to change, and she knew from experience that once she told the truth about her past, everything did. Here, right now, tending a bar in Texas was the most normal life she had ever lived, and it was a life she wanted to keep the way it was. She was searching for something to say that might acknowledge all this without requiring her to explain it when a boom of thunder shuddered overhead. Immediately, the lights went out.

The outage was accompanied by the blanketing silence that always seemed to Clara more pronounced than the lack of light: the hum and whir of every machine in the room turning to a stop.

Julián sighed. "Really?"

"You guys want us to go so you can close up?" Barb asked.

"No," Julián said. "We need to stay until the power's back on anyway. I think we have a flashlight in the back." Clara heard the tread of his Doc Martens recede down the hall, followed by the creak of the office door. Presently, a beam of light shot out of the hallway.

"What's this?" Julian trained the flashlight on the mahogany box.

"That's the metronome," Clara said.

"The mystery metronome." He set the box on the bar, then pulled a fistful of half-burned tealights and a tin of matches from the pocket of his apron. Soon, their side of the room glowed in candlelight.

Julián nudged a candle toward the box. "Can we open it?"

Clara hesitated. In her mind, she had already relegated the metronome to the back of the guest room closet where she kept her old records and the programs of her performances—the boxed-up remains of the first twenty-one years of her life. But she knew that to refuse would only draw more inquiries. She inclined her head toward the metronome. "Go ahead."

Julián took the box into his hands, feeling around for the groove of the lid. Finding it, he palmed the top and pulled. In the silent room, the lid separated from the base with a vacuuming rasp.

"Wow," Julián said when he'd set the metronome on the bar. "It's— pretty. Kind of."

The bronze casting gleamed in the luster of the candles, the angels with their blank eyes appearing faintly monstrous as they lifted the hourglass like a sacrifice. The gold bun feet reflected the darting flames.

Lisa tilted her head to the side, scrunching up her nose. "It's just a little bit . . ."

"Over the top?" Barb said.

"Yeah."

"It feels, like, weighed down or something," Julián said. His face lit up. "Maybe it's haunted!"

Clara rolled her eyes. Julián had spent an entire winter thinking his attic was haunted. It turned out to be a squatting raccoon. "Maybe you can ask the ghost what I'm supposed to do with it," she said.

Julián peered into the velvet interior of the box as if looking for something better. Not finding it, he returned to the metronome and slid off the faceplate. The lion's mouth gaped wide.

"How do you make it go?"

Clara released the pendulum hook, then turned the winding key three times. The beam began to swing back and forth. The tick reverberated into the corners of the room.

"That's all it does?" Julián asked.

"That's it."

Barb slid a candle closer to the winding key and squinted at the Roman numerals engraved on the lion's tail. "What number is this?"

"Seventy-two."

"What's it mean?"

"I assume it's a tempo marking, but honestly I don't know."

Julián watched the pendulum swing, then turned to Clara. "Why'd she give it to you? Were you two close?"

Had anyone been close to Madame? Clara had been her longest-running pupil, and even when she was going to Madame's house once a week, the woman had remained as shrouded and unknowable as a vision from a bad dream.

"No," Clara said. "We weren't close at all."

She saw a question on Julián's face and knew he was wondering why she had traveled to Chicago at the last minute for someone she wasn't close to. She was grateful he didn't ask it.

"So what do you think she meant by giving it to you?" Lisa asked.

Before Clara could answer, the candle nearest the metronome went out.

"Christ!" Julián exclaimed. "What is up with tonight?"

He lit another match and tried to reignite the wick, but the wax was gone. The flame on the candle beside it had withered to a halo of light around a spark. Julián tossed the box of matches on the bar. "I'm going to look for some more candles," he said. "And after that, I'm having a drink." He flipped on the flashlight, then followed its white beam down the hall.

"Well," Clara said to Barb and Lisa, "how about another round before I can't find the bottle?"

She mixed their gin and tonics, then pulled two clean glasses from the shelf and poured a bourbon for herself and Julián. She set the glasses on the bar just as the final flame expired, a sudden darkness. They all laughed.

"Cheers." Clara lifted her whiskey in Barb and Lisa's direction, but instead of the clink of glass, she heard a loud thud, followed by a hollow toppling sound. Barb cursed, then something hit the floor with a terrible *thwack.*

"Was it the metronome?" Clara asked, surprised by the anxiety that gripped her when the wood smacked the floor.

"The box," Lisa said, from somewhere farther away. She groaned. "I hit it with my elbow."

Just then, the electricity surged on. The refrigerator beneath the bar clicked, then hummed to life; the air conditioner revved and churned. Julián whooped in celebration from the back office.

Lisa stood a few feet away from the bar, holding the lid of the box. She blinked in the bright light. "It was just the top, I guess." She nodded toward the base, which had tipped over on the bar, half of it jutting perilously over the edge. Quickly, Clara reached over and set it upright.

"Thank God," Julián said, emerging from the back. "I was starting to feel like we were homesteading. There's not even any more candles back there. What are we supposed to do in a real emergency? Make lanterns out of the whiskey bottles?" He stopped when he saw Lisa staring down at the lid.

"What happened?"

"The box fell off the bar," Barb said.

"I knocked it over." Lisa pointed to the damaged corner where the wood had buckled.

"So much for the resell option," Julián muttered.

"Clara, I'm so sorry," Lisa said.

Clara shrugged, though she had a powerful urge to reach out and remove the lid from Lisa's hands. "Don't worry about it. It's really okay."

Barb walked over to examine the damage. "The lining came loose a little, but we can probably fix it." She studied the edge of the stiff velvet, peering at the wood beneath. "There are some rusted staples holding it in there on the sides. Hey—" She brought the lid closer to her face, squinting into the seam. "There's some kind of writing in here." She held it out to Clara. "Take a look."

Clara peered beneath the velvet. On the inside panel of the lid, she could just make out the letters *k-n-o* etched into the wood. She slid a finger beneath the fabric to pry it up further: *piękno*.

"What language is that?" Julián asked.

Clara squinted at the tail on the letter *e*. "Looks like Polish."

"How do you know?"

"My mom's family is Polish. My great-aunt Pauline speaks a little."

"Can you tell what it says?"

Clara shook her head. "I only know a few phrases. I can't really see anything except the end of what's in here anyway."

"Should we take off the fabric?"

Clara shrugged. "It's already loose." She plucked a pencil from an old pint glass they kept beside the register and used the tip to pry the rusted staples from the wood. When she had removed the velvet, all four of them bent to look. The wood here was darker, not faded by time. But the inscription was worn. Certainly not recent.

Musimy przekuć ból w piękno.

Julián leaned over her shoulder. "What's it mean?"

Clara brushed her fingers over the engraving. "I told you," she said. "I don't speak Polish."

"Call your Aunt Pauline then!" Julián said.

Clara wrenched her eyes away from the inscription to look at him. "It's ten o'clock at night. She'll think somebody died."

"You've got this creepy box with a hidden mystery message in it, and you're just going to take it home without knowing what it says?"

She peered at the engraving, whose unfamiliar letters in their looping script held the allure of forgotten history, and also a strange disquiet. A word from her musical past rose to her mind. *Pesante.* Heavy. Sad.

She looked up at Julián, shrugging the feeling away. "It's been in there a long time. I think it can wait." Suddenly drained, she put the metronome back in the box, then placed the damaged lid on top. The dented corner drooped like a sagging eyelid.

"Clara, I feel terrible," Lisa said. "I broke your inheritance! Let me have the box repaired for you."

"Don't worry about it," Clara said, really meaning it. "I'm just going to put it in the closet anyway."

"Don't be silly," Barb said. "Of course we'll have it repaired."

"No," Clara said. Her voice was firmer than she intended it to be, and she softened it. "Really, please don't worry about it. I promise I don't even want the thing."

It was the most truthful statement she'd made since walking in the door.

Barely forty-eight hours had passed since she left for Chicago, but standing in the doorway to her house later that night, she had the unsettling sensation of seeing her home as a stranger might. Her eyes flitted from the mismatched furniture to the dining room table piled with the miscellany of a solitary life: unread mail, a collection of Dickens novels she bought at a used bookstore, a burnt light bulb from the back porch she needed to replace. The living room was painted sage green, with white cotton curtains around the picture window and built-in bookshelves on either side of the fireplace. A yellow couch she bought at a thrift store faced the mantel, covered with Bingo's blue dog blanket. Clara had always liked the room, where the morning light angled in on a table of plants. But after the opulence of Madame's house, everything appeared small and rundown. She noticed the gray dust that had accumulated on the shade of a porcelain lamp she bought on tour in Hong Kong, and how bare the walls seemed with only two hung pictures—photographs Clara had taken of the fall foliage at McKinney Falls State Park. For the first time, the house made her sad, and she hated herself for it. This was what Madame had always done: made her feel like an impostor in her own life.

Bingo had no such compunction. He trotted past her and bounded onto the couch, circling once before dropping onto his blanket. Clara left her suitcase at the door and walked to the kitchen, gathering a bottle of Maker's Mark and a glass from the cabinet. She sipped the whiskey while looking around the room, trying to reclaim the sense of it as home. After a while, she pulled the metronome box from her canvas backpack and put it on the table, then lifted the lid.

Musimy przekuć ból w piękno.

She ran the tip of her index finger over the engraving, feeling its craggy depressions in the wood, then rose and walked to the bookshelf.

In the corner of the bottom shelf, beside long-closed travel guides to Tokyo and Moscow and Madrid, were a collection of pocket phrasebooks in various languages. She fingered past the guides for Russian, Spanish, and Portuguese and pulled out the one for Polish.

When she opened it, a train ticket from Warsaw to Kraków fluttered to the floor. She picked it up, ambushed by a memory of drinking cappuccino in a cozy train car while snow fell on the frozen grass outside. It had been one of the first tours she took without her parents, the year she was eighteen. The freedom of aloneness had thrilled her.

Nestling the ticket carefully in the back of the book, she skimmed through the pages, scanning past phrases for how to ask what time it was or how much something cost, searching for any of the words engraved on the lid. The whiskey in her glass was long gone by the time she found one clue, in the final section of the book. *Useful phrases if you need to see a doctor.*

I do not feel well.
Nie czuję się dobrze.

I have a headache.
Boli mnie głowa.

cough
kaszel

pain
ból

She looked back to the inscription. *Musimy przekuć ból w piękno.*

Ból, she wrote on the back of an old grocery list. Pain. She made a little sound, a snuff borne from a chill in her chest, then rose and turned off the light.

Chapter 5

AT TEN O'CLOCK THE NEXT MORNING, Clara wheeled her bike up Julián's front walk. The brick bungalow with cobalt blue shutters had belonged to Julián's grandmother. Her old rocking chair still sat in the corner of the porch beneath a hanging fern, only now its needlepoint cushion was embroidered with the words *Park It*. Beside it, two Adirondack chairs painted turquoise sat around a table, where a stick of incense tilted in a mason jar. Eyeing a cigarette butt wedged in the bottom of the glass, Clara knocked on the door.

Julián answered in green gym shorts and a Dolly Parton T-shirt. The red sunglasses she had given him last night were perched atop his head.

Clara pulled a white paper bag from her backpack. "They only had one jelly, so I got you a bear claw." She tilted her head to the mason jar. "Have you been smoking again?"

Julián frowned guiltily. "Of course not. Who could live with themselves with such a disgusting habit?"

Clara gave him a look.

"Fine," Julián groaned. "Paul called last night."

Paul had moved out of Julián's house last Christmas. A flight attendant who was gone for days at a time, they had lived together two years before Julián discovered Paul had another house, complete with another boyfriend, in Fort Worth. Recently Paul had been calling, asking for another chance. Every time, Clara had to stop herself from driving to Fort Worth and ripping his phone out of the wall.

"How'd it go?" she asked.

"I didn't answer. I came out here and smoked instead."

"Probably less toxic in the long run," she said, and handed over the donuts.

She followed him inside, where the furniture was pushed to the center of the room, draped in old sheets. Since Paul left, Clara had participated in a ceremonious throwing-out of his left-behind belongings, a systematic culling of all furniture Julián found too nostalgic to keep, and several energy-clearing rituals that involved burning sage through all the rooms of the house. Painting, according to Julián, was the final step to signal the universe he was ready to invite something new into his life. Clara observed the sample strokes on the walls—electric teal and pineapple yellow—then looked down at the brown carpet.

"What if the universe doesn't approve of the color scheme?"

Julián gave her a withering look. "A lack of boldness is never rewarded by the gods." He led her to the kitchen table. "What's going on with the metronome? Did you find out what the inscription meant?"

"Just one word." She pulled two napkins from a pile in the center of the table and slid one toward him. "Pain."

Julián scrunched his nose. "That's not very uplifting."

"No." Thinking about the metronome doused the warmth of the morning in a cold wash.

Julián noticed the shift. "Are we going to keep pretending that you're not hiding something? Because I have to warn you—I kind of have baggage with that type of thing."

Clara had pulled an éclair from the bag but set it on the table without taking a bite. She had gone to sleep the night before dreading how to explain to him that another person in his life had lied. Hers were lies of omission, but as she well knew, sometimes omissions were the most painful types of injury.

"You're going to be mad I didn't tell you earlier."

"Absolutely I am," he said emphatically.

Clara sighed. "You know I was in a fire."

"Yes." He looked at her with the type of intense eye contact that she knew from experience meant he was trying hard not to look at her scars.

"Well, last night when I told you I used to play piano, I didn't just play like it was a hobby. I did it professionally."

Julián looked confused. "Like Jerry?"

Clara shook her head. "Like on stage."

Julián had taken a bite of his jelly donut, but now stopped chewing. "Excuse me. *You* got on a stage? You can't even stand it when *other* people get on stages. You basically hold your breath all the way through open mic night!"

"I'm afraid the performers are going to humiliate themselves," Clara said. "It was my greatest fear all through childhood."

Julián eyed her warily. "All right," he said, waving his hand toward her. "Keep going."

"Ten years ago, there was a fire at the Warsaw Symphony Concert Hall in Poland," she said. "It was a festival for the hundred and forty-fifth birthday of the composer Aleksander Starza. I was performing on stage when the alarm went off."

The ominous opening bars of Starza's *Fire Concerto* thundered into her mind. Clara had played four measures to a background of silence before realizing the rest of the orchestra had stopped. Her hands were still on the keys when she looked up at the conductor, confused, and finally heard the alarm.

"My teacher and I were both invited to perform at the festival, but we'd had a falling out over it."

"Zofia Mikorska to return to Warsaw with Starza descendant Clara Bishop," the headline in *Classical Times* had read.

Clara's manager, a woman named Kerry with eyeglasses and hair nearly the same color of cherry red, had looked up from the article and frowned.

"We need to separate you from her. You're your own artist."

Clara, who was used to being described in terms of Madame—whose entire life, in fact, had been outlined against Madame's achievements—disagreed.

"That's how they always bill me. I don't mind."

Kerry studied Clara through the red glasses. "You've been performing with world-class symphonies since you were twelve. You need to start minding."

It was a month past her twenty-first birthday. Clara marked the occasion with a visit to her lawyer. There, she signed the papers needed to take possession of the trust her parents had begun with her competition winnings when she was ten, then used the phone in the lawyer's office to call her parents and tell them she was moving out. The Bishops weren't home, as she knew they would not be. Thursday mornings they went to water aerobics and a massage at the health club. Clara left the message on the answering machine: The trust was hers, and so now also were her touring schedule, calendar, and business decisions. She had bought a condo in Lakeview and had also hired Kerry. Her parents could retire as her business managers.

In later years, Clara apologized for the heartlessness of this abrupt severance, for which she gave virtually no warning. At the time, she was too immature to understand that her parents had controlled her life so closely because their lives, too, had been usurped by her startling fame. There was not even so much as a regular newspaper in the Bishop household. For all of them, life orbited around Clara's performance schedule rather than the natural milestones of a family. Clara had never had the time to be a child; nor had she had the agency to grow up.

"Why would you want to waste your time at a high school?" her mother said when Clara announced she wanted to attend the local public school. "Your tutors say you're a year ahead already. Do you really want to spend all that time away from practicing? You won't have anything in common with the other students."

Or, when Clara suggested, at age nineteen, she wanted to move into her own apartment: "You can't take the Steinway to an *apartment*, Clair de lune!" her father chuckled. "The neighbors wouldn't stand for all that practicing. Your mother and I have to wear earplugs to get through the day, and we love you!"

By the time she was twenty, Clara had exhausted seven passport books with her international travels but had never gone on a date or slept over at a friend's house. Even something as simple as driving herself to the supermarket was unattainable; there had never been time to practice for her driver's test ("Clara, honey, where would you even *go*?").

Everyone has a period of life they return to and thumb like a beautiful stone found on a beach to warm them with past happiness. The first few months of life in her condo were the dream Clara held up when she mourned all she later lost. In six months, she lived out all the unrealized plans she had missed from adolescence. She watched TV until late at night and smoked cigarettes at the piano and ate all her meals at a dingy poetry café down the street. She hired a driving instructor and got her license, then bought a blue Volkswagen convertible. Even as she flew to concert dates across the globe, she dreamed about driving it across the country, to the wide, anonymous west.

Unused to happiness and the suspension of reality it can bring, there ensued a series of bad decisions that led, in some ways at least, to the worst moment of her life. One of these was Kerry.

"You should decline the invitation to the Starza Festival unless they allow you to play the *Fire Concerto*," Kerry urged.

Clara was appalled. Starza's Third Concerto was Madame's signature finale—the performance that launched her to fame, the recording that swept the Grammys, the piece that made her career. Never had Clara dared do more than study the score in the privacy of her bedroom, so cowed was she by the possibility of ever measuring up.

"Madame is going to play it. I play the Second Concerto."

Kerry cast her an exasperated look. "You have to play it eventually. All your peers have already played it. Tony Park played it two years ago. If she were really interested in your career, she would be happy for you to play it."

It was true that the *Fire Concerto* was a rite of passage. But unlike many of her contemporaries who had moved on from their mentors long ago, Clara had not yet broken with Madame. She still went to her lessons every Tuesday as she had since she was six years old. Madame told her what to play, when to stop, how to do it better. Never once did Madame ask if she was well or ill or tired or defeated. Madame commanded and Clara played, and though Clara hated her for calling her fingers "like pokes on a typewriter" and her interpretation "as cold as a fish," now that she had the power to leave, somehow she could not.

"Let me talk to her about it," Clara said.

Kerry picked a piece of lint off her pink blazer and flicked it to the floor. "Don't expect it to go well with a megalomaniac like that."

The next Tuesday at the conclusion of her lesson, Clara rose as usual from the piano, but instead of thanking Madame and saying goodbye, did not walk out of the gallery.

"I want to play the *Fire Concerto* at the Starza Festival," she said.

Madame had been gathering scores from the ledge of the piano. She shook her head without looking up. "You are not ready," she said, and began to walk away.

Clara held to the side of the red Steinway for strength. "I think I am," she called after her.

Madame looked at Clara over her shoulder the way someone might toss a backward glance at a table they had risen from at a restaurant to ensure they had not forgotten something.

"Why do you want to play it?" she asked. "Because you have such passion for the music? Because you wish to distinguish yourself? Because you think it will further your career?"

Clara felt the muscles in her neck twitch and wondered if Madame knew she had hired a new manager. Still, she kept her voice strong. "Starza was my ancestor. I should be playing his work. All of his work."

Madame regarded Clara for an unblinking moment, her chin slightly lifting. Then she shook her head in one decisive movement. "You do not have the fortitude."

With this, she turned and walked away, the wooden soles of her mules clacking across the parquet.

"The fortitude!" Kerry exclaimed. "You played Tchaikovsky's First for three nights back-to-back! She's bullying you."

"I'll just play the Second," Clara said. "I'm more prepared for it anyway."

"We can't back down *now*," Kerry insisted. "Let me take care of it."

Within a week, Kerry had spread word that Clara was refusing to attend the festival unless she was invited to play the *Fire Concerto*. *Classical Times* ran a story headlined "Pupil seeks to unseat master."

Clara read it from the bed of her condo, horrified.

"Tell them it was a mistake," Clara said. "Tell them you were wrong."

"I will if you really want me to," Kerry said. "But ask yourself—do you *really* want me to retract it, or are you just afraid of her?"

Clara could not explain that her feelings toward Madame went far deeper than fear.

"Retract it," she insisted.

But it was too late. That afternoon, a letter arrived by messenger.

It is my last duty as your former teacher (Madame had underscored "former" with two bold strokes) *to inform you that you do not have the fortitude to perform this piece as the master intended. I take no responsibility for your failure, now or in the future.*

Clara looked up at Julián. "I tried to undo it immediately. I had my manager call the festival organizers to tell them to remove me from the bill. I called my teacher and told her I was sorry and begged her to take me back. She said she was no longer interested in working with someone 'whose ego had surpassed her abilities.'" Clara's fingers curled into her palm, remembering the words. "I have told you repeatedly that you are not ready," Madame had said before she hung up the phone. "Now you will show the world that you are not. And from that, you will not come back."

Clara picked up a napkin from the table and balled it in her fist. "It was the only time I stood up to her in fifteen years. I called a few more times, wrote her a letter, went to her house. After a while, I gave up. When the festival called a few weeks later and told me Madame had decided to play the Second Concerto and that the *Fire Concerto* was still available if I wanted to perform it, I said I would."

In the months leading up to the festival, Clara did what she always did when life overwhelmed her. She practiced. From early in the morning to late at night, she rehearsed the concerto's endless runs and flashing octaves. The piece held all the frustration she had harbored for years—toward her parents and her stifled, stunted childhood, but mostly toward Madame. Kerry was right. It was time to break with Madame's legacy. Or possibly—in Clara's wildest dreams—supersede it. Searching for a way to distinguish herself, Clara listened to every recording of the piece Madame had ever made. Where Madame held back on the tempo, Clara played as fast as Starza's *Allegro con fuoco* could permit. Where Madame slowed with generous *rubato*, Clara pressed forward with urgency. But still it wasn't right. Every time she returned to the piano, all she could hear were Madame's recordings. Or worse, Madame's words: *I take no responsibility for your failure.*

"You're too in your head," Kerry counseled. "Stop thinking about her. Think about *you*. You've got Starza's blood in your veins, for Christ's sake!"

Clara didn't bother explaining that she had about as much in common with her distant ancestor as she did with Madonna. Starza had once thrown a lit candelabra into an audience because two men were whispering in the front row. If any of his fiery blood still beat in the family veins, it had been cooled by generations of politeness.

Yet Clara's family relation to Starza did offer one advantage. Starza's house and other worldly belongings had been donated to the city of Warsaw after his death, but his original manuscripts—every draft and scrap he ever composed—were owned in full by Clara's family. The scores were housed in a humidity-controlled room at the Starza Museum in Warsaw, but the family alone, along with the handful of scholars who worked at the museum, had unfettered access. Even as a young child, Clara had wondered if this was the reason Madame agreed to take her on as a pupil. Madame had often asserted that the only way to know the true heart of a piece was to see the evolution of the manuscript in the composer's hand, and there was no composer Madame had written about more extensively than Aleksander Starza. As the matriarch of the family, Clara's Aunt Pauline was their representative on the museum board, but Clara, as the professional musician, was the person to whom Aunt Pauline deferred all matters related to the archive.

Two months before the festival, Clara phoned Tomasz Górski, the director of the Starza Museum. At Kerry's urging, Clara had decided to give a pre-concert lecture about the *Fire Concerto* showcasing the composer's original scores. It was the kind of elbow-rubbing with audience members Madame had always disdained.

Tomasz hesitated. "Of course I am happy to accommodate you, Clara. But the scores are very fragile, as you know. Might we use the facsimiles instead of the originals?"

"People don't want a facsimile," Clara insisted. "They want the real thing, and I can provide that for them. I'll lock everything up in my dressing room afterward. Don't worry. I'll take good care of them."

By the time the festival came around, she hadn't seen Madame in almost a year.

"I didn't expect her to come to my performance," she said to Julián. "But when the fire alarm went off, I saw her backstage."

Julián sat up straighter in his chair.

The night of her performance, Clara walked on stage to an audience already on its feet. Here she was, Aleksander Starza's famous young relative, come to play his most famous piece. Clara blew a kiss to the audience, letting their admiration fill her up, and sat at the piano. The fire alarm went off three minutes into the first movement.

"I don't think anybody thought it was a real fire at first. All the orchestra members were annoyed because it was raining outside, and they were worried about their instruments getting wet. There wasn't any smoke yet, and I think most of us figured we'd be back inside in a half hour to start the piece over again. But I had done my lecture earlier that afternoon, and the scores to the *Fire Concerto* were in the safe in my dressing room. I felt like I couldn't leave them there if the building was unattended. They were priceless. So I decided to go downstairs to get them."

She rushed down the steps to the dressing rooms, the heels of her slingback pumps clicking on the white marble. The basement was deserted, the practice rooms on either side of the hallway bearing signs of hasty departure. A winter coat lay crumpled on the floor; an open viola case leaned against the wall. The alarm bleated from the ceiling, white light flashing.

"The hallway was laid out in a big square, with rooms on either side. I had just turned the corner to the main corridor when I saw Madame."

Clara's voice caught as she remembered the relief that had lapped against her when she glimpsed Madame disappear through a metal door at the end of the hallway. Through all the guilt and shame of the last several months, and the resentment of the years before that, all Clara had been longing for was one indication that Madame cared about her in some small fraction of the way that Clara cared for her. In the months without her, she had come to understand that every award she ever received or competition she had won was because of Madame, and not just because of Madame's unreachable expectations. Madame had dug a well so deep inside Clara that she didn't recognize it anymore than she recognized her own stomach until it was empty. She had given

Clara hate, and pain, and sorrow. With Madame listening, Clara had played her anger into the room, reaching into the bowels of her unlived life to feel the triumph of Beethoven and the alienation of Chopin, the exquisite fury of Starza. Long past the time when Madame had ceased attending Clara's concerts, Clara had been playing for only one listener. And now here she was: she had come to hear Clara play. She had not given up on her after all.

"I don't know if it really slowed me down," she said. "I don't remember stopping. But all of a sudden, I smelled smoke, and I knew I had to get out. I ran the rest of the way to my dressing room. The electricity went out as soon as I unlocked my door."

Her dressing table was littered with lipstick tubes and eye shadow palettes. A bouquet of roses still in the cellophane slumped against the mirror. Her spare dress hung from the garment rack in a cascade of emerald silk. All of it looked sinister in the glow of the red emergency lights, which began to pulse with the sound of the alarm, total darkness followed by eerie red. Clara lunged for the safe. She unlocked it and slid the fragile scores into her arms just as the door behind her whooshed shut.

She looked up at Julián miserably. "I got stuck in the room."

Julián's eyes filled with horror. "You got *stuck*?"

"The fire started in the electrical room, on the other side of the basement. The heat had built up pressure in the hallway." Her mouth was dry, and she swallowed to clear her throat. "When the door slammed, it jammed the doorknob."

Her palm prickled with heat, remembering how she had gripped the knob and turned with all her strength. It had not yielded at all. *Help me!* she screamed, banging her fist against the wood.

Somewhere down the hall she heard a low roar, like the lowest bars of the piano growling in a menacing crescendo. And also, she was sure of it, the sound of footsteps. Her stomach dropped, recalling how she heard the quick steps pause and then begin to retreat.

Madame! she screamed. *I'm in here!*

Julián was searching her face. "Hold up. She was *out* there?"

She looked into Julián's stricken eyes. "I heard her. I know she heard me, too."

At the sound of the steps dying away, Clara began to hurl herself against the door, each red flash of the emergency lights growing cloudier as smoke filled the room. On the fourth attempt, she tried turning the knob at the same time as she slammed her weight against the door. Searing heat entered her flesh as it finally gave way. Clara stumbled into the hallway, where flames soared to the ceiling. Holding her burned hand against her chest, she grabbed the concerto from where she had dropped it on the chair and plunged into the smoke. She only made it a few feet before a flame reached for her arm. She fell to the ground, the score coiling in her arms.

Julián put a hand over his mouth. "Oh, Clarita. How did you get out?"

"The firefighters found me in the hallway."

Julián was staring at her in disbelief. "What caused it?"

"An old electrical cable. The concert hall installed new stage lights for the festival, but they didn't update the cables. One got overloaded. It melted and caught a box of programs on fire."

"Precious score to Starza's *Fire Concerto* burned to ash," the headline had read. Clara's injuries were not mentioned until the third paragraph.

"Did your teacher get burned, too?"

Clara shook her head. "Not a mark."

"Did she explain what she was doing down there?"

"She told the firefighters she went downstairs to get her coat when the alarm went off, then noticed the smoke and exited the building along with everyone else."

"She went and got her *coat*, but left you in a burning room?" Julián cried. "Did you ever confront her about it?"

Clara brushed crumbs off her lap so she would not have to look into his anguished face. "We never spoke again."

"Never?"

"Never." She thought of the note Madame had sent her a year after the fire. Two sentences, after fifteen years together. *Find a way to play again, whatever you must do. Otherwise, your life will be a waste.*

"Well, Clarita, now I know why you're so messed up," Julián said. Seeing that Clara wasn't smiling, he squeezed her hand. "I'm joking. So why do you think she gave you her metronome?"

"That's the big question."

"Maybe she was trying to make amends," Julián said.

Clara shook her head. "When I got the invitation, I thought that too. That's why I went to the stupid thing in the first place. I thought maybe she wanted to apologize. But this feels more like a task. Like she wants me to do something with it."

"If that's the case, she obviously trusted you to figure it out. Maybe you meant more to her than you think."

"No. She resented me my whole life. For a while, I was egotistical enough to think it was my talent—like I was so good for being so young or something. Toward the end, I started to think it was because I was a woman, which doesn't make sense unless you consider that she was the first woman to win all the big competitions, and the first to be respected in the same way as men. Sometimes I wondered if she thought my path was too easy, and she wanted me to suffer more for it, like she did."

Julián was looking at her thoughtfully. "You must have been pretty good, huh?"

Clara's throat caught. "Not as good as her."

"I can't really see it," Julián said softly. "To be honest, I didn't even think you *liked* music."

Clara shrugged, trying to seem like the person Julián knew. Clara the bartender, who liked bourbon and donuts and digging in the garden. "That was the point of moving here. I just wanted to be normal."

"Well, it's too late for that." He gave her a sidelong look. "So, what are you going to do with it?"

"I haven't decided. I don't want it."

"Why don't you sell it, then? Go to an antiques store or something. I'm sure somebody would buy it."

She thought of Madame's letter in the will. *Each of you should understand why you were selected for the bequest you received.*

Before her mind had a chance to decide on her words, she was already shaking her head. "I want to figure out why she gave it to me first."

It was nearing sunset when Clara headed home. She walked slowly, ladened with misgiving. She and Julián had painted the living room as planned, but the afternoon had been quiet, Julián uncharacteristically somber. She had been right: things were different now that she had told him.

Inside, Bingo bounded to the door to meet her, then returned to his throne on the yellow couch. The metronome was on the kitchen table where she had left it last night. Next to a bowl of half-eaten corn-flakes and a *VISIT TEXAS* coffee mug, it appeared both ornately out of place and vaguely tatty. The brass looked tarnished, the gold feet dull, the lion's tail ridiculous. Clara picked up the lid with its tatter of blue velvet, then walked to the phone.

"Clara!" Aunt Pauline's smoky voice came through the receiver. Clara imagined the old woman sitting in her living room among the piles of books and magazines that accumulated around her pink armchair.

"I was just talking to your mother earlier today," Pauline said. "She tells me she's going to try to lock you in for Christmas this year. Is she right?"

Clara blew a sigh out the corner of her mouth. Only Ruth would plan for Christmas in June. "I haven't really thought about the holidays, to tell you the truth."

"No one has, except your mother. She's probably already called the catering people and ordered up her turkey. I told her I might be dead by Christmas, so she might as well wait to ask me again until October. How are you, dear? Still bartending?"

"Still bartending."

"You know, my father made bathtub gin during Prohibition. Apparently, it was quite coveted among the neighbors. Maybe it runs in the genes. Of course, you've got something better in your genes than mixing liquor, but what do I know? If you want to make gin in your bathtub, too, you go ahead and do it. But how can I help you, dear? The long-distance rates are scandalous."

Clara nodded, observing that Pauline and Ruth had more in common than perhaps Pauline was willing to admit. "I was wondering if you could translate some Polish for me."

"Ah!" Pauline's voice brightened. "I could certainly give it a go. Do you know the Polish alphabet? Can you read out the letters?"

Clara dutifully read the letters. Pauline paused, then emitted a grunt of curiosity.

"It's a strange saying."

"What does it mean?"

"*Musimy przekuć ból w piękno.* 'From pain, we must make beauty.' A bit dark, I'd say, but you know, the Poles have suffered horribly, historically speaking. Where did you find it?"

Clara hesitated, unwilling to explain the metronome and from where it had come. "I came across it in an old book."

They talked for a while longer about their gardens and the travails of Pauline's bridge group, which had been beleaguered by hip replacements, then Clara hung up.

"From pain, we must make beauty," she repeated, studying the inscription.

On the couch, Bingo lifted his head.

A lost memory was finding its way to the front of Clara's mind. The day before her debut with the Chicago Symphony Orchestra the year she was twelve, Madame had given her some advice. *Just before you go on stage, close your eyes and let the music fill you with its pain. When you are ready to scream or weep, you are ready to perform.*

What if the piece is happy? Clara had asked. *What do you do then?*

Madame looked at her as if she were a fool. *Without pain, there IS no music.*

Clara ran her fingers over the engraved wood, a sadness heavy and old gathering around her heart. Shaking the feeling away, she put the metronome back in the box and, with more heft than was required, closed the lid shut.

Chapter 6

JOHN LAFLEUR HELD A JEWELER'S MONOCLE to his eye and peered at the metronome. A slight man of about fifty with hair the color of a blackbird wing and a complexion like milky tea, his face contained a stillness that Clara found reassuring. When he had spoken, which was now so long ago it seemed like an aberration, she detected a Creole accent.

Clara and Julián had chosen LaFleur Antiques from the other stores in the Yellow Pages because the graphic in the advertisement featured a violin. *Clocks, Fine Furniture, Musical Instruments, and Curios*, the ad had read. *We treasure the treasures of the past.* Clara wondered who came up with the bubbly tagline. John LaFleur did not seem capable of anything as playful as verbal puns. For forty minutes, he had worked without speaking, inspecting every inch and filigree of the metronome. She knew it was forty minutes because there were clocks on every available surface of the store: clocks ticking and clocks stilled; grandfather clocks and mantel clocks and tiny porcelain clocks in the shape of cats. Dusty shelves behind the counter held clocks in various states of dismantled disrepair—faces off, hands askew, cogs stacked in metallic towers like columns of coins. The glass display case beneath Clara's hands held what must have been a hundred gleaming watches. The ticking was clamorous. The only reprieve from the sound was the occasional squeak of an office chair from a small room behind the counter, where LaFleur's wife, a tanned Frenchwoman with elegant short hair and a cigarette coiling smoke from her fingers, sat writing in a ledger. Clara wondered how two people who seemed so deliberately quiet could stand such cacophony.

"Remind me of the translation," LaFleur said without looking up.

"From pain, we must make beauty."

"Odd." He straightened and looked at Clara. The monocle magnified his eye, which was unsettlingly blue, the color of a wilted cornflower.

"The first metronomes date from the early nineteenth century," he said. "Based on the bronze casting and all the Romantic imagery, I'd place this one around midcentury, 1850 or 1860. The box seems to be from around the same time, though from the differences in style I'd guess they were made by different craftsmen. The metronome was made by an artist. The box is finely constructed but looks like more of a tradesman's work to me."

Julián popped out from behind a seven-foot carving of a humanoid bird that had a man's long legs and a yellow pelican beak. "Do you think it's valuable?"

LaFleur set the monocle on the counter and pulled a clove cigarette from a pack of Djarums near the register. "The craftsmanship is impressive." He lit a cigarette and inhaled deeply before blowing out the smoke in a smooth line. "The materials seem to be original, aside from the repair to the rear foot." He tapped the metronome's back right corner. "It must have taken a tumble at some point. If you look closely, you can see that the grain of the wood doesn't quite match." Clara leaned forward and could barely make out a slight difference in the wave of the grain. She looked up at LaFleur, impressed. "I would never have seen that."

LaFleur nodded. "Whoever repaired it did a skillful job. Hopefully you can find someone just as good to fix the box." He tapped a finger on the buckled corner of the lid. "I'd say it's worth something. It'd be better if you knew more about it. People like objects with a story." LaFleur flicked the clove over a glass ashtray shaped like a seashell. "You say you inherited it from your piano teacher?"

"Yes."

"And she never told you anything about it?"

"No."

"Hold on." Julián placed a tortoiseshell back on a shelf and walked forward. "I think we're leaving out some important bits of the story here. The piano teacher wasn't some old bitty teaching kids in her living room. She was a famous pianist, and Clara was her star student. And not like, at-the-school-talent-show star student, but like, touring the world. The teacher and Clara weren't on good terms, but in the will, the woman said the gift was chosen especially for Clara, even though Clara has never seen this thing in her life. Oh, and it could be haunted."

LaFleur looked at Clara.

"He thinks everything old is haunted," she said.

"It is." LaFleur lifted the cigarette to his mouth. Clara and Julián both stared at him, waiting for some additional explanation, but LaFleur simply pursed his lips around the clove and inhaled. "You said some people have been asking about it?"

"Just one, I guess."

Yesterday after she hung up with Aunt Pauline, Clara's postman had arrived with a certified letter from Mr. Borthram. The unsettling missive was what had spurred her and Julián to LaFleur Antiques.

Dear Miss Bishop,

Our office has been contacted on behalf of an anonymous party interested in the metronome bequeathed to you by Ms. Mikorska. To protect your privacy and preserve the wishes of Ms. Mikorska, we have declined to respond to these inquiries. However, I am sorry to say that an intern did regrettably acknowledge that a metronome of nineteenth-century origin *was* in Ms. Mikorska's possession at the time of her death. On behalf of our firm, I apologize for this indiscretion. The mistake was met with swift reprobation. Your name was in no way mentioned as the beneficiary of the metronome; however, given that your fellow beneficiaries are aware that you are the new caretaker of the piece, it seems possible that this anonymous party may discover the means to contact you. I spoke with the gentleman myself on one occasion and found him to be quite disagreeable. He would not reveal what personal stake he had in the metronome, though by his agitation a personal stake does seem likely. I do not wish to cause you alarm. I simply advise you to be circumspect. It is the lawyer in me to plan for the worst-case scenario—an unfortunate consequence of the work.

Warmly,

Vincent Borthram

Clara looked at LaFleur. "I was advised to keep it safe."

LaFleur exhaled smoke in a slow, ruminative line. "In my experience, people don't inquire about objects that aren't valuable. From what I can tell, what you've got is a nice piece of art, but it's fairly lousy as a mechanical tool. May I?" He reached a hand to the winding key. Clara nodded. LaFleur slid the lion's head weight to sixty beats per minute, then turned the key three times. He pointed to a grandfather clock near the seven-foot bird. "Watch." He released the pendulum, and the metronome began to tock.

Julián leaned his head toward Clara's ear. "What are we watching for?" he whispered.

Clara jabbed him with her elbow. She watched the second hand move steadily around the face of the grandfather clock, passing two, then three, then four. Just as it swooped past five, Clara heard it. The metronome was not beating with the grandfather's second hand.

"It's fast," she said.

LaFleur nodded. "It's fast when you set it to a slow tempo like sixty. But listen to what happens when you set it to a fast one." He slid the lion's head toward the bottom of the pendulum alongside the marking for 200 beats per minute. "You watch the clock," he said to Julián. "Tell us when a minute has passed." Then he pointed at Clara. "You count the beats."

Julián looked annoyed. "Okay," he mumbled, looking at the clock. "Start."

For a full minute all three stood still, counting different ticks.

"All right, that's sixty seconds," Julián said. He looked at Clara. "How many beats?"

"One hundred eighty-two." She looked at LaFleur. "Too slow."

"How is it too fast at one end and too slow at the other?" Julián asked. "That doesn't make sense."

"It makes perfect sense," LaFleur said.

Seeing their confused stares, he slid open the back panel of the glass display case and removed a gold pocket watch.

"A metronome is a kind of pendulum." He held the watch from the end of its chain and the clock face began to sway back and forth. "The speed of a pendulum depends on the length of the beam. The longer the beam, the slower the swing. The shorter the beam"—he moved his fingers down the gold chain, pinching it two inches closer to the watch—"the quicker."

Clara observed the watch swing faster, thinking of the high school physics class she had never taken. She shook her head. "I still don't follow."

LaFleur stilled the watch and laid it on the counter. "A metronome is like an upside-down pendulum. Technically, it's called a double-weighted pendulum. There's a lighter weight on top"—he pointed to the lion's head—"and a heavier weight on the bottom concealed in the cabinet." He gestured to the base of the metronome. "Instead of swinging from a point at the top like my fingers on the watch chain, a double-weighted pendulum swings from the heavy weight at the bottom. The reason a metronome is shaped like a pyramid is because that bottom weight needs room to swing back and forth. That weight is supposed to stay fixed in the same spot. But if something is wrong with it—say the weight has moved on the beam over time, thereby shortening or lengthening the effective length of that beam—the time will be inaccurate."

"That still doesn't explain how the metronome would be fast on one end and slow on the other," Clara said.

"Any time anomaly will be exaggerated at the extreme ends. In the middle"—LaFleur slid the lion's head halfway up the beam to 160—"the discrepancy will be negligible, if it's noticeable at all. But the farther you get on the ends—the larger the swing of the pendulum or the tighter—the more pronounced the inaccuracy will be."

"So basically, you're saying this thing is broken," Julián said.

"It's not broken. It's inaccurate."

"But what would cause that to happen?" Clara asked.

LaFleur shrugged. "A lot of things can interfere with mechanical parts over time. Obviously, it fell or was dropped at some point if the back foot had to be repaired. That could have jarred the weight loose. But really, with an instrument this old, it could have been anything. I could open it up and take a look if you want, but sometimes with these old pieces, it's hard to get them back together in the same way." He gestured to the graveyard of clock cogs on the shelf. "You can't necessarily make it perfect, and trying to do so could ruin what makes it unique."

"Sounds like a metaphor for life," Julián said.

LaFleur slid his blue eyes to Julián. "Isn't every metaphor a metaphor for life?"

Julián's smile dropped. "Well, is it worth the risk?" he asked disagreeably.

"Not in my opinion," LaFleur said. "It's one thing if you want to use it to rehearse music. But if you're thinking of it as an antique, the time inconsistencies make it more distinctive. Someone who wants a perfectly operating metronome is going to buy a new one."

A growing disquiet was stirring in Clara's stomach. From the moment she heard the metronome accelerate ahead of the grandfather clock, a memory had been inching to the surface of her mind: Madame in the gallery, crossing out the metronome marking on Starza's *Dark Angel Sonata* with a lash of her pencil. Madame, who held sacred a composer's original intent the way Constitutionalists revered the Founding Fathers, scribbling in a new tempo. To Clara's look of incredulity, Madame had offered only the simplest of explanations. *It is too fast,* she had said. *His metronome was not right.*

Julián was watching her closely. "What is it?"

"I was just thinking of something Madame said once, but it's not relevant."

"We don't have anything relevant. What did she say?"

"It was about Starza. The composer." She looked at LaFleur, who nodded his recognition. "The metronome markings on some of Starza's faster pieces are basically unplayable. As in, it's physically undoable to play them as fast as he wanted. Most pianists disregard them. It's assumed that his metronome must have been faulty."

"Hold on." Julián turned to Clara. "Isn't Starza the guy you're related to?"

"Yeah."

Julián blinked. "And you *still* don't think it's relevant?"

"You're related to Aleksander Starza?" LaFleur asked.

"Distantly. He and my great-grandfather were cousins."

"Well, then." Julián lifted his arms triumphantly. "Mystery solved!"

"No," Clara shook her head. "Starza's metronome is gone."

She could still see clearly in her mind the plaque at the Starza Museum in Warsaw describing the scandal of Starza's death. The museum had been the composer's home, donated to the Starza Society of Warsaw by his sister Marianna after his murder in 1885. The parlor where Starza died had been reconstructed to look the way it had in the final days of his life. The plaque was mounted to the fireplace above the spot where his brutalized body was discovered by his butler. It described in Polish, German, and English how Starza's pupil, the pianist Constantia Pleyel, had on the night of December 4, 1885, bludgeoned him to death before attempting to flee the city. One of the most popular attractions of the museum was a magnifying lens attached to the treble end of Starza's Erard grand piano, which revealed dried splatters of the composer's blood. When Pleyel was apprehended the day after the murder attempting to board a train to Vienna, her luggage contained five hundred rubles taken from Starza's desk, as well as the composer's silver pocket watch. At the bottom of Pleyel's trunk, wrapped in a blood-stained petticoat, was the composer's metronome.

"It must have been worth a lot of money if she stole it," Julián said after Clara finished the story.

Clara shook her head. "It was the murder weapon. That's what she killed him with."

"Holy *shit!*" Julián raised both arms to the ceiling like a football player who had scored a touchdown. "I *told* you the thing was haunted!"

The bells on the shop door clanged against the glass. Julián jumped. A young man of about twenty stood in the doorway, wrestling a dolly of boxes over the threshold.

"Get sidetracked?" LaFleur said drily.

The young man glowered at him beneath a wave of silky black hair, then rolled the dolly behind the counter. He winked at Clara as he passed, then grimaced when he saw the other side of her face. She glared at him.

"So, you're saying this was involved in a *murder?*" Julián said after the young man had wheeled the dolly into the office.

"No," Clara insisted. "Starza's sister kept his house and all his belongings the way they were at the time of his death, but she insisted the metronome should be destroyed. She said if she kept it, it would become a spectacle, and that people would focus on her brother's death rather than his life. She burned it herself the night Pleyel was sent to the asylum. There's a newspaper story about it in the museum."

Julián's face lost its brightness. "Are there any other famous Polish composers who had a broken metronome?"

"Not that I know of."

All three of them stared down at the instrument, which had stopped oscillating and now pointed out the window, toward the setting sun.

"Why'd she do it?" LaFleur asked. "The woman who killed him."

Clara shrugged. "She went crazy, apparently. Starza was known to be abusive to his pupils. I guess one day she just snapped."

"That's a pretty extreme snap," Julián said.

Clara recalled the last lesson she had attended at Madame's, the day before her twenty-first birthday. Distracted by her plans to take over her trust and move out of her parents' home, she fumbled a note of Beethoven's "Tempest." She felt the whish of air as Madame flashed a hand into her pocket for the tuning wrench. Before the socket collided with the back of her wrist, Clara spun around and knocked it from Madame's fist, sending it skittering across the parquet. She saw a blood vessel in Madame's nose grow a deeper red as the two stared at each other. Then Clara turned back to the keyboard and finished the piece, perfect to the very end. Nothing about that lesson had been different from any of the hundreds that had come before it. It was as if her body reacted independent of her mind, deciding for itself that it had had enough.

"Starza was a pretty extreme guy," she said.

Julián rested his elbows on the glass counter. "Let's just say this is it," he said to LaFleur. "The sister never destroyed it. What would it be worth now?"

LaFleur placed another clove between his lips, squinting as he lit it with a struck match. "If this was the metronome of a famous composer, that automatically takes it up to the five-figure mark. If this is also the murder weapon that killed the guy, that'll take it up further. If it's been missing for a hundred years, that would make it worth even more." He looked at Clara as he blew smoke out the side of his mouth. "Maybe a hundred, maybe more."

"A hundred *grand*?" Julián's mouth dropped open.

"I can do a little research if you want, no charge," LaFleur said. "Call around about other metronomes with these types of features. Usually, craftsmen don't do something just once. In the meantime, you might consider storing it somewhere more secure. And not just because of accidents." He nodded reprovingly at the dented corner of the lid. "If people are asking about it, it's a good idea to keep it safe."

"Thanks," Clara said. "I will." She reached for the metronome, taking more care with it now than when she'd laid it on the counter an hour ago.

She and Julián got in the car without speaking and pulled out of the lot, driving past a wide expanse of cornfield into the orange dusk. They drove fast down the curving road, a hot wind whipping through the open windows of the car.

After a while, Julián looked over at her from the driver's seat. "Your teacher sounds insane. But it doesn't seem random to me that she gave you this thing."

Clara watched a strip of sycamore trees agitate in the breeze. "Believe me. Starza was a hero in Warsaw when he died, just like he is now. The museum has locks of his hair in a glass case. If the metronome existed, it would have turned up long before now, and it never would have made it out of Poland."

"But what if it did somehow? You're related to him. If that was his metronome, who better than you to have it? Maybe your teacher felt like she was returning it to the rightful owner."

Clara shook her head. "How would she have gotten it? And why wouldn't she tell anyone if she had? Anyway, if she thought I was the rightful owner, she could have given it to me years ago. Whatever this metronome is, she didn't give it to me for my sake. She did it for her."

Julián threw up both hands, letting the steering wheel go unmanned. "Are you sure you're not letting your emotions get in the way?"

Clara reached out to steady the wheel. "She left me in a burning room. Of course I'm letting my emotions get in the way!"

Julián put his hands up in a gesture that said *okay, okay*. They passed a tractor moving slowly down the road. The farmer at the wheel tipped his hat as they sped by. Clara waved in return, then let her arm drape out the window, buffeted by the warm wind.

"Obviously other people have an idea of what the metronome's all about," she said. "Otherwise, they wouldn't be calling the lawyer about it, right? So, let's go find Mr. Anonymous and ask him."

Julián shook his head vigorously. "The lawyer said to be circumspect. Even I know what that means. It's gay-man-in-a-Texas-saloon behavior. You keep your head down."

Clara leaned back against her seat. Anonymous seemed like the quickest way to extricate herself from the metronome, but she had to admit that she, too, had been chilled by Mr. Borthram's letter.

"Do you have any ideas?" she asked.

Julián shook his head, his face glum. "Not really."

Outside, a hawk traced a circle in the orange sky. It dove to the ground, the sun glinting off its copper tail. When it swooped out of the cornstalks, a rodent hung from its talons. Clara turned to Julián to ask if he had seen, and instead found him looking at her.

"What is it?"

"I have an insensitive question," Julián said.

"When do you not?"

But Julián wasn't smiling. "Do you ever play anymore?" he asked.

Clara's smile fell. "No."

"Because of your hand?"

"Yes. Mostly. At first it really hurt. But even when it stopped hurting so much, I couldn't play the way I used to." Pain flickered across her hand as she remembered sitting at the piano day after day for months, trying to make her fingers play pieces she had mastered when she was seven years old. No matter how many times she started over, her fingers would not do it right. "After a while it was too hard."

"Do you ever miss it?"

Clara looked out the window, searching for the hawk. When she was young, she had felt that sounds were housed within her in a catalog so deep and varied she sometimes imagined them as a store of records in a vast warehouse, stretching into unlit corners. She could name the pitch of a doorbell or sing with perfect accuracy the melody of a song she had heard only once. To her it wasn't special; it was just the way she experienced the world. The piano had hitched a buggy to the soundscape in her head, harnessing it to structure and order. Who knows what might have become of her gift had it not been for her famed ancestor Starza. Would Clara have been a violinist? A trumpeter? A marine biologist who studied the calls of whales? But Aleksander Starza loomed behind her. The piano, like her blonde hair and pale skin, was inscribed on her DNA before she ever took a breath. Then, a year or so after the fire, Clara woke one morning and the music in her head was gone. In its absence was a silence as blank as a dark room.

"Yes, I miss it," she said. "But it's not pure, you know? It's like missing someone you loved who betrayed you. You can't remember the good parts without inviting the whole avalanche of bad ones."

Julián nodded knowingly. "The piano is like your toxic breakup."

"Pretty much."

"Well, in that case, I know exactly what to do."

He looked so pleased with himself that Clara couldn't help but smile. "What's that?"

"First, you eat ice cream and drink a lot of tequila."

Clara laughed. "I think I've been in that stage for a while."

Julián looked at her archly. "I agree. That means it's time for step two."

"What's step two?"

He turned to look at her, the playfulness gone from his face. "You pick yourself up off the floor and go find something better."

They drove on toward the city, the cornstalks waving behind them in the wind. After a while, he glanced at her. "So, what are we going to do with it?"

Clara shook her head. She was already tired of asking herself this question. "I don't know."

Chapter 7

THE WEATHER WAS HOT, and The Andromeda Club was full. Outside, heat steamed up from the oily pavement, gusting into the bar with each swing of the door. Gin was the order of the night—gin martini, gin gimlet, gin and tonic, gin fizz. Every time Clara went to the back for another bottle, she heard the wheeze of the air conditioner straining to keep up. Jerry had chosen a heat-themed medley for the night and was playing "Too Darn Hot" on the Yamaha, bouncing to the rhythm in his Hawaiian shirt.

"You should tell Jerry you play piano," Julián said, pumping a cocktail shaker in his hand.

Clara shoveled ice into a pitcher, sweat gathering at the top of her belt. "Why?"

Julián paused the shaker mid-lift. "Because you have something in common, and that's what normal people do when they have something in common?"

Clara watched Jerry slide a finger up the keys in a jaunty glissando. "It seems like an awkward conversation to have five years after the fact."

"It is." Julián popped the top off the shaker. "But not as awkward as having it *six* years after the fact." He gave Clara a pointed look, then poured the frothy contents of the shaker into two cocktail glasses. He carried them out into the bar, passing Barb and Lisa, who were on their way in.

Clara pulled two highball glasses from the shelf. "The usual?" she asked.

Barb nodded as she slid onto a stool. "With extra ice."

"How's the metronome, Clara?" Lisa asked as Clara poured the gin. "Have you decided what to do with it?"

Julián walked back behind the bar carrying a stack of empty glasses. "I was just going to ask the same question."

"I hid it in the guest room," Clara said.

Lisa looked between them. "Why are you hiding it?"

"You two have missed a few episodes." Julián pushed off the counter and headed toward two women waving at him down the bar.

Barb raised an eyebrow. "So, what's the news?"

"Well, first we figured out what the inscription meant."

"What does it say?"

"'From pain, we must make beauty.'"

"Intriguing!" Lisa said.

"We thought so, too. So we took it to an antiques dealer out near Wimberley, where we learned that it doesn't keep accurate time."

"Isn't that its only job?" Barb asked.

"Yes. And in the meantime, an anonymous guy contacted the lawyer who's handling my teacher's estate. Apparently, he got wind of the whole thing and is trying to find it."

"Trying to track us down and kill us for it is more the impression I got." Julián was back from mixing the drinks.

"He's exaggerating," Clara said.

"We're still talking about a metronome, right?" Barb wagged her finger back and forth.

"Exactly. So we're wondering if maybe it has a deeper history than we thought."

Clara remained unconvinced that the deeper history had anything to do with Aleksander Starza. Nonetheless, the mahogany box was now at the back of the guest room closet, concealed at the bottom of a crate of Beethoven records. All weekend, she had felt its presence growing, filling the house like the burgeoning heat.

Julián put his hands on his hips. "You are truly terrible at narrating events!" He turned to Barb and Lisa. "The *real* story is that it might be involved in a famous crime and is probably haunted, like I've said from the beginning. Meanwhile, Clarita here keeps trying to pretend it's just some normal old clock."

"What famous crime?" Lisa asked.

"Ignore him," Clara said. In her peripheral vision, she noticed a man walk into the bar. She registered his height, the breadth of his shoulders, the smooth dip of his head as he took a stool two seats down from Barb. "It *is* just an old clock. It's just turned out to be more complicated than we thought." She smiled at Lisa, then turned to the man to take his order and felt her smile die.

"Hello, Clara."

Tony Park's giant hands rested on the burnished oak. He wore a black leather jacket and a collared shirt the color of a deep merlot. Sitting among the other patrons in their jeans and tank tops, he looked absurdly overdressed, and also as if he belonged to a life better than all of them, where he was used to making a disturbance and getting what he wanted.

Barb, Lisa, and Julián were all staring, waiting for her to explain who Tony was and why he was sitting at her bar. All she could come up with was "What are you doing here?"

Tony smiled broadly. Even in shock, Clara recognized it as his stage smile. Anger flared within her. He had wanted to make a grand entrance.

"I had a conference in Dallas and thought I'd stop in to say hello," he said.

Clara realized her mouth was hanging open and quickly closed it. "Dallas is two hundred miles away."

Tony laughed as if this were a great jest between them. "I figured that out on the drive here."

"How did you know where I worked?"

Tony leaned forward to rest his elbows on the bar. "Your mother told me. She said to tell you hello."

The exhilaration with which Ruth must have received an unexpected phone call from Tony Park infuriated Clara anew. But she would not permit Tony to see. She wiped her hands on her apron, gathering up what was left of her performer's reserve of poise.

"Two hundred miles is a long way to drive to say hello. What are you having?"

Tony looked past her to the liquor shelf. "What's your specialty? The Clara Bishop I remember always had a signature style."

This was the problem with Tony Park. He invariably sought out the things that mattered and twisted them around to make them seem stupid.

"The Vieux Carré," Clara said, looking him in the eye. She would not allow Tony Park to make her feel small. "It's a whiskey cocktail."

"The Vieux Carré," Tony repeated, mulling the words in his mouth. "I do remember you had a fondness for whiskey. Scotch, if I'm correct." One corner of his mouth lifted.

Fury stirred in her chest. "That was a long time ago."

"So it was." Tony smiled, but the silk had flowed out of his voice.

Clara pulled bottles of rye, cognac, and vermouth to the counter, glad to have an excuse to turn her back on him. Julián stepped beside her and began wiping his rag along an invisible wet spot near the register. "Care to explain?" he whispered.

She poured the rye and cognac into a mixing glass, keeping her eyes on her work but her attention behind her, where she could hear Tony introducing himself to Barb and Lisa.

"He was Madame's student, too," she said. "The one I told you about."

"The jerk from when you were a teenager?"

"Yes."

Julián snuck an appraising look at Tony. "Why do jerks always have to look like that?"

"Like what?"

Julián made a face. "Look at that jawline. He's like an Armani model! I hope you've had sex with him."

Clara shaved a lemon peel with her knife and twisted it onto the rim of the glass, seized by a vision of Tony standing behind her in his Brussels hotel room, sliding the strap of her black dress down her shoulder with his teeth. "I haven't."

Julián had seen the memory on her face. "You're blushing!" he whispered gleefully.

"I'm not *blushing*. We had a thing. Once."

"A *thing*?"

Clara looked over her shoulder at Tony, who was talking warmly to Barb and Lisa. "We were together." Clara shook her head. "Not *together*, but—" She dumped the Vieux Carré into a cocktail glass. "It was just for a week, a million years ago. We were at the same competition and had a thing. That's all."

"Looks like maybe it's not *really* all if he drove all the way from Dallas for a drink. What happened?"

Clara stabbed a brandied cherry with a toothpick and dropped it in the glass. "I won the competition and he never spoke to me again."

She picked up the drink and walked it to Tony, who was talking to Lisa about the new Sonic Youth album. Imagining Tony Park listening to Sonic Youth made her feel like the disjointed halves of her life were sliding together like two slabs of Jell-O.

"The Clara Bishop Vieux Carré," she said. She set the glass on the bar, a little too hard.

"Tony was just telling us that you two know each other from child-hood," Lisa said.

"Not just childhood," Clara corrected. She turned to Tony with false brightness. "You're forgetting about Brussels."

Tony's smile blanched, and she felt the situation shift back in her favor.

"So how long will you be in Texas?" Clara asked, hoping to get to the point of this surprise visit. She wanted him out of her bar. Out of the state. Out of her life.

"Just the night," Tony said. "I'm staying at the Driskill Hotel. I thought I would take you to breakfast before I fly out tomorrow."

Behind her, Julián coughed. Clara wanted to kick him.

"I have to take my dog to the vet," she said, latching onto the first excuse that entered her mind.

Tony shrugged. "I'll have to settle for a drink, then." He took a sip of the Vieux Carré, frowning a little as he tasted it. Impatience quickened her pulse.

Barb and Lisa had sensed the tension and were drinking their gin and tonics quickly.

"Another round?" Clara asked, wanting them to feel welcome but also wishing everyone in the bar would leave. She did not feel equipped to contend with a surprise visit from Tony, much less while sweating through her shirt.

"We have dinner plans," Barb said, rising. "We were just popping by for a quick one." She laid a ten on the bar. "Nice to meet you," she said to Tony.

"Same." Tony tipped his head.

After they'd left, he looked around the bar, taking it all in. "It's nice here," he said to Clara. "Do you like it?"

"I do."

"You know, if you ever want a career change, I'd be happy to have you on the faculty at Northwestern."

"I already changed from that career."

Tony shrugged. "You should think about it. I've been riding Madame's coattails for years, and I studied with her for half the time."

"Like I said, I'm happy here."

"Sure." Tony set down his glass with a click. "Speaking of Madame, how's the metronome?"

From behind her, Clara felt Julián's head tilt up.

Clara kept her eyes very still. It was the only useful skill she had ever learned from Kerry, to be deployed when dealing with the press. Pick a vein in their eye to stare at while you lie.

"I had it checked out by an antiques dealer," she said.

Tony's forehead contracted a little. "Are you thinking of selling it?"

"I don't have much use for it."

"You're not putting any stock in Madame's instructions, then."

"Why should I? I don't even know why she gave it to me."

"I'd be interested, if you're selling."

Clara let her eyes float to Tony's. For an instant she saw in his guarded look the ruthless teenager she had spent so much of her childhood trying to beat. "What do you want with it?"

Tony looked at her over the rim of his glass and took a sip from the Vieux Carré. "I'm starting a collection of Madame's manuscripts at the university. I thought a dedicated place for some of her belongings would be a draw for scholars."

Tony Park, music altruist. Clara had to stop herself from scoffing. A desire to crush him rose within her, as familiar as if she were seventeen waiting in the wings to go on stage.

"What a great idea," Clara said, bobbing her head. "I mean, the metronome's not particularly valuable or anything, so why not donate it to the cause of music?"

"That's exactly what I was thinking," Tony said eagerly. "Don't get me wrong, she was impossible as a person, but her legacy is her brilliant playing. Adding her metronome to the collection would be a nice personal touch."

Clara had been nodding enthusiastically. Now she let her smile drop. "What are you doing here, Tony?"

In a millisecond, Julián was beside her.

Tony looked between them, his face assuming an expression of practiced bafflement. "I told you. I had a conference in Dallas and wanted to say hello."

Clara tossed her bar towel over her shoulder. "In that case, hello. It was great to see you. Good luck with your project. Your magnanimity is inspirational." She turned to walk away.

"Oh, hold on," Tony groaned. "You're always so *dramatic.*"

"Excuse me, Mr. Hugo Boss," Julián interjected. "Who's driving here from *Dallas* to try to steal a freaking *metronome?*"

Tony lifted his palms in a gesture of innocence. "I'm not trying to steal anything! I just offered to buy it!"

Julián crossed his arms over his chest.

Tony sighed. "Okay, okay! I don't know anything *for sure.* I just have some suspicions that maybe it's—" He glanced behind him into the bar. "Important."

Julián turned to Clara. "You were right about him."

"Right about what?" Tony asked.

"Hmm." Julián walked to the register, where he began tallying receipts.

Tony looked at Clara probingly. "Listen, Clara. I've been going through the stuff Madame gave me. There's boxes of papers. Scores, notebooks, old concert bills, everything. Her edition of the *Fire Concerto* is the same one she's used since the forties. There are notes all over it. *Rubato* here and *more adagio* there, that sort of thing. I'm thinking of publishing a critical edition, actually. But anyway, I noticed that at the top of each movement, she crossed out the metronome marking and made her own notation."

Clara's heart began to thud a little faster.

"At first I didn't think much of it. Everybody changes the tempo on Starza, right? But do you remember the marking he gave the second movement?"

Clara didn't remember at all. And yet she knew exactly the number that Tony was about to say.

"Seventy-two," Tony said. "Madame marked it out on the score. Her note at the beginning of that movement puts the tempo at eighty-eight. But the seventy-two stuck with me. And then the other day I had the score out in the archive room at the university. They have these bright reading lights in there, you know. You can see every pencil mark. And I noticed that there was another marking right next to it. It was so faint I had to get a magnifying glass out to see it. It looks like she wrote it in pencil a long time ago and then erased it."

Tony reached across the bar for a pen and scribbled on a napkin, then held it up to Clara:

$$\flat = 88 = Sza\ 72$$

"It says eighty-eight *equals* Starza's seventy-two," he said. "That's not a guess. That's an assertion of fact."

Clara looked away from the napkin and began swabbing the bar. "Madame said everything as if it was an assertion of fact. She didn't believe in gray areas."

"In music she did," Tony said emphatically. "All her articles are about gray areas, especially when it comes to Starza. She wrote about *all* his gray areas. Except one. I've read every article Madame ever published. Not one of them is about Starza's metronome."

"Maybe because it's not worth writing about a broken clock."

"Or maybe it's because she didn't want to draw attention to it. Clara, what if the metronome she gave you is *that* metronome. You know—" Tony lowered his voice. "*His.*"

Clara rolled her eyes. "It's okay, Tony. I don't think anyone in here knows who *HE* is."

Tony's eyes widened. "Is it true, then?"

"No," Clara insisted. "That metronome was—"

"Destroyed, I know, I know." Tony waved it off. "But what if somehow it wasn't? What if it survived?"

Clara shook her head. "If Madame had Starza's metronome, she would have displayed it in her collection and bragged about it like she did all her other historical stuff."

"She didn't brag about having a Guarneri violin."

"But it was still in the display case," Clara retorted. "We all knew it was there, we just didn't know it was a Guarneri. Nobody at her house the other night had ever even seen that metronome."

"Isn't that all the more reason to investigate? Don't you want to know what you've got?"

How many ways did she need to explain that she did not?

"What would we even be looking for?" she said. "As far as I can tell, there's no way to know if it was Starza's or not."

Julián had busied himself with counting money from the drawer. Now he stopped abruptly, a pile of twenties in his hand. She knew he was thinking about the inscription.

"I know some music historians," Tony said. "They could help us."

"*Us?*"

Tony looked exasperated. "Fine. *You.*"

Clara studied him, trying to determine what he was up to. "Why are you so interested? And don't give me some tall tale about your devotion to music history."

Tony leaned back on his stool. "I'm up for tenure in the fall." He eyed Julián disagreeably before looking back at Clara. "Some of my colleagues on the hiring committee don't want me to get the job."

"How surprising," Julián piped in from the register.

Tony shot him a dirty look. "If I can publish something significant in the field, you know, something that would enhance the prestige of the department, it could help."

"I guess your job offer was bogus, then," Clara said.

"Not at all. I still have my position until December. I meant what I said. I don't care what the state of your hand is, you're wasting your talent here." Tony waved dismissively at the bar. "Come on, Clara. All personal ambition aside, don't you want to know if it's his? Even if you don't want me involved, at least promise me you won't sell it to some antiques dealer who doesn't know its historical value. Put it in a museum or something so people can study it." He tossed a twenty on the bar and laid his business card on top. "Think about it, okay?"

He nodded goodbye to Julián, then strode out of the bar. Clara watched him stroll past the picture window, head lifted, his gait easy and unhurried, as if he knew all the coin tosses of life would fall in his favor.

Julián leaned against the counter. "He might be right, you know. Maybe he could help you figure it out. He's no dummy."

"No. He's not." Clara hadn't remembered Starza's metronome marking on the second movement of the *Fire Concerto*. She had to admit it was an interesting coincidence. "But I don't really want to help Tony Park become even greater than he already is."

Julián nodded thoughtfully. "And if it is the guy's—Starza's—it still doesn't help you with the real question."

"What's the real question?"

The look Julián gave her said *Are you dumb?*

"How did your teacher get it, and why did she give it to you?"

It was after two a.m. when Clara got home. Bingo ambled sleepily to the door to nose her hand, then plodded back down the hall to the bedroom. The red light on the answering machine blinked from the kitchen counter. Clara thought immediately of Tony, but when the tape played back, it was just the click of a receiver hanging up. Relieved, she turned off the lights and followed Bingo to bed.

She jolted awake a few hours later to the sound of the phone. In the bands of moonlight coming in between the blinds, she could see the silhouette of Bingo's lifted head, his ears pricked in alert. Clara lay still as the answering machine beeped on and the sound of her own recorded voice drifted down the hall. After the beep, there was only a click. She closed her eyes. When the phone rang again, she sat up.

Still wading through the fog of sleep, she stumbled out into the hallway, where the nightlight flickered its wavering yellow flame. She picked up on the fourth ring.

"Hello?"

"Clara Bishop?" It was a woman's voice, throaty and weathered, with a breathy wheeze after each word as if every syllable were a labor to get out.

Clara looked at the clock on the microwave. It was 5:07. "Who is this?"

"Do you have it?" The woman began to cough, a gasping, hacking sound choked of air. In the background, Clara heard what sounded like someone banging on a door.

"Who is this?" Clara demanded.

"She . . . *stole* it," the woman wheezed.

Clara shook her head. "Who stole what?"

"Mikorska," the woman panted. "She . . . stole it from my father. We're going to get it back, you know. We'll get it—"

Clara heard a clatter in the background, then the line went dead.

Bingo had followed her out of the bedroom and stood at the mouth of the hallway with his head cocked to the side as if asking what was wrong. Now he padded up to her and butted her hand with his large head. Clara crouched down and hugged him around the neck. When the phone rang again, they both jumped. She stared at it until the answering machine clicked on and the caller hung up.

Knowing she would not be able to sleep, she made coffee and drank it sitting on the porch, listening to the birds begin to titter in the trees. Should she call the police? Mr. Borthram? The phone company? She deliberated a long while before finally rising to walk inside. The sun was just coming up when she wheeled her bike out of the gate, headed for the Driskill Hotel.

Chapter 8

Starza at 150: A Timeless Genius, A Man of His Times
Harold Young, Princeton University

Few composers of the Romantic Age have garnered more renown than Aleksander Starza. His name stands boldly alongside the other luminaries of the nineteenth century, yet unlike many of his fellow Romantics, Starza the man remains largely unknown. In his life, he sought always to retreat from the public eye. A hundred and fifty years after his birth, he looks away still. An international star by the time he was twelve, he was comfortable performing in the grand concert halls of Europe but felt "dumb as a fish" at dinner parties held in his honor. He roared at conductors over the smallest mistake, yet answered fan mail with gracious kindness. He terrified and, in some cases, physically threatened his pupils, yet was described by his sister Marianna as "the most tender man who has walked this earth." To some, he is that quintessentially Romantic symbol—the misunderstood and tragic genius, gone too soon (see "Tarry Not, Ye Burning Star" by Frederick E. West, page 178). Others have argued that Starza was a mentally unstable narcissist whose violent death was an unsurprising end to a disturbed life (see "The Pugilist of Sound: Violence and Madness in Starza's 'Delicate Genius'" by Zofia Mikorska, page 243). What no one disputes is that Starza's music stands among the best ever written. His work was described by his contemporary Johannes Brahms as "pure human feeling caught in the net of a stave."

Aleksander Karol Starza was born in Warsaw on December 21, 1844, in what was then Russian-occupied Poland. The Starzas were respectable but poor, both parents hailing from old families that had once been Polish nobility. Michał Starza was a physics and mathematics teacher who taught at one of Warsaw's secondary schools for boys; Starza's mother, Zuzanna, was a pianist and opera singer who had once performed in Warsaw's Grand Theatre. Zuzanna was her son's first piano teacher, and recognized early his prodigious musical talent. By the age of three, Aleksander was inventing compositions of his own, which Zuzanna transcribed since the little boy could not yet fully manipulate a pen.

Tragedy struck the Starza household in 1850 when Zuzanna died from tuberculosis. "It was as if a snow fell over the house, though outside roses bloomed in the yard," Marianna Starza wrote later of that time. "The year of mourning never ended in our father's house." A stern man even before his wife's death, Michał Starza shut himself in his study with his newspapers and books. Equally devastated, the five-year-old Aleksander fell silent, refusing to speak for three months. A concerned Marianna assumed responsibility for nurturing her brother and his talent. She found him a new teacher, the pianist Casimir Mikuli, and persuaded her father to pay for the lessons. Deeply impressed by his young pupil, Mikuli arranged for Aleksander to give his first public concert at the hall of Warsaw's Philharmonic Society in 1852. Within a year, the reputation of Aleksander's talent earned him an invitation to Vienna, where his virtuosic performances transformed him into an overnight star.

Despite the welcome income Aleksander's fame brought the struggling Starza family, Michał failed to muster support for his son's achievements. A talented but frustrated academic who had been routinely passed over for advancement in favor of his Russian colleagues, the senior Starza resented his son's early success, and was equally frustrated by Aleksander's sensitivity. From an early age, Aleksander was known in the family for his "melancholic disposition." As a child, this melancholy manifested in outbursts of tears that would enrage his father. In Starza's adolescence, the tears turned to anger. Marianna often found herself between father and brother, serving as "translator between two separate languages the other could never seem to learn."

Whether it was due to this enduring paternal conflict, his mother's early death, or simply the "melancholic disposition" with which he was born, Starza soon earned the reputation as a difficult genius that would follow him the rest of his life. "It is a regret," wrote one reviewer in 1858, "that a young soul in possession of such divine talent seems possessed of a demon's spirit. To watch the boy perform is as to watch Lucifer and Michael battle for the fate of man." Starza did little to counter such opinions. Upon reading the review in the Vienna newspaper, the fourteen-year-old boy promptly sent the man the contents of his chamber pot.

"Do you play?"

Clara looked up, startled. The plane was descending over Chicago. Below, gray grids of neighborhoods spread out in the misty morning, anonymous and small. Across the aisle, a skinny teenager in khakis and a swallowing navy polo shirt was looking at the book in Clara's hand.

"Sorry to interrupt you," he said, his Texas drawl thick. "I don't see people reading about composers very often. I'm a pianist. Or, trying to be, anyway," he said, blushing. "Do you play?"

"I used to," Clara said. "I don't anymore."

The boy beamed. "Starza's my favorite composer. The *Dark Angel Sonata* especially. What's your favorite piece?"

"Probably the 'Sister' Nocturnes," she said. "And the *Fire Concerto*."

"Oh, I could never play that," the boy exclaimed, laughing.

"If you're playing the *Dark Angel*, you could."

"Nah," the boy laughed. "I don't think so. My mom and I are going to Chicago to tour music schools—the University of Chicago, Roosevelt University, Northwestern." He ticked off each one on a long, slender finger. "But I doubt I could get into any of them, to be honest."

"You never know," Clara said.

"Sometimes you do," the boy said amiably. "But it's good life experience. That's what my mom says. Anyway, I won't bother you anymore. You can get back to your book. My name's Peter," he said. "Peter Juniper."

"Clara Bishop," she said. "Nice to meet you, Peter."

They shook hands, then Clara picked up the book and continued reading.

The early 1860s saw renewed political unrest in Warsaw as Poles increased demands for political and social reform. After a deadly protest in Warsaw's Castle Square left over one hundred praying protestors dead, the Starzas determined it was best if Aleksander left the tumult of Poland. Marianna had planned to go with him, but that summer, Michał, like his beloved wife before him, fell ill with tuberculosis. Accepting her role as the matriarch of the family, Marianna decided to remain in Warsaw to nurse him.

Starza settled in Paris, where their father had distant relations. A young man of seventeen, already famous but uncomfortable in the spotlight, lonely but debilitatingly shy, Starza was adrift in France and desperately homesick for Poland. In a letter to Marianna, he called Paris "a city of elegance and indifference." He was besieged by requests to perform, but never overcame the feeling that he was an impostor among the Parisian musical elite. "I am like a farmhand come to the dinner table," he wrote to Marianna in 1862. "They delight at the spectacle I make, and no doubt laugh at my expense when I am gone."

To support the family back in Warsaw as well as a growing taste for finery, Starza supplemented the money he made from performing by teaching pupils from well-to-do French families. It is here that the reputation of his volatile temper grew. Starza had little patience for novice pianists, and less for undedicated ones. He was known to lose his temper at as little as an incorrect note. "I have practiced for three days without sleeping," one young woman wrote. "If I do not play perfectly, Monsieur Starza is sure to kill me."

Despite or perhaps because of his sense of alienation, it was in Paris that Starza came fully into his compositional powers. In 1862 alone, the composer wrote what are now known as the "Early" Nocturnes, the op. 6 Mazurkas, the Fantasy in E-flat Major, and Sonatas Nos. 3–7. News of the January Uprising in Poland in 1863 only intensified his compositional focus. During the eighteen months of the Polish rebellion, Starza composed twenty Polonaises, including the beloved *Liberty* Polonaise destined to become one of his most famous works. When in 1864 he received word of the quashed rebellion, he wrote to Marianna that the news "brought pain to my chest the same as if my heart were pierced by a Russian bayonet." Barely a month later, Michał died. Aleksander had not been home in three years. Plagued by guilt, he wrote his three Elegies, op. 11, as well as the famous *Mourning Variations*, which he dedicated, simply, "To Poland."

Starza's spirits temporarily lifted in 1866. In March he wrote to Marianna that he had fallen in love. Referred to in his letters only as "Annabelle," the young woman of Starza's affection was likely Anne-Marie Brodeur, the daughter of a low-level official in the French army. Starza met Annabelle in the kitchen yard of the home at which he was living. She was a friend of one of the maids. Correctly believing that Marianna would not approve of the match, Starza wrote: "She possesses not the grace of a lady, but her mind and heart are pure and true as Bach."

Marianna wrote immediately to her brother to caution him against becoming "ensnared by someone unworthy of your genius." Disregarding his sister's advice, Starza proposed. Annabelle accepted, but soon discovered that Starza was not the gentleman of great fortune she had thought him to be. She abruptly ended the relationship and married a lieutenant in the French army. "I have been deluded," a miserable Starza wrote. "Neither her body nor her mind were true." Starza never forgave the betrayal, and never loved again. "With the exception of you, my faithful sister, and our mother," he wrote to Marianna years later, "there is no woman on earth whose beauty might persuade me that she is worth the inconstancy of her heart."

A few weeks after Annabelle broke the engagement, Starza suffered the first of many episodes of severe depression he was to endure in his life. Reports Marianna received from the Paris relations suggest that the composer was drinking heavily, often to the point of unconsciousness. In October he wrote to Marianna that he feared himself "on the precipice of death." Elliptical references in her journal suggest that Starza may have attempted suicide. Marianna traveled immediately to Paris to nurse him, and in the spring of 1867, the siblings returned to Warsaw, where, Marianna wrote, "The Russians may be in the streets, but the blue Polish skies are a balm to my brother's heart."

Starza returned to a changed Poland. Russian was now the official language, Polish schoolchildren were forced to memorize the names of the Russian Imperial Family, and Poles faced new obstacles gaining positions in the vast Imperial bureaucracy. Despite new restrictions on Polish history and customs, however, Warsaw was a cosmopolitan city with robust industry, first-class hotels, and a thriving musical culture. Starza returned to the city of his birth a hero. When he went out, which was infrequently, he was treated as a celebrity by Poles and Russians alike.

Marianna had served as her brother's amanuensis since the mid-1860s, when his publisher printed an incorrect edition of Sonata No. 2 as a result of the composer's famously illegible handwriting. Upon returning to Warsaw, she took on more responsibilities as his business manager and began scheduling concerts and managing correspondence with Starza's publisher, the venerable Breitkopf and Härtel in Leipzig. During this period of domestic companionship, Marianna also worked tirelessly to maintain her brother's fragile mental health. The household operated on a strict schedule that included "waking promptly at seven, bed no later than eleven. No poetry after dark. No melancholy visitors."

The composer regained his health, and by 1870 was writing prolifically and once again touring Europe. Yet even in this time of relative calm, he was prone to melancholy moods during which he would frequently vow to abandon composition forever, often throwing whatever work he had in progress into the nearest fire.

In February 1881, Starza suffered a fever that left him fearful for his life. When he recovered, he announced that he was finished with performing and would devote himself wholly to composition. In a letter to his publisher Christoph Windscheid at Breitkopf and Härtel, he wrote, "Many can perform. Only I can create the music that beats so wildly about my mind. There is no time to waste."

Waste time he did not. The year 1881 ushered in what many historians believe to be the composer's golden period of composition. Lasting until his early death in 1885, the Golden Years were fertile ground for no fewer than twenty-six of the composer's greatest works for piano. Among these were such masterpieces as the *Dark Angel Sonata*, the two "Sister" Nocturnes in

A Minor, and the composer's crowning achievements, Concerto No. 2 in F# Minor and Concerto No. 3 in E Minor, the masterful *Fire Concerto*, named for the tempo marking of the opening movement—*Allegro con fuoco*, "fast, with fire."

Unfortunately for Starza, the Golden Years of composition did not correspond to happy ones in the composer's personal life. In May 1881, a dispute with Marianna led Starza to vacate the family's Foksal Street home and establish residence in his own house on Freta Street. Marianna, normally voluble about the details of the Starzas' domestic lives in her journals, is silent on the source of the rift between the siblings. For this reason, scholars have often concluded that the origin of Starza's complaint was with Marianna herself. Whatever the source of conflict, it had reverberating effects on the composer's life. Though she continued her responsibilities as his amanuensis and business manager, her stabilizing influence on her brother was gone. Without Marianna to manage his domestic affairs and lacking the income from performing, the notoriously profligate Starza soon found himself in financial straits and opened his home to private students. In the fall of 1881, one of those students was Constantia Pleyel.

Constantia Baranowska Pleyel, youngest daughter of the violinist Stanisław Baranowski, had herself been a renowned prodigy. A young Starza saw her perform in Vienna in 1859 when she was just eleven and was deeply affected by the girl's artistic powers. According to Marianna's journal from that time, "Aleksander refused to play for well near a month, claiming he would never approach Baranowska's mastery." Pleyel's career as a pianist ended in 1869 after she fell from a horse while on honeymoon with her husband, the French opera singer Olivier Pleyel. The accident resulted in a broken wrist as well as two broken fingers of the right hand. The injuries never fully healed, and Pleyel retired from performance life at the age of twenty-one.

Pleyel and Starza met in February 1881 at a salon at the home of one of Starza's benefactors, Valeska Holland. In their initial exchange, Pleyel reportedly called Starza's recently debuted Piano Trio in D "wooden and rote." Starza in turn called Pleyel a "deformed impostor of the piano" among other epithets "impugning her female character." The incident soon became a topic of gossip in the Warsaw newspapers. At the direction of Holland, who threatened to withdraw her financial support of Starza, the composer wrote Pleyel a letter of apology in which he suggested a regimen of finger exercises that might improve Pleyel's injured hand. The two began a correspondence about Starza's proposed rehabilitation plan, and in September 1881 Pleyel began weekly lessons at the composer's Freta Street address.

The relationship was tumultuous from the start. Known for her own temper, Pleyel quit her lessons no fewer than three times, writing in one colorful letter to Starza, "Were it not for these pathetic fingers, dear sir, which leave me bonded to you like a servant to his master, I would use my good hand to strike you in your sniveling mouth." Starza held no shortage of animosity in return, saying in a letter to Christoph Windscheid that Pleyel was "as much a demon as any man could ever be, without even the veneer of Eve." The arrangement continued nonetheless, as Starza, continually draining his finances with his taste for fine clothes and, increasingly, fine liquor, needed money, and Pleyel was desperate to return to the stage. Marianna disapproved of her brother's arrangement with Pleyel, writing in a letter in 1882 that "she is the sort who will never be content until she has stolen all she can of your own light, that yours might shine a little dimmer." Unfortunately, her advice proved eerily prescient.

In October 1885, Pleyel gave birth to her second child. A maid who worked in the Pleyel residence described the change that came over her mistress soon after. Pleyel fired most of her domestic help, refused to allow her husband near the child, and stayed up all night playing her piano, practicing until she slept on the keys. Weeks later, on December 4, 1885, Pleyel went to her regular lesson at Starza's home. Reports from her maid suggest she left that evening in a state of agitation, with her hair and clothes disheveled. Alarms were raised by her husband when she did not return home later that night. At eleven o'clock, Starza's butler, who was off for the evening, returned to the composer's residence to find Starza on the floor of his parlor in a bloody scene the butler described as "a battleground." The composer had suffered a massive blow to the head. Pleyel was apprehended the next morning at Warsaw's Vienna Station attempting to board a train with her infant daughter. In her possession were five hundred rubles stolen from Starza's desk, the composer's silver pocket watch, and the murder weapon: the composer's own metronome.

Reports from the chief inspector who interrogated Pleyel in the days after the murder describe her as disoriented and volatile. While in custody, she screamed for hours on end, refused food, and physically attacked a prison guard who delivered her dinner, thereafter requiring forcible restraint. The team of psychiatrists appointed to evaluate her declared her a psychopath. She was deemed mentally unfit to stand trial and lived the remainder of her life in an asylum, where she died of the Russian Influenza Epidemic of 1889–1890.

Constantia Pleyel's fatal actions on December 4, 1885, inflicted not just one, but two great tragedies: she silenced that night not just the man, but countless unknown works the world will never—

Clara shut the book and slid it into her backpack, where it settled against the metronome with a quiet thud. *When Genius Speaks: The Life and Music of Aleksander Starza* was the fourth collection of essays about the composer she had checked out from the Austin Public Library. None of them had yielded any new information about Starza's metronome, though reading about Constantia Pleyel's injuries and subsequent psychological decline never failed to cause Clara a moment of queasiness. The feeling grew as the plane dropped closer to the tarmac and skidded onto the runway.

Her mother was waiting at the gate.

"Oh, darling!" Ruth cried, loud enough that the people in front of Clara looked up. "Welcome home!"

Clara tensed. Her mother's public displays of emotion had always made her uncomfortable. Even as a child, she had sensed that Ruth's gushing was a cover-up of the deeper disconnect that had always existed between them. The louder Ruth fawned over her in front of others, the longer the silences when they were alone.

"Hi, Mom," she said.

They stood opposite each other beside a reuniting family embracing a teenage girl. Clara held her suitcase in one hand and her jacket in the other, the luggage saving them from the awkward moments of first meeting, when neither knew what to say or where to put her hands.

"You look wonderful!" Ruth said. "Have you been using the creams I sent you?"

"Every now and then," Clara lied. One of the rules she had set for her life in Austin was to stop trying to improve the look of her scars. Every expensive cream Ruth sent her was contributed directly to Julián's expansive medicine cabinet.

"They certainly haven't disappointed," Ruth said. "I told you you'd look better with time."

"You did." Clara inhaled, trying not to make it look like the calming breath it was. "It's good to see you, Mom. Let's go home."

They walked through the terminal, Ruth with her quick gait just slightly ahead of Clara. Her mother had turned sixty since Clara had last seen her, and yet somehow looked younger. Clara found herself sneaking glances at Ruth's neck, searching for evidence of a facelift. For as long as Clara could remember, her mother had dressed for each day with full makeup and hair, and accessories to match. For every occasion and weather, there was a scarf to drift behind her in the stir—real or imagined—she created when she walked into a room. Now her copper hair was tastefully highlighted and cut into "The Rachel." Her arms were toned and sunned with the fake tanning lotion she purchased by the boxful. Her white tunic was perfectly complemented by navy pants and a matching silk scarf. With her sunglasses hanging from the collar of her shirt, she looked ready for a day at sea.

"How's that young man you were seeing?" Ruth asked as they rode down the escalator. "Eli?"

Eli had been a prolific creator of abstract paintings that appeared indistinguishable from one another and reminded Clara, always, of winds blowing across a snowscape. Clara broke it off after he asked if he could paint a portrait of her face "in all its tortured beauty."

"We broke up last fall," Clara said.

"You didn't tell me that!"

"We weren't that serious. How's Dad?"

"Oh, you know your father," Ruth said brightly. "Always into something."

Clara had never known her father to be into anything but day-trading and managing the Bishops' impeccable lawn. How he spent his time in retirement was a source of perpetual bafflement to her.

"He'd like to have dinner if you're free," Ruth said. "I called Giuseppe's, but they didn't have any tables at such last minute, so we'll have to go someplace regular."

"Regular is great," Clara said. "We don't have to do anything fancy."

"You haven't been here in over three years!" Ruth exclaimed. "We need to celebrate."

Clara felt the skin around her scars tighten. "It was two years, actually," she said.

"No, three. Two years ago would have been our anniversary party."

They had made it to the parking lot, where Ruth's navy-blue Saab was parked in the very first row. Clara gripped the strap of her backpack as she waited for Ruth to unlock the door. Her failure to attend the twenty-fifth anniversary party had resulted in a six-month silence that only thawed when Clara's father had required an emergency appendectomy.

"Well, I'm glad to be here now," she said, with as much enthusiasm as she could conjure.

"And your father and I couldn't be happier about it either." Ruth started the car and pulled out of the lot. For a while the only sound was the whir of the engine and the *clip-clop* of the windshield wipers. Clara couldn't think of any safe topic—not work, or Bingo ("feral beasts," Ruth had always said of dogs), or her social life. Certainly not her clandestine trip to Chicago for Madame's final concert or the phone call that had jarred her awake in the middle of the night last week. For years when Clara spoke to her parents, there hadn't been anything to report. Now there was so much to say that to acknowledge any of it would have been an admission that her parents knew less about her life than a handful of near strangers.

"What are your plans while you're here?" Ruth finally asked. "Anything in particular?"

Clara shifted in her seat. "I'm meeting someone tomorrow morning."

"Oh, how nice! Who?"

Clara braced for impact. "Tony Park."

"To-ny *Park*!" The three syllables held the delight and surprise of an entire romance. "I was wondering if it might have something to do with him," Ruth said knowingly. "He called here last week asking for your address. I didn't realize you two were still friends."

Clara resisted the urge to admonish her mother for handing out her address without permission. "We weren't ever friends. Madame willed us some things when she died. We're meeting to talk about what to do with them."

Ruth gripped the steering wheel a little tighter. Madame had become an off-limits subject between Clara and her parents years ago. "What kinds of things?"

"Tony inherited her scores and papers." Clara looked out the window at a train traveling parallel to them along the highway. "I got a metronome."

"That's odd." Ruth opened her mouth to say something more, and Clara could tell she wanted to ask about the invitation she had forwarded to Austin. Ruth seemed to think better of it and veered back to Tony.

"I was just at the mall and saw Tony's new album at Sam Goody. He's awfully handsome now."

Clara groaned. "Mom."

"I'm just *observing*, Clara. He was such a sour-looking child. Always scowling. It just goes to show."

Ruth's favorite expression was "It just goes to show." She applied it liberally and indiscriminately, like the wrinkle cream she slathered on her skin.

"Goes to show what?" Clara asked.

"Sometimes handsome results bloom from unfortunate beginnings. I always did like him, you know."

"You didn't. You thought he was a sore loser. Which, by the way, he was."

"He was just a *child*, Clara. People grow up! What is Tony doing in Chicago? His bio in the CD booklet said he was still in New York."

Clara did not miss that her mother had stopped to read the liner notes in Tony's album. "He teaches at Northwestern now."

"How prestigious!"

Clara did not reply. When she knocked on the door of Tony's hotel room last week, he had seemed her best option for determining what to do about the metronome and the mysterious five-a.m. caller. He answered the door in a Driskill Hotel bathrobe. Underneath, he was bare to the waist. Clara noticed he had a six-pack, and wished she hadn't. Of course Tony Park found time between touring and teaching to do sit-ups.

"If you help me identify the metronome, what do you want in return?" Clara had asked.

Tony blinked, his eyes still bleary with sleep. "If it's Starza's, I want to buy it."

"What if it's not his?"

Tony shrugged. "If it's not his, I don't care."

Ruth pulled the Saab into the Bishops' driveway. A two-story brick in the Federalist style with a hedge of evergreen bushes lining the front, it had always seemed to Clara like a house for old people, which she supposed it now finally was. Everything from the tuck-pointed brick to the tidy paving stones exuded control. The gutters were painted a respectable brown that matched the shingles of the roof. The lawn featured unimpeachable edging. Even today, with the wind and rain blowing through the trees, there wasn't a leaf on the bright green grass. One of Clara's most distinct memories from childhood was her father bent over in the yard, picking up leaves by hand every day before breakfast.

Ruth parked in the garage next to a freshly waxed Volvo. The metal shelves against the walls were labeled with laminated signs for each tool: SNOWBLOWER, SHOVEL, EDGER, SPADE.

Mr. Bishop met them at the door to the house. "Clair de lune!" he said, pulling the door wide.

Clara was surprised at the surge of emotion she felt at hearing her old nickname. She hugged her father tight to hide her face, noticing that he felt frailer than the last time she embraced him. Whereas Ruth seemed to have a resistance to age, he was sliding in the other direction. His hair had gone completely gray. An old-man paunch gathered at his middle. The collared shirt he wore beneath his maroon sweater made him look like he was on his way to church.

"Doesn't she look wonderful?" Ruth asked. "I told her she looks wonderful."

"When did she ever not?" He kissed Clara on top of her head, then took her backpack and led their quiet party into the house.

Chapter 9

Tony drove a black BMW. It was sleek and shiny with white leather interior. When Clara got in the car outside the coffee shop where they met for breakfast, she had asked if he only felt comfortable with large equipment that looked like a grand piano. The comment had not been well received. Now they drove in testy silence downtown, listening to, of all the music two classically trained pianists might enjoy together, Pearl Jam.

"You don't really fit into the whole grunge-rock ethos." Clara waved her hand to encompass Tony's tailored jeans and leather jacket. It was the most casual outfit she'd seen him wear, and he still looked like a model for a men's fashion retailer.

"And you look like you *do* fit into the grunge-rock ethos, and yet you actually don't," he said, tipping his head toward Clara's own ensemble. She had left her ripped jeans and Chuck Taylors at home, unwilling to attract the extra disapproval they would garner from Ruth. She wore a black long-sleeved T-shirt and black jeans with her black cowboy boots. She had thought when she dressed that morning that she looked polished.

"They're comfortable," she said. "I spent my whole childhood wearing dresses."

"And I spent *my* whole childhood wearing my cousin's hand-me-downs and listening to Bach," he said.

Clara thought of the young Tony Park in his ill-fitting Oxford shirts, which he sometimes wore with a *Star Wars* T-shirt underneath. For years, his lesson had been right before hers, every Tuesday afternoon. Clara had spent hours in the wooden chair opposite the portrait of Starza listening to Tony play behind the closed door of the gallery. But in the way of awkward adolescents, they barely ever spoke to one another. At the exchange in the hallway each week, Tony slouched past her as if she were another portrait on the wall. Clara, for her part, stared at whatever book she had brought. She wondered now if Madame had stacked their lessons on purpose, to stoke their rivalry.

"I've been sorting through Madame's papers," Tony said, turning down the volume on the stereo. "I found an old copy of that article she published in the seventies about the 'Sister' Nocturnes. Do you know which one I'm talking about?"

"I do," Clara said. "She made me annotate it when I was twelve years old. I had to go home and look up the word *annotate* in the dictionary, if that gives you any indication of how well it went."

Starza's two nocturnes in A Minor, op. 48, were among the composer's most popular works. Known as the "Sister" Nocturnes because they were published together in 1885, the nocturnes were as different from one another as sisters who had been separated at birth. One had been nicknamed "The Melancholy Sister"; the other, "The Vengeful." Clara had always preferred the rocking harmony of *The Melancholy*. Madame, of course, had favored *The Vengeful*.

"One of the topics she wrote about was the discrepancies in the tempi," Tony said. "The metronome marking of both nocturnes is sixty, but the tempo description of *The Melancholy* is largo, and *The Vengeful* is larghetto. It's a little odd, right? The metronome marking is the same, and yet he wanted *The Vengeful* to be played faster."

Clara sighed inwardly. She did not miss the music world's obsession with pointless minutiae. "We know his metronome was broken. Maybe it got worse between the composition of the first and the second nocturne. What did Madame have to say about it?"

"Nothing, really. She hardly addresses it in the article, but she had some more of those metronome calculations in the margins of her draft. In her notes about *The Melancholy*, she wrote '60 not S's.' What do you think that means?"

"That it wasn't his marking?" Clara suggested. "Maybe she's saying the publisher added it later."

"Maybe." His face concentrated in thought. "It's just had me thinking about that letter she wrote me last year. Did I tell you about it?"

"You mentioned she wrote you a letter. You didn't tell me what it was about."

"I published an article about how Starza's sonata form evolved over the course of his life. I made a comment about the *Dark Angel Sonata*—how it's different from all the other ones. Weirder. Less organized. I had just read a paper about Starza's time in Paris, and how some of his letters to Marianna suggest he was frequenting an opium den. Anyway, I was hypothesizing that maybe the 'Dark Angel' in the dedication wasn't a person but opium."

Clara shook her head. "That sonata was from late in his life. Not the Paris period."

Tony gave her an exasperated look. "I know that. I was just *saying* that maybe if he liked opium in the 1860s, he was still liking it in the 1880s. Anyway, it was a passing comment—a sentence, at most. But a week after it was published, I get this letter from Madame, totally out of the blue. It was three sentences long." Tony squeezed his eyebrows together, mimicking Madame's contemptuous scowl. "'The *Dark Angel Sonata* was published in 1881, years after Starza's return from France. It is anomalous from previous sonatas because of Starza's renewed interest in counterpoint (well documented) beginning that same year. If you are looking for Starza's so-called 'Dark Angel,' you would do better to examine the reasons for the dramatic shift in his music at this time, as embodied by such pieces as the Second Concerto and *The Melancholy Sister*, rather than run a scholar's tired errand across overtread work.'"

"Ouch," Clara said.

"Yeah. A real warm fuzzy. Anyway, the fact that she called out *The Melancholy Sister* in particular, and then was obviously focused on it in her metronome calculations—I don't know." He shook his head. "I guess I'm still trying to figure out why she gave me all her papers. I mean, you're the one with the connection to Starza's manuscripts. If she wanted somebody to have her scholarship about his music, it seems like it would be you."

Clara did not immediately respond. "That one actually makes sense to me."

Tony glanced away from the road to look at her. "How do you mean?"

Clara trained the AC vent on her face, feeling suddenly warm. "I revoked her access to the Starza archives."

"What?" Tony turned to face her. "When?"

She blushed, ashamed of how petty it sounded. "A couple of years after the fire. The museum called to tell me she wanted to do some research and was asking permission to spend some time with Starza's manuscripts." Clara cringed, remembering the rage that had quaked through her the day she received the call. "I said no."

Tony was silent for a minute. "And you never restored it, after all this time?"

Clara looked out the window. "I resigned from the board after that. But no, I never did."

They had driven into the old manufacturing district of the city. Brick warehouses from the turn of the century sprawled on every block, the bustle of their glory days long silenced. Tony parked before a plain redbrick building with arched limestone windows. Clara leaned her head out the window to read the sign etched above the door: FERRIELL & SONS STONE CO.

"I thought we were going to a museum," Clara said.

Tony opened the car door. "We are."

She followed him to the side of the building, where a wooden sign hung over a glossy paneled door. *Chicago Museum of Historical*

Instruments, the engraved lettering read in looping copperplate script.

A gust of cool air blew into the street as Tony pulled on the heavy door. He held out a hand. "After you."

The room she stepped into was cold and windowless, with wood-paneled walls and soft track lighting. A harpsichord stood beside her, its open lid painted bright red. ITALY, 17TH CENTURY, a sign propped on the yellowed keys read. DO NOT TOUCH. Beyond it, glass display cases created a maze of walkways in every direction. Just in her immediate line of sight, she could see wooden flutes and painted harps and a collection of Chinese pipa. Her eye lingered on an ancient-looking xylophone mounted to the back of a carved dragon. On every wall and surface of the room, instruments sat, hung, or stood, their sound suspended. Not even an electric fan disturbed the quiet.

"I guess it's a slow day." Her gaze landed on a piano in the corner. STEINWAY & SONS GRAND PIANO, the placard resting on the lid read. PLAYED BY IGNACY JAN PADEREWSKI ON HIS FIRST AMERICAN TOUR, 1892.

"How many people want to pay to see old instruments?" Tony rang a brass call bell resting on a console table.

"Coming!" someone shouted.

Clara heard heavy footsteps approach from the back of the room, then a woman emerged from behind a display of woodwind instruments. Barely five feet tall, with black leather pants and a maroon pleather vest cut low into her décolletage, she looked more like a bass player in a punk band than the historical instrument curator Clara had expected. A constellation of silver earrings studded the cartilage of both ears, and her hair was swooped into a high, black ponytail. A tattoo of a viola covered one exposed tricep.

"Tony!" Her lipsticked mouth opened in a bright smile. "I thought that might be you."

"Good to see you, Jess," Tony said, bending down to kiss her on the cheek. The woman pulled away quickly when the kiss was over, a tinge of color in her pretty face, and Clara experienced a jolt of recognition. It was an exchange she had witnessed dozens of times at The Andromeda—the awkward meeting of former lovers. She glanced at Tony, surprised, then looked away when he caught her watching.

"You must be Clara." Jess turned toward her and stuck out a hand. A silver bangle engraved with the Star of David slid down her wrist, clinking against a charm bracelet.

"Nice to meet you." Clara took the outstretched hand.

Jess blinked, her hazel eyes clear and curious beneath thick cat-eye liner. Clara saw them take in the scars on her cheek before making eye contact again. "So." Jess looked between Clara and Tony. "You said you wanted help identifying an instrument?"

Tony glanced at Clara. "A metronome, actually. Do you have some time?"

"With all the visitors clamoring at our doors?" Jess gestured to the back. "Let's go to my office. It's Aaron's turn to get the door next, which means I'm yours until the end of the day."

They followed her past a display of lutes to an unlabeled door on the back wall, then up concrete stairs to the second floor. The stairwell opened onto a carpeted hallway that smelled of musty paper and ancient mildew, with a tang of instrument varnish. Framed photos of instruments leaned against both walls as if waiting to be hung.

"No time for aesthetics up here," Jess said to Clara over her shoulder. "We only have funding for me and Aaron. We have to prioritize our time for the lovelies."

She nodded toward an open door, where rows of metal shelves held what Clara presumed to be "the lovelies"—case after case of instruments, paper tags hanging from their handles.

"That's Aaron," Jess said as they passed another open door. A balding man with a pair of magnifying goggles on his head was bent over a stringless violin. He lifted a hand in a wave but didn't look up.

Jess entered a room at the end of the hall, where a white drafting desk sat in the light of a small lamp. She dragged a scuffed piano bench from the corner of the room. "Have a seat," she said, then plopped onto a stool on the other side of the desk, her small figure dwarfed behind its enormous hulk. "So." She folded her hands. Tattoos on her fingers merged to form a braid of mermaid tails. "What have you got?"

Clara pulled the metronome box from her backpack and set it on the desk.

"We were hoping you could tell us."

"I saw one similar to this in grad school," Aaron said. He leaned over the metronome, studying the lion's head on the pendulum. Jess had called him in for his opinion, and now all four of them crowded around the desk, following the pinprick of light coming from his magnifying goggles.

"It was on loan from a private collection in Vienna. The pendulum looked like this almost exactly."

"And you're sure it wasn't this one?" Jess asked.

"Absolutely. The casting wasn't nearly this elaborate. It was in the shape of some kind of plant—hawthorn branches, I think. And it definitely didn't have any numbers on the winding key." He tapped the *LXXII* gently with a pair of fine-pointed tweezers. "This one looks more intricate, like maybe it was a later model by the same artist."

"What about the box?" Clara asked, nodding toward it. The blue velvet lining had been once again removed and folded into a ziplock bag.

"I agree with your antiques guy that it's somewhat newer," Aaron said. "The engraving, though, that's hard to say. Do you know what the inscription means?"

"Beyond what it says?" Clara shook her head. "No."

"Where did you get it?" Jess asked.

Clara and Tony exchanged a glance. "I inherited it," she said. "From Zofia Mikorska."

Now it was Aaron and Jess's turn to exchange a look.

"We were just working with some violins from her collection a few weeks ago," Jess said.

"Alan Feldman?" Tony asked.

"Yep. He wanted us to date the instruments. It seems like she had quite the collection." Jess turned to Clara. "She didn't tell you anything about the history of this metronome?"

"No," Clara said. "Never."

"Clara is related to Aleksander Starza," Tony said. "We were wondering, maybe, if this might have belonged to him."

Jess lifted a perfectly plucked eyebrow. "I've only heard of one metronome associated with Aleksander Starza."

"Yes," Tony said.

Jess snorted a disbelieving laugh. She looked between Clara and Tony. "You think you have Aleksander Starza's death metronome?"

"We know it's unlikely," Clara said.

"But it seems possible," Tony added. "Based on other findings."

"Findings like what?"

For the next half hour, Clara and Tony explained the metronome's inaccurate timekeeping and the revised tempo markings in Madame's score of the *Fire Concerto*, as well as the mysterious inquiries at Mr. Borthram's office and the five-a.m. phone call Clara had received last week. Jess and Aaron listened attentively but not, Clara thought, very excitedly. When all the relevant facts were divulged, Jess once again folded her hands on the desk.

"I think it would be good to find the owner of the sister metronome—the one Aaron saw from Vienna. See if we can find out a little more about the maker."

"I can do that," Aaron said.

"He's good for it," Jess said, seeing Clara's hesitation. "We deal with a lot of sensitive materials around here. Aaron's discreet."

"Okay," Clara agreed, relieved that at least something in the search for the metronome's origins was not her responsibility.

"Do we know anything at all about the characteristics of the metronome Starza had?" Jess asked. "Distinguishing features, maker, that kind of thing?"

"I bet the Starza Museum in Warsaw has that information," Tony said. "We could check with them."

"Let's start there and see what we can find. But I'll tell you"—Jess leaned forward on the desk, the viola on her tricep bulging with the flex of her arm—"I think you should lower your expectations."

Clara nodded enthusiastically. "I agree. Everyone knows Starza's metronome was destroyed."

"Sure, and that's foremost. But I mean for other reasons." She paused. "I think we all agree that everything we're talking about here is sensitive information. Like doesn't-leave-this-room information. With that understanding, I have some sensitive information of my own that I'll share with you under the same agreement. As friends." She looked pointedly at Tony.

"Of course," Tony said.

"Feldman wanted us to authenticate the instruments he got from Mikorska, like I said. I think he left here wishing he hadn't."

"Why?"

Jess blinked her long eyelashes. "Aaron thinks her Guarneri might be stolen."

"Stolen?" Clara asked. "Why?"

"The instrument passes as a convincing del Gesù," Aaron said, pushing the magnifying goggles further up on his forehead. "The f-holes look like Guarneri's, and the archings fit with his style too. But the label has been messed with. The date on it says 1736, but when you look closely, you can see that the part of the label with the '36' on it is not original. In Guarneri's time, labels were made from something called 'laid paper'—essentially linen rags that were boiled to make a paste and then laid to dry on a wire sieve. You can identify it because of the faint outline of the wire sieve on the paper. Most of the label on Mikorska's violin was laid paper, but not the very end of it. It looks to me like someone removed the part that had the *actual* year and added a *different* piece of paper with the '36.' So either the whole instrument is a fake—which is certainly possible, as there are some fantastic imitations out there—or it was stolen, and someone doctored the label to disguise its true identity. I'd need more time with it to know. The label anomaly would certainly have been discovered if she had ever tried to sell it."

"So you're saying maybe the metronome could be fake, too?" Tony asked.

"Could be," Aaron said. "Or maybe a copy. People in the nineteenth century had copies of art and famous objects just like we do today. I could certainly see someone making a side business out of selling imitation Starza metronomes."

Jess slid the metronome carefully into its box. "It's a beautiful piece," she said, handing it back to Clara. "And worth looking into. But I'd say it's pretty unlikely that you've inherited the metronome used to kill Aleksander Starza."

"We should talk to the people at the Starza Museum," Tony said on the walk back to the car. "Maybe they have details about what the metronome looked like from his papers or something."

The afternoon had grown dark, the humidity bearing down as rainclouds gathered in the sky. Clara tugged her backpack higher on her shoulder. It felt lighter than it had in days. "Why don't we wait to hear back from Aaron first?"

"Because that could take a while, and people are making threatening phone calls about it now."

"The woman didn't threaten me. She just said she was going to get it back."

"You certainly felt threatened when you knocked on my door at six in the morning."

"And now I think I overreacted. The woman could barely breathe. I don't think she's going to come hunting me down. Anyway, it doesn't matter now. You were in there too. The metronome is probably just a fake."

Tony stepped in a wad of gum on the sidewalk. He looked at her with annoyance as he scraped his shoe across the concrete. "If it's an imitation, how could it have the same time anomaly as Starza's?"

"Because it's a hundred and fifty years old? The parts are probably going bad."

He dragged the shoe along the sidewalk in a long rasp. "You're looking for reasons to deny that it's Starza's."

"And you're looking for reasons to *confirm* that it's Starza's, despite the fact that everyone who knows anything about his metronome knows it was destroyed."

A delivery truck gusted past them, spewing a cloud of exhaust in their direction. How had she ever liked it here? When she was younger, she had adored cities—their noise and bustle and anonymity, the smell of diesel and old snow. Now it made her claustrophobic.

"You're letting your feelings about Madame cloud your judgment," Tony said.

"No, I'm listening to logic and reason and the experts who know that Starza's metronome is gone."

"I still think we should talk to the people at the Starza Museum. I have a concert coming up in Warsaw. Maybe you could come."

Clara glanced up, trying to gauge what kind of invitation this was, but there was no hint of flirtation in Tony's drawn expression. She shook her head. "I've taken enough time off work for the whole summer."

Tony stopped on the sidewalk. "We might have the murder weapon to the greatest crime in the history of music, and you're worried about skipping a night at the bar? What are you going to miss? A big night of margaritas? Madame obviously wanted you to look into it."

"Did you forget what happened to me the last time I went to Warsaw, Tony?" She thrust out her hand, with its strange, white flesh. Tony flinched.

"Madame was down in the basement that night when I was trapped in that room. She knew I was in there, and she left me. So frankly, I don't care what she wanted me to do about her metronome."

Tony's face screwed up in confusion. "But the papers said—"

Clara shook her head to stop him. "I saw her in the hallway right before the lights went out. I heard her outside the door while I was screaming for help. If it were her in there, I would have died trying to save her." She turned and walked alone to the BMW, where fat raindrops began to smack the hood in uneven succession. When he caught up with her, he paused, looking at her over the roof of the car. "I'm sorry," he said quietly. "I didn't know."

"You couldn't have." She noticed she was clenching her burned hand into a fist and dropped it to her side. "But even if Madame had expressly asked me to take this metronome to Warsaw—which she didn't—I still wouldn't go. Don't you see that this is exactly how it's always been with her? She wants me to anticipate her wishes and do her bidding just like she always did. She *wants* me to get involved."

"I don't disagree," Tony said. "I guess the difference is that I don't think that's necessarily a bad thing."

Traffic was slow on the way back to Oak Park, complicated by the increasing rain that drummed on the hood of the car. They were quiet for a while, listening to the hiss of the tires on pavement. Was it true, what she had said? If Madame had asked her to go to Warsaw to investigate the metronome, would she still have refused? A month ago, she would not have hesitated in her answer. Now she wasn't sure, and it bothered her that she wasn't. Since it arrived in her life, the metronome had felt like an extension of all that was unresolved between her and Madame. And while part of her was desperate to find out what it meant and why Madame had given it to her, as if the answers might heal all the wounded years that had elapsed, another part was outraged. Madame had been audacious enough to give her this mystery object and all its concomitant problems, and yet had still withheld the one and only thing that Clara actually wanted from her—an explanation.

Embarrassed by how emotional she felt, she turned to Tony, anxious to redirect the conversation. "I like her," she said. "Jess. How do you know her?"

"We were together for a while." Tony kept his eyes on the road. "I messed it up."

"Shocking," Clara said, then, seeing the look on his face, regretted it. "What happened?"

"It was back during all that stuff with my mom. I kind of lost my way for a while. Not my proudest moments." He turned up the stereo, where the CD player had switched to Glenn Gould playing the *Goldberg Variations*. The storm was blustering now. Darts of rain cut through the beams of the car's headlights as Tony turned onto the Bishops' street. Seeing him backlit by the rainy light, Clara recalled another stormy evening years ago when she had exited Madame's house after her lesson and found Tony standing on the porch, smoking.

"What are you doing?" she had hissed, pulling the door quickly shut. "What if Madame sees you?"

"I missed my bus." Tony glanced at her and took a drag off the cigarette. "Besides, what's she going to do about it? Like me less? Tell my parents?" He shrugged, but his face clenched a little at the mention of his parents.

Clara looked down the rainy street, worried her own parents might see him.

"It smells terrible," she said, waving the smoke away.

He moved to the edge of the porch, so that runoff from the awning began to drip onto his shoulder. "I think that's what I like about it," he said.

Clara was bewildered. "How can you like something you think is terrible?"

He studied the cigarette in his hand, then looked straight at her for what felt like the first time ever. "I guess I like to do something wrong that I'm choosing, instead of being told I'm doing something wrong when I'm always trying to do everything right."

This, to her fourteen-year-old self, had seemed like profound and adult wisdom, and she had wanted to say something equally important in return. But Ruth's Volvo had turned onto Madame's street then. Tony flicked his cigarette instantly into the grass, and Clara opened her umbrella and ran down the path. The next week she had looked forward to her lesson, wondering if maybe now she and Tony would be friends. But that afternoon when he opened the gallery door, he walked past her as if she weren't there, impassive as ever.

Now, he pulled into the Bishops' driveway and parked the car. "I always wondered where you lived," he said. He peered at the house through the bleary windshield. "I imagined it something like this."

Clara regarded the stately brick. It was a house of privilege, with money and opportunity and love. She knew she should be more grateful for it. But just looking at it made her feel trapped.

"I wondered about your house, too. For some reason"—she laughed, remembering it—"I wondered if you were allowed to watch TV. And I wondered if you had friends."

Tony tilted his head to one side. "I grew up in Albany Park. We lived in the apartment above my parents' upholstery store. I watched a ton of TV, and I think I had a friend over exactly once. I tried to impress him by playing Rachmaninoff."

They laughed, and Clara felt herself recalibrating. She considered again the BMW, the Rolex, the expensive leather jacket.

"Luckily for me," he said, "my college roommate was the most social person on campus. I learned how to be a human by watching him."

The image of Tony in a college dorm room pricked her with a stab of jealousy. She had contemplated going to college herself in the early years after the fire. Her plans were quashed by the stream of rejection letters that came back in the mail. On her applications, she had refused to give any indication of her previous career. As a result, on paper she was a twenty-three-year-old with a GED but no high school diploma or job experience. Life had prepared her for nothing except playing piano and ordering room service.

Tony was looking at her thoughtfully. "It wasn't all bad, you know. We were lucky. Both of us."

Of course she'd been lucky. For a while.

"It doesn't matter now, I guess," she said.

Sadness drifted over Tony's face. He turned in his seat to face her. "I was a jerk not to reach out after what happened to you in Warsaw. I thought of it a bunch of times. I was worried you wouldn't believe I was sincere."

Clara watched rain pour down the windshield in thick rivulets. "I probably wouldn't have, back then."

"I called Madame to see how you were." He glanced at Clara uncertainly. "She said, 'Many great performers have lost more and come back. The little bird will be fine.'"

Clara snorted. "I guess that was her softer side."

"You know, she was always telling me to watch you perform—how the music took you over. *Possessed* is the word she used. You had that thing—the artist's gift, natural talent, whatever you call it. She thought so too." He hesitated. "My manager told me what happened between you two, over the *Fire Concerto*. How you stood up to her and everything. I was proud of you. You were right to do it. She was holding you back."

Clara could not look at him. "I guess we'll never know."

"She was really down there that night?"

"She was."

"Maybe she didn't hear you."

"Yeah," Clara said, unconvinced. "Maybe."

Tony paused. "Do you really not play anymore?"

"I don't."

"At all?"

"It's a good enough hand for anything a normal person might want out of life, but not a musician. Once you were where we were—" she stumbled. Tony was still there. She was the one who wasn't. She recalled a PBS program she had watched in the months during her recovery. Stroke survivors with aphasia were relearning how to talk. All the sophistication of language had been taken away, and they were left with three-word sentences. "You can't go backward," she said.

He pointed at her hands, which were twisted in her lap. "Your fingers still move a lot."

"They don't."

"They do. I noticed it at Jess's office."

Tony reached out and grazed her hand. The shock of his warm skin on the cold flesh made her arm tingle.

"Can I see?" he asked.

Clara's breath hitched in her lungs. Reluctantly, she turned over her hand. The burns on her palm where she had gripped the hot doorknob had been the most painful. The skin here was uneven, like candle wax had pooled and hardened in her palm. With the tip of his index finger, Tony traced the raised edge where the graft from her thigh had been attached to the damaged skin. His eyes drifted to her forearm, where the scars coiled up from her wrist in a rope of white flesh.

"Your arm, too?" he asked.

Clara nodded, resisting the urge to pull down her sleeve. "And my face. Obviously."

"You're still beautiful. It doesn't change that."

The earnestness in his eyes made her want to weep.

"That's not true."

"It is. Before, you were always so perfect, with the makeup and hair and everything. Then you would play, and it sounded like it was coming from somebody who'd had their heart broken a thousand times. I think you look more like who you really are."

"Somebody damaged?" She tried to laugh, but it came out sounding choked.

"No," Tony said. "Somebody with a story worth sharing. Somebody I'd want to know." He raised his head to look at her just as the porch light flipped on. The interior of the car lit up. Clara pulled her hand away.

"Thanks for your help today." She unbuckled her seat belt, the warmth of his touch dissolving. "Let me know what you hear from Jess. Oh, and if you meet a kid named Peter Juniper from Texas who's coming to tour your program, give him a real chance."

"Sure. Anything." He looked out the window, waving a hand at the rain in a gesture of helplessness. "I wish I could offer you an umbrella or something," he said. When he turned to look back at her, his eyes were mournful. "Clara, I'm so sorry."

She swallowed, trying to find her voice. "It's just rain, Tony," she said, opening the door. "I'll be fine."

Chapter 10

CLARA RAN DOWN THE DRIVEWAY in the twin beams of Tony's head-lights. Ahead, the windows of the garage were illuminated, three yellow squares in the rainy night. She could see her father within, holding a pair of gardening shears up to the light as he ran a whetstone along the length of the blade.

Inside, the kitchen smelled of baked salmon and broccoli. The counters were immaculate. A single empty teacup sat in the sink. Sorrow wedged in her chest at the sight of the orderly life here, cleared of any evidence of hunger or mess. It made her sad to think of her parents in their impeccable house, where dishes were done three times a day and the floor was swept every night after dinner. It saddened her even more that she had never noticed how lonely someone must be to spend their time making the perfect even more perfect.

"Clara?" Ruth's voice meandered from the den.

"Hi, Mom," Clara called. She removed her wet boots and set them on the shoe tray by the door, then headed further into the house.

Ruth sat in a gray Ethan Allen armchair, a navy throw over her lap despite the warm weather. The book on the side table next to her was titled *MAXIMUM ACHIEVEMENT: Strategies and Skills That Will Unlock Your Hidden Powers to Succeed.*

"How's Tony?" Ruth asked. She had washed her face for the night, and her skin looked softer without the foundation gathering in the lines of her forehead. Clara couldn't remember the last time she'd seen Ruth without her mask of cosmetics. It made her look younger but also more tired, as if she'd been strained all day and was now worn out.

Clara felt a pang of remorse, realizing that the source of that strain probably had something to do with her.

"Tony's good."

"Is he married now?"

Clara sank onto a pale gray loveseat. "No, Mom."

Ruth smoothed the throw on her lap. "I'm just making small talk, Clara," she admonished. "I always thought he had a thing for you, is all."

"He didn't," Clara said, though her mind was walking backward to examine the look in his eyes when he had turned to her in the car. She had seen the same expression on his face once before, standing by the fountain in the Parc du Cinquantenaire in Brussels, right before he said *I'm going to kiss you now, Clara Bishop.* She found she was touching the inside of her wrist and dropped her hand.

"Like I said," she said to Ruth, "we were never close."

"I won't say anything more about it," Ruth said primly. She stroked the fringe of the navy throw. "Your father suggested maybe we could go to Texas for Christmas this year. We still haven't seen your house, you know."

"That would be great," Clara said, though the thought of her parents sitting on her thrift store couch seemed as improbable as Bingo curling up on Ruth's white rug. "I'll check with work."

Ruth's mouth turned down. "You always say that."

Clara stiffened, sensing a coming argument. "We'll find a time, Mom. I promise."

"We've tried hard to support you, you know," Ruth said. "I don't understand why you don't want us in your life."

"I *do* want you in my life. And I know you've tried hard to support me."

"Then why don't you ever come home?" Ruth exclaimed, an edge of exasperation in her voice. "We practically have to beg you to see us."

She knew she should lie, and promise that she would visit more often, and say that her parents were always welcome in Austin. But the emotional sprint of the day had worn her out, and she was tired of pretending. She wished she felt comfortable here, just like she wished her parents could visit her house and get a drink at The Andromeda and see that her life there was good. But she knew all they would see in Texas were deficits—what she wasn't doing, and who she hadn't become. More than anything else about being with them, it was this need to prove that she was okay that made her feel like she had failed.

"My whole life here was about being a prodigy, Mom. I spent my entire childhood in that room." She gestured down the hall, where the French doors to the piano room had remained closed since she arrived. She knew everything inside would be just as it had always been—the black Steinway, the shelves of music, all hostage to the past. "It brings up too many memories."

Ruth fell quiet, and for a moment Clara allowed herself to believe that stating the truth might thwart the usual outcome of this conversation. Then Ruth's mouth hardened.

"No one shackled you to the piano, Clara. We didn't force you to practice."

Clara squeezed her hand into a fist to prevent herself from raising her voice. "It doesn't mean it was good for me. It doesn't mean *she* was good for me."

"Oh, *please*." Ruth threw up her hands. "You pranced around this house talking in a Polish accent for years! You wanted to be exactly like her!"

"Everyone idolized her! All you guys ever talked about was how lucky I was to get to study with her. You never gave me another choice."

"Excuse *me* for giving you the kind of opportunities most children could only dream of," Ruth scoffed. "Is that what you want me to say? That I'm sorry we gave up our own lives so yours could be remarkable?"

"I was a child!" Clara exclaimed, anger surging to her face in a flood of warmth. "You should have let me be a kid, have friends, go to school! I didn't have anything else. There was nothing to fall back on."

"There was *us*!" Ruth shouted. The veins in her neck bulged. "*We* were here to fall back on. It's not our fault you're a bartender living alone in some backwater town! You could have gone to college. You could have taught. You could even play."

"I can't."

"Dr. Rickman said you could."

"He's a surgeon. Not a pianist."

"You barely even tried."

Clara rose to her feet. "How do you know what I tried to do? You were too busy trying to fix my face."

"Don't be ridiculous! I was trying to help you move on!"

"You were trying to pretend it didn't happen. That's not the same."

The click of the back door made them fall silent. Glaring at each other, they listened to Clara's father remove his shoes, then stop at the stove to turn on the kettle. Soon he appeared in the doorway.

"Anyone want some tea?"

He had always done this—intervene, whitewash, buffer. When she was a child, she had thought of him as the more loving parent. Now she knew he had just been the hands-off one.

"I was just heading to bed," Clara said.

He kissed her on the head. "Maybe we'll all get breakfast before you go tomorrow." He looked between them—first Ruth, then Clara, sewing a thread of peace.

The phone rang from the kitchen before anyone was forced to agree.

"I'll get it," Ruth said, and huffed out of the room. "Clara," she called, her voice flat. "It's for you."

Clara forced a parting smile at her father, then trudged up the steps to her bedroom, listening to her mother complaining urgently in the kitchen, followed by her father's hushed, soothing tones.

"Clara, hey, it's Jess," a melodic voice said when Clara answered the phone. "I know you're headed out in the morning, but I did some research after you left. I found something I think you should see."

The Blue Serpent was an unlikely establishment for Oak Park. With its strip mall parking lot and neon blue sign, it appeared from the outside more like a nail salon than a bar. Inside was dark and overly air-conditioned. A reassuring smell of bleach wafted from the bathrooms. Above the liquor shelf, a mechanical blue iguana turned its head on a swivel at intervals before ejecting its pink tongue.

"I used to date a guy who worked here." Jess sipped a vodka tonic through a cocktail straw, eyeing the iguana. "It always annoyed me that that thing wasn't a serpent. Shouldn't the place be called The Blue Lizard?" She shook her head, then popped open the silver clip of her purse, withdrawing a scratched CD case. "After you left, Aaron and I were talking about Mikorska. He didn't know a lot about her, so I dug up one of her albums." Jess passed the CD across the table. It was the recording of Madame's performance of the Third Concerto at the 1948 Starza Competition. *MIKORSKA PLAYS THE FIRE CONCERTO* white capital letters read across the top of the cover. The photo of Madame on stage in the red silk dress was printed in the background.

"Something about her was familiar," Jess said. "It was nagging me, because I never saw her in person. Of course I'd heard her recordings, but I don't think I've even seen any pictures of her except this one, and even then, I never really paid attention to what she looked like. Then I was on the train on the way home and realized where I recognized her from." Jess wiped the surface of the table with a cocktail napkin and pulled a ziplock bag from her purse. Inside was a plain piece of white cardboard.

"Have you ever heard of the *Sonderstab Musik*?"

Clara shook her head.

"It was one of Hitler's pet projects. It translates to 'Special Task Force for Music.' He wanted to gather instruments and other musical artifacts for a university he was planning in Linz. He wanted the special ones—Stradivari, Amati, Guarneri—all the Cremona gems. Everywhere the Nazis invaded, they confiscated property from the Jews they rounded up—art, furniture, instruments, you name it. Then they had musicologists and other experts come in to assess what they'd found. The really valuable instruments were sent to Berlin. Others were sold to fund the war effort. They still turn up every now and then in the collection of some old person who's passed away. It's kind of a side project for me, helping Jewish families who are looking for a lost instrument. My great-grandparents' home was looted during the invasion of Hungary. The soldiers took my grandmother's violin."

"That's terrible," Clara said.

"Not as terrible as dying at Auschwitz, but yes. My grandmother made it out, luckily. She's still alive. Anyway—most of those instruments are worth close to a million dollars now, if not more, but between the records that were destroyed in the war and all the chaos that came afterward, the families who owned them can't prove that they were theirs. There's no serial number or anything on those old instruments, so it's hard to identify them definitively. A lot of times the best we can do is go by an old certificate from a dealer, or a letter describing it, or, if one exists, a photograph."

Jess slid a purple fingernail beneath the lip of the ziplock bag, breaking the seal. She withdrew the cardboard interior, which turned out to be two pieces of cardstock pressed together, and removed a photograph that was nestled between them. The picture was old and faded, with ragged edges thinned by time. A brown burn mark marred one corner. In it, two women and a boy stood beside a piano in a sunny apartment. Jess set it on the table beside Madame's album.

"A Jewish family in New York is trying to track down this violin." Jess pointed to the instrument in the hands of the boy, who held it proudly beneath his chin, his bow hovering above the strings. A smiling woman in a floral puff-sleeve dress stood beside him, her hands on the boy's shoulders.

"The woman in the picture is Sonja Rademakker. That's her son Samuel. The violin was confiscated when the Germans invaded the Netherlands. Sonja died of starvation at Bergen Belsen. Samuel survived and emigrated to the States. He died a few years ago. His daughter is the one searching for his violin. She says this is a picture of the day the family bought it. They know it's an Amati. They think it was made in 1671. They don't know anything about this other woman in the picture." Jess tapped the figure on the edge of the photograph.

Part of the young woman's face was obscured by the burn mark. She stood before the mantel in a belted dark dress, her short hair curled in the fashion of the 1930s. She was slimmer than Clara had known her to be. Just a girl, really. But the look on her face was unmistakable. No one else regarded the world with such unmasked contempt.

Clara reached out to take the photo, but Jess pulled it back. "I really shouldn't have it out of the museum," she said. "But that's her, right?"

"Yes." Clara didn't have to look at the album cover for comparison. She could feel Madame's gaze crossing all the years. "Where was this taken?"

"Rotterdam, we think sometime in early 1940. Based on the fact that a Jewish woman is smiling, we're assuming it was before the Nazi invasion on May 10. That's all we have to go on. Or it was, until I saw Mikorska's CD. Do you know anything about where she spent the war?"

Clara shook her head. Madame had never spoken about her past. Like everything else about her life, it was vaulted and inaccessible. "I know she was at the Warsaw Conservatory before the invasion," Clara said, "and that in 1946 she came to New York and went to Juilliard. I don't know anything about where she was in between."

Jess swilled the ice in her glass. "That's not unusual for refugees from that time. Most people moved around a lot before finding somewhere safe to settle down. My question is, how did a refugee from Poland—an *orphan* refugee with no family and ostensibly no money— get ahold of an Amati violin?"

Clara looked up. "You mean she was the one who sold it to them?"

Jess nodded. "Samuel Rademakker said he remembered a woman with black hair coming to show them the violin. He didn't recall where the woman said she had gotten it. All he remembered was that she played piano. Apparently, she accompanied him while he played a Paganini concerto, and she was annoyed that he couldn't keep accurate time. She brought out a metronome from her bag to keep him in line. This photo turned up in an archive in Rotterdam two years ago. Samuel had already died, so he never saw it to verify if it was Mikorska, but I'd say it's pretty unmistakable, wouldn't you?"

Clara peered again at the grainy photo. Light from the apartment windows angled in on the piano, illuminating half of Madame's face so that she looked split, like a statue in partial shade. Behind her, barely visible in the burned edge of the photo, was a shadow on the mantel. A pointed structure, like the top of a pyramid. Clara's heart ticked faster.

"You see it, don't you?" Jess asked. "Over in the corner."

Clara leaned closer to the photo. "It could be any metronome."

"It could be." Jess took a magnifying glass out of a case in her purse and passed it to Clara. "But I don't think so."

Clara peered through the magnifying glass. Despite the poor quality of the picture, it was obvious that there was something reflective on the face of the metronome that glinted in the sun.

She looked up at Jess. "There's something on the front."

"A gold lion, perhaps?" Jess arched an eyebrow. She slid the photo back into the ziplock bag and sealed it.

"It doesn't change what I said earlier, about the metronome probably being a copy, but based on this, I think it's likely that Mikorska had the thing when she left Poland. And *maybe*, also, an Amati violin, provenance unknown. When you guys came to the museum today, I thought you were a little nuts. But I agree that something about all of this is weird. I called Aaron already. He's going to contact his advisor from grad school tomorrow to see if we can find that sister metronome in Vienna. Hopefully that will give us some kind of lead to work with." She put the ziplock carefully in her purse, then pulled out her wallet and laid cash on the table.

"You and Tony must have met through Mikorska, right?" Jess said. "Have you been friends for a long time?" Her tone was casual, but she began to twirl one of her silver rings with her thumb.

Clara felt herself flush, the memory of Tony holding her hand making her suddenly guilty. "I think it's more accurate to say we're former enemies."

Jess laughed. "He has more than a few of those. It's a shame. He's really a great guy. But the ambition. It gets in the way every time. I think his mom really did a number on him. She was really depressed for most of his childhood. I think he felt like his success was the only thing that made her happy. I'm glad she wasn't around for the big debacle, or I don't think he would have recovered."

Clara frowned. "What debacle?"

Jess's eyes widened. "The London thing?"

"What London thing?"

Jess gawked. "You really have been out of the loop, haven't you? He showed up drunk to a performance with the London Symphony Orchestra. And I mean *drunk* drunk. He flubbed the opening of the Chopin First Concerto, and it went downhill from there. He had to be escorted off the stage."

Clara felt her eyes bug. "Escorted *off*?"

Jess nodded. "For shouting at the conductor. Apparently, Tony thought the guy was going too fast."

Clara cringed, imagining how the critics must have eviscerated him. "That's awful."

"Yeah. In his defense, it was four days after his mom died. Everybody tried to convince him to cancel the performance, including me, but you know how he is. He lost a bunch of contracts after that. The university didn't look too kindly on it, either. He's been trying to come back from it ever since." Jess finished the rest of her drink in one gulp, then set the glass on the table with a *thunk*. She looked at Clara a little abashedly. "I know I sound like a jealous ex, and to be fair, I probably am. But just so you know, his interest in this metronome sounds like part of his comeback plan to me."

Clara stood in her parents' driveway and watched Jess's beat-up Camry recede down the street. The house was dark except for the glow of the desk lamp coming from her bedroom. She had a sudden, wrenching memory of sitting up late at that desk, staring at the red skin of her burned hand in the bright light, every cell of her body clamoring with dismay. Two days ago, she would not have remembered these things. The body had its own memory haunting it, even if the mind had tried to excavate it all.

She let herself in the back door and crept through the dark, listening to the familiar breath of the house—the whir of the ceiling fan in the den, the buzz of the refrigerator, the gin bottles quietly clanking against each other in the next cabinet. She paused at the bottom of the staircase. At the other end of the foyer lay the French doors to the music room. She hesitated, staring through the glass panels at a square of silvery moonlight shining on the wall, then walked forward and pulled open the doors.

The Steinway stood in the center of the room the way she had always insisted upon ("To hear the complete sound," she had told her parents, the way Madame had said it). The yellow chaise lounge Clara had sat on while she studied scores between practice sessions was still beneath the window. Artificial orchids bloomed from the fireplace mantel. The whole room looked stiff and formal, as if awaiting someone to come look at it. Standing in the center of the room, she realized that person was her.

She walked toward the instrument, the slight uptick in her heartbeat surprising her. It felt as if she were approaching someone she had once loved whom she had not been ready to see again, and yet here they were, whittling the years of absence down to nothing. Ruth had always kept the lid of the piano closed when Clara was a girl, complaining of the noise in the house, but now that it was never played, the lid was flung wide. Moonlight shone on the lowest octave.

"Clara?"

She whirled around. Her father stood in the doorway wearing his pajamas and bathrobe.

"You okay, honey?"

"Yeah," she said. "I just came in here to—" She looked at the piano. Why had she come? She gazed around the room. "It looks the same."

Her father pulled his bathrobe tighter around his shoulders. "We wanted to keep it the way you liked, in case you ever want to play while you're home."

The idea that this was home and the piano awaiting her infrequent visits made her chest hurt. "You don't need to do that for me," she managed to say.

He took a step toward her. In the silence that followed, she could feel him struggling to find words. "You loved it so much. Sometimes I worry we took that away from you."

Clara felt a sting in the back of her throat. What was there to say? That it wasn't their fault? That it was Clara's own? Madame's? That maybe everything would have been different if it weren't for the fire, and she might have loved music forever? In the end, all she could manage was the simplest of the many truths she felt.

"I don't want you to feel guilty," she said. "It's not your fault what happened."

Her father nodded, then walked forward and kissed her on the head. "We could ship the piano to Austin if you want, you know. It's your instrument. Your mother would have a field day redecorating the room."

Clara laughed, brushing a tear from her cheek. "It wouldn't even fit through the door."

Her father laughed and folded her into a hug. "We'll hang on to it then. You might find room for it someday. Just if you want." He kissed her on the head again. "Good night, Clair de lune."

Clara listened for the trudge of his footfalls up the stairs, then turned back to the piano. Carefully, like brushing the petal of a flower, she allowed her index finger to sink middle C to the keybed. *Pianissimo*, so softly. A sob fought its way up the back of her throat as the sound rang into the room and died. She choked it down, then pulled her hand away and retreated out the door.

Chapter 11

CLARA STOOD ON THE SECOND FLOOR of the Austin Public Library. A rack of periodicals in front of her displayed the week's magazines. *Should He Die?* asked the front cover of *Time*, alongside a photograph of Timothy McVeigh. Down the row, Tom Cruise stared dreamily from the cover of *People*. *The 50 Most Beautiful People in the World*, the bubble text next to him read. Death and beauty, Clara thought. Selling headlines through the ages.

"You're back."

Clara jumped. She turned to see a hulking teenager coming toward her, pushing a metal cart piled with books.

"Hey, Jerome," she whispered.

"You don't need to be quiet," he replied, his voice booming into the room. "There's nobody here." He parked the cart at the end of an aisle. "No one cares about reading when the weather's good."

He was giantly tall, with a soft middle that pooched his black T-shirt over his jeans and a red cardigan with a diamond-shaped bleach stain on the elbow. Short dreadlocks sprouted jubilantly from his head.

"I was gonna call you today. I had my boss help me dig up some stuff on your composer dude." He waved for her to join him. "Come on."

Clara followed him through the wending aisles to the reference desk, which formed a rectangular hub in the center of the room. Jerome walked around the counter and dropped into a swivel chair, then pushed back from the table and sent the chair sailing to the end of the desk.

"First the bad news." He picked up a stack of papers and sailed back to her, bumping to a stop. "I didn't find much else about your piano teacher lady." Jerome pushed his black plastic glasses further up his nose. "My boss Jeff, he's like a research *genius*, and even *he* couldn't find anything. It's kind of like she just showed up at Juilliard one day after the war, and then *bam!*" Jerome made a popping sound with his mouth. "Two years later, she won that competition and became a star. Crazy, right?"

"Crazy," Clara agreed. When she first approached the reference desk last week and asked for help finding a description of Starza's metronome and background information on Madame, she hadn't even known what questions to ask about Madame's past. Jerome had happily zigzagged his way to some discoveries anyway—the recital bill of a concert Madame gave at Juilliard in 1947; an article in the Juilliard student newspaper about her rapid ascent to fame; even a brief interview she'd given to *The Daily Telegraph* after she won the 1948 Starza Competition. Clara read the article hungrily, eager for information, but it hadn't held any surprises. When the interviewer asked how an orphan had managed to become one of the most famous young musicians in the world, Madame's response was characteristically self-congratulatory: "The sisters at the orphanage nurtured my interest, but I believe that talent, like so much else of who a person is, is determined at birth. My parents were not musical, but my grandmother was a very talented pianist. I believe my gifts come from her." The article mentioned that Madame left Poland in 1939 on one of the last trains out of Warsaw, but it had not yielded any information about where she spent the rest of the war.

"Your composer guy, on the other hand"—Jerome held up a finger—"there's some *really* interesting stuff about him. Jeff sent a fax to this library in Poland. You'd better believe the main librarian will flip her *shit* when she sees that one on the phone bill, but hey, you're a taxpayer, right?"

"A modestly contributing one, but yes."

"Well, this guy Jan in Warsaw. I guess you say it 'Yan,' though, with a *Y*?"

"Yes."

"Jan sent us these articles from a newspaper archive from 1885. Jeff and I don't speak Polish, but I guess Jan figured as much because he sent translations in English. He speaks four languages! You need to read it for yourself, but basically the guy's butler discovered the murder scene, like you told me. But what I *didn't* read about in any of the books we have on Starza was that apparently the butler was arrested first. The cops were pretty convinced the chick couldn't have done it because the scene was so grisly. The article talked about 'bits of scalp on the rug.'"

Clara grimaced. "Gross."

"Right?" Jerome grinned, dreadlocks bouncing. "Anyway, this dude the butler said he came back from his day off and found the dead guy and the scalp bits on the carpet—"

"Stop saying 'scalp bits,'" Clara said. "It's disgusting."

"Sure. Anyway, he calls the cops. The cops come in, see the dead body, the blood everywhere, furniture broken, the whole bit. Obviously, there's been a huge struggle. There's a piano bench across the room, papers on the floor soaked in blood, a couch upside down, all this stuff. But what's *really* interesting is that he notices that in the middle of all this chaos, there's one part of the room that looks totally fine. Any guess what it is?"

"The piano?"

"No. The piano had some scalp bits on it too, I think."

Clara didn't bother to disguise her eye roll. "Okay, what then?"

Jerome leaned forward, his eyes bright. "The fireplace. 'Swept clean' is how the inspector guy described it. Every piece of wood from the woodpile was gone. And the room, they noticed, was really hot."

Clara frowned. "What was burned?"

Jerome leaned back and shrugged. "They never found out."

Clara threw up her hands. "Then what's the point of the story?"

"The point is that it's interesting! And kind of suspicious, don't you think? I mean, how many girls do you know who can throw furniture?"

To Clara's warning look, Jerome held up his hands. "I mean, sure, if you're really in a crazy situation, like those women who pick up cars to rescue their babies. But somebody was obviously burning something in the fireplace. Don't you think that's weird?"

"It was December," she offered. "Maybe he caught a chill."

"Maybe," Jerome said. "Or *maybe* there was something more to it. The butler smells weird, don't you think? If I were the butler and *I* wanted my boss gone, I might wait for the crazy lady to come over on my day off, too. *If* she was actually crazy. I've been reading about her." He picked up a book from the bottom of the stack and held it up. Unlike the tomes Clara had been reading about Starza, it appeared to be new, with a pristine laminated library jacket around the glossy black cover. *She, Too, Played,* the title read. *Female Musicians of the Nineteenth Century.* A grainy photograph of Fanny Mendelssohn Hensel seated at a square piano filled the center of the jacket.

"Pleyel doesn't seem all that crazy to me," Jerome said. "I think she was just royally pissed." He passed Clara the book and the sheaf of faxed pages.

She took them, feeling her burden growing. "Was there anything at all about the metronome?"

"Oh, right! I almost forgot." Jerome sent the swivel chair rattling across the linoleum to the other side of the counter.

"Sorry, I got caught up in the exciting parts." He opened a large clothbound book. "One of the books I read on Starza mentioned this portrait of him by a dude named Piotr Biliński. I guess they were kind of friends or something, or 'mutual admirers' of each other's work, is what the book said. So Biliński offered to paint Starza's portrait, but when Starza saw it, he was so insulted he threw Biliński out of his house and the two never spoke again. I was kind of wanting to see the painting, right? I mean, what could be so bad about a picture of your own face?"

Clara thought immediately of Eli and his request to paint her portrait. The last thing she would ever want was an artistic rendering of her own face.

"Anyway, I tried to find a reprint of the painting in a book somewhere. So far it hasn't turned up. But I did find *this* about Biliński." He held up the clothbound book and began to read: "'Piotr Biliński was known primarily as an early influencer of impressionism in Poland. As a young man, he supported himself by making paintings of Polish intelligentsia, especially artists, writers, and musicians, in which he liked to capture the artist at work. Some of his famous subjects include the writers Boleslaw Prus, Adam Somebody-With-An-Unpronounce-able-Last-Name, and also'"—he smacked the page triumphantly—"'a portrait of the composer Aleksander Starza in his music room, metronome and pen at hand.'" Jerome flashed a proud smile. "Not bad, huh?"

"It's perfect." Clara took the book, scanning eagerly down to the sentence about Starza. "Where is the portrait now?"

"No idea," Jerome said cheerfully.

Clara felt her shoulders slump.

"Biliński kind of lost prestige after he died. The only surviving pieces I can find are in a museum in Warsaw. None of them are portraits. But if you *do* track it down, you can see what the metronome looked like."

"Right," Clara said, wondering how she was supposed to locate a painting that may or may not still exist to study a picture of a metronome that may or may not have belonged to Starza. All promising leads seemed to dead-end in similar fashion. Jess had called yesterday to report that Aaron finally hunted down the sister metronome he had told them about from the collection in Vienna. It had been made in Paris in 1863 by an apprentice of Phillipe-Nicolas Paquet. Starza spent the early 1860s in Paris, but Aaron hadn't found any link at all between the maker and the composer. As was the case with everything else, the unknowns multiplied the further she went.

"Why are you so interested in this metronome, anyway?" Jerome asked.

Clara looked up from the book. "I'm related to Starza."

"No *way!*" Jerome regarded her with new appreciation. "I hadn't ever heard his music before, but he sounds like a pretty awesome dude. Other than the temper tantrums and all that."

Clara thought about her ancestor and his many contradictions. "He wrote some incredible music, but he wasn't a nice guy."

"Isn't that true for all geniuses? It seems like it goes with the territory."

"I don't think it has to be that way," Clara said. "Bach was a pretty good guy. Chopin, too. Clara Schumann managed to compose amazing music while going on world tours and raising eight children. They were geniuses just as much as Starza was." She passed Jerome her library card and he took it, pausing to look at her scarred hand.

"I've got a wicked one, too." He pulled down the collar of his shirt, revealing a spear of rippled skin around his collarbone. "Car accident when I was eight. Pretty badass, huh?"

Clara peered at the marred skin, unsure how to play this exchange of *look at my scar*.

"Looks like it hurt."

Jerome shrugged. "I was unconscious most of the time. What happened to you?"

"Fire."

Jerome whistled. "Clara the Fire Walker." He scanned her books and handed them back, admiration in his eyes. "Bad*ass.*"

"No cheating this time," Barb said. "When the timer's out, it's out!"

"Oh, stop it," Julián complained. "It's Taboo, not the Chess Olympics. We're not at a regulation tournament."

"Olympi*ad*," Barb said. "It's the Chess Olympi*ad*."

"As I said," Julián retorted, "we're not there!"

They sat around Clara's kitchen table with beers and a bowl of tortilla chips, the contents of the Taboo box scattered around them. Game night had been Julián's idea, begun last winter after Paul moved out. Tonight was Clara's turn to host. It was the first time Barb and Lisa had come over, and that afternoon as she washed dishes and vacuumed dog hair off the couch, she had experienced a moment of gratitude for her ordinary life. It was not the life she had thought she would have when she was a girl, but it was a good one, with good people in it. How could her parents not understand that?

"Clara, how was your getaway with the handsome pianist?" Lisa asked.

Clara popped a bottle cap off a beer. "First, it was definitely *not* a getaway."

Julián lifted a finger. "Notice that she did not object to the fact that he is handsome, however."

Clara pretended not to hear him. She did not need any further reminders of Tony. Since returning from Chicago, she had found her mind reaching for him more often than she wanted.

"We took the metronome to an expert," she said. "There's a theory—a long-shot theory—that it belonged to Aleksander Starza."

Lisa gasped. "The famous composer?"

"That's why Tony came here," Clara said. "If the metronome is Starza's, he wants to buy it from me."

"I *broke* the metronome of a famous composer?" Lisa said.

"It's probably not even his," Clara said. "The people we talked to in Chicago said it's likely just an imitation."

"What are you going to do with it?" Barb asked.

"I don't know. Right now it's still in the closet. I have an appointment on Monday to put it in a safety deposit box at the bank."

"Can we see it again?" Lisa asked. "It might be our last chance before it ends up in a museum."

Clara rose from the table. "Sure."

"Let someone else hold it," Barb called after her.

The room Clara called "the guest room" did not house a bed. Nor had it ever hosted an overnight guest. In the seven years since she'd bought the house, the room had always been used as a storage closet. The floor was littered with dog toys Bingo had long-since abandoned, the baseboards obscured by stacks of books. The tiny closet in the corner of the room was thrown open to accommodate trash bags of designer gowns from her performance days that were now too out of style to put on consignment. Behind these, crates of records—her own recordings among them—were stacked to the ceiling, dusty and untouched. She pulled the furthest crate from the back of the closet and lifted the Beethoven records to the floor. The metronome box was at the bottom, swaddled in a nubby bath towel. She unwrapped it and slid the metronome out, then walked it back to the kitchen and set it on the table.

"Wow," Lisa said in a hushed voice. "I feel like I'm looking at Shakespeare's quill or something."

Julián held the metronome aloft like a crystal ball. "Spirit of Starza," he said in a spooky voice. "Speak to us."

Lisa giggled. "You really don't want this?" she asked Clara.

"I really, really don't."

"What if you decide to play again?"

Clara looked up, caught off guard. It was an innocent question. But something about the expression on Lisa's face reminded her of Ruth—like she was trying, ineffectively, to mask disappointment.

"I won't."

"But weren't you, like—" Lisa glanced uncertainly at Julián. "—a star, or something?"

Julián looked apologetically at Clara. "Sorry. I felt like they needed to know the missing pieces of the story."

"It was a long time ago," Clara said. "I stopped playing after my hand got burned." She kept her voice light. Still, the room fell quiet.

"Are we going to get back to this game anytime soon, or have we moved on to the *Antiques Roadshow*?" Barb asked.

"I need a snack break first," Julián said, standing.

"Me too," Lisa said. "Ooh, let's make grilled cheese."

"With tomato!" Julián exclaimed.

Barb rolled her eyes and pushed back from the chair. "Let's go outside and let these drunkards try to cook."

"Sorry about Lisa," Barb said when they were settled on the porch. "She gets nosy when she drinks."

"It's fine. I don't mind if you guys know."

It wasn't true, and by Barb's silence, they both knew it.

Barb leaned back on the swing. "It's a big deal, to turn away from the person you spent most of your life being. It's hard to remake yourself. Something always gets left behind, doesn't it?"

It was a rhetorical question, and one Clara didn't want to consider any more than she already had. "That's not always a bad thing," she said.

"No, I don't think it is. I guess I see you as someone who has some ghosts to clear out of her closet, is what I'm saying," Barb said, and laughed.

Clara laughed with her. "Since I'm hiding a creepy metronome in my closet, I guess that's fair." She tossed Bingo's ball into the yard, and they watched him canter after it. "What did you do to remake yourself?" Clara asked. "You sound like you're speaking from experience."

Barb looked thoughtfully out into the yard. "It wasn't remaking myself so much as becoming myself, I guess. My mother died about ten years ago. She was a devout Catholic and was totally in denial about who I was. Before she died, I decided to tell her I was gay."

"What happened?" Clara asked.

Barb smiled sadly. "She said she wished I had never told her. She insisted on calling Lisa my roommate until her dying breath."

"I'm sorry," Clara said. "That's awful."

"It was. Eventually Lisa helped me see that even if I never got the validation I wanted, at least I held to my truth. It was like, here I am, standing before you, and I can either let *you* break my heart, or I'll break my own, and there's nothing worse in this world than breaking your own heart."

Julián and Lisa stumbled out onto the porch then with plates of grilled cheese, and soon they all went back inside for another round of the game, but the frivolity of the evening was muted. Barb's story had left Clara sad, and also with the feeling that even here, among friends who had never heard her play a note, she was being judged for leaving music behind.

She stayed up late at the kitchen table after everyone left, winding the metronome again and again. The sound seemed loud in the silent room among the beer bottles and game cards, the suggestion of the departed friends and their bright noise making the hollow tick sharp in her ears. Still, each time it oscillated to a stop she wound it again, until after a while the sound was as regular as her breath, necessary and taken for granted at the same time, a random beat and a measure of the ticks of her life passing by. And here I am, she thought, rising finally in disgust to turn off the light, just sitting by and watching it go.

Chapter 12

WATER GUSHED DOWN THE CLOGGED GUTTERS of Fourth Street, shooting along the asphalt in a spume of trash and leaves. Clara sat behind the bar and watched rain stream down the windows. The Andromeda was quiet. A young couple from Fort Worth—newly engaged! they told Clara when they arrived—were her only customers. They sat in the booth farthest from the bar, holding hands across the table.

Clara poured herself a bourbon and pulled the pile of xeroxes Jerome had printed out for her from her backpack. She awoke that morning agitated and unrested, with an urgent need to move. Leaving the mess from game night where it was, she left the house with Bingo and walked nearly ten miles trying to outrun the feeling that the fractured halves of her life were slowly colliding, ready to crush her in between. It hadn't helped. She returned thirsty and depleted but still primed like a bird dog, alert to every ragged emotion that crossed her mind. The minute she got home, she pulled the stack of library materials from the dining room table and shoved them into her backpack, ready to find answers and get the metronome out of her life for good.

A shrunken facsimile of a newspaper dated 6 December 1885 sat on top, proclaiming *SLUZACY OPISUJE SCENE ZLA*. Someone—the helpful polyglot Jan, presumably—had scribbled an English translation in the margin. *Butler describes scene of evil.* Clara flipped through more grainy xeroxes: *Poland's musical prince laid to rest; Constantia Pleyel declared insane; Marianna Starza proclaims miscarriage of justice.*

She scanned Jan's translations about the murder, which, she noted, had a striking absence of "scalp bits," then turned to the book *She, Too, Played.* Jerome had placed a bookmark in the center, with a note scribbled on top: *Read this!* Clara flipped to the marked page. *Before Him: Constantia Baranowska Pleyel, Woman and Artist*, the chapter title read. A young woman seated at a piano smiled at Clara from the facing page. Wearing an off-the-shoulder gown that emphasized her long neck, hair pinned up in an elaborate cascade of dark curls, she looked at the aperture with a smile that was almost flirtatious. *Constantia Baranowska on tour in Vienna, 1866,* the caption beneath the photo read.

Clara took a sip of whiskey and began.

Before Him: Constantia Baranowska Pleyel, Woman and Artist
by Eleonora Konopnicka, Warsaw University

Few women in music history are more notorious than Constantia Pleyel. In the late 1880s, it was fashionable to burn photographs of her likeness in the streets of Warsaw. She was, in her shortened life, a child prodigy, composer, iconoclast, and finally, murderer. Nothing about Pleyel was ever straightforward, and nothing, to those few scholars who have sought in recent years to rehabilitate her reputation, is that way now. An eccentric who by historical accounts defied her prescribed gender roles, Pleyel's refusal to conform to societal expectations earned her a reputation years before she ever met Aleksander Starza.

The paucity of scholarship devoted to Pleyel has fixated on her crime and her femaleness at the expense of her achievements as a musician. Indeed, the first series of newspaper reports about Starza's murder describe a woman deranged by jealousy and unhinged by recent childbirth, thus emphasizing a narrative of female hysteria that has followed Pleyel more than a hundred years after her death—

"Right," Clara muttered, reaching for her whiskey. "Blame it on the hormones."

But this narrative of female otherness was already at work in Pleyel's lifetime, determining the fate of her career, her relationships with men, her creative talent, and ultimately, her crime and early death.

Constantia Baranowska was born 24 January 1848 in Warsaw to the violinist Stanisław Baranowski and his wife, Duchna. A renowned teacher as well as performer, Stanisław recognized the prodigious talent of his youngest daughter when the three-year-old could replicate on the piano any melody he played on the violin. Soon a young virtuosa, Constantia began touring Europe with her father at age six and was selling out concert halls by the time she was ten. She garnered widespread admiration throughout the important musical cities of the continent, but was always seen as a female first, musician second. "What brilliant playing!" one reviewer from Vienna wrote. "A listener would never know she was a child, much less a girl!"

The bias inherent in this assessment was not singular. Critical reviews of Baranowska's performances, and later her compositions, enthuse about her talent while expressing skepticism such talent could belong to a woman. A Rhapsody in E Minor she composed and debuted in 1866, at the age of eighteen, was deemed "the most inventive, pleasing, compassionate of musics. Upon listening, one cannot help but be transported, but also to wonder if Mademoiselle Baranowska's father might have been at her shoulder while she held her pen."

Rather than defending his daughter's talent, Stanisław encouraged such accounts, touting himself in letters to his wife and to the press as instrumental to Constantia's success.

Unfortunately, Constantia seems to have internalized these views. Discouraged by reviews such as the one above, she continued composing only intermittently, for the private entertainment of family and friends. Her sister Nadia, Constantia's closest confidante throughout her life, describes in her journals an oeuvre of mazurkas, waltzes, lullabies, and as many as ten nocturnes. Sadly, none aside from the Rhapsody in E Minor survive.

In 1869, while on tour in France, Baranowska met the French opera singer Olivier Pleyel. Her father disapproved of the match, rightly fearing a marriage would derail his daughter's success in a world in which women, and especially married women, were relegated to domestic life. In a letter to his wife, Stanisław describes Olivier Pleyel as "a second-rate imbecile with no musical talent. That he can sing is purely a gift of God and no credit whatsoever to any industry on the part of the man." Constantia, famously single-minded, married Pleyel anyway, defying her father with a secret ceremony just three months after the couple met. The elopement was the first of many scandals in her short life.

It was while on honeymoon in the south of France that Constantia suffered the injury that would determine the rest of her years. While out riding with her new husband, she fell from a horse, injuring her right clavicle, right wrist, and at least two fingers of her right hand. "Oh, Papa," she wrote to her father in a rare moment of vulnerability. "I have been such a fool. If I cannot mend my hand, I will never be happy again." Unfortunately, her fears were realized. Years after Constantia's death, Nadia would still refer to the accident as "the sorrow that launched all future sorrows."

Stanisław rushed to his daughter's aid with two of the best doctors in Europe, who agreed she would never play piano again except "in the parlor style of most ladies." Constantia refused to accept this prognosis. The Pleyels settled in Paris, where she sought the advice of the best physicians the city had to offer. She was prescribed treatments that ranged from poultices and herbal soaks to laudanum and custom splints. One doctor even advised immersing the injured hand in a mixture of warm brandy and tea for four hours at a stretch. Correspondence with her childhood friend, the Warsaw socialite Valeska Holland, reflects Constantia's growing despair as each remedy failed. The marriage, too, seems to have soured. Monsieur Pleyel, who once described Constantia as "a fire burning so hot I cannot touch her for fear of alighting," wrote to his brother that "Constantia is no wife. All she speaks about is her despair that she cannot play. I dare not even sing around her lest she begin to shout or weep."

In 1876, the Pleyels welcomed their first child, a son Constantia named Stanisław after her father. Accounts from her sister Nadia's journals attest that Constantia adored her baby, but that her low spirits worsened in the months after his birth. Then, in 1879, Constantia's father fell ill. Constantia and her son relocated to Warsaw, leaving Olivier Pleyel in Paris. Stanisław died quickly. In a letter to Holland, Constantia blamed herself: "My playing was his hope. My silence sunk into his body and killed him, the same as it will kill me."

Constantia met Aleksander Starza at a dinner party of Warsaw artists and intellectuals hosted by Valeska Holland in February 1881. Much has been made of the hostilities the two exchanged at their first meeting. Of her own impression of the encounter, however, Constantia was more balanced. "He is just as I imagined him," she wrote to Nadia. "Tall and angry. Very irritable. He can barely look anyone in the eye, and when he does, there is such vitriol burning there that one cannot but look away. His manners are intolerable, with no sense of pleasantry or kindness. Nearly his first words to me were about my hand, and in the unfeeling manner with which he spoke of my 'lost talent,' I was taken aback. But then he spoke of hearing me play years ago in Vienna, and for the genuine regret in his eyes, I forgave some of the rest."

Even still, the supposed "duel of words" made the society pages of the local newspapers. Holland, anxious to quell the gossip, urged Starza to write Pleyel a letter of apology. Thus, Starza and Pleyel began a correspondence in which the composer suggested a regimen of exercises designed to rehabilitate Pleyel's hand. Pleyel's interest was piqued, and in September 1881, she became one of Starza's private pupils. A letter Constantia wrote to Holland shortly after the lessons began reveals a relationship that was contentious from the beginning:

19 September 1881

Dearest Valeska,

You ask how the lessons proceed with Starza. I must tell you that the man is more intolerable than even you suggested. "The Maestro," as his ridiculous butler calls him, has more tantrums than my little Stani! He spends half our lessons shouting about my playing and the other half pouting that I haven't made better progress. His maid cowers through the house terrified to come near him, and thus the music room looks as if a team of mules had trampled through day after day. Then he blunders about the room grumbling that he cannot find his pen, or his ink, or his watch, or his scores, grousing like a dyspeptic bear! I admit I derive satisfaction from remaining sanguine in the face of such petulance. Starza is accustomed to people being afraid of him, but what have I to fear? I won't be an Ophelia any longer. Besides, it's rather fun to watch <u>The Maestro</u> squirm!

Yet do not think me ungrateful, dear Valeska. Already my pathetic hand is improved, and with it, my amputated spirit

begins to mend. At present I apply myself to a tedious process
of playing scales with my second and third fingers bound by a
piece of string to force the fourth to learn to move on its own.
Starza has also begun writing a concerto for the left hand
that I can play until the little duds are ready. Olivier says
it will lead only to heartbreak, but I hear my father's voice
rasping from the grave. I'd rather die than give it up.

Yours,
Constantia

One can hear in this letter the mixture of hope and resolve in Pleyel's words, as well as a beginning—if reluctant—reliance on "The Maestro's" support. And indeed, Starza's assistance was substantial. In addition to the rehabilitation regimen that gave Pleyel hope of returning to the stage, he composed the concerto for the left hand and later helped set up a reintroduction concert that Pleyel, sadly, never performed. But the relationship became increasingly antagonistic. Barely two months into her association with Starza, Constantia wrote to Holland announcing she had resolved to quit her lessons:

27 November 1881

Dearest Valeska,
Starza is the most loathsome man! This afternoon we were
rehearsing the first movement of the concerto for the left hand,
which he finally completed after weeks of my nagging. I was
not one minute into the piece when Starza began to shout that
the tempo was incorrect. His tempo, which he set! And yet it is
my fault that the music does not match the sound in his head,
which is, to hear him recount it, a work of unparalleled genius.
Let me assure you, dear friend, that it is not. The outrageous

tempo is only the beginning. When I pointed out that perhaps the problem is not <u>my</u> interpretation but <u>his</u> deficient metronome, he picked up the dastardly thing and threw it across the room! I departed immediately and have determined I shall not return. Some say a genius is the voice of God transmuted to human understanding. I hear God in Starza's music, but I see a beast in his eyes. I refuse to be treated as the dog who limps to the kitchen door for scraps.

Yours,

Constantia

Despite these strong words, Constantia did return a few weeks later, perhaps deciding that a revival of her career was worth whatever unpalatable treatment Starza chose to mete out.

Valeska Holland left Warsaw in February 1882 for an extended tour of America. Whatever correspondence the two women may have maintained while she was abroad is lost. Holland returned to Warsaw in October 1885 in time to congratulate her friend Constantia on the birth of the Pleyels' second child, a baby girl. In a letter Constantia sent thanking Holland for a baby gift, one can hear the high spirits of 1881 given way to despair.

23 October 1885

Dearest Valeska,

How wonderful to see you, if only for a moment. Your face brightened the shadows of this cold house. Helene adores the blanket. When I see her wrapped in it, I see the peace I might have enjoyed had my life been different. I have written her a nocturne, that she and I both might never forget the perfection of this time of innocence, when she is too small to know the cruel inequities of the world.

*You must think me melancholy for a new mother who
treasures her beautiful girl. But there is no easy path for a
woman in this life. You were wise to never bind yourself to any
man. If I prayed—and you know I do not—I would pray that
the men who will determine my girl's life are at least kind,
and that she might have a daughter to love as I love her. All
my own happiness now depends on her, and on Starza, whose
darkness I fear more than anything in this world. Oh, Valeska.
His eyes are terrible to behold. I cannot bear to ponder the
demons they possess.*

Your loving friend,
CP

A mere six weeks later, on 4 December 1885, Pleyel went to
her lesson at Starza's home for the last time. By the time she left,
the composer was dead. Her own fate had been almost equally
determined.

At the time of her arrest on the platform at Warsaw's Vienna
Station, a police officer seized Pleyel's infant daughter from her
arms. Pleyel lunged after the child and was immediately detained
by three men, who dragged her away from her wailing baby. Pleyel
was told nothing of her daughter's whereabouts and reportedly
screamed for her child day and night. When a guard told her it would
be fitting if the child died for the crime she had committed, Pleyel
struck him. She was thereafter tied to a chair and denied access to
food, water, or even a place to urinate. When finally the baby was
revealed to be safe—not by anyone employed by the jail, but by the
jailer's wife—Pleyel agreed to speak to the chief inspector.

According to his reports, Pleyel first claimed Starza's death to
be an accident but soon confessed, alleging she had killed him in
self-defense. The inspector found this variation in Pleyel's version

of events to be "evidence of a mind steeped in either confusion or deceit." But his primary reason for suspicion of Pleyel's veracity came from her failure to offer a compelling motive for why Starza might have attacked her. He called Pleyel "as much of a liar as any sane criminal, but too hysterical to keep her story intact. Her mind is weak, unable to reckon with the depravity of her actions." Thus, Pleyel's claim of self-defense—and any truth it might reflect—was forgotten in the drama that played out in the ensuing weeks, as Pleyel's mental fitness became the central focus of the case.

News of Starza's murder spread rapidly. If Constantia Pleyel was before a name familiar only to the musical in-the-know, it was now in the headlines of newspapers throughout the world. Reports describing the gruesome state of Mr. Starza's parlor, Pleyel's dramatic arrest at Vienna Station, and her purported "violent disposition" quickly churned the public into a frenzy.

It was customary at that time in the Russian Empire for female murderers to be assessed for psychological fitness—the assumption being that a woman who killed someone must obviously be deranged. Pleyel was likewise evaluated by a team of psychiatrists who observed her after her arrest and took statements from witnesses—no one who had actually been in the vicinity of the crime, but rather persons who had "relevant information regarding Mrs. Pleyel's state of mind." Chief among these were her lady's maid, who testified that in the weeks since giving birth, Pleyel had been agitated and paranoid, refusing to allow the staff alone with the children and locking herself in her music room for hours on end.

More titillating for the public were the statements from Starza's butler. Marek Poldowski had been the first suspect in the murder and was arrested and briefly detained before Pleyel was discovered with Starza's metronome. Now he presented colorful tales to the medical board and the press about Pleyel's jealousy of the composer, complete with a sensational story of how Pleyel, on one occasion, set fire to one of Starza's compositions and left it on his piano to burn. Even Olivier Pleyel offered testimony about his wife's "deranged" state of mind, which allegedly included a physical attack on his own person when he visited her while she was in custody.

The psychiatrists declared Pleyel to be a psychopath "in the throes of puerperal insanity." A "disorder" that ceased to be a credible medical diagnosis barely a decade after Pleyel's death, in Pleyel's time as many as 10 percent of female asylum patients were institutionalized as a result of this specious condition. Believed to arise in the days or weeks after childbirth, indications of puerperal insanity could include anything from expressing hostility to one's husband and showing disregard for one's appearance to more serious behaviors like self-harm and violence. Not to be confused with postpartum depression or postpartum psychosis, which are real and treatable disorders, "puerperal insanity" was instead a blanket term used to confine and, in some cases, condemn nineteenth-century women who did not conform to their expected roles as wives and mothers. As is perhaps unsurprising, many women sent to asylums for puerperal insanity were committed against their will, at the behest of their husbands or other male relatives.

It is certainly possible that Pleyel suffered from a medical condition that could have contributed to the events of 4 December 1885. The facts, however, allow for the possibility of a different narrative. Raised by an egomaniacal father who insisted on perfection, then quickly married to a man who seems indifferent to her thwarted ambition, then forced to rely on the patronage of a man like Aleksander Starza, Constantia Pleyel spent her life bending to the will of difficult men in a world that did not believe she should have attained the fame she did. Like her trailblazing

predecessor Clara Schumann, Pleyel's talent was restricted by
the expectations of women in the nineteenth century. To assume
that she was simply a mad or jealous woman sent over the edge by
the hormonal imbalances of pregnancy is to ignore the improbable greatness to which she ascended and the tragic decline she
fought off for years. We will never know what might have become
of Pleyel had she returned to performing. Would she, like Clara
Schumann, have performed into old age, mesmerizing the crowds
of Europe and inspiring admiration around the world? Perhaps
not. But perhaps.

Pleyel was deemed unfit to stand trial and was sent to Ragin
Mental Hospital. Records indicate her repeated petitions to be
given permission to see her children and her sister, and to be freed.
These hopes were never realized. Like so many of her fellow inmates,
she died of the Russian Influenza Epidemic of 1890. The last medical record of her time at Ragin, recorded by her psychiatrist on
8 November 1889, was summarized thus: "The patient continues in
her delusions that Mr. Starza's murder was not her fault."

Clara flipped back to the photo of Pleyel. Constantia had been just
twenty-one when she injured her hand, the same age as Clara when the
fire ruined her own career. Like Clara, she wasted years on promises
of recovery that went nowhere. Clara understood the desperation that
would drive Pleyel to study with Starza if she thought it would get her
back on stage. Clara could remember being willing to trade anything
for her life to go back to the way it was. It was the type of longing that
could kill you.

The phone by the cash register rang, jarring her from her thoughts.
The young couple was gone, their champagne flutes half empty on the
table. She reached for the phone, her mind still stuck in the nineteenth
century, and was startled to hear a familiar voice on the other end of
the line.

"Clara, it's Tony."

She glanced at the pea-green alarm clock they kept hidden on a low shelf so patrons wouldn't know how much time they were wasting. It was past midnight.

"Hey," she said. "What's going on?"

"Sorry to call so late. I tried you at home first. Do you have a second?"

Clara looked outside, where the rain drove toward the pavement in unrelenting streaks. "I have many, as it happens."

"Listen," Tony said. "I've been sorting through more of Madame's papers. My assistant has been cataloguing it all. She found a notebook with a draft of an article Madame was writing about Constantia Pleyel."

Clara did not miss that Tony's assistant was a "she." She imagined an adoring graduate student with trendy glasses and glossy hair.

"Weird. I was just reading about Pleyel. What's the article about?"

"It's just notes, so it's kind of hard to say. There's a paragraph about how Starza heard Pleyel perform in 1859 in Vienna, and some other stuff about how the two of them were both influenced by Polish folk music, and then a bunch of stuff about how Pleyel and not Starza was the preeminent pianist out of Warsaw until she hurt her hand. It's all over the place, really, but it seems like Madame is making the case for Pleyel influencing Starza's music. Listen to this." Clara heard the shuffling of papers through the phone. "'Much has been made about what Constantia Pleyel took from the world when she murdered Aleksander Starza. Little has been thought about the ways in which Pleyel's own artistic sensibilities may have influenced the composer's late works.'"

Clara frowned. "It seems logical, I guess. Pleyel was apparently kind of a bigshot in her heyday."

"Kind of, right? But that's not why I called. The notes in here talk a lot about how Pleyel's own compositions have been lost through the years, and how since they're gone it's impossible to know how much Pleyel might have composed, and when, and who might have been influenced by it, et cetera. But what's *really* interesting is that there's a list here in the notebook. At first, I thought it was a list of museums. Then I realized it's a list of music archives. Clara, I think Madame was looking for Pleyel's music."

"But you just said Pleyel's works are gone."

"They're *mostly* gone. That night at Madame's house when I walked in, you were in front of the instrument case. Did you happen to see that there was a new score in the manuscript collection—right in front?"

The image of the fragile score open on the wooden stand flashed easily to her mind, followed by a recollection of the sparkling music—a constellation sweeping across a night sky.

"Yes," Clara said. "I couldn't remember who wrote it."

"That's because you'd never heard it before. I hadn't, either. It's a first edition of Pleyel's Rhapsody in E Minor."

Clara's eyes darted to the open pages of the book: *A Rhapsody in E Minor composed and debuted in 1866, at the age of eighteen.*

"There aren't that many copies left," Tony said. "The publisher stopped printing it after Starza's murder. Madame bought it at auction last year, from a private collection in Prague. I found a letter in her papers about it." Tony cleared his throat. "'*Dear Ms. Mikorska, It is my great pleasure to inform you that a first-edition printing of Constantia Pleyel's Rhapsody in E Minor has been discovered in the archives of a private collector. As I know you have been most eager to obtain a copy for many years, I have notified the representative of your enthusiasm for the piece and have procured for you the first right to purchase.*' There's also another letter in here from 1918. It's in Polish, so I don't know what it says yet. I've sent it to one of my colleagues in the Languages Department to translate. But it's addressed to someone named Helene."

Clara frowned. "That was the name of Constantia Pleyel's daughter."

"I know. I'm wondering if it might have information about Pleyel's music." The tempo of Tony's words accelerated. "And here's the *really* insane part."

Clara poured herself another whiskey. Tony needed to rethink his definition of *insane*.

"This list of music archives," Tony continued. "She has the Starza Museum on there. It was crossed out in blue ink, then she crossed out the cross-out and wrote the museum at the top of the list, with a note beside it that says *Clara*."

Her heart quickened.

"Just 'Clara'?"

"Just 'Clara.'"

"Is there a date on it?"

"No. I looked everywhere in the notebook. There's not a date on any of it. Listen, I know you don't want to go to Warsaw, but all signs are pointing there. We need to go to the Starza Museum and talk to the people over there about what we've found. I get it that you have baggage with Madame and with Warsaw. But we could be on the precipice of something huge."

Clara recalled what Jess had said about Tony's stake in the metronome. On one of her trips to the library, she had looked through past issues of *Classical Times* for news of Tony's calamitous performance with the London Philharmonic. It hadn't been hard to find. The review in the magazine called the incident "career-ending misbehavior."

"You can go," Clara said. "If you want to go hunting around Poland, you have my blessing."

"No." Tony's voice was firm. "Madame gave the metronome to you. I don't understand it, but it's clear she thought you were the one to figure it out."

Clara thought of the supposed portrait of Starza by Piotr Biliński, which had been nagging her since she left the library yesterday. If anyone had knowledge of when it was made and what it depicted, if not where it actually, physically was, it was Tomasz Górski, the director of the Starza Museum. She knew Tony was right, and that the answers, if there were any to be found, were in Warsaw. But just thinking about going made her sweat.

"If she wanted me to figure it out, she should have left more explicit instructions. I'm sorry, Tony. I'm not going."

Tony sighed. "At least take a look at these notes, will you? Maybe you'll see something in them I don't."

"Fine. You can fax them to the bar. I'll be here all week."

She hung up feeling heavy with the past—Madame's, Constantia Pleyel's, and her own. She cleaned up the bar slowly, trying to put order to the chaos in her mind. Clara had never restored Madame's access to the archives at the Starza Museum. Was that all Madame had wanted from her? If so, why not pick up the phone and ask while she was still alive to go look into it herself? Why goad Clara into doing it by bequeathing her a metronome that may or may not have belonged to Starza? And on the subject of Starza and his metronome, what had happened on December 4, 1885, to cause the beautiful and talented Constantia Pleyel to decide to kill him with it? Clara thought of the day she had raised her arm to Madame's tuning wrench, ready to fight back. Was it crazy to defend yourself against a man who hurled objects across the room? Or was the real madness in taking it day after day, year after year?

It was after one when the bus dropped her off at the end of her street. Rain was falling so hard it popped up from the sidewalk, dampening the cuffs of her jeans. She hurried down the desolate streets, dreaming of a hot shower. Somewhere in the distance she heard a barking dog, its frenzied woofs muted beneath the drum of the rain. It was only as she neared her house that she recognized Bingo's rich tenor. She froze, hearing the note of fear in it, then lowered her umbrella and ran.

She saw him as soon as she turned onto her street. He stood on his hind paws with his head straining over the gate, the chain link bowing beneath his weight. When he saw her coming, he bellowed a woof of relief and hurled himself against the fence.

She hugged him around the neck. "What are you doing out here?" She looked past him to the house, fear prickling the backs of her arms. The porch light was on as she had left it, the swing and the flowerpots undisturbed.

Bingo whined and thumped his tail against her leg.

"Come on," she said.

Together they mounted the steps. Through the gap in the front curtains all she could see was the glow of the hallway nightlight. She turned the doorknob to confirm it was still locked, then pulled her keys from her backpack and unlocked the door. Holding her breath, she pushed it open.

Bingo bounded past her, howling.

"Bingo!" she hissed. "Get back here!" But he disappeared into the house.

Clara stood on the threshold, listening to the skitter of his nails on the wood floor. Then she heard a high-pitched yelp.

She plunged into the room, fumbling for the light switch. When the overhead light flooded on, she gasped.

The coffee table was upended, a potted philodendron crushed beneath it. The bookshelf was on the floor. The porcelain lamp she'd bought on tour in Hong Kong was beside it in a pile of blue and white shards. Even the sofa had been assaulted. It lay tipped on its back, the undercarriage ripped to shreds.

She stood in the doorway, too astounded to move. Then Bingo limped from the hallway. Clara let out a cry at the blood trailing from his front paw. Two daggers of blue porcelain sprung from the pink flesh. She sank before him and held his head in both hands.

"I have to get it out," she said.

Bingo whined and looked away but allowed her to grasp the injured paw. She gripped the tip of the larger shard and pulled. Bingo whimpered. The betrayal in his eyes made her want to weep.

"I'm sorry," she said, and reached for the other shard.

He scrambled away from her and hid behind the upended coffee table, yelping as the porcelain drove deeper into his paw.

"Bingo," she begged, crawling toward him over the crust of glass on the floor. "Please. I have to get it out."

He growled.

"I'm sorry." She clung to his wet, thick neck. "I'm sorry." Holding him close, she pinched the porcelain between her fingers and pulled, the jagged edge slicing her flesh. Bingo squirmed away from her, then limped beneath the kitchen table.

She sat on the floor, looking around at the destroyed house—her European treasures and secondhand mishmash, the vintage floor lamp she'd bought after moving to Austin that felt like the fresh light for a new life. Eventually her eyes settled on the hallway, where the night-light flickered its false yellow flame. Unsteady, she rose and walked toward it, hearing Madame's voice in her mind.

Each of you should understand why you were selected for the bequest you received.

She knew Bingo would never have rested if someone remained in the house, but she flipped on every light on the way to the guest room, wanting to fill the horrible darkness.

You are its temporary caretaker, charged with shepherding it to the next generation.

Clara barely registered the dresser drawers on the floor and the books strewn in every direction. Her eyes went straight to the closet. The trash bags of old dresses had been emptied. The boxes of records, too. At the very back, the crate of Beethoven records she had pulled out last night sat empty.

Clara lunged toward it, the opening bars of the *Fire Concerto* rushing over her in a thunderclap of sound. Pulling back the closet door, she yanked the chain for the overhead light and dug through mounds of satin and splintered vinyl, the runs and arpeggios of the concerto lashing through her mind. She found the sleeve of one of the Beethoven records, half the vinyl of another. The mahogany box was gone.

She staggered to the kitchen and called 911, then ran to the front door, where she had dropped her backpack. Slipping on the fragments of a shattered fruit bowl that had once sat on her kitchen table, she fell to the ground. Crumbles of broken glass lodged in her arm, but Clara barely felt them. She reached for the backpack and clutched it to her chest as if it were the only thing holding her together.

She had walked so long and so far that afternoon that she was running late when she came back. By the time she dressed for work and ran to the kitchen to fill Bingo's bowl, it was ten minutes until the beginning of her shift. She was on the porch locking the door when she glimpsed the metronome through the window. It stood on the table just where Julián had left it last night, between the open Taboo box and the bottle of Maker's Mark she had finished alone after everyone left. She dashed back inside and shoved it into the nearest hiding spot she could think of.

Clara pulled the metronome from her damp backpack, simulta-neously cursing and thanking herself that she had been such a fool. Huddled on the floor, she cradled it in her arms. In her mind, the concerto barreled on to its final, wondrous note.

Chapter 13

MORNING SUN STREAMED THROUGH the open windows of the living room. It carried on its pale beams a sweet wind that smelled of cut grass and dew. With every rustling breeze, the white curtains billowed, and the dust that hovered over the wreck lifted and settled again, blanketing everything.

Clara stood in the doorway, coffee in hand for fortification. Jumbled on the floor was nearly everything she owned. She was struck by how much she had accumulated, and also how little the assortment of belongings said about what she had accomplished. There were no photographs of family. No diplomas or treasured gifts. No keepsakes from a beloved friend. The waste of it ached.

Bingo woofed grumpily from the backyard. Last night he refused to take his usual place at the foot of her bed. It was his absence that caused her to wake early, dread seeping in through her cold feet.

She set the coffee mug on the windowsill and pulled a garbage bag from her pocket. Julián was coming at eight. At nine, they were going straight to the bank to rent a safety deposit box, where she had planned to take the metronome on Monday. Where she should have taken it weeks ago.

"It's not a bad idea, in case that's really what they were after," the older police officer had said last night. He hadn't bothered to conceal his skepticism. Even when she brought out the metronome and told them where she got it and what it might be, she had seen their eyes glaze over.

"I saw somebody break into a car last week for a pickle jar of change," the younger cop said when she finished her story. "But all the perps really took in your case was this wooden box you're telling us about. When most of the valuables are left intact, we usually think more along the lines of a revenge motive." His eyes darted over Clara's scars. "Or teenagers. Some kind of prank."

"What's funny about destroying someone's house?" Julián had asked.

"Same thing that's funny about TP'ing a tree, I guess." The cop shrugged. "I haven't asked."

They'd had dozens of questions about who it might be. Anyone with a grudge? Anyone who knew this "supposed artifact" might be valuable? Clara thought immediately of the woman who had called in the middle of the night. If she had discovered Clara's phone number, surely she'd found her address as well. But the woman was clearly old and sick. She would have had to convince someone else to break in on her behalf. Then there were the anonymous caller to Mr. Borthram's office and John LaFleur, who both knew about the metronome and its possible storied past, but who seemed equally unlikely candidates. They would have been smart enough to know they were stealing an empty box. In the end, there were so few people in her life that the conversation was very short. It was probably just some rowdy teenagers looking for a thrill, the older cop said. They were sorry. There wasn't much they could do.

Clara plucked her copy of *Great Expectations* from the floor and shook slivers of glass from the pages. The binding collapsed, sending half the book sliding to the ground. Clara chucked it in the trash bag so hard the spine tore through the plastic. When they said there wasn't much they could do, what they really meant was that the break-in didn't matter enough to warrant doing anything. The metronome was just an old clock to them, its case a decorative box. They didn't care to whom it had once belonged, or who it may have injured along the way.

The phone rang from the kitchen. Clara wiped her grimy hands on her jeans and rose to answer.

"Two glazed and one jelly," she said when she picked up. "I've already made coffee, but it tastes like dust, so you'd better get some of that too."

Silence on the other end. Then, "Clara?"

"Jess?"

"Oh, good! For a minute I thought I called the wrong number. Sorry to bother you so early. I was up all night!"

"Me too, incidentally," Clara sighed. "What's up?"

"This is big. *So* big." Jess was almost breathless. "I've been trying to figure out how Mikorska might have come into possession of that Amati violin she sold the Rademakkers in 1940."

Clara leaned against the kitchen counter, feeling weary. She did not have energy this morning for anyone's misfortunes but her own. "Okay."

"So I was thinking—Mikorska's last known location before the photo was taken in Rotterdam was the Warsaw Conservatory. That would be a logical place for a pianist to obtain a fine violin if she were so inclined, right?" Jess took an excited breath. "So I asked the conservatory to send me a list of instruments they knew to be lost or confiscated during the German occupation. And guess what? The list they compiled after the war includes"—Clara heard a jubilant shuffling of pages—"a Guarneri del Gesù violin, dated 1738, property of the pianist Jozef Zamoyski. And right beneath *that*: 'nineteenth-century metronome with lion pendulum,' also property of J. Zamoyski! Remember what Aaron said, about Mikorska's violin? He thought the instrument looked like a convincing Guarneri *except for* the last two digits of the label, which he thought had been replaced with a fake year. Mikorska's violin says 1736. Zamoyski lost a 1738. Clara, what if she got both the Guarneri and the metronome from him?"

Clara rolled through the chronology in her mind. Zamoyski had been Starza's preeminent pupil, but he was just a boy when Starza died. That he would have ended up with the metronome seemed even more improbable than Madame getting ahold of it.

"How would he have gotten Starza's metronome?"

"That I don't know. The better question is, how did *Mikorska* get it, if it was thought to be confiscated by the Germans? So I did some digging. I called the conservatory for all the records they had on Mikorska during her time there. Did you know she was expelled from the school?"

"Expelled?" Clara shook her head in confusion. "What for?"

"The records aren't clear. There's just a form dated 26 May 1939 that says 'Zofia Helene Mikorska is hereby dismissed from the studio of Jozef Zamoyski for failure to meet the standards of the conservatory.' It's signed by Zamoyski himself. There's a tuition statement on the reverse side showing that she owed the school a balance of 346 zloty."

Clara's head began to hurt. She plucked a fragment of a broken plate from the counter and tossed it in the garbage can. "I thought she left because of the war."

"That's what everyone seems to think. And that would be my story, too, if I got expelled from school by the most influential pianist in Poland. But the Germans invaded on September first. Mikorska was expelled three months earlier. It's especially curious because I also found an announcement in the Warsaw paper from May fifteenth that said Mikorska was invited to give a concert with the Warsaw Symphony that coming October. She was going to perform Starza's *Fire Concerto*. That doesn't sound like someone who's failing to meet the standards of the conservatory." Jess paused. "So my question is this: How did an *orphan* who couldn't afford her school tuition in May turn up in Rotterdam eight months later peddling an Amati violin? I'm cooking up a pretty scandalous hypothesis over here, so stop me if you think it's nuts."

"Go on," Clara said.

"Jozef Zamoyski was the owner of a Guarneri violin that was thought to be stolen by the Germans, as well as a nineteenth-century metronome with a lion's head on the pendulum. Sixty years later, it turns out that his student, Zofia Mikorska, had in her possession a Guarneri violin and also a nineteenth-century metronome with a lion's head on the pendulum. And here's the part I didn't tell you yet."

Clara leaned forward, though Jess was a thousand miles away.

"Jozef Zamoyski died on September 1, 1939."

Clara relaxed, unimpressed. "I know. He died during the invasion."

"No," Jess said. "Or yes, but no! September first *was* the day the invasion began, but Zamoyski was found dead that morning in his studio. The conservatory hadn't been touched! Apparently, he was drunk and fell and hit his head. The official cause of death was suffocation. He choked on his own vomit."

"Gross," Clara said, unsure how all this was related.

"Right? In the chaos of the invasion, there wasn't an investigation into Zamoyski's death. I guess he was known to have a drinking problem, so everybody just assumed he was wasted and fell and hit his head. But the janitor who found him had gone back to the conservatory the night before because he forgot to lock one of the doors. He told Zamoyski's widow that he heard Zamoyski playing the piano in his studio around midnight. But it turns out Zamoyski was out drinking with the violin teacher until at least two in the morning. The janitor insisted he heard him at the school. The violin teacher insisted Zamoyski was at the bar with him. So who was in his studio playing the piano?"

"Hold on." Clara shook her head, struggling to follow Jess's logic. "Are you saying you think Madame had something to do with his death?"

"Not necessarily," Jess exclaimed. "But maybe! I guess it's possible he gave her the metronome and violin and *then* fell and hit his head, but from what I've read about him, he wasn't the most generous guy. Clearly there was some bad blood between them if he expelled her."

"I don't know," Clara said, doubtful. "That's a lot of what-ifs." It wasn't that she couldn't imagine Madame killing someone. That part was disturbingly easy. It just seemed too complicated.

"She had both the Guarneri and the metronome when she died," Clara said. "She obviously didn't sell them to finance her escape from Poland, so she couldn't have needed money that badly."

"I know. I thought the same thing. So I went back to the list of missing instruments from the Warsaw Conservatory. The violin teacher, the one Zamoyski was out drinking with the night he died? He was killed in the bombing of Warsaw during the invasion, but his widow reported that one of his violins, an Amati, had been at the conservatory and was never recovered after the war. Guess what year it was made?"

A chill traveled up the back of Clara's neck and lodged in the base of her skull. "1671."

"1671," Jess repeated. "The same year as the violin she sold the Rademakkers. Clara, I think she stole it."

Clara leaned against the counter, recalling the accusations of the five-a.m. caller.

"Did Zamoyski have a daughter?"

"He did. Her name was Maria. She was fourteen at the time of his death, which means she could definitely still be alive."

Clara shook her head. It still didn't add up. "But why steal the metronome? Violins, sure. They were clearly valuable back then. But the metronome couldn't have been, unless Madame knew it was Starza's."

"Who's to say she *didn't* know? And even if she didn't, everybody but you who's laid eyes on that thing wants it. Tony would chew off a finger to get it. And if she *did* suspect it was Starza's—and that certainly seems possible since Zamoyski was Starza's student—that would give her even more motivation. All I know is, the actual value of the metronome doesn't matter anywhere *near* as much as the emotional value of what people see in it. That would be just as true in 1939 as it is in 1997. It's still possible the thing isn't Starza's at all, but the bottom line is this: however Mikorska got ahold of that metronome, it seems feasible that it's stolen property. As a purely ethical matter, I can't keep this information to myself. I'll give you a little lead time to avoid people coming out of the woodwork, but you need to get in contact with Mikorska's lawyer and tell him what you know."

Clara's eyes fell on the remains of a cereal bowl pulverized in the bottom of her sink. "I think it's too late to avoid people coming out of the woodwork."

After she'd told Jess about the break-in she hung up, feeling more tired than she had when she went to bed last night. If Jess was right and Madame had stolen the metronome and had a hand in Jozef Zamoyski's death, then Clara's intuition had been correct: Madame had been a monster all along. But that didn't answer why Madame had given her the metronome. Surely Madame knew that its history might come to light once she gave it away. Why not come clean and return it to the Warsaw Conservatory, or donate it to a museum and let the experts handle it? Why involve Clara at all? It was this question that had gnawed at her all night as she lay awake in her desecrated room, burning with fury. She knew her anger should be directed toward whomever had broken into her house, or to Mr. Anonymous, who had been the first to frighten her, or to the five-a.m. caller. Instead, her rage had coalesced around Madame, who had left her this precious object with no instructions and no tools, and who wasn't here anymore to take the blame.

She turned back to the disaster of her living room, where the narrow walkway she had cleared was barely visible amid so much ruin. Feeling she could not face it, she walked out the front door and sat on the stoop beside the red hibiscus that had just begun to bloom. She ran her hand over the silky petals to soothe her mind. When the metronome first intruded into her life, all she wanted was for it to disappear. But last night, any doubt she felt about whether the metronome was actually Starza's had dissolved the moment she saw her mangled living room. This was the metronome he held in his legendary hands, the metronome that had tocked back and forth as he wrote the sorrow and fury of his life into music. A hundred years later, Clara had felt that sorrow and fury in her own body as she played his nocturnes and scherzos, his pain pulsing within her from decades away. But so had thousands of other pianists. Why had Madame, who had scorned and belittled Clara from the moment she entered her studio, given it to her?

You are only here to convey the music! Madame used to hiss in Clara's ear as she played. *You are a gnat on the glass of history. Your job is to disappear and let the music take the stage!*

The opening bars of the *Fire Concerto* rumbled in the back of her mind. Clara shook her head to silence them, then rose and walked into the house, the screen door slamming behind her.

Dusk was falling out in the street, where weekend partiers passed by on the sidewalk, their voices lilting and bright. The smell of damp asphalt and smoked barbecue wafted into the bar from the open door. Clara could not muster appreciation for the fine summer night. She had come straight to work after hours of cleaning her ravaged house and could still feel dust coating her arms and hair. By the end of the day, all that remained of her belongings were a bed, a chest of drawers, clothes, and a few plates. Everything else—broken, torn, shattered, ripped—was piled on the curb in a mound of ruin. Her life had been reduced to a bedroom suite.

"You sure you want to be here?" Julián asked. "I can cover for you if you want."

Gratitude momentarily overcame her bad mood. Julián had helped her clean all afternoon. Clara and Bingo were going to stay with him until her house was put back together. "Thanks. I think I'd just cry into the dust heap."

She mixed a round of old-fashioneds for a group of graduate students in the back booth. When she returned to the bar, Julián was talking to a man in a navy suit. Both of them were looking at Clara. The sight of the man's dour expression made her shoulders tense.

Julián walked over. "That guy's here to see you."

"Who is it?" Clara asked.

Julián grimaced. "Some kind of lawyer." He put his arm around her. "All the bad news over with on the same day, right?"

Clara flinched. What other bad news could there possibly be? She walked over to the man in the navy suit, wishing she could walk past him and out the door. "You wanted to talk to me?"

He was in his forties, with a humorless face and pale blond eyelashes he blinked frequently, as if there were something in his eye. He shifted his leather briefcase into the crook of his arm and stuck out a pale hand. "Brooks Ptarmigan," he said. "I'm from Borthram and Adams, in Chicago."

Clara slumped. "What's going on now?"

"Is there somewhere private we could talk?"

She led him down the hallway to the office and sat on a pallet of beer that had been delivered that afternoon, gesturing to the desk chair. The man cast a dubious look at the holes in the green upholstery before perching on the edge of the seat.

"I wouldn't have intruded on you at work, but I went to your house, and it looked like you'd moved out."

"Moved out?" Clara exclaimed, thinking of the mess of splintered furniture stacked on the curb. "No. My house was broken into last night. What's going on?"

Mr. Ptarmigan withdrew a large white envelope from his briefcase. "I'm in Austin for my niece's wedding. Mr. Borthram knew I would be in the area, so he asked me to make sure you got this." He held the envelope toward Clara like it was a plate of bad food he was passing down the table. "I'm sorry to be the bearer of bad news, but we've received a demand letter contesting the estate's ownership of the metronome bequeathed to you by Ms. Mikorska."

Clara accepted the envelope with reluctance. She didn't know what a demand letter was. She targeted the more comprehensible second point. "Contesting the estate's ownership? What do you mean?"

"Someone is claiming the metronome wasn't Ms. Mikorska's to give away." Mr. Ptarmigan blinked. "They're threatening to sue you."

Clara felt the room lurch as her eyes bugged. "*Sue* me! For what?"

"They're saying the metronome is stolen property."

The force of her disbelief propelled Clara off the crate. "Did you talk to Jess? Because I told her already—if somebody else has a legitimate claim, they can just *have* the thing! I don't even want it!"

Ptarmigan eyed Clara as if she were dangerous. "I don't know who *Jess* is," he said slowly. "The petitioning party is a family by the name of Dabrowski, in New York. The matriarch claims that the metronome belonged to her father and was stolen during the German occupation of Poland. We're going to investigate their claims and try to resolve it before it comes to litigation, but they're making aggressive threats. Ms. Dabrowski is ill and is anxious to see the metronome returned to the family before she dies. If it does belong to her, you'll have to return it in the same condition in which you received it."

Panic was rising up the back of Clara's throat. She looked into his pallid face, feeling lightheaded. "The box," she whispered.

Ptarmigan looked confused. "What about the box?"

Clara tore open the envelope and read the letter uncomprehendingly, feeling as if it were a piece of a puzzle she didn't know she was supposed to be solving. In the second paragraph, her eyes paused on a familiar name: . . . *Jozef Zamoyski, Ms. Dabrowski's father, obtained the metronome in 1937. It was noted missing from its last known location at the Warsaw Conservatory in late 1939.* The letter was dated four days ago. She looked up at Ptarmigan, afraid she might throw up.

"The people who broke into my house last night," she said. "They took the box."

Ptarmigan blinked three times in rapid succession. "It's my understanding that the box is a signature element of the piece. Did you have it insured?"

Clara felt too heavy to stand. "No. What does that mean for me?"

Mr. Ptarmigan blinked several more times before responding. "It means you need to find that box if you want to avoid a lawsuit. I'll call the local police on your behalf and tell them to alert the antiques stores in the area that we're looking for a potentially high-value artifact." He stood. "If the metronome turns out to be the Dabrowskis', you could be liable for anything you did to diminish its value. In this case, that could mean thousands of dollars."

Clara watched him exit the room, alarm clanging through her body. She didn't have thousands of dollars. She didn't have *a thousand* dollars. She didn't even have a sofa.

Dazed, she walked out into the bar. Jerry was playing "I've Got Rhythm" on the piano. Every bar stool was taken, Julián working in a frenzy to fill the orders. Clara didn't even register the attempts to wave her down. She poured herself a stiff drink, then walked back to the office, where the fax machine was spitting papers onto the desk. They accumulated in a sloppy pile, then slipped to the floor, fanning over the linoleum. She glimpsed her name on the top page.

> Clara,
>
> Copies of Madame's papers. Reconsider Warsaw.
> You know it's where this ends.
>
> Tony

Clara groaned. She sank to the chair and laid her head on the desk. In less than twenty-four hours, every good thing in her life had been ruined, and now she was being sued by someone she had never met over an object she had never wanted. She closed her eyes, feeling like she might scream. Above her head, the fax machine began to screech and whir again, and presently another piece of paper slid off the printer and landed on her head. She sat up and found that she was staring at a copy of a faded letter written in Polish. An English translation was typed at the bottom of the page.

Dearest Helene, it began.

> If you know me at all, it is as either stranger or villain. Please read this letter until its close, that I might convince you I am neither. I have searched for you these long years, and wish to speak to you about your mother, my dear sister Constantia.

Clara straightened in the chair.

> No doubt you have been told many tales about your mother, and perhaps most especially about her actions on the night of 4 December 1885. I do not know all of what transpired that night. My sister did not tell me while she lived, knowing I would plead for her freedom at all cost to myself and perhaps even to you. But I do know this: What the world believes about that night is untrue. I hesitate to divulge more here for fear you will find my story too fanciful to believe, but when I meet you and, God willing, hold you to me, I will tell you all.
>
> If you are reading this, the lawyer Mr. Narbut has found you and given to you the small sum I put aside, as well as a keepsake from your mother I have saved for you these many years. Know that there is more waiting for you here—a modest inheritance, as well as a few mementos of your father's. Above all, there is love. Perhaps you do not know that it was your mother's wish that I should have raised you, and my great heartbreak that this wish was denied. Should you ever want to reunite with your family in Łódź, we will welcome you forever.
>
> Your loving aunt,
> Nadia Brzezińska

Clara glanced at the date at the top of the letter: 19 December 1918. Something buzzed on the periphery of her consciousness, like a mosquito she could hear but not yet see. She sat still, trying to grasp it. *Zofia Helene Mikorska,* Jess had read from the record of Madame's expulsion from the Warsaw Conservatory. The name in Madame's will was Zofia *Helena* Mikorska. But *Zofia Helene,* Jess had said. *Helene, Helene, Helene.* When the realization hit her, she leapt from the chair. She rushed into the bar and lunged for her backpack.

"Clara!" Julián looked concerned. "Everything okay?"

"Fine!" She raced back to the office.

Back at the desk, she dug *She, Too, Played* from the bottom of the backpack and flipped to the letter Constantia Pleyel wrote about her infant daughter. *Dearest Valeska, Helene adores the blanket.* Clara scanned to the bottom of the page, where a tiny footnote ran across the margin: *Constantia Pleyel's daughter Helene was born 9 October 1885.*

Clara looked up at the ceiling, recalling Madame's letter to the beneficiaries. *As an orphan who was also the child of an orphan, I have lived my life without the bonds of family.* She closed her eyes, calculating. *My parents were not musical, but my grandmother was a very talented pianist.* Clara's heart guttered in her chest. She picked up the desk phone and dialed Jess's number.

"The record from the conservatory, where Madame was expelled," Clara sputtered when Jess answered. "Are you sure it was Zofia *Helene* and not Helena?"

"Yeah," Jess said. "I have it right here. Why?"

"Helene is the French variant of that name. It's weird that a Polish girl would have it, right?"

"I guess," Jess said. "Why? What's going on?"

"I'll call you back!" Clara hung up and immediately called Tony.

"Clara. Hey. Did you have a chance to look at my fax?"

Clara squeezed her eyes shut, trying to catch hold of the thoughts racing through her mind. So much had happened since she talked to him twenty-four hours ago, she didn't know what to say first.

"Tony!" The words dammed up behind her mouth. "She's her granddaughter!"

"What? Who?"

"Madame. She's Constantia Pleyel's granddaughter. That's why she wanted the metronome. That's why she stole it from Jozef Zamoyski."

"Hold on, hold on. She stole the metronome from Jozef Zamoyski?"

"Yes. Maybe! Jess thinks so. That's not important right now. Listen to me! Madame's middle name is Helene. Did you know that?"

"I thought her middle name was Helena."

"Me too. But it was there, on a form Madame signed when she was expelled from the Warsaw Conservatory! She must have changed it when she emigrated." -

"I don't know." Tony sounded skeptical. "It's just a name."

Clara shook her head. "No. Madame said she was an orphan who was also *the daughter of an orphan*. In an interview in 1948 she said that her grandmother had been a talented pianist. Helene Pleyel was born in 1885. She would have been thirty-five in 1920 when Madame was born. It's not just a name, Tony. It's a name Madame changed to disguise her past, and a lifelong obsession with Starza, and the fact that she had a copy of Constantia Pleyel's Rhapsody, and the metronome, and this letter to Pleyel's daughter—all of it! She was trying to—"

A shiver went up Clara's arm.

"What?" Tony asked. "What was she trying to do?"

Clara flipped through the rumpled fax pages until she found the list Madame had made of music archives in Europe. At the very top, Madame had written *Starza Museum*. Scrawled next to it, underlined three times, was her own name. *Clara.*

"She was looking for her grandmother's music," Clara said. "And she wanted me to help her find it."

PART II

Chapter 14

Warsaw was a city where old had been made new. As good as leveled by the Nazis, Warsovians spent the postwar decades restoring their beloved city to the way it stood before a Panzer ever rolled across the border. Baroque palaces rose from the foundations of their bombed predecessors. Gothic steeples speared the sky as if they had never been toppled by Nazi shells. Since Clara had last been here, the country had seen the end of Communist rule and the explosion of a new modernity. The highways were crowded with honking cars and tour buses. High-rise Sheratons and Marriotts towered on busy street corners. It was a vibrant city, rich with the past, humming with the promise of the future. Clara watched it all from the window of the taxi as if peering through gauze. In every young woman sipping espresso at a sidewalk café or strolling with a shopping bag, she saw the last days of her old life: a twenty-one-year-old who could have had a limitless future had she only made different choices.

"You're quiet."

Clara looked over at Tony, who sat next to her in the back seat of the cab. They hadn't spoken much on the flight. At one point, Clara fell asleep and dreamed she lost Bingo in Madame's house. When she startled awake, she was clutching Tony's arm. She abruptly withdrew her hand, but he took it back and squeezed it, holding on until they both fell asleep. Now she turned away from him, embarrassed by how jittery she was.

"It looks different," she said, watching a band of teenagers in brightly colored tracksuits exit a Burger King.

"A lot changes in ten years."

Clara didn't need reminding of that.

The taxi pulled to a stop before a cobblestone street. The Starza Museum was in New Town, a part of the city that had been "New" in the fourteenth century. Like the adjacent Old Town, New Town was closed to vehicles. Clara paid the driver, beginning a mental tab. Tony had bought her plane ticket and hotel room. She was resolved that this was all he would pay for.

They proceeded on foot, tugging their luggage across the cobblestones. Starza moved to his Freta Street address in 1881 after the falling-out with his sister Marianna. Both Starza's home and the Starza family residence on nearby Foksal Street had been badly damaged in the war. The Foksal Street house was now an apartment building, but Starza's home had been rebuilt as if suspended in 1885. A three-story stone building with a red tiled roof and white-framed windows, it rose from the street in much the same way it had when the composer last exited its doors. The original cast-iron carriage hitch stood at the curb. A gas lamp flickered beside the arched door. The house was a shrine to the composer, and to the city's past. Crowds swarmed the sidewalk, snapping photos of the home and pausing reverentially at a bronze statue of Starza erected in the center of the street. The composer stood in a top hat and morning coat, one hand lifted to the sky as if channeling music from heaven. Bouquets of flowers and pages of musical scores rested at the base of the pedestal. As Clara and Tony neared, a woman in a bright red jacket knelt before the statue and bowed her head.

Tony watched with uncharacteristic solemnity. "You do forget, don't you? How much he means to people." He looked up at the tall house, taking in the black shutters and the window planters blooming with purple mums. "I've actually never been here."

Clara followed his gaze up the length of the elegant house, thinking of the last time she had come here, the day before the fire, to view the score of the concerto. Her scars itched beneath her shirt. "I'm surprised Madame didn't require a pilgrimage."

"Starza was always her thing," Tony said. "And yours, of course."

They joined a line of visitors waiting to get in the door, and the dread that had congealed in Clara's stomach when the plane landed gained a little mass. For months after the fire, she had received hate mail from strangers as far away as Istanbul and Moscow decrying her irresponsibility at allowing the score of the *Fire Concerto* to burn. Facing the Starza scholars at the museum was the easiest on the list of difficult encounters of this trip, and it by itself made her want to run. But the metronome box was still missing. Maria Dabrowski and her sons were still threatening to sue. How they had learned that the metronome had resurfaced in Madame's estate remained unknown. Though there had been a knot in her gut since the day she decided to come here, she'd concluded that her best chance of avoiding a lawsuit and any further unwanted incursions into her life was to prove that the metronome was Starza's. She had finally heard back from Tomasz Górski, the museum director, last week. The Biliński portrait was in their archives. Tomasz warned her that it had suffered water damage and was in bad shape. Clara hoped the view of the metronome had not been obscured. If she could demonstrate that the metronome was Starza's, she could argue that, as his heir, it technically belonged to her, leaving her perfectly within her rights to lose its custom box worth thousands of dollars.

There was also, of course, the draw of Constantia Pleyel. Madame had thought some clue about Pleyel's lost work might be found here. Clara had visited the museum at least a dozen times. Today as she regarded the house, she thought not of her ancestor coming and going through the heavy mahogany door, but of Constantia Pleyel. How she might have parked her carriage before the iron hitch and descended to the curb in a bustle dress, the hem of her skirts grazing the brick walkway. She experienced a strange out-of-bodiness imagining Constantia lifting her head to look at the brass knocker on the door. How could she explain this affinity she felt for the most notorious woman in the history of classical music, or the sympathy that swelled in her chest when Pleyel spoke of her damaged hand and "amputated spirit"? Or, late at night, alone in her emptied house, the slinking dread that crept up her neck when she wondered what had tipped Constantia's life from a tragedy into a horror. Maybe Pleyel really was a deranged, violent, evil person who deserved to die alone in an asylum. Or maybe she was just a desperate woman trying to get back the one thing that mattered most to her who one day made a huge mistake. Like a dumb twenty-one-year-old ignoring a fire alarm, it was a moment of irrevocable decision that determined the rest of a life.

She was unaware that she had stopped at the bottom of the porch steps and was holding up the line. Tony looked back at her from the door, his expression concerned. "You need a minute?"

"No." Clara shrugged off the haunted feeling and ascended the steps.

The foyer had been converted to the museum's welcome area. A woman with bright pink lipstick smiled at them from behind a white ticket counter.

"*Dzień dobry! Witamy w Muzeum Starza!* Welcome to the Starza Museum," she said. "Two tickets?"

Clara realized she was clenching her fingernails into her palm and released her fist. "We have an appointment with Tomasz," she said. "My name is Clara Bishop."

Clara watched for changes in the woman's smile, wondering if she knew who Clara Bishop was or the crime she had committed against the museum, but the woman only regarded her pleasantly. "Yes, he said to expect you. You can go through the museum if you like." She gestured toward the hallway. "He will come down to meet you."

Clara and Tony joined a line of tourists milling past black-and-white photographs of Starza, many of which Clara recognized from the books she had checked out from the library. Of more interest to her were the photos of Marianna, whose face until now Clara had only imagined. In contrast to her brother's dark hair and countenance, the elder Starza was fair and diminutive, with pale eyes and a frankness about her expression that lent her an air of capability. Clara paused at a portrait of Marianna encased in a thick wooden frame. In it, Marianna sat at a giant desk wearing a high-necked gray gown with a fur collar, her pale hair braided in a crown atop her head. She held a pen in her hand, the look on her face distracted, as if sitting for the portrait were drawing her away from more important matters. *Oil painting of Marianna Starza by Jakub Rostworowski, 1878*, the placard beneath the painting read. *The French walnut frame of this portrait was made from the Starza family's Boisselot et fils piano after a flood in 1895 rendered the instrument unusable.* Beside the painting hung a triptych of framed pages from the original score of Starza's Nocturne in G-sharp Minor in the composer's famously illegible hand, alongside Marianna's neatly transcribed edition. *An amanuensis for the ages*, the sign above the transcriptions read.

Tony had moved down the hallway and was straining to peer over a tour group of seniors stopped before a pair of open French doors. The most popular attraction of the museum was the first.

The composer's music room had been recreated according to the portrait of Starza by Jakub Rostworowski that hung now over the fireplace. The walls were covered in a faded red damask that made the light coming through the arched front window seem like evening rather than midday. An escritoire stood beneath the window, its ebony top covered in glass to protect the letter beneath—a missive from the composer to his publisher Christoph Windscheid in Vienna, informing Windscheid of the delay of Starza's final and unfinished work, a Piano Trio in G Minor. A chaise lounge of gold velvet sat nearby, as if ready to accommodate the composer should writing become too exhausting. The needlepoint carpet was a pattern of red, black, and cream diamonds, each with a center red rosette. In the middle of the long wall facing the French doors was the white marble fireplace, wood stacked in its cold grate. Two high-backed chairs upholstered in red velvet sat on either side of it. But all of this was incidental to the main feature of the room. A square grand piano of gleaming rosewood with ornate curved legs and painted gold scrollwork stood in the center of the room. An unfinished score rested on the music rack, an open inkwell ready on the rim beside it. On the leg nearest the fireplace was the glass magnifying lens illuminating the famed drop of blood that had spurted from the composer's head. Behind a cordon of black rope, a plaque entitled *A Fateful End* described the events of December 4, 1885.

Clara's eyes settled on a pair of matching end tables with long, curved legs standing near the red chairs. She imagined them easily hurled at an unsuspecting back.

"Clara!"

She turned at the sound of her name. A slender, bespectacled man with a trim black beard hurried forward with arms extended. He folded Clara into a hug that smelled of Earl Grey tea and musty papers. "It has been such a long time."

Clara thought she saw him sneak a look at her scars as he pulled away, but he was so quick it was hard to tell.

"And, Mr. Park, it is an honor," Tomasz said, turning to give Tony's hand a vigorous shake. He reached for Clara's suitcase. "Let's go upstairs, away from all the chaos," he said, gesturing to the tour group of seniors, who were talking around the plaque. "I have prepared a tea for you after your travels."

Tomasz led them past the reconstructed dining room, set with china for one, and up a back staircase—the servants' staircase, Clara realized, thinking of the butler whose testimony had helped determine Constantia's fate. The second floor of the house had been converted to offices to house the museum's administrative arm. Tomasz turned into a room on the right and gestured to three chairs set around a Victorian tea table. "Please," he said. "Sit down."

The canvas backpack was still on Clara's shoulder. She noticed she was holding it across her body like a shield and set it on the floor.

"All of us at the museum were so saddened to hear of Ms. Mikorska's death," Tomasz said, pouring tea into blue china cups. "The world has lost one of its greatest musicians, and one of Starza's greatest interpreters." Tomasz handed Clara a cup with a tender smile that she did her best to return. Tomasz loved Starza the way an indulgent parent loves an untamable child—with completeness and abandon. She wondered what he had thought of her embargo against Madame visiting the archives and felt suddenly and intensely ashamed.

"Thank you for taking the time to meet with us," she said, forcing herself to look him in the eye. "I know I've caused the museum a lot of trouble."

Tomasz's face softened, though it was not without a vestige of pain. He looked at her as someone might regard a Judas they had worked hard to forgive. "You are always welcome here, Clara," he said. "We are very grateful to your family for allowing us to house the scores. One was lost, yes, but so many more are safe because your great-grandfather and all your relatives since have seen the value in keeping them in Warsaw. It was a terrible accident, what happened to you the last time you were here. I cannot blame you for what is not your fault."

They were all quiet a moment, then Tomasz set his cup on the table. "I must say I was surprised to hear that you are interested in the Biliński portrait. We had to pull it out of storage. It is not very good, I'm afraid. In fact"—Tomasz chuckled as if sharing gossip—"Aleksy sent it back and refused to pay. I believe he called it"—Tomasz lifted his eyes to the ceiling—"'an abomination of my likeness.'"

Clara saw Tony's eyebrows lift when Tomasz called Starza "Aleksy."

"And is it?" she asked. "An abomination?"

Tomasz laughed gaily. "Well, it's not exactly flattering. You'll see. It's rather dark. It was made in 1879, during one of his episodes."

Clara glanced at Tony. "Episodes?"

"That's what we've taken to calling them. Things have been quite exciting around here in the past year." Tomasz leaned forward giddily. "We recovered a new batch of letters between Starza and the violinist Henryk Wieniawski. They met in the 1850s, you know, when they were both young prodigies touring Europe, and wrote to each other periodically through the 1860s. The letters were discovered five years ago but have been tied up in Wieniawski's estate. My colleagues and I disagree on our interpretation of them, but some of the letters do seem to reveal a kind of—shall we say *clinical* moodiness. The dates align with some of the less gentlemanly behavior we learn about in Marianna's journals. My colleague is developing a wild theory of his own. Ah—there he is himself! Gregor!" Tomasz lifted a hand as if he were summoning the help. The sound of books thudding to the ground boomed in the hallway, then a man leaned into the room.

He was tall and large in a farmhand kind of way, with a broad ruddy face and thick arms that strained the sleeves of his tweed jacket. His light brown hair needed a cut and drooped over one eye in a way that made him look boyish, though Clara suspected he was about forty. His face broadened into a jolly smile.

"This must be Miss Bishop! And Mr. Park, of course." He lumbered forward and pumped Clara's hand.

"Gregor is our resident expert on Marianna," Tomasz explained. "I was just telling Clara and Tony about the Wieniawski papers. Gregor is convinced Aleksander caught something in his Paris days that he couldn't quite shake, if you understand me." Tomasz looked at them slyly.

Clara groaned inwardly. Some things hadn't changed enough since the nineteenth century. "You mean a venereal disease," she said.

Tomasz nodded. "Gregor believes Starza contracted syphilis in Paris, and that he was suffering the neurological effects as early as the late 1870s." Tomasz cast a look of exasperated tolerance at Gregor, whose thick eyebrows jumped in a gleeful lift.

"Ah, yes. It is all madness and mayhem here these days, hahaha!" Gregor laughed heartily.

"You think Starza was going mad from syphilis?" Clara asked.

"Well, I don't *know* it, but I do think it, Miss Bishop," Gregor said cheerfully. "A terrible fate, terrible! But it was very common in those days, you know. We citizens of the twentieth century forget how lucky we are to have penicillin."

Clara was slightly disturbed by the apparent joy Gregor took in his discovery but was anxious to know more. "What in the letters leads you to believe he had it?" she asked.

"Well." Gregor clasped his hands behind his back and leaned forward as if Clara had just entered his lecture hall. "The letters to Wieniawski written in 1866 mention the end of the engagement with Annabelle, and suggest that Starza had been unwell. Scholars have always known about Starza's struggles after Annabelle, of course, but we assumed it was a depressive episode. However, Starza describes mostly physical symptoms to Wieniawski—fever, headache, rash, and a 'gnawing' pain throughout his body. These could be symptoms of many diseases, to be sure, but it's the language he uses to discuss Annabelle that gives me pause. I believe the exact words he employs are 'deceptive Jezebel.' The writing is very colorful!" Gregor laughed merrily, then resumed his scholarly frown.

"It made me curious, of course. I have studied Marianna Starza's journals for years, and I have always thought that there was something that changed for her around 1878. She knew we would be reading, you see, and I feel she knows I am looking over her shoulder." He smiled distractedly, as if he were imagining Marianna's ghost there with him in the room. "But I can see that she is troubled by a change in her brother's behavior. She writes in her journal of a day Starza lost his temper with the cook over some minor trifle—a spoiled pudding, I believe—and how he raged around the house for hours throwing dishes at the walls. Marianna was appalled, and in disbelief how her dear brother could contain such fury. Of course, we could also surmise that she was simply in denial about who her brother truly was, but when I read the letters to Wieniawski, it made me reflect on Starza's illness in 1866. Early syphilis infection, you see, includes symptoms such as fever, rash, and headache—many of the complaints Starza wrote about to Wieniawski. After these resolve, a person might appear to have had a full recovery. Luckily for everyone around him, after a period of years he is also no longer contagious. But the disease is still latent, you see, and over the course of many years it can begin to attack the brain. As you may imagine, this can lead to all manner of troubles—mood changes, depression, headache, fevers, paranoia, delusions, hallucinations— terrible, terrible things!"

"I think our guests understand you, Gregor," Tomasz interjected. "Their time here is limited."

Clara had to stop herself from protesting. She longed to corner Gregor without Tomasz and ask more questions. If Starza had been losing his mind, it was possible, as Clara had been wondering for weeks, that Constantia Pleyel really *had* killed Starza in self-defense. But Gregor accepted Tomasz's interruption with a good-natured shrug.

"Forgive me. Tomasz and I disagree on the findings, of course. It is a theory only. We can never truly know. Very glad to have met you," Gregor said to Clara and Tony. He offered an awkward bow, then backed out of the room.

"I'm not persuaded myself," Tomasz added when Gregor had departed. "My feeling has always been that Aleksander was a misunderstood poet of deep feeling, which sometimes meant deep darkness. Sometimes the china was a regrettable casualty." He smiled thinly. "Regardless, the fall of 1879, when he sat for the Biliński portrait, was a particularly bad time for him. He was ill in September and struggling with the tepid reviews of his first concerto. After he saw the portrait, he sent it back and refused to pay. It was Marianna who requested it from the artist and paid the bill. I don't think she ever hung it, and to honor her wishes we haven't either." He placed his teacup in its white saucer. "Not many people know it exists. How did you come to learn of it?"

Clara felt Tony turn toward her. She did not look his way. She wasn't ready to reveal the metronome. Not yet.

"I've read some new research on Constantia Pleyel," Clara said, keeping her face decidedly blank. "It led me to want to know more about the murder. I happened to come across a mention of the portrait. It said Starza's metronome was in it."

Tomasz's smile vanished as soon as Clara mentioned Pleyel. "There *is* a metronome in the portrait," he acknowledged, with a reluctant tip of his head. "Whether it is or is not *that* metronome, we do not know. Of course, some people have speculated, but there is no physical description of Starza's metronome in the composer's papers for us to compare. But tell me—this *investigating* you are doing into Constantia Pleyel. Would you perhaps be referring to Ms. Konopnicka and her new research?" His mouth puckered.

"Yes," Clara said, surprised by the bitterness in his voice. "We have an appointment to talk with her tomorrow, actually. Have you read her work?" Clara did not add that the appointment with Eleonora Konopnicka to discuss the article she had written about Constantia Pleyel was the only thing about this trip that Clara had been remotely looking forward to since the airline ticket had been booked.

"I read all the new research about Starza." Tomasz removed his spectacles and began to polish one lens with the edge of his napkin. "I am not in support of Ms. Konopnicka's revisionist take. Constantia Pleyel had a tragic life. It does not excuse the murder of one of the greatest composers ever to have lived."

"No," Clara began, "but I think it's worth—"

Tony leaned forward abruptly. "I couldn't agree with you more, Tomasz," he said, setting his teacup on the saucer in a decisive click. "As you know, I publish some articles of my own here and there. I've been interested in writing a piece about representations of Starza through the years—in art, literature, that sort of thing. When Clara told me about the painting, I asked if I might come along to take a look." He turned to her with a smile that told her to shut up.

Tomasz visibly relaxed. "Yes. Well, we do have it. But I would direct you to the Jakub Rostworowski portrait down in the music room. It's so much warmer. I like to think it is the more accurate portrayal."

"I spent some time with it downstairs," Tony said. "It would be fascinating to compare the two."

Tomasz glanced at them sideways, clasping his hands in his lap. "Of course. Well, I had Darek bring up the Biliński from the basement for you. It really *is* in bad shape. I'll have to ask that you don't touch it." He looked pointedly at Clara.

"Of course not," Clara said, her face warming. "We'll just look."

"Then I will take you to it." Tomasz rose from his chair.

"One more question, if you don't mind," Clara ventured as she stood. "In the archive, is there any unpublished music, or partial drafts—anything that seems a departure from Starza's style?"

Tomasz frowned. "Well, we do have a few scraps here and there. Melodies on the back of a bill for candles, that sort of thing. Anything complete we would have published, of course, for the world to enjoy. Why do you ask?"

Clara shook her head, trying to conceal her disappointment. "Just curious."

Tomasz led them down the hall, past modern rooms with desks and computers where air conditioners hummed in the windows. Clara followed, only half listening to Tomasz's explanation of the renovations the museum planned for spring. She knew Tomasz must be correct about Starza's manuscripts. Clara had been in the archives many times. It was all thoroughly documented and catalogued. There was nothing down there that the museum scholars could not identify exactly. Madame would have known the same thing. So, what was it Madame had thought would be at the museum?

"And here it is!" Tomasz said, pushing open a door to a large room with a conference table in the center. At the far end of the table, too far away to see in detail, a painting no larger than a cereal box was propped on an easel. "Again—no touching, please," Tomasz said. "I'll leave you to take it in." With that, he smiled and closed the door.

When they heard his footsteps recede down the hall, Tony whistled a sigh. "Geez. You'd think he was the guy's brother. I thought he was going to fight you to defend Starza's honor."

But Clara was hardly listening. She had walked to the end of the table and was now standing before the portrait. Tomasz had been right to call it dark. Despite its small size, it exuded a foreboding that seemed to dim the room. The bottom third of the painting was indeed damaged. The canvas was rippled and cracked from where the linen had separated from the wood backing. In places, only dark smudges revealed that there had ever been paint on the canvas at all. But the part of the portrait Clara cared about was vividly intact. The composer loomed before his fireplace staring into the flames, one side of his face shadowed in darkness. His giant hands rested on the mantel as if commanding the fire to rise.

"No wonder he didn't like it." Tony walked up behind her. "He looks like a demon."

"Maybe Biliński saw the real side of him," Clara said.

They stood side by side before the portrait, awed to silence by what they saw. After a while, Tony spoke. "You see what I see, right?"

Clara's voice caught in her throat. "I do."

They both leaned in at the same time. A metronome stood on the mantel beside the composer's right hand. Positioned as it was on the periphery of the painting, the winding key faced away from the portraitist's view, but Biliński had taken time rendering the ornate casting on the cabinet and the shining gold feet. The unmistakable head of a lion gleamed in the firelight.

Tony laid a hand on Clara's arm. "Clara," he said, "before this goes any further, I need to tell you something."

Startled by the urgency in his voice, Clara looked into his face just as the door behind them swung open. Tomasz sailed into the room. "So what do you think? Macabre, isn't it?"

Clara glanced again at Tony, but whatever he had been about to say or do was gone. He lifted his eyebrows in an expression that seemed to say *What now?*

Clara turned to Tomasz. "Tomasz, I'm going to show you something, but I need to ask for your discretion."

Tomasz's eyes turned quizzical as he watched Clara reach inside her backpack and remove the plywood box Julián had built that Clara had then encased in Bubble Wrap. When at last she withdrew the metronome from its protective layers, Tomasz only stared. Then his mouth opened wide. "No!"

Clara and Tony laughed.

"But how could it?" Tomasz sputtered, shaking his head. "It is impossible!" Even as he said it, he reached toward the metronome, his hand quivering. Finally, he turned his eyes to Clara, his voice barely a whisper. "Can it be?"

Clara set the metronome on the table beside the portrait so the two lions stood beside each other.

"Yes," she said. "I believe it is."

Chapter 15

"CONSTANTIA WAS A REMARKABLE WOMAN. Her talent was compared to that of Clara Schumann and Liszt. Until she injured her hand, of course." Eleonora Konopnicka sat behind a tiny wooden desk in her basement office. Blonde and slender, with hazel eyes and a golden luminescence to her skin, she seemed freshly returned from modeling in a Noxzema commercial rather than the fluorescent depths of an academic library. Had she walked into The Andromeda Club some Saturday night, Clara would have spent the evening reminding herself of all the resolutions she had made about accepting her own face as it was. But if Eleonora knew of the disturbance her beauty caused, she gave no indication. She seemed hardly to occupy the present world at all, so absorbed was she by the past. She had met Clara and Tony in the lobby of the Warsaw Conservatory, an expansive 1960s building of concrete and glass, and led them to her office in the cramped wing of the basement dedicated to music history, musicology, and music therapy. Now they sat squeezed across from her in two folding chairs, their knees grazing the xeroxed pages that draped like wilted petals over every edge of her cluttered desk.

"What was the exact injury, do you think?" Clara tried not to sound as desperate to know as she felt. She didn't want to admit to anyone, most especially Tony, how badly she needed to understand the circumstances of Constantia's unraveling.

"She broke her clavicle and wrist," Eleonora said, in clipped Americanized English. She had done her postgraduate work at NYU, she explained. "But most of the doctors I've asked think that the persistent problems came from a fracture of the fourth and fifth fingers. In her letters to Valeska Holland, she calls those her 'little duds.' She also talks about how the fourth finger is crooked, which would seem in keeping with a bad break. But of course, so much of the correspondence of that time one must read with the expectation of obfuscation. No one talked about what was really going on."

Tony cleared his throat. That morning when he and Clara met in the hotel lobby, he had looked with appreciation at her black jeans and sweater and told her she looked nice. Clara had been dismayed by the way her face had warmed, wondering for the tenth time in so many hours what he had felt such urgency to share with her at the museum the day before. The expression on his face before Tomasz walked into the room reminded her of the way he had looked in her parents' driveway back in June—a tinge of desire coupled with a longing to go back and amend the past so that things might have turned out differently. Now she watched him stare at Eleonora with the awestruck admiration of a teenage boy and felt ridiculous for thinking that whatever he wanted to say could have had anything to do with herself.

"What was really going on?" he asked.

Eleonora turned both palms to the ceiling in a good-natured shrug. "Who's to know for sure? I have my theories, based on what the family has allowed me to read of Nadia Brzezińska's journals. That's Constantia's older sister." Eleonora passed Clara a xeroxed photograph of two teenage girls in matching gowns standing before a fireplace draped with evergreen boughs. The younger of the two Clara recognized instantly as Constantia Pleyel, who appeared to be about sixteen in the photograph. She stared boldly at the camera, the corner of her mouth lifted as if she were suppressing a smile.

"This is Nadia," Eleonora said, pointing to a dark-haired girl of around eighteen or nineteen. Taller than Constantia and more beautiful, with large, dark eyes and a cascade of shining curls beneath her feathered hat, the older girl stood slightly behind her sister, peeking over Constantia's shoulder as if shy of being photographed.

Clara passed the photo back to Eleonora. "What are your theories?"

"Well, as a woman of talent and relative power in those times, Constantia had a complicated relationship with the men in her life, in particular with her husband. Everything I've read about Olivier Pleyel suggests a man who was unwilling to share the spotlight with a woman. This applied to the sopranos he worked with on stage as well as to his personal relationships. There are some coded mentions of violence against Constantia in Nadia's journals." Eleonora folded her hands on the desk and regarded them frankly. "I think it's possible that a fall from a horse was not the real reason for her injury. Like maybe a horse was never involved at all."

"You mean you think he hurt her?" Tony had regained himself enough to assume his usual skepticism. "Do you have any proof?"

"Only that Pleyel did hit her on at least one occasion before their wedding, and that she and her father quarreled about it. I believe this is the primary reason her father forbade the match. He wasn't the picture of benign paternity by any stretch of the imagination, but I think he realized correctly that Olivier Pleyel would not tolerate two stars under the same roof. Also, Constantia seemed to blame Pleyel for what happened to her hand. She wrote to Nadia shortly after the injury and said she would never forgive him."

Tony frowned. "That's not a lot to go on."

"There's not a lot of open discussion of domestic abuse even now," Eleonora said. "Much less so in the nineteenth century. And yet we know it occurred. Why not to Constantia Pleyel?"

"You see her more as a victim, then," Tony said, his voice taking on a new edge.

Eleonora's face remained placid, but Clara saw in the languid shift of her eyes the fatigue experienced by women everywhere who are called on to explain to men what is obvious. "I see her as a complex human being who was at the mercy of difficult men. I'm not saying she was innocent of killing Starza. I don't know what happened that night.

But I do think there's more to the story than a hysterical woman who couldn't contain her jealousy."

Clara was reminded once more of Gregor's hypothesis that Starza had been going mad. Since yesterday, it had circled her mind like an unresolved melody. The theory could certainly account for some of the worst stories about Starza. But it didn't explain the inconsistencies of Constantia's story after her arrest, or what became of her music, or how the metronome ended up with Madame. For every mystery solved, a new case was opened, with fewer clues and more convolution.

Tony seemed to have the same thought. "If there was really more to the story, why didn't she explain it? Why not defend herself?"

"Maybe she did," Eleonora said. "When she was first arrested, she said Starza's death had been an accident, but pretty quickly, she changed her story and said she killed him in self-defense. No one believed her. The chief inspector's main issue with her version of events was that she couldn't explain why Starza would try to attack her. He also thought it was suspicious that she had taken Starza's watch. The money she stole from his desk he understood as a means to escape, but the watch seemed to him like some sort of trophy. Then the witnesses started coming forward and talking about her mental state, and he concluded that she either had been hallucinating during the crime or was making it all up."

"But doesn't it seem like her mental state *was* in question?" Tony persisted. "It sounds like everyone agreed she was losing her mind."

"It does *sound* that way, but you have to remember: Starza was a celebrity. The entirety of Warsaw was outraged by his death. And if you step back and look at the list of witnesses, it's easy to see how they all could have an agenda—the lady's maid, Starza's butler, the guard whom she reportedly attacked while in custody—they all had reason for a grudge. And then there was her husband. It was his statement that really sealed her fate."

"What did he say?" Clara asked.

"He told the doctors that she had been violent before and that he feared for the children's safety. Having read Nadia's journals, I find that very hard to believe. He left the family for months at a time to do operas and didn't seem to worry for their safety then. Then there was the incident when he visited her in the hospital after her arrest. According to the records, he asked if he could speak to his wife in private. After a few minutes, a guard heard a scuffle in the room and went in. Constantia was unconscious on the floor. Olivier claimed she tried to attack him and that he knocked her down to protect himself. He was reportedly distraught while he gave his statement to the doctors, crying that his wife had been lost to him forever, but then left the country with the couple's son before her case had even been decided. Constantia disputed his version of events, of course, but it's obvious the doctors didn't put much credence in what she said. If anything, her hostility toward her husband further convinced them that there was something wrong with her. This was a time in history when women who acted outside the bounds of acceptable female behavior were often seen as mentally unstable. A woman could easily be committed to a mental institution if her husband made a convincing case that she was crazy, and Constantia was being accused of a violent crime."

A pressure was forming in Clara's head. She couldn't grasp one end of a thread before another came loose. She focused on the one at hand.

"What do you know about Constantia's daughter? Helene?"

Eleonora shrugged. "Not much, other than the fact that she was another point of contention between Constantia and her husband. Constantia wanted the baby to be raised by Nadia. Olivier Pleyel forbade it, but then sent Helene to live with an aunt of his near Tarnów and never saw her again. He died ten years later of a heart attack. The son, Stani, died in the Battle of Verdun. Nadia spent years trying to get in touch with Helene but was always rebuffed by Pleyel's aunt. She eventually tracked her down after World War I, when Helene was working as a governess in Kraków. Unfortunately, by the time

Nadia contacted the family, Helene had left the household. Nadia never found her again. Really, it's just one more mystery from a family with a bunch of skeletons in the closet. I've interviewed Nadia's granddaughter Amelia several times, but she's very protective of the family's privacy. She's let me read a few of Nadia's journals but won't let me photocopy them or even quote more than a few sentences in my work. She's also alluded to a collection of letters between Nadia and Constantia, but whether there are two or two hundred, I have no idea. Amelia is firm in her belief that the past should stay buried. I think she's wary of a backlash, and rightfully so. You wouldn't believe the hate mail I've gotten since publishing that article on Constantia. It's vitriolic."

"Oh, I would," Clara said, thinking of the letters she had received after the score to the *Fire Concerto* had burned. "Do you know if Helene had any children?"

"None that I know of, but again, I hardly know anything about her. Why do you ask?"

Clara glanced at Tony. "We have a theory that maybe Zofia Mikorska was Helene's daughter."

Clara was expecting astonishment or disbelief. Instead, Eleonora smiled. "Ah," she said, with a scholar's squint of revelation. "Well, that would explain it."

Clara leaned forward on her chair. "Explain what?"

"Mikorska wrote to me. A year ago, right after my first article about Constantia came out. She had a lot of questions about my research. She was especially interested in Amelia. She said she wanted to come to Warsaw to meet with me but was sick at the time and hoped to be well enough to travel in the spring. I was flattered by her inquiry, of course. Mikorska is a legend around here. She's never been back to the conservatory, despite numerous invitations. When I told the dean she might come, he was practically planning a parade. But what is your evidence? She did not mention anything about being a relation of Constantia's in her letter to me."

"Well, she was born in 1920 in Kraków," Clara began. "Her middle name is Helene, though it seems she changed it to Helena when she emigrated to the States. She said that she was an orphan of an orphan, but also that her grandmother had been a talented pianist. She had in her collection one of the only existing copies of Pleyel's Rhapsody in E Minor. We also found notes she made about music archives in Europe she had visited, we think looking for Pleyel's music. And she had these." Clara withdrew the metronome and the photocopy of Nadia's letter to Helene from her backpack. She set both of them on the desk.

Eleonora peered at the metronome with confusion.

"We verified yesterday that it belonged to Starza," Clara said. "The letter is from Nadia to Helene Pleyel."

Eleonora picked up the letter, her eyes widening as she took in the date and signature. "This is definitely Nadia's handwriting," she said. "I recognize it from the journals." Clara saw her scan down to the bottom of the page, her posture becoming more alert. When she finished reading, she looked up at Clara with bewildered excitement.

"The story I've been told is that Nadia searched for Helene but never found her. But if Mikorska had this letter, Nadia and Helene must have made contact." She read the letter again, quickly this time. "We should show this to Nadia's granddaughter."

"Do you think she'd agree to meet with us?" Clara asked.

"I think she'd be interested to know more about what you've found. If you really think Mikorska was Constantia's granddaughter, that means they're related."

A mounting sense of urgency was building inside Clara's chest. "Mikorska seemed to believe that Pleyel's unpublished music might have survived," she said. "Do you know if Nadia's granddaughter has any of it?"

Eleonora's face fell, and from the sorrow in her eyes Clara knew the answer.

"I'm sorry," Eleonora said. "It wasn't much—just a few pieces Constantia wrote as gifts for birthdays and such. It was all destroyed in a flood in 1934. It's gone."

It was a somber walk back to the conservatory entrance. Tony and Eleonora traded stories about teaching; Clara followed behind, contemplating the day's discoveries. For weeks, she had been convinced that Madame's sole purpose in willing her the metronome was that she wanted Clara to uncover Constantia's music. Now she was here, in Poland, and had authenticated the metronome, but all of Constantia's music was gone. The thought of Pleyel's last pieces disintegrating in a flood left her with a profound sense of failure. She was mulling this over, headed for the exit, when Tony called out.

"Hey, look. It's Madame."

He had stopped before a glass case of photographs like one might find in a high school vestibule. He tapped a long finger on the glass. "That's her, right?"

Clara stepped forward to a black and white photo. A man of imposing height stood beside an open piano, his long arm spread across the lid in a way that seemed to suggest that the instrument, the room, and everyone around it belonged to him. He was flanked by a half dozen stoic young men in ties and jackets, their hair, she noticed, all featuring the same severe side part as their teacher. In the corner of the photo, shrinking against the curve of the piano, stood a young woman whose head barely lifted to meet the camera. Small and slight in a long-sleeved belted dress with buttons up the front, her eyes looked over the photographer's shoulder to something behind him. Clara scanned down to the engraving plate affixed to the wood frame. *Studio Jozef Zamoyski, 1938.*

"She looks . . ." Tony's voice drifted.

"Young," Clara said. The girl in the photo was unlike Madame in every way. Timid and retreating, as if she wanted to flee.

"That would have been her first year here," Eleonora said, leaning in to look. "I don't envy her situation. Zamoyski thought women shouldn't be permitted in his studio. Mikorska was the only woman he ever allowed in, and it was only because the dean of the conservatory forced him to. Apparently, the dean was on the board of the orphanage where Mikorska grew up and insisted Zamoyski give her a chance. Zamoyski agreed to take her on, but it must have been awful for her."

Clara had moved closer to the glass to peer at the piano. A book of music was open on the music stand. On the ledge beside it stood a metronome. Gleaming in a beam of sunlight, Clara could just make out the lion's head pendulum tilted away from the camera. Her heart began to pound.

"Look." She pressed her finger to the glass. "On the piano."

"So Zamoyski *did* have it," Tony said. "But how would he have gotten it? He was only eight years old when Starza died. Who would give a kid a murder weapon?"

"Here she is again." Clara had moved down the case to another photo. In it, Madame stood on a stage between two middle-aged men in tuxedos. The contrast between the jubilant young woman in this picture and the one cowering in Zamoyski's studio was so stark that Clara barely recognized them as the same person. With her dark lipstick and dazzling smile, she looked like a movie star out of a black-and-white film. A man in wire spectacles stood beside her, lifting her arm in a triumphant clasp. In his other hand was a glossy violin, its lustrous wood glowing in the lights of the stage.

"Tony." Clara tapped the glass urgently. Barely visible on the lower part of the instrument was a familiar curved scratch.

Eleonora was peering at the photo. "What is it?"

"This looks like a violin Mikorska had in her possession when she died," Tony said. "A Guarneri del Gesù we think she may have gotten from Zamoyski. Do you know where this picture was taken?"

Eleonora leaned in. "That's the stage of the old performance hall. The man on the left is the cellist Janusz Eisenstadt. He was killed at Auschwitz. The man holding Mikorska's hand is Bronislaw Ossendowski, the violinist. Mikorska must have really impressed someone to be able to play with him."

The pressure had returned to the back of Clara's head. Madame, Zamoyski, the violin. Something wasn't right. She peered at the date etched into the silver plate at the bottom of the photo frame, which read *5 Maj 1939.*

"*Maj* means 'May,' right? Mikorska was expelled later that month. So she was good enough to play with a world-famous violinist, then Zamoyski kicked her out a few weeks later?"

Eleonora shrugged. "Maybe he was jealous. Like I said, everyone knew he didn't want women in his studio. Maybe he thought she didn't deserve the recognition."

"And yet a few months later, she left Poland with the metronome and his violin," Clara said. "It doesn't add up."

They stood in silence, staring at the photo as if it would offer answers before turning one by one to walk toward the door. Clara was the last to leave. She lingered a long while before the smiling young woman on stage, so radiant and full of life. It was only as she walked out into the bright September sun that she realized why the Madame in the picture had been so unfamiliar. Clara had never before seen her smile.

The bar of the Hotel Bristol was, like the rest of the hotel, breathtaking. The chairs were made of soft white leather, the tables of polished hardwood. A red lily, so perfect it looked fake, bowed its waxy head from a clear glass vase on the table. The elegance of the room left Clara with both a profound sense of alienation and—she cringed to admit it—bitter jealousy that she had barely missed her chance for this life. In Warsaw, she had found, there were always, everywhere, regrets.

She and Tony drank gin martinis at a booth in the back corner. Clara had wanted a bourbon, craving the familiar, but the only American whiskey available was a shot of Maker's Mark that cost sixty-four zloty. She ordered what Tony was having instead. Not that he would have noticed the tab. By the time they returned to the hotel, Eleonora had left a message for them at the front desk with the news that Nadia Brzezińska's granddaughter had agreed to meet with them. They would go with Eleonora to Łódź the next morning. Suddenly, Constantia Pleyel was all Tony wanted to talk about.

"What if Madame was right and there really *is* another story to Starza's murder?" he said eagerly. "It would transform the whole landscape of music scholarship! Imagine if there's actually some unpublished Pleyel music out there somewhere. It could change everything!"

Clara was unable to match his enthusiasm. Leaving the conservatory that afternoon, all she had felt was deepening confusion. The Madame she had seen on that stage had looked so happy and triumphant, completely unlike the person Clara had known all her life. What had happened to change that? How could Madame have spent two years with a teacher who disdained her talent and undermined her confidence—only to become that herself? And how could a brilliant woman's compositions just be lost in one fell swoop, her talent erased from history? It aggravated her that Tony seemed impervious to these implications. They were barely in the taxi on the way back from the conservatory when he began rhapsodizing about the article he wanted to write on the process of authenticating Starza's metronome, and perhaps a second on "the tragically lost works of Constantia Pleyel. With your permission, of course," he had added. A little belatedly, in Clara's view. Since leaving the Starza Museum yesterday, she had seen his ambition ignite the same way she'd watched him psych himself up for competitions when they were teenagers by doing push-ups backstage.

In the days leading up to the trip, there had been a few moments when she allowed herself to graze against the memory of the night he'd held her hand in the driveway of her parents' house, and what might have occurred next had she not gotten out of the car. She had felt the same frisson yesterday at the museum, and this morning when they met in the hotel lobby. Now she realized that even if there was some shared electricity when their arms touched or their eyes locked, she would never be able to trust whether it was real or if he was simply trying to keep in her good favor. They weren't on equal footing and hadn't been since the moment he realized what the metronome might be, or maybe even back years ago, from the night her future in music had been foreclosed on for good.

"I was just thinking," she said, unwilling to hide her annoyance, "that it's tragic, all these lives touched by the metronome. Starza's, Pleyel's, Helene's, Madame's—" *Mine*, she almost said.

"Isn't it?" Tony said excitedly. "It's like a Shakespearean tragedy. Bodies piling up everywhere."

Clara frowned. "Don't be so flippant."

"I'm not being flippant. The history of music is of greatness accompanied by tragedy. Beethoven, Schumann, Tchaikovsky, Starza—they were all miserable. I don't envy their lives, but it's hard to argue that their challenges weren't formative for their music. And I, for one, think it was worth it. Look what they brought us."

Clara finished her drink and wished she had the money for three more. "Maybe it wasn't worth it to the people who knew them."

Tony shook his head decisively. "Every genius has an accompanying support system that works for the greater good. Look at Starza's sister. She obviously thought it was worth it."

"Do you really think Starza was working for the greater good when he threw chairs at his students? Or Jozef Zamoyski when he said women shouldn't be allowed in his studio? People like Starza and Zamoyski are megalomaniacs. Madame, too."

"Maybe. But without her, I'd never have become the musician I am. She was a difficult person, but you can't deny that she was a great teacher."

"Maybe she was. I still wish I'd never met her."

Tony's mouth tensed as she saw him hold something back. "And yet you're here, in Warsaw, because she wanted you to come," he eventually said. "You went to her final concert after getting a random invitation in the mail. You love to hate her but won't let that metronome out of your sight. I even think—" He stopped.

"What?"

Tony thumbed the edge of his cocktail napkin. "I talked to my friend who's a hand surgeon. He said that it would have been a long recovery, and maybe not the same, but that you could have come back." He looked up at her. "I think the real reason you quit is because you were always trying to upstage her and now you know you can't."

"Up*stage* her!" Clara pushed back against the booth so hard it thumped. "I was trying to separate myself from her. And at least I did. You've spent your whole life trading on her name."

"Sure." Tony nodded, but his eyes took on a new glint. "Madame made my career. What's wrong with that? Anybody who survived a year with her deserves a medal. You didn't pick the noble path because you decided to deny who you are."

"I'm not ashamed of what I'm doing with my life."

"Did you ever stop to think that maybe you should be? Whatever happened between you and Madame, she gave you that metronome because she wanted you to play again. It's like she said in the will—*we're* the legacy. You have all this talent, and all this training, and instead of doing something with it, you're wasting your life at a bar!"

Clara's entire body flushed with heat. "I'm not obligated to do something because Madame wanted me to be her legacy. I chose the life I have. Not everything is about climbing the ladder."

"Oh, so because I stuck with it, I somehow don't have principles?"

"Your whole life is about doing whatever it takes to get ahead!" Clara exclaimed. "You're wining and dining me to get the metronome so you can keep your job!"

Tony paled, but his voice remained low. "I paid for you to come here because you couldn't afford to. I think I'd know better than to try the wining and dining route after what happened in Brussels."

"Brussels!" Clara cried. "You dumped me because you couldn't stand it that I won!"

Tony laughed darkly. "I think you're missing a few steps in the middle, don't you? I told you I'd been in love with you since we were kids, and then you sabotaged my whole performance!"

Clara swelled with indignation. "I didn't force you to make a proclamation ten minutes before you went on stage!"

"And I didn't dump you because you won! I dumped you because you didn't have a heart. Or are you so used to playing the victim that you can't remember how it really went?"

Clara stood, jostling the table. Tony's glass tipped, splashing gin onto the tablecloth.

"Thank you for setting the record straight," she said. "When you write your big article, you should mention how you financed the great authentication of Starza's metronome without any regard for your own self-interest."

She shoved a hand in her back pocket and threw a handful of zloty notes on the table, where they wilted in the spilled gin.

"Go get drunk," she said, pulling her backpack over her shoulder. "I hear that's all you're really known for these days anyway."

Chapter 16

THE HOUSE THAT NADIA BRZEZIŃSKA had lived and died in was situated on a pastoral hill outside the city of Łódź. Nadia moved to the estate in 1868 after her marriage to Adam Brzeziński, a wealthy textile merchant. Within the walls of the house she had raised four sons, passed the darkness of the First World War, and mourned, always, the loss of her sister Constantia. A once stately home of white painted brick with a tiered mansard roof, the house now seemed to retreat into the small wood that surrounded it. Towering pine trees occluded the second floor, and the formal garden in front of the house was a tangle of wildflowers aflame with the energy of neglect. Down the hill, a meadow that had once been farmland was the site of a new housing development. Yellow bulldozers beeped in the distance with the sounds of progress.

Nadia died in 1920 on the precipice of her seventy-fourth year. The house was now inhabited by her last living descendant, her granddaughter Amelia. A frail woman in her eighties made to look frailer by a clunky silver wheelchair, Amelia wore lilac slacks and a white sweatshirt that said *Barcelona!* in red italic letters. Her sunken cheeks bloomed with a lacework of broken blood vessels. She had welcomed the trio into her house with kindness if not enthusiasm, her smile wavering only when Eleonora introduced Clara as a relative of Aleksander Starza's. Now they sat in the parlor surrounded by furniture that looked as old as the house, sipping tea and eating crumbling slices of poppy-seed cake Amelia had produced from a wrap of waxed paper.

"I explained that you have a letter from Nadia to Helene that you discovered in your piano teacher's papers," Eleonora said. "And that you came to Poland because you believe some of Constantia's music may have survived."

Amelia shook her head decisively and gestured out a pair of French doors to the slope of woods behind the house.

"She says Constantia's music was all destroyed in 1934," Eleonora translated. "It rained for three days. They woke one morning and water was gushing down the hill into the house. Constantia's music was on the bottom shelf of a cabinet. Everything inside was ruined. It was only a few pieces. A couple of waltzes and some lullabies."

"Gone," Amelia said in heavily accented English. She turned to look at Clara and Tony, her faded eyes shifting from one to the other.

"There's nothing left at all?" Tony looked around the cavernous room, his eyes lingering on a pair of dusty curio cabinets that looked like they hadn't been opened in a century. "Not a draft, or a page, anything?"

Amelia eyed him without warmth, then spouted off a string of impatient Polish.

"Everything left of Constantia's is in a trunk in Grandmother Nadia's bedroom. It is just letters and a few trinkets. There is no music."

Clara glared at Tony, who looked away. They had managed to avoid saying a word to each other all morning as Eleonora drove them to Łódź in her blue Peugeot. Clara found herself both furious with him and repentant for how they had left things. Last night she had lain awake in her hotel room wondering what she was really doing here in Poland. Was it the opportunity to revisit the site of her tragic undoing? A chance to get close to Tony? The relief of having a purpose? Or was Tony right? Had she come simply because Madame wanted her to? Finally, she'd turned on the light and pulled Madame's papers from her backpack. Tony had brought Madame's leather-bound notebook to Warsaw. Its contents had not eased Clara's restless night. Someone— Clara could not help but imagine Tony's female assistant—had flagged a page near the end with an orange Post-it. When Clara opened to the marked section, Madame's bold handwriting lashed the paper with disjointed notes, all scribbled with the same furious intensity.

CP met Sza September 1881: Golden Years, 1881–1885

Who is Dark Angel? Starza? Pleyel?

Posthumous works are in Marianna's hand.
Where REAL originals?

Melancholy and Vengeful—different metronomes?

A dozen pages went on in the same disconnected manner until the final entry, which held only one note, in all capital letters:

CONCERTO NO. 2, SECOND MOVEMENT. BARS 345–500.

The scrawled pages felt desperate and chaotic—so unlike Madame's antiseptic control. It took several minutes for Clara to realize they were the notes of someone who knew they were running out of time.

She passed the remainder of the sleepless hours with a photocopy of Constantia's Rhapsody in E Minor. Examining the pages, Clara understood why the reviewers from 1866 had been dubious that an eighteen-year-old had composed them. She read the score with amazement, ferried from a bottomless longing to pent-up fury. She saw again a constellation sweeping across a night sky like an exploding firework. And yet just like the first time she'd glimpsed the score, there was something familiar about the piece that floated like a wisp of dandelion seed just beyond reach.

She turned to Amelia. "We recently discovered a copy of the rhapsody Constantia wrote when she was young. Have you heard it? She was incredibly talented."

Amelia listened to Eleonora translate the question, then turned to Clara and shook her head. "All I know of Constantia's music was a lullaby she wrote for my Uncle Stefan. My grandmother would sing it to me sometimes before I went to sleep." She hummed a few bars tunelessly.

"Have you read the letters in the trunk?" Clara asked. "The ones between Nadia and Constantia?"

Amelia regarded her warily. "I have."

Clara glanced at Eleonora and Tony before pressing on. "We think that if we understood more about Constantia's life, we could help to rehabilitate her reputation. Would you be willing to let us look at them?"

"No." Amelia shook her head, her face resolute. "No one would believe what those letters say. I do not know if I believe them myself. Perhaps Constantia *was* truly mad. It is impossible to know. There is no one alive to ask."

The room fell quiet.

"We would be very respectful," Tony said gently. "We are pianists, too." He gestured to Clara without, she noticed, actually looking at her. "We want Constantia to be known as a composer, not a murderer."

Before Eleonora had finished translating his words, Amelia interjected. "It is too late for that," she said sharply. "The best thing that can happen now is for her to be forgotten. The young people nowadays are right to want to leave the past behind. If I had the money, I would leave this old house and move somewhere new. As it is, I will die here like my grandmother, and then all of this"—she waved her hand at the musty walls—"will be forgotten."

Clara shifted in her chair, deliberating what she might say to change Amelia's mind. Sometime around four a.m., she had decided that the real reason she had come to Poland was not for Tony or Madame or even herself, but for Constantia Pleyel—that one less misunderstood, underappreciated woman would be relegated to the footnotes of history. And now here she was, in a house Constantia had probably visited countless times, drinking tea on a creaking old chair Constantia had maybe even sat in—so close she could literally breathe the dust of the past. She could not allow the vestiges of Constantia's life to rot in an old trunk.

"I know what it's like to feel trapped by the past." Her voice qua- vered unexpectedly, and she blushed, feeling exposed. "I always felt like my life was decided before I was born, because of an ancestor I never knew. Your family must have suffered a great deal because of what Constantia did."

Amelia studied her closely, as if measuring the truth of her words. "Constantia's life was tragic," she finally said, "but her decisions cost all of us. My grandmother grieved for her sister her entire life. When my father was a boy, the whole village shunned the family. People said there was insanity in our blood. He grew up terrified he would go mad and drank himself to death trying to keep it away."

Clara was quiet, unsure what to say in the face of this sadness. The human toll of Constantia's actions was undeniable. Her tragedy had followed the family, bleeding out across generations.

"Yes," she finally said. "I think Constantia was unlucky too. But I also think she was very special. And your grandmother seemed to love her very much. Would you like to read the letter we brought? The one your grandmother wrote to Helene?"

After a second's hesitation, Amelia nodded, and Clara removed the xeroxed letter from her backpack. They all watched as Amelia began to read, the wrinkles on her forehead furrowing like cracks in parched dirt. When finally she reached the end, she looked up at Clara, a combi- nation of shock and accusation on her face. She began to speak rapidly.

Eleonora looked at Clara, alarmed. "She wants to know where you got this."

"It was in the papers of our piano teacher, Zofia Mikorska." Clara pointed to the photographs of Madame from the conservatory display case that Eleonora had set on the coffee table. "We think she may have been Constantia's granddaughter. Did you ever meet her?"

Amelia took the photos into her lap and studied each one. "No." She looked up at Clara, consternation in her eyes. "I have never seen her before."

"What about Helene?" Tony asked. "Did you ever meet her?"

Amelia's mouth twisted on one side. "Yes," she said after a moment. "Once."

They all became still, waiting for her to continue.

"She came here, the day of Grandmother Nadia's funeral." She looked up at them. "My mother died when I was a baby, you see, and my father had always been preoccupied with his own troubles. When he came back from the Great War, he was worse. My grandmother raised me, and I could not accept that she was gone. I was hiding in the larder feeling sorry for myself when I heard our cook speaking to a woman at the kitchen door.

"She could not have known it was the day of the funeral, because she was not wearing black," Amelia said. "I remember her dress clearly because it was blue, with brass buttons up the front, and it was obvious even to me as a child that she was pregnant. I knew she was poor because of her handbag. A piece of carpet had been sewn into the bottom where the leather had worn through. She waited by the door while our cook went to fetch my father. She did not know I was watching her. I remember how she patted her belly and whispered things down to her baby." Amelia's face softened. "I felt jealous of that baby, that she had a mother who loved her so much."

"What year was this?" Tony asked.

"Grandmother died when I was ten years old. That would have been 1920."

Tony looked at Clara for the first time all morning, his dour expression from earlier giving way to excitement.

"When my father entered the kitchen, he asked the cook to leave," Amelia said. "The woman introduced herself as Helene, and I became very agitated. The whole family knew that Grandmother had tried to find Helene for years. Sometimes when she fell asleep sitting by the fire, she would say Helene's name over and over until she woke. But my father and his brothers did not like to talk about her. They thought

Constantia had brought shame upon the family, and they had no wish to associate with Constantia's daughter. I could see immediately that my father was angry Helene had come. He demanded to know what she wanted. Then Helene brought out a letter from her bag and said that it was from Grandmother. My father took it from her and read it, then began to shout. He said it was a forgery, and that Helene was an opportunist who had heard that Nadia had died and had come to try to get some of the family money.

"Helene looked very tired when she heard the news, but I admired her, that she did not seem afraid of him. She said she would not intrude on a home where she was not wanted, but that she was not a liar or a thief, and that she could prove the letter was not a forgery because Nadia had already left her something that had belonged to Constantia. Then she reached into the mended handbag and brought out a wooden box. Inside was a metronome."

Clara and Tony exchanged a breathless look.

"I knew then that she was telling the truth," Amelia continued. "When I was a little child, I found that metronome hidden in my grandmother's trunk. I recognized it instantly because it had a lion on the beam. Grandmother caught me playing with it and became very angry. Later she came to find me and told me the metronome had belonged to her sister, and that it made her sad because she missed her sister so much.

"But my father claimed he had never seen the metronome before. Perhaps he was telling the truth, I do not know. It would not have mattered. He ordered Helene out of the house. He said that even if she really was Constantia's daughter, the family would never acknowledge the child of a murderer." Amelia pressed her lips together, the wrinkles around her mouth gathering in pain.

"I remember how Helene put her hands on her belly as she left, as if she was protecting her baby from his words. I wanted to run out from behind the door and tell him what I knew, and to beg him to allow

Helene to stay, but I knew he would be furious if he caught me spying, and even more if I contradicted him." Amelia looked up gravely. "I was too afraid. I never saw her again.

"I forgot about it for many years, but after the war, when all my family was gone, I thought about her, and wondered what had happened to her and her baby. It has been with me for a long time, like a rock in my shoe I am so used to I forget it hurts. But I never knew what was in the letter until now. Now I feel my shame again, that my grandmother told her we would accept her, and still she was turned away." She looked up at Clara. "Do you know what happened to her?"

Clara glanced uneasily at Tony. "She died, we think sometime in the late twenties or early thirties." She hesitated before continuing. "Her daughter grew up in an orphanage near Kraków."

"An orphanage!" Dismay broke over Amelia's face. Seeing there the same regret for Helene and Madame that Clara now felt, sadness sank through her body like a plummeting weight. To hide the emotion on her face, she reached for the backpack at her feet. Carefully, she withdrew the metronome and set it on the table.

"Is this the metronome Helene had that day?"

Incredulity flickered on Amelia's face. She began pointing at the metronome, then at Clara, directing a salvo of urgent questions to Eleonora.

"Yes," Eleonora said. "That's the metronome she found in Nadia's trunk when she was a child. She wants to know how you have it."

"Zofia Mikorska gave it to me when she died. We thought previously that she got it from this man." Clara pointed to the photo of Jozef Zamoyski in his studio. "But now it sounds like it belonged to Helene, at least for a time."

"And you're certain Nadia said it was Constantia's?" Tony asked.

Amelia nodded. "That is what she told me."

Tony looked at Clara in bewilderment.

Clara leaned forward in her chair. "Amelia, I know you are protecting your family. But Constantia's granddaughter thought that some of

Constantia's music might still be out there somewhere. She was trying to find it before she died, and she wanted us to keep looking. We think that if we read her letters, maybe we could find it and let the world finally hear it."

Amelia stared into Clara's face for what seemed like a long time, her eyes taking in the scars on Clara's cheek without embarrassment or hurry. Finally, she spoke.

"This woman. My second cousin. You knew her?"

Clara nodded. "She was my teacher for many years."

"It is a terrible thing, to grow up without a mother. Did she have a good life?"

So many emotions sought purchase on Clara's heart that for a moment she could not speak. What did it mean, to have a good life? Certainly Madame had not been happy. Nor had her life been easy, or filled with love, or blessed by companionship. Learning about Madame's experience at the Conservatory yesterday, Clara had been forced to consider for the first time what Madame's life had been like before she became the great Zofia Mikorska, when she was just an orphan at the mercy of a domineering man, and then a refugee escaping a war. Madame had become one of the greatest musicians the world had known, but she'd died alone in a hospital, willing her most beloved objects to near strangers. Had it been a good life? The answer was painfully clear.

She took a breath to steady her voice. "She became famous," Clara said. "She was one of the greatest pianists of the twentieth century, just as her grandmother was one of the greatest before her."

Tears brimmed in Amelia's eyes, but she smiled at Clara for the first time that morning. "Perhaps then she is the one in the family who was lucky among us." She sighed, wiping her eyes, then patted Clara's hand. "If reading Constantia's letters is what my cousin wanted, I will not turn her away."

She said something to Eleonora, then slowly wheeled down the hall toward the kitchen.

"She says she's going to get the keys to Nadia's bedroom," Eleonora whispered excitedly. "Well done, Clara! I've been trying to read these letters for five years."

Clara smiled but felt shaky inside. She knew Tony was watching her but could not meet his eyes.

When Amelia wheeled back down the hall, she held a brass key ring in her lap. She led them to the front of the house, where a scuffed staircase ascended to the second floor.

"She can't afford a safe," Eleonora explained, "so she keeps the door and the trunk locked. She wants us to know that no one but the family has been through these papers, and she is trusting in our goodwill."

Amelia held the key ring out to Clara, who took it gently. "We will honor it in every way," she said.

She turned to mount the stairs, but Amelia shot out a spotted hand with surprising vigor and grabbed her arm. She spoke with urgency, her face suddenly stern.

"She says that we must remember that this was a person's life," Eleonora said, glancing at Amelia, who had leaned forward in her wheelchair to deliver her admonition. "A real person who did a terrible thing. Not a terrible human being."

Clara nodded, surprised at the constriction in her throat. "I understand," she said. "No one should be remembered for their worst moment."

The instant the words left her mouth she looked up and saw Tony watching her and knew they were both thinking of what she had said last night about his mistake with the London Philharmonic. She looked away in shame. But Amelia smiled, then patted Clara's hand and wheeled back down the hall. They watched her turn into the kitchen, then together mounted the weary staircase.

The broad landing of the second story was empty, the windows bare of curtains. Sun shone on the pine floor, where scuff marks on the wood suggested the memory of furniture that had once sat to capitalize on the light.

"Last door on the right," Eleonora said.

They walked without speaking until they reached the closed door.

Clara held up the key ring. "Well," she said, looking between them. "Let's see what we've got."

The key turned easily in the lock, a faint *ting* of metal on metal, then Clara pushed the door open on a darkened room. On the far wall, cracks of sunlight peeked through the sides of heavy curtains.

Tony swept his arm over the wall. Clara heard the empty click of a light switch.

"No electricity," he said.

They lingered on the dark threshold, all of them feeling, Clara imagined, the same sense of trespass; then Eleonora walked forward and threw back the curtains, flooding the room with sun.

A four-poster bed stood in the center of the room, the mattress draped with a forest-green coverlet of the same velvet brocade as the curtains. A massive armoire hulked on the opposite wall, its double doors thick with dust. In the corner nearest the windows was a dressing table, its oval mirror warped, one of the drawers strangely gone, like a missing tooth.

Eleonora whispered something in Polish, causing Clara and Tony to turn. She had wandered over to the wall beside the bed, where a gilt-framed photograph hung on delicate brass chains from the crown molding above. "It's them," she said. "Nadia and Constantia."

Two girls of about ten and twelve sat on a picnic blanket holding hands. Behind them, sun glinted off the surface of a lake.

"So much history," Eleonora murmured.

The comment seemed to focus their energies, and all three turned at once to the trunk at the foot of the bed. Clara's first thought on beholding it was that it did not have the appearance of a container of mysteries. Plain compared to the opulence of the bed and curtains, it was covered with a cognac-colored leather that had darkened around the brass latch. Its curved top was mottled and nicked and inlaid with darker leather arranged in the shape of a rose. Clara walked forward to unlock it, but Eleonora stopped her with a high-pitched "No!"

She pulled three pairs of white archivist's gloves from her purse. "These documents are over a hundred years old," she said. "We must be careful."

When they had slipped on the gloves, Eleonora nodded. "Okay," she said nervously. "Open it."

The key scraped against the lock. When Clara pushed open the lid, it creaked on an old hinge.

Four stacks of envelopes bound in twine sat in the bottom of the trunk. Beside these were a dozen or so leather-bound books—Nadia's journals, Clara presumed—the binding swollen with age. A small wooden box with a pearl inlay on the lid was the sole remaining item. Clara's heart sank. Whatever Amelia might have been concealing, she had not been wrong about the music.

Clara reached for the envelopes and lifted them to Eleonora, who took them with a tiny cry of joy. Next, she picked up the wooden box. She brushed her fingers over the pearl inlay in the center, then pushed open the lid.

The horse caught her attention first. It was a child's toy carved of wood, the paint worn around the flank where it must have been often carried. Beside it lay a gold locket, its chain twined with a single lock of fine brown hair.

Careful to keep the hair wrapped around the chain, Clara picked up the locket. A miniature portrait of a boy of about five years old wearing a blue shirt and a white hat smiled from within. Clara passed the locket to Eleonora. "Is it her son—Stani?"

Eleonora shook her head. "I don't think so. He was very blond. Nadia describes his hair as almost white."

Tony leaned over Clara's shoulder to pick up a photograph nestled in the bottom of the box. In it, Constantia sat in a high-backed chair gazing at a swaddled baby in her arms. The smile on her face was incandescent.

Tony turned the photo over, where the date penned at the bottom read *3 November 1885.*

"It's Helene," he said, turning the photo so Clara and Eleonora could see. "This was just a month before . . ." He trailed off.

"If we'll ever know what happened, it's now," Eleonora said firmly. She laid the stacks of letters on the bed. Carefully, she sorted them by date, finally gathering fourteen envelopes into a small pile. "Pleyel began her lessons with Starza in September 1881. Let's start then, shall we?"

With a nod to Clara and Tony, she unfolded the first letter.

"'Dear Nadia.'"

Chapter 17

30 September 1881

Dear Nadia,

You have asked what it has been like, and so I sit to tell you. What I might say is this: All you have heard of Aleksander Starza is true.

I will not waste ink enumerating his talents. That a man such as he should have so much while I have been left to wither only proves once more that justice does not exist. He has no mind toward gratitude, no susceptibility to kindness, no awareness of what others might give for a fraction of what his hands can do. Knowledge of his own greatness has twisted his soul like a rope blowing about a mast. As for his opinion of me, he complains that my playing *lacks spirit*. That *I* lack *spirit*! Today I had prepared the Sarabande from the Bach French Suite in D Minor. It is slow enough that the little duds can keep up, and even Olivier concedes that to hear me play it no one would know I couldn't do more. But Starza listened with disdain.

"There is fear in it," he proclaimed when I had finished. "I can hear you trembling."

I do not need to assure *you*, dear sister, that not a quiver overtook one hair on my head! Who am I to cower to a brute like Starza after the misery I have waded through?

"You have grown too accustomed to the fainting ladies at your concerts, sir," I said. "You hear timidity where in fact there is feeling."

He grimaced as if I had forced him to sip spoiled milk.

"I do not challenge your courage, Madam," he announced coldly. "But twenty years ago when I heard you in Vienna it was not your technique that enthralled the theater, but your spirit. The spirit is what is missing. I cannot help you with that."

I burned with rage all the way home. When I came in, I sat at once at my piano and played until my hand contorted in spasm. But here, recounting it to you now, I weep with bitterness. He is a terrible man, but he has seen the truth of me. Even if my fingers should mend, there is no remedy for my wretched heart.

Your Loving Sister,
Constantia

28 January 1882

Dear Nadia,

I shall *never* return to that beast's home, even if he should fashion me a hand after Apollo himself! Today when I arrived, he made me wait a full hour before he admitted me into his parlor, leaving me standing in the entryway while I heard him in the next room scratching away with his pen. When finally he flung open the door, his fingers were covered with ink, his collar crooked, his shirtsleeves rolled to the elbows. He ordered me to sit at the piano and bade me play his newest composition. The piece was impossible to read with his horrendous handwriting, and each time I stumbled over a note he flinched as if I'd struck him! Eventually he shouted for me to stop and sat to play it himself. When he had finished regaling me, he turned, seeming to await my applause. I suggested that the theme was dull and sounded too much like Chopin. At this he looked so crestfallen that I nearly pitied him, until he began to demand what *exactly* echoed Chopin and which part *precisely* was dull, and argued with my every example until the fool grew so indignant that he gathered up the pages and threw them into the fire!

"Don't be a child!" I shouted. "Get those out at once!"

But Starza only sat sulking on the bench. So I plucked the nearest one from the flames and set it on the lid of the piano.

Had I not been so furious, I would have burst my corset laughing at the way he threw himself on his precious instrument. When this absurd theater was over, a black mark was left on the lid of the piano. Starza was attempting to regain his dignity by scowling at me with *great* severity and lecturing me about the damage I might have caused.

"You should not be so frivolous with your gifts," I admonished him.

"Nor you, Madam," he roared. "As I wrote the piece for the improvement of your detestable hand!"

I admit I suffered a slight—<u>slight</u>!—pang of compunction at this, but before I could begin to assemble an apology he ordered me from his presence, pointing to the door and bellowing at me to leave! *Impossible* man!

Your Loving Sister,
Constantia

5 March 1882

Dear Nadia,

Forgive my delayed reply to your letter. I could not write until now. Olivier has taken Stani to Moscow. He says the boy has grown too tender left alone with me and needs toughening. My protests were dismissed, my wails ignored. When I did not relent, I was forcibly silenced. Stani witnessed it all, and for the first time did not shed a single tear. Oh, what have we made of our dear, sweet boy?

Today I resumed my studies with Starza. You will think I am mad for returning after all I have said of him, and perhaps I am. Some weeks ago, he sent me a revision of the piece he threw in the fire—atonement, no doubt, for the ungentlemanly manner in which he ejected me from his house. I had resolved to ignore it, but the silence of this house without Stani was a madness of its own I could not bear.

The piece is an etude in C-sharp Minor. It almost pains me to tell you how clever it is. Every measure is designed to place demand on the fourth and fifth fingers, yet a listener would never know she heard anything but stunning music. Starza believes that once I can play the etude, I will be ready to challenge myself with something longer. I have my sights on one of Beethoven's sonatas—op. 28, perhaps, in D Major, or the op. 26 variations. I get ahead of myself, however, for the etude is quite a gauntlet, especially with Starza's excitable metronome. I have told him repeatedly the thing is useless, but it was a gift from his sister and now he, who can countenance throwing his own music into flame, cannot abandon it for an instrument that actually works. But this is a small matter. Now I see the results of his vision, I find it easier to forgive his flaws. Starza's exercises have the little duds moving faster than they have since—. Such a strange turn, that one of such disagreeable temper has unending patience for my clumsy little fingers. He is rather like a mother to them, forgiving all their iniquities and believing the best is still yet to come. Today I came to my lesson feeling particularly low and found my fourth finger could play nothing. I declared I would leave so that I might attend my sorrow in private, but Starza said to me, with a countenance so grave it nearly redoubled my tears: "You will never be what you were. You must be someone new. You must take your pain and make from it beauty."

You will be quite astonished by this show of gentleness. I confess that I was. It gives me hope, Nadia, to see that no man is singular. Not Starza. Not my Stani.

I have not ignored your entreaty to come at Easter. I will speak to Olivier when he returns, though you must gird yourself, etc.

Your Loving Sister,
Constantia

16 April 1882

Dear Nadia,

Oh, to be a woman in this wicked world! Lucky you have four sons, for if all your dear children were girls, I would proclaim there is no hope of happiness for them or their mother. Two weeks Olivier has been home, rescuing me from one misery and inflicting another. He has forbidden me—*forbidden!*—from continuing my work with Starza. He says it has pulled me away from my duties in the house. This after it was discovered one of the maids, our dear Lucia, has been found to be with child. I venture Olivier himself could be the father and has invented the scenario just to have cause to dash my ambitions. I can feel you blushing, dear sister, but I tell you, it is the truth. He hears my pained improvements on the piano and fears I will supersede him again. Let him forbid all he wants. Whatever his threats—and surely those are to come next—I will not stop. I would die first. Don't lecture me with your Christian doctrines. I'd do it, if it weren't for Stani, and for you.

Could you have imagined, back when our world was mother and father's warm parlor, that your happy sister would come to this? It is the cruelest punishment. But then, Olivier's punishments are as cruel as his words were once sweet. Had Stani been a girl I would raise her to trust no man. A domestic worker of independence would be better than my lot now, so long as she never marry.

I thought of you and the boys at Easter, eating your poppy-seed cake in the garden. We, here, were silent and solemn.

Yours Always,
Constantia

17 July 1882

Dear Nadia,

Olivier has been summoned to Paris! M. Perrin has invited him to sing *Rigoletto*. He will be gone at the least six months. Receiving the news, it felt as if my corset had been loosened by three ties. He has insisted I accompany him, but I have already decided an illness will leave me behind. You know how he is so fearful of harm to his lungs. Had he shown my fingers the care with which he attends his precious voice, all would be different. As it is, prepare rooms for Stani and myself! We will come to you for my *convalescence*!

Your Loving Sister,
Constantia

3 November 1882

Dear Nadia,

When I close my eyes, I can still see your roses swaying in the wind. Each morning at breakfast I long for your sunny table and for you sitting at it, waiting for me before you pour the tea. Still, I am gladdened to return to my work with Starza. In my absence, he has taken on a new pupil, a boy of merely six, already arrogant but remarkable, nonetheless. I am overcome with jealousy of his agile little fingers. Starza asked me to listen to him play a Scarlatti sonata, and when it was finished, I complimented the boy's execution with genuine admiration, but told him not to forget the feeling behind the music, for the playing lacked warmth. He sulked until his mother arrived to collect him. Clearly, he is used to being praised. If he but cures himself of that—and who better to cure oneself of self-importance than Starza?—the world will see young Jozef Zamoyski become famous, without doubt.

Starza has been working on a new concerto in my absence, his second. To hear it is to feel a February gale blowing through the frosted trees. He played it for me today and imagine my astonishment when in the second movement I heard the theme from my own Rhapsody quoted in the melody! Oh, Nadia. To hear it brought me to a time when I was so full of passion and belief. Starza watched me as he played, and when he saw the wonderment on my face, he smiled. It quite changed the look of him.

He tells me that in my absence he dreamed of my spirit as a starling in a turbulent wind, cast about but still striving to fly. When he woke, he says the concerto was ready, as if flowing from his pen. History will forget me, whatever once may have been, but at least you and I will know that my spirit now will forever sing.

I have decided I will give a concert in the spring. Starza agrees that I am ready and has offered to assemble an orchestra for the left-hand concerto. At last, it is happening! You must come, with all the children. More than anything, my heart soars to think of Stani watching me perform. I want him to know his mother as she once was.

Yours in hope,
Constantia

20 February 1883

Dear Nadia,

Olivier has returned early. A surprise, he says, though there was no mirth in his reunion for any but Stani. The way the boy ran to his father sealed my jail. Olivier has insisted Stani and I accompany him back to Paris. We leave tomorrow, with barely time to dash off these notes of sorrow. The concert has been canceled. Oh, how it aches to write it. Next time I will know better than to tempt his fury.

Constantia

27 September 1883

Dear Nadia,

To be back in Warsaw after the hot streets of Paris! I hope I shall never go to France again as long as I live. Olivier leaves in a week for Petersburg, and as soon as the carriage departs, I will fly to you in Łódź!

I called on Starza today for the first time since my return. He had not expected me, and I was surprised by the agitation on his face when he found me standing in his parlor. He seemed quite flustered and offered me tea three times. Our visit was brief, as Olivier thought I had been to see Bronya Gładkowska and her new son, but in the minutes we shared, Starza showed me what he accomplished in my absence. While I have been wasting time at teas and dinners, Starza has been busy writing. The number of pieces he has produced in just these few months both awes and—I can admit it— torments me with envy. To have his freedom, his talent, his gifts.

I draw now to the most curious incident of our encounter. I had bid him good day and was already in my carriage when suddenly Starza flew out the door with a stack of pages in his hand. He placed them in my arms through the carriage window just as the horses were drawing away. "For you" was all he said, then stood back on the paving stones and watched the carriage depart.

It was the slow movement of another new piano concerto. He wrote to me in Paris of the first movement, a work of storm and fury to be played *Allegro con fuoco*. If the opening is half as wonderful as the music I beheld today, it will crown him among the most accomplished composers to have lived. It is a piece of tender longing such as I have never heard. I read it in the carriage on the way home, weeping at its beauty. When I came to the end there was a note. It said but this:

The weight of being away from you, now and always.

The moment I returned home, I burned the note in the kitchen fire lest Olivier should ever see.

Your Loving Sister,
Constantia

19 February 1884

Dear Nadia,

I read your letter with a heart that is both guilty and relieved. You are correct that I have not been honest. My conscience has been heavy some months, not for the reasons you might think, but because I have lied to you, and because I have been so very wrong in my judgment. I know you understand the reason for my reticence. It is the same as the last time I concealed my feelings from you. Only I hope you have confidence I would not make the same error twice. You won't think so, based on the stories I have told these many months. Oh, I wish you would burn those letters! All they show is that your sister is a fool. It is true that Starza is an imperfect man. Assure yourself that no one judges his character with more stringency than he, though there is more reason for his distemper than the world understands. Whatever his flaws—and I concede there are many—there is a wellspring within him from which his music flows. From that same outpouring, there is feeling of the kind that would burst a heart. Do not worry after me, dear Nadia. I am no silly girl indulging in fantasies. I go forward with the wisdom of a weathered heart.

Yours in Truth and Courage,
Constantia

13 April 1884

Dear Nadia,

You say you have burned my last letter in the kitchen fire. Does the smoke make the words evaporate into the sky? I tell you now that it is the wrong letter to have burned. Listen to your sister. I am alive in a way I was never before living. No Bible verse or promise of redemption could sway me, nor plea, even from you. I know what evil I court, and I care not. I know what I said of him before, and I aver that my judgment was too swift.

I have copied out a nocturne I have written of late, in A Minor. It is my first in more than ten years, and yet the music came to me effortless and complete. I send it to you as proof that whatever promises I have made before God or anyone else, this music surely counters those in the court of Heaven. I have sent it in a parcel of linens so that Olivier would not intercept it. Read the music, and you will understand your sister's heart.

I know you fear for me. Rest your mind. Olivier leaves in a week for Paris. His rages of late convince me he knows I am afraid no more. Perhaps this time he will stay.

Your Loving Sister,
Constantia

4 November 1884

Dear Nadia,

I know you read my letters even if you do not reply. I imagine you hiding the envelopes in the drawer of your desk and vowing to burn them once the cook is out, then opening them in a fever rush the same as when Mother set the plums on the table to ripen when we were girls. You always ate yours first. You are trying to protect me, I know. But we have all failed to protect me from the real serpent. I am no foolish girl anymore. My hair is graying. Even my good hand aches. I care not. Blood beats through me again, all the way to my pathetic fingers. Do you understand what I am telling you? Your sister is back from the dead. Celebrate the same as you would on your precious Resurrection Day. I tell you, I am back.

Rest your mind in the knowledge that you are not the only one to be concerned. Your same admonitions I hear in his mouth. I must convince you both that I know my own choices. You are wrong, as I once was wrong. Come to Warsaw and see for yourself your lost sister restored.

Yours Forever,
Constantia

12 October 1885

Dearest Nadia,

Do you remember that day at Lake Śniardwy when we vowed to never love anyone more than the other? I've only broken it once, the day Stani was born. And now again.

Helene has her father's eyes, the color of a morning storm. I call her my Little Tempest. She is strong, like me. When she is angry, she pushes me away with her tiny hand, and I resist her to make her do it again. A woman must have anger to survive in this world.

Today she met her father. The tears he wept would have been enough to soften even your decided heart. I know you do not approve, and perhaps this I must accept. But know this: he held her as if God Himself had been placed in his arms.

She is not all that blooms within me. A new intermezzo flows from my hand as tears once flowed from my eyes. When I have the time, I will write out a copy so you can play it. As it is, I have sketched the first few bars that you might know what sings within me now.

Your Loving Sister,
Constantia

"Helene was *his*?"

Clara looked up from the letter and saw on Tony's face the same astonishment that had overtaken them all. They sat on Nadia's bed like three children being read a story, forestalling the end when the magic must disappear. Clara above all had been shocked into silence. In the span of a half hour, everything she had suspected about Starza and Constantia Pleyel—violence, coercion, degradation, abuse—was proved utterly wrong. It had been like arriving home at night after a long absence, then pushing back the curtain in the morning to discover that while she was gone, the garden had bloomed and the trees had gotten their leaves and now everything was different. If Helene was Starza's child, that meant Madame was Starza's grandchild—and also—the realization washed over Clara in a wave not unlike nausea—that she and Madame were related. Had Madame known? Or had she taken her last breath convinced that her grandmother had been unfairly treated by the monster Aleksander Starza?

All these thoughts sought hold in Clara's mind, but they fell instantly away when Eleonora pulled a second paper from the envelope. Sixteen bars of music penned in jubilant, bold strokes leapt across the fragile page. They rose instantly to Clara's ear, unspooling in a sparkling arc of sound. In the silence of Nadia's long-cloistered bedroom, the music soared within her, fresh as a rain-washed morning.

"Tony," she whispered. But he, too, was staring at Constantia's intermezzo in amazement.

"It's incredible. Is there more?" Tony sorted through the stack of envelopes, but Eleonora had already opened the final letter.

"No." Eleonora shook her head. "There's nothing more."

The knowledge that this was all that remained of Constantia's music sank into the bones of Clara's hands. She looked down at the faded letters and the box with the sad wooden horse.

"I don't understand what happened," she said. "All this time, I thought he had mistreated her or something. And now—she *loved* him?"

Eleonora muttered something in Polish, looking down at the letters with a stricken expression. "It is something my mother used to say: 'You look so hard, you cannot see.' I did not expect this either."

"In the other letters," Clara said, "the ones you published in your article, he sounded so violent. She was afraid of him."

Eleonora shook her head. "That's never how I read them. She had contempt for him. She found him ridiculous. But she enjoyed baiting him. I don't think she felt threatened."

"But then—" Clara felt the narrative she had built—the evil, maniacal Starza coming after Constantia, Constantia fighting back in self-defense—dissolve in an instant. "But if she loved him, why did she kill him? It doesn't make any sense."

Eleonora picked up the last letter. "Let's see."

19 November 1885

Dear Nadia,

Our plans for London have been delayed. A is not well. He warned me this day would come, but I did not realize how terrible it would be. He begs me to leave him, and wounds me with the most terrible insults to spur me to go. But I know it is the fever in his mind that speaks. I would no more abandon him than I would you.

Olivier has been detained in Paris, and this remains our only good fortune. Once he arrives . . . I cannot think of it. I have told Stani we are going to England. If Olivier returns, I will not be able to keep him from telling our secret.

Your Loving Sister,
Constantia

Eleonora looked up, her brow furrowed. "That's the last one."

"That was just two weeks before he died." Tony looked at Clara, bewildered. "What could have happened?"

"Maybe the husband did it," Clara offered. "The letter said if he came back, Stani would tell him they were planning to leave. Maybe he found out."

Eleonora shook her head. "Olivier Pleyel *was* in Warsaw the night of the murder, but he performed at the Grand Theatre that night as part of a benefit concert for the Warsaw Benevolent Society. That's why he came back from Paris. He was still on stage when Constantia returned to the house to get Helene. Stani had gone to the performance to see his father, which I've always assumed is why he wasn't with her on the train platform the next morning. Her return home was ultimately how she got caught. A maid found her petticoat, soaked in blood." She looked down at the letters in her lap. "These change so much, but not what ultimately happened." She looked at Clara, her expression sorrowful. "Constantia said it was self-defense, but she never denied that she killed him. I'm sorry, Clara. I know you wanted it to be different. But she's the one who did it. She's the one who killed him."

Clara and Tony exited Eleonora's Peugeot at the curb of the hotel, their doors closing in a unified click. Eleonora was headed back to her office to record all she could of the day's events. Amelia had not permitted them to remove the letters from Nadia's trunk, but she had agreed to allow Eleonora to take Nadia's journals, and to return the following week to photograph everything else. Facsimiles would be the next step. One day, the world—or at least those who troubled themselves to know—would see the broader picture of Constantia Pleyel. Mother. Sister. Composer. And now—Starza's lover. Who was this Starza who had rushed from his door to pass Constantia the tender piece he wrote for her, and who wept holding his newborn daughter? What did it mean about the music? The murder? Was it any better to have killed the man you loved than a man you hated?

They entered the lobby in silence, pushing through the revolving doors in a whoosh. Now that it was just the two of them, it was hard to know what to say. Their fight from the night before seemed inconsequential considering the day's discoveries. As the elevator door closed before them and began its slow ascent up to the ninth floor, she turned to him, gripped by a need to apologize for what she had said last night. They both spoke at the same time.

"I'm sorry for—"

"I was wrong to—"

They fell silent. Clara spoke first. "I'm sorry for what I said last night, about the thing with the London Philharmonic. I meant what I said today about worst moments. For what it's worth, I never judged you for it. I felt bad for you. I haven't judged."

"And I shouldn't have presumed to know what it's been like for you," Tony said. "You were right about the metronome. I've had too much invested in proving it was Starza's. I was hoping it would turn things around for me, and I haven't always behaved in ways I'm proud of as a result."

Apologies dispatched, they turned and faced the elevator door and rode in silence until it dinged on the ninth floor. The doors slid open, and they walked together down the corridor to the suites that faced each other across the hall.

"So what now?" he asked.

"Maybe it's out of our hands." She was strangely saddened by the thought.

Tony nodded. "Maybe it is."

They stood with this for a moment, then Tony took her hand. Her heart fluttered, and she squeezed his hand back. Then he let go. "Good night, Clara," he said, then turned and unlocked his door.

She watched him go inside, then turned toward her own room. She placed the metronome on the nightstand and set it to seventy-two, then lay down in the dark. It must have been only five minutes later when she woke from a dream in which she sat on the floor of Madame's music room surrounded by blood. Constantia's intermezzo was on the floor, the paper soaked through. Constantia sat at the piano, scribbling music. Behind her, Starza watched the metronome tock on the mantel. Clara sat up, heart racing. The metronome had stopped, but a rhythmic beat still pulsed in her ears. Someone was knocking on the door. Tony.

She rushed across the room and flung it wide.

"Good evening, Miss Bishop."

Clara's shoulders sagged. The concierge from the front desk smiled politely and held out an envelope. "This message arrived for you."

Clara looked past him to Tony's closed door. "Thank you," she said, reaching for the envelope.

"Can I help with anything else, miss?"

"No, thank you," Clara said. "Good night."

The message was from Ruth, requesting that Clara call home. *Not an emergency*, it said. *Just need to talk.*

Clara set it on the entryway table and stood in the doorway, breathing fast. In the moment before she opened the door, she had been convinced it was Tony standing on the other side. Now she stared across the hallway at his room, adrenaline shuddering through her. All her life, she had been imagining how things could be different—with other parents, with normal friends, without Madame, without her scars. She didn't want to spend the rest of her life catching up, or reliving her mistakes, or haunted by what might have been. Constantia's words rose to her mind, taking hold like a root. *Blood beats through me again, all the way to my pathetic fingers. Do you understand what I am telling you? Your sister is back from the dead.* Before she had even consciously decided what to do, she marched across the hall.

Tony opened the door immediately.

"Clara." He looked surprised, but also—pleased?

Her heart was beating so fast that when she spoke, she was out of breath.

"I keep thinking about Brussels and wondering—"Already the words were failing her. She cleared her throat. "I want—" *I want to be different. I want to come back from the dead, too.*

"What?" Tony searched her face. "What do you want?"

Finally, she took a step toward him. "I'm going to kiss you now, Tony Park," she said, and reached her hand to his face.

On the precipice of sleep, Clara bolted awake. The opening bars of Constantia's intermezzo echoed in her mind. Then another melody whispered in the darkness. For a moment, it sang inside her, just out of grasp. It faded as she sat up.

"What's wrong?" Tony asked.

But the music was draining out of her, flowing back into the sea of sleep.

"Just a dream," Clara said.

He reached up a hand and pulled her back down.

Chapter 18

CLARA WOKE IN A BROAD BEAM OF SUNLIGHT. They had fallen asleep without drawing the curtains. Tony's arm was around her, his hand resting on hers. Her arm tingled beneath his warmth. She had not realized until last night how unaccustomed it was to being touched. Everyone she'd slept with had avoided her scars, maneuvering around them as if they might hurt. Tony had wanted to touch all of her. Now she lay still, afraid to break the spell, knowing from the way his breaths had shortened that he was awake. Then he spoke.

"You remembered," he said into her hair. "About that day at the Parc du Cinquantenaire."

Clara's face warmed. "Of course I remember." Her chest ached at the recollection of the happiness of that afternoon and the girl she had been, so nervous and hopeful. "It was a great day."

"*Great?*" Tony rolled her toward him, incredulous. "I practically had to beg you to come with me! I was sweating through my suit jacket trying to work up the nerve to kiss you, and meanwhile you acted like I was going to push you into the pond!"

"What did you expect?" she said, tossing a pillow at him to disguise her pleasure. "You'd been a jerk to me the entire time I'd known you."

"I was a jerk to everyone. It was an unfortunate side effect of thinking I was God's gift to music. We have Madame to thank for curing me of that." He bent to kiss her, his body pressing into hers. It was not the type of kiss, she decided, that anyone might regret.

When it was over, he pulled back, a teasing smile on his mouth. "Though my favorite memory from that week is when you threw your shoes in the fountain."

Clara groaned and pulled the sheet over her head. "I was too embarrassed to tell you I'd never drunk whiskey before. I had to leave my rehearsal three times the next morning to throw up in a garbage can backstage. I couldn't have scotch for ten years without wanting to vomit from humiliation."

"I tried to stop you." Tony laughed. "You just kept shouting that you were never going to wear high heels again."

"I was so ridiculous," Clara moaned. "Those shoes could have made my first mortgage payment."

When their laughter subsided, she looked up at him. "I'm sorry about what happened, the day of your performance. I promise I wasn't trying to sabotage you. I just—" Regret wilted some of the warmth in her chest. "You told me how you felt about me, and I wanted to believe you, but I kept hearing Madame's voice in my head, telling me there are no friends in competition." She shook her head. "I was afraid you didn't mean it."

"It's okay." Tony shrugged matter-of-factly. "It didn't matter in the end. You would have won anyway."

"That's not true."

Tony regarded her soberly, the playfulness draining from his face. "I was in the hall for your performance. You would have beaten anyone."

He studied her a moment longer, seeming like he had something more to say. Instead, he tilted his head toward the door. "I have to leave in a few minutes. I'm having breakfast with Damian Szymanowski."

"Who's that?"

Tony raised an eyebrow. "The conductor of the Warsaw Symphony?"

"Oh." She had forgotten that tonight was the night of his concert.

He paused. "You should come to the performance."

Clara regretted the way her body tensed.

"I was just thinking that maybe it would be helpful for you to go back," he said. "For closure. You could come early, before anybody gets there. I'm not going to beg you to play again. I just want you to make your peace with it, if you can."

Clara picked up her sweater from the floor. She did not want to go to the Warsaw Symphony Concert Hall any more than she wanted to walk across the room naked in the sunshine. But she did not want to cast off the courage she had slipped on last night when she knocked on his door. She pulled her sweater over her head.

"Okay," she said, glad he could not see her face.

He came around to her side of the bed and kissed her. "I'll take you to dinner after. Maybe you'll even be brave and order a scotch."

Soon she heard the shower begin to run, then the faint sound of Tony humming Constantia's intermezzo. The melody soothed and nagged her as she combed her hair with her fingers in the mirror over the bed. For the first time since waking, she remembered the music that had soared within her last night in her dream. She closed her eyes, trying to recapture it. A melody rose from the dark lake of her memory, so distant she had to strain to hear it. She leaned toward it, but the harder she listened, the further it receded.

The door to the bathroom swung open. Clara opened her eyes as Tony emerged, pulling a black T-shirt over his head. The music sank into darkness.

"Everything okay?" he asked.

"I was just—" Clara shook her head, trying to jar the music back to the surface. "There's something about Constantia's intermezzo. I woke up in the middle of the night feeling like it was . . . familiar." The music returned for a fraction of an instant, surging to her mind on the legato strings of a cello.

Tony saw the change on her face. "What is it?"

"I don't know." She reached for her boots from where they had tumbled beneath the bed, a sense of urgency beginning to beat within her. She needed to get to the Starza Museum. Going there had not been her plan when she woke that morning. Now it beckoned, a radar pulsing in the fog.

She pulled on her boots. "I'm going to the museum. I want to look at the archives."

Tony was looking at her with bewilderment. "Do you think Starza quoted the intermezzo in one of his pieces like he did her Rhapsody?"

Clara fastened the buckle of her boot. "I'm not sure. I just keep hearing this melody—" She paused as the cello began and faded again, this time with the accompaniment of a double bass. "I don't know what it is."

"But there's something you've recognized," Tony persisted. "So you're going there looking for something." His eyes were sharp, and she felt their old rivalry, forgotten for the night, invite itself back into the room.

She rose from the bed and stood before him. "I don't know *what* I'm looking for. I just have this hunch that something of hers is there. I can't explain it. I just feel like I need to go there and look. I'll come to the concert hall after. If I find anything at all, you'll be the first to know. I promise."

She kissed him on the cheek, then turned and walked toward the door. A question made her hold back.

"What were you going to say the other day at the museum?" she asked, turning to him. "Before Tomasz came in the room?"

The tenderness of the morning had made her bold, and she was expecting something good. She was surprised when instead his smile fell.

Tony ran a hand over the back of his head, ruffling his wet hair. "I was going to apologize, for the way I behaved this summer when I came to Austin." He paused. "I should have told you my suspicions outright. I've regretted it ever since. I worried that you thought maybe the metronome was all I was in it for, and it never was. I'd be lying if I said I don't want it. But that's not why I got so involved."

Pleasure trilled up the back of her neck.

"For the record," Tony said, "I never would have bought it from you without telling you I thought it could have been Starza's."

"You definitely wouldn't have," Clara said, and smiled. "I wouldn't have let you." She turned to leave once more and was almost to the door when he said her name.

"Last night, when you knocked on the door," he began.

Clara braced herself, hearing a note of uncertainty in his voice. But he looked at her steadily, and with a vulnerability she had seen on his face only when he held Constantia's intermezzo in his hands, said, "I was hoping it was you."

Clara felt her mouth hang open, astonishment and bashfulness and a sudden, stupefying joy flooding her all at once. "I'll see you this afternoon," she stammered, and walked out of the room.

Halfway across the hall, she stopped, mortified. *I'll see you this afternoon?* Should she go back and say thank you? Tell him she'd been wondering about that night in her parents' driveway for months like a silly teenager? Sleep with him again before their budding romance collapsed beneath the weight of their historic competition? For a paralyzed moment, she stood in the hall listening to the silence behind his door, then decided against all of them and walked on.

The lamp beside her made bed was still on, the metronome next to it on the nightstand. She had been foolish to leave it out, especially now that the circle of people who knew of its existence had grown, but the discoveries of the past two days had lifted the burden of Madame's admonition to keep it safe. The metronome was more resilient than all its possessors had proved to be. Even if she lost it now, she would trust it to survive.

The first hot blast of water from the shower released the smell of Tony's aftershave from her skin, sending a shiver of desire down her back. Pressed against him last night in the velvety dark, her body had not been damaged, but alive. Sleeping with him had felt both intimately familiar and electrically new, as if it had been destined to happen and on the verge of never happening at all. Had she never walked across the hall last night, maybe it never would have. The thought caused her to open her eyes into the streaming water. For the last decade, she had been waiting for life to happen again—for her scars to heal, her wounds to anneal, her hatred toward Madame to fade. Yesterday, reading Constantia's letters, she had realized that she was the one who had to make it happen, right now, no matter the obstacles. The longing for that new start was what had propelled her across the hall last night to Tony's room. No one was going to show her the way to the rest of her life. She had to find it herself.

She raked the lush hotel shampoo through her hair, hurrying through the rest of her shower. Once out, she dressed in a clean pair of jeans and another black sweater, packing a pair of black slacks in her backpack for the concert. She slipped the metronome in her backpack before walking out the door. The tumult that had broken over her life when she received the invitation to Madame's final concert was nearing a crescendo. She could feel its culmination building. From here to the end, it would be nothing but *prestissimo* and fire, but the end was coming. All that remained now was to maintain her stage presence until the final note.

Freta Street was empty, with only the faint clink of glasses from a café down the street to suggest the tourists who would flock here in a few hours. Standing alone on the cobblestone before Starza's house, Clara could imagine Constantia stepping down from her carriage for the first time, hoping the great Aleksander Starza would heal her hand and thus change her life forever. And then stepping down from that carriage again and again, each time revising the man inside, her feelings changing from suspicion to contempt to exasperation to jealousy to love and then—what? It was 7:55. She had an hour before Tomasz arrived at the museum. She had to make it count. She mounted the steps and knocked on the door.

Silence. Clara knocked again.

From somewhere above her, she heard a familiar voice.

"Muzeum będzie otwarte o dziesiątej!"

Clara stepped back on the cobblestone. A window on the second floor of the house was open.

"Gregor?" she called up to it. "It's Clara Bishop."

Gregor appeared at the window. His ruddy face broadened in a smile.

"Miss Bishop! I did not know we were expecting you!"

"You weren't. I'm leaving tomorrow, and I wanted to look into something before I go. I was hoping I could spend some time in the archive."

"A scholar's errand!" he called back joyfully. "But Tomasz is not in yet. I can phone him if you like."

"Like I said, I don't have a lot of time." She shaded her eyes and tilted her face up to him, offering her best smile. "Could you maybe let me in?"

Gregor hesitated, then held up a finger. "We do not need to shout to each other out the window like Romeo and Juliet!" he said. "I will come down."

Presently, he opened the door, but did not, she noticed, invite her inside. "Perhaps I could show you the restoration plans for the Biliński painting while we wait. The archive is Tomasz's domain, as you know."

Clara weighed which tactic of persuasion would be most effective. She thought of the way Tony had charmed Tomasz with flattery, then thought better of it. She had always been more comfortable with frankness.

"Gregor, I want to look at the archive without Tomasz. I won't take anything, I promise. But I have a hunch I want to look into, and I don't think Tomasz would approve. I think you can appreciate what that's like."

Gregor regarded her soberly for a moment, and Clara was sure he was going to deny her. Then the corner of his mouth tilted upward.

"You have your ancestor Marianna's persistence, Miss Bishop," he said, and with a good-natured wink widened the door. "But you must defend me to Tomasz when he arrives. I will tell him you threatened to move our collection to the United States."

The house smelled musty after being closed up for the night. They walked past the portrait of Marianna seated at her desk and the cordoned-off music room, past the formal dining room with its place setting suspended in 1885, to a door in the back of the house. It would have passed for a closet if it weren't for the three gleaming deadbolts fastening it closed. Gregor pulled a set of keys from his pocket.

"We don't allow visitors down here, as you know," he said, unlocking them one at a time. "But you are no regular visitor, of course."

The door opened onto a metal staircase. Clara followed Gregor to a lower level that resembled a storage facility. The walls were white drywall, with white recessed lighting. The suspirations of an HVAC system whirred overhead.

"Very striking, isn't it?" Gregor said as he led her down a carpeted hallway to another locked door. "The difference between upstairs and down?"

"Incredibly," Clara agreed, wishing he would hurry.

Finally, he pushed open the door to the archive room. The walls were white, the floor white tile. The light overhead was dim to protect the manuscripts from fading. Most of the room was consumed by a large wooden table, cleared except for three brass reading lamps. Against the far wall were the metal cabinets that held Starza's music. They stood chest-high across the length of the room, each containing dozens of shallow metal drawers so the scores could be stored flat.

Gregor lifted a pair of gloves from a wire basket beside the door. "The paper is fragile," he said, handing them to her.

"I'll be very careful," Clara said, the image of the burned concerto coiling in her stomach. "I promise."

Gregor pointed to the far left. "They are organized by year and opus," he said. "I would ask if you need help, but I have a feeling you know what you are looking for. Tomasz will arrive at nine," he continued, glancing at the clock. "I will leave you until then." He turned to go.

"Your hypothesis about Starza and syphilis," she called after him. "How sure are you?"

Gregor paused in the doorway, his face assuming a tender thoughtfulness. "My interest in the Starza family has always sided with Marianna. My brother was a great athlete, you see. He went to the Olympics for Poland as a sprinter. I have always been interested in the people 'behind the scenes,' as they say." He chuckled, then his face grew serious.

"Marianna was very troubled by the change she saw in her brother in his later years. She had raised a boy who once wept that he could not save the life of an injured bird. She could not understand how her gentle brother could sometimes be so filled with rage. Do you have children, Miss Bishop?"

Clara shook her head.

"Ah." Gregor's face lit up. "One day you may, and then you will know the worries a parent has. Four years ago, I had a child. A beautiful boy, sweet like his mother. One day he hit her with his toy truck and gave her a black eye. It is normal for children to do such things, but I thought of Marianna, and how her sweet brother who wept for a bird became a man who throws chairs. I thought, what could have changed him? You ask how sure I am, and the scholar in me will never tell you he is certain. But in my feeling as a human being, I believe there are only two possibilities to explain the change in Starza."

Clara shook her head. "Syphilis and what else?"

Gregor smiled. "Love and madness. Though to some they are one and the same." He winked, then pulled the door closed.

Clara turned to the cabinets. The drawers seemed to hum in concert with the buzz of the fluorescent lights. She walked along their cool expanse until she reached the cabinet from 1881, the year Constantia and Aleksander met at Valeska Holland's house, the first year of Starza's so-called Golden Age. Certainly anyone who might read Constantia's letters could no longer imagine this as mere coincidence. The question now was this: Had Constantia been Starza's muse, or had she written some of the works herself? Clara slid on the white gloves and pulled open the first drawer.

The opening page of the *Dark Angel Sonata* stared up at her. *August 1881*, the label on the inside of the drawer read. The ink was faded and the paper yellowed, but Starza's pen strokes remained thick and bold, the ink lashing the page in hurried scrawls. She imagined him hunched over the piano, hand tense with the speed of his effort, racing against the unknown time when his mind would begin to fail. For the first time since accepting the metronome into her arms, she felt pity for this man whom she had so sorely mistaken, who had run from his house to hand a piece of music through a carriage window to a woman who did not know he loved her. Gently, she closed the drawer and moved on to the next.

There were the Opus 32 Sonatas, the C-sharp Mazurka, the B Minor Ballade, the concerto for solo left hand. A bolt of sound shot up the back of her neck with each page she passed, the music tunneling into her spine and up to the bones of her ears in flashes of sound and memory. But there was nothing here that departed from all the music Starza had written before. Quickly, she began pulling on other drawers. *CONCERTO NO. 2. SECOND MOVEMENT*, Madame had written in her notebook. *BARS 345–500*.

There! The opening measures rose to Clara's ears as the drawer glided open. *Starza has been working on a new concerto in my absence . . . imagine my astonishment when in the second movement I heard the theme from my own Rhapsody quoted in the melody!* Clara pulled the pages of the second movement to the table and began counting the bars from the beginning. When she reached 345, she cried out.

It had been disguised, dressed up with a richer harmonic progression and a sonorous violin solo that sung out over the original melody, but it was clear now that she recognized it. *He claims he dreamed of my spirit as a starling in a turbulent wind, cast about but still striving to fly.* Madame had recognized the Rhapsody in the concerto. But this was not the music Clara had heard last night in her dreams.

Energized, she reached for her backpack and the list of dates she had scrawled on the inside cover of *She, Too, Played*. Yesterday, Clara had made one amendment to the timeline, backing up nine months from Helene's birth to add *January 1885* in pencil. She turned again to the cabinets, looking for the pieces from late 1884.

What do you hope to find? Tony would have asked if he were here. Clara did not know what her answer would be. She did not know what crumb or hint of Constantia's presence she expected to see in the scores, only that she might recognize it once she saw it.

The first piece from late 1884 was the Fantasia in E Major, begun in October of that year. Clara scanned back to her notebook. *Do not worry after me, dear Nadia,* Constantia had written in November. *I am no silly girl indulging in fantasies.* Clara laid the fantasia on the table. Colors rose to her mind. Purple shores with seabirds. A water-soaked garden. It showed a change in Starza's style—a more tender, less bombastic approach—but there was nothing at all to betray another mind other than a few penciled notes in Marianna's small, neat hand. Frustrated, she laid the fantasia aside and bent to the next drawer. The Scherzo in C-sharp Major. Clara had last performed it in Tokyo in 1986. It had rained so hard that night she had needed to bang out the notes to be heard over the drive of the rain on the roof. The music swept in and out of her mind like a choppy tide. But no trace of Constantia.

Next came the "Sister" Nocturnes from early 1885. Constantia had sent Nadia a nocturne in March of that year hidden in a parcel of linens. What had become of it? *The music came to me effortless and complete.* Clara laid the pieces on the table side by side, the eight pages of *The*

Melancholy, the nine of *The Vengeful*. Both were in the key of A Minor. Both had a metronome marking of 60. Her eyes lingered on Starza's scrawled tempo at the top of each piece: one largo, one larghetto. *60 not S's*, Madame had written in her notes. *Melancholy and Vengeful—different metronomes?* Clara shook her head, frustrated. What did it mean? That Starza had used a different metronome on each, or that one nocturne was not written by Starza at all? Clara scanned them both, hearing their familiar arcs and valleys of sound. There was nothing in either nocturne reminiscent of the sixteen bars of Constantia's intermezzo they had discovered in Nadia's trunk. She closed her eyes and conjured them again, the opening like a church bell echoing across a misty vale. The slow crescendo rising like a fire revived after a rain. Dusky blue, cornflower, smoke. She hummed the sound in the silent room, all the way to the final bar, waiting for the seventeenth to appear. Nothing.

"What came next?" she said aloud. Last night, she awakened from a deep sleep with the certainty she had heard the music before. Where?

Frustrated, she yanked on the next drawer. When she saw what lay there, the breath left her lungs. *Concerto No. 3 in E Minor, op. 64*, the label affixed to the inside of the drawer read. *Completed January 1885. Original destroyed December 1988.*

Protected between two pieces of thin glass were the singed scraps of what remained of the original score, twenty bars of music in total. Her hands involuntarily clutched her chest, remembering how the brittle paper had curled in her arms. For a moment, she felt heat enter her body. The sound of footsteps clomping across the wooden floor upstairs jarred her from her terror. There was no time for mourning now. She laid the piece of glass aside and pulled out the facsimile reproduction Tomasz had created from photos of the original. Clara was thumbing past the trombone solo halfway through the second movement when she heard it. A slow, mournful song, plodding but beautiful, like a distant bell echoing across a misty vale. Her heart skipped a beat.

The sparkling melody was less recognizable in the plaintive tones of the trombone, but there it was—all sixteen bars of Constantia's unfinished intermezzo, as unmistakably beautiful as the first time she had seen it. Clara laid the next three pages of the score on the table, following the theme as it meandered to the cellos and bass before the piano took the lead again. There the thread disappeared. Dismayed, Clara scoured the rest of the concerto, looking for something more. When she did not find it, she whirled to the cabinets and began pulling out drawer after drawer in growing despair. By the time she reached the Polonaise in E, the last piece Starza completed before his death, the hope that had clamored within her on the way to the museum was silenced. All she had were sixteen bars of an unpublished intermezzo and a similar trombone solo in the second movement of the *Fire Concerto*, which wasn't enough to prove anything. Madame had been convinced that the museum was the answer to finding Constantia's music, and that Clara was somehow integral to that discovery. But here she was, and all she had found was circumstantial, at best. Already, Clara could hear the objections mounting—Constantia Pleyel was not just a murderess but also a plagiarist. She sat on the floor, dejected.

The sound of the door opening made her look up.

"Clara!" Tomasz strode into the room, followed closely by Gregor, who shot Clara an apologetic look.

"I'm sorry I wasn't here to help you." Tomasz looked past her to the scores on the table and the many open drawers of the cabinet. Clara thought she saw him shudder.

She stood. "And I'm sorry to come so early," she said. "I promise I've been very careful." She gestured to the cabinets, feeling desperate. "Is this everything the museum has? Everything Starza wrote?"

Tomasz looked exasperated. "Yes, everything! Truly, Clara, we are professionals, you know."

"What about the scraps you told me about? Where are those?"

Tomasz's mouth puckered, but he bent to the lowest drawer of the cabinet and pulled out a folder. "Scraps," he said, laying it on the table.

All hope sank at the sight of the slim folder. It was truly only scraps: half a page with a bar of music scrawled on the corner, a melody scratched on a piece of wax paper that might have been used to wrap a rind of cheese. There was hardly any music at all.

Tomasz stood next to her as she peered at each one, his hands clasped behind his back as if he were using one hand to restrain the other from yanking the papers from her arms.

"What's this?" Clara held up a piece of paper about the size of a greeting card. The front appeared to be an invoice, dated 8 January 1885. On the back was a brief letter in Starza's hand.

Tomasz looked over her shoulder. "A bill from the furniture maker," he said. "Starza had several chairs repaired at the shop."

"What does the letter say?"

Tomasz sighed. "'Dear Sir,'" he read. "'The accompanying parcel encloses the instrument, for the additions of which we spoke. As it is intended for a gift whose occasion draws near, please return with haste.—AS'"

The instrument. A gift. Quickly, she thumbed through *She, Too, Played* to the opening pages of Eleonora's article. *Constantia Baranowska was born January 24, 1848.* Her heart guttered. She looked up at Tomasz.

"Does it say anything else about what the gift was?"

Tomasz read the invoice side of the bill. "There is one charge listed here for 'construction' and one for 'engraving.'" He looked at her warily. "What have you come searching for, Clara?"

Clara removed her white gloves and placed them in a basket near the door.

"Something that wasn't here." She picked up her backpack and hitched it over her shoulder. "I'm sorry to inconvenience you, Tomasz. Can I ask you for one more favor?"

His smile strained. "Anything."

"See if you can find out anything about that furniture maker, and if they might have ever serviced a metronome for Starza. I think that's the bill for the creation of its box."

The mention of the metronome seemed to have a tonic effect. He straightened a little. "I will look into it this morning," he said.

Clara turned to go, but he called after her. "I had a message waiting for you this morning. From a Mr. Sanchez, in Texas?"

The sound of Julián's name in Tomasz's Polish accent unsteadied her so thoroughly she wobbled on her boot. "Julián called here? Is everything okay?"

"I'm sorry, I do not know," Tomasz said. "The message said he tried at the hotel first. He has asked that you call him at *the bar*?" he said distastefully. "You are welcome to use my office if you wish. Gregor can show you up."

She joined Gregor at the door and followed him back down the sterile hallway and up to the sunlit rooms of Starza's house, now bustling with tourists.

"You did not find what you were seeking?" Gregor asked.

Clara shook her head. "No."

"Sometimes with mysteries from the past, you don't see the whole for many years. That is the pleasure of the work," he said cheerfully, leading her into Tomasz's sunny office. "A lifetime's worth of mystery."

Clara looked at him in disbelief. Who had a lifetime to solve the mystery of anyone's life but their own? She thanked him, then sank into Tomasz's desk chair. She found herself staring at a framed photograph of Starza on the opposite wall. He stood on stage, one fist on his hip, appearing to scoff at the audience. Trying to imagine that face weeping at the sight of his newborn child was almost impossible.

She pulled the calling card she had purchased at the airport from her wallet and entered the code before dialing The Andromeda Club. Julián picked up on the first ring.

Her heart lifted at his voice.

"Clara! My god, girl. Where have you been? Your mother and I were about to book a flight to Poland!"

The thought of Julián and Ruth spending any fraction of a moment together made Clara balk.

"Why have you been talking to my mom? Is everything okay?"

"She's been calling me for the past two days! The woman is relentless. Where have you been? I called you five times last night!"

"I didn't spend the night in my room."

Julián paused. "Does that mean you were in someone *else's* room?"

"Yes, obviously! Julián, what's going on?"

"Sorry! Distracted by the headline. A detective from the police station came by the bar last night. They found the people who broke into your house."

Picturing her house in Austin while sitting in Tomasz's office at the Starza Museum felt like conjuring an imaginary world from childhood. The recollection of her bare living room made the back of her neck tight.

"Did they find the box?"

"Yes. It's fine. I have it here, in the safe. It was just some teenagers, like the cops thought. He showed me their mug shots. They've been arrested before for breaking into cars. They're just kids, Clara. Like, eighteen years old. I guess they tried to take the box to an antiques shop in Dallas, and the owner had seen the bulletin the cops issued about it. They didn't know what it was. They were paid to go steal it."

"Paid by who?"

"The cops are still working that out. The guy who hired them approached them back in June. It was dark when they met, and he was wearing a hat and sunglasses, so they don't have much of a description, but the guy explicitly told them that you were a bartender and would be out at night, that you had a dog—everything. When they brought him the box without the metronome, he refused to pay them for it. That's when they took it to Dallas."

Clara shivered, feeling as exposed as her pilfered house. "What does all of this have to do with my mom?"

"Well, she's talked herself into thinking you're being hunted by an international crime ring, for one. Next time you decide to lie to your parents about your house being broken into, you should probably tell me."

Clara winced, imagining Ruth's reaction to the news. "Sorry. I thought it would just make her worry."

"You were correct about that. But mostly she's got something she needs to tell you about your aunt."

"Aunt Pauline?"

"Yeah. Your mom went to visit her up in Wisconsin. They found some family papers while they were cleaning out the attic. She said she thought they would help you on your quest."

"My quest?"

"Her words. Soooooooo." He stretched out the word in two long syllables. "You and Tony."

She smiled. "Me and Tony."

Clara waited for his barrage of questions and was surprised when instead he fell quiet.

"I just have a thought, Clarita," he said softly. "I don't want to have it, but I do."

Her smile vanished.

"I can't help but wonder how many people back in June knew you had this metronome. And how many of *those* people know you have a dog, or are a bartender? As far as I can tell, outside of us, there's really only one."

Clara leaned back in the chair. "You think Tony put on a hat and sunglasses and roamed the streets of Austin searching for some thugs to break into my house?"

Julián sniffed. "Well, when you say it like that, I guess it sounds a little farfetched. I don't know, maybe nobody would be good enough for you in my eyes. I just wanted to say it out loud. You know, before you fall in love with him or whatever."

"We're a long way from love," Clara said, though somewhere inside of her, a tiny part hoped she was wrong.

After they'd said their goodbyes, she hung up, the dissonance of the two worlds sliding away as she rose from the desk and walked to the photograph of Starza standing on stage.

She had been so sure that Constantia's music was in the museum, concealed somewhere in the archive. After all Constantia had fought to claw back to music, there was no way she would have left it in her own home, vulnerable to her husband's discovery. And Amelia avowed that the only music in Nadia's family home had been the waltzes and lullabies destroyed in the flood—not the nocturne Constantia had sent in a parcel of linens. That meant that Constantia's music must either have been with her at the time of her arrest or was left at Starza's home the night he died. Clara stood before the photograph and peered into her ancestor's face. Where did she hide it?

Chapter 19

CLARA STOOD IN THE VESTIBULE of the Warsaw Symphony Concert Hall, faltering. A cool wind wisped through the glass of the revolving doors behind her, but her lungs felt squeezed of air. She had walked the two miles here from the museum to work up the courage to enter the door. Having arrived, she felt unable to go on.

The concert hall of her recollection, its details fixed and clear in the way of all terrible memories, was gone. The fire had taken out the west wing of the building, ravaging the stage and orchestra pit before destroying half the auditorium. The exterior of the building had been refurbished to replicate the arched windows and classical columns of the original, but inside had been made new. The lobby was a bright atrium with vast skylights that seemed to signify the upward promise of the future. Minimalist paintings hung on every wall. A giant sculpture of a woman strumming a harp towered above the box office. All that remained of the building's tragic past was a plaque on the vestibule wall that commemorated the fire in Polish, German, and English. Placed as it was in the breezy entryway, only someone waiting out of the cold for a taxi might have stopped to consider it. She turned away, feeling like a ghost in a house she had once inhabited, and pulled on the heavy glass door.

The lobby was empty except for an old man in coveralls pushing a vacuum over the maroon carpet. He turned it off when he saw her lingering near the door. In the silence that followed, Clara heard from deep within the building the sounds of the piano. Tony was rehearsing the *Fire Concerto*.

The old man gestured toward the box office, where the metal grate was closed. "*Kasa biletowa będzie otwarta o piątej,*" he said.

Clara pointed to the closed doors of the concert hall. "I'm here to see Tony Park," she said in English. "He's expecting me."

When the old man shook his head, Clara reached in her backpack for the Polish phrasebook that three months ago she had pulled from the dusty corner of her bookshelf. They spent a few long moments in silence as she cobbled together a phrase. "*Jestem tu dla* Tony Park," she said. "*Oczekuje mnie.*"

The old man screwed up his wizened face to squint at her before finally tilting his head to the back of the lobby. "*Chodź ze mną,*" he said, and gestured for her to follow.

Clara saw him glance at the scars on her cheek as she neared. He led her past the box office and the shuttered lobby bar to an unmarked door obscured behind a potted lemon tree. Lifting a ring of tightly packed keys from his belt loop, he unlocked it, then pushed the door open on a bright hallway. Clara hesitated, beginning to sweat. The old man lifted his white eyebrows as if asking whether she was coming. His gray eyes were the color of dull water, but his expression as he held the door was patient. Nodding a thank-you in his direction, she stepped across the threshold.

The corridor was new, the carpet maroon with dizzying black zigzags. Clara noticed the silver heads of a sprinkler system glint from the ceiling. Dread coiled in her stomach—mistakes remedied. Photographs of performers on the stage of the old concert hall lined the walls: Itzhak Perlman, Artur Rubinstein, Martha Argerich, Madame. Clara turned her head to look as she passed, cold spreading down her arms to the palms of her damp hands.

The hallway turned sharply right and then left, through another door and past a second corridor. With each step, the piano grew louder, the barriers of sound falling away until at last the janitor pushed open a final door into the darkness of backstage. The sound of the concerto gusted past her like a wave of heat.

Never once in all these months had she heard Tony play. She hadn't wanted to know how good he had gotten. Part of her had harbored a wish that his playing would be wanting in some way—overly showy or lacking depth, the way he had seemed to her at Madame's house back in the spring. She saw immediately that this was not the case. His articulation was as exquisite as it had always been, but the expression had grown deeper, as if the music came from somewhere more visceral within him. Clara stood in the shadow of the curtains and watched his hands race over the keyboard, his head bowed and intent. She recognized it as the moment when the music was flowing through you onto the keys, lifting on its unstoppable wave every longing you had ever held and every sorrow you had ever mourned, rinsing you clean and filling you up all at once. It lent him the appearance of deep stillness despite his rapidly moving fingers, and she realized with equal parts pride and envy that despite all the months of phone calls and visits and even last night, she had underestimated him. He had achieved everything they both had wanted, back when they were young and so hungry to become great. He had done it all.

The old man had seemed to decide that she was not an interloper. He gave her a nod of farewell before walking back toward the corridor. The metal door clanged shut at the same time Tony landed on the closing chord of the concerto. He turned, shading his eyes from the bright lights.

"Clara? Is that you?"

"It's me." She stepped out from the curtains, remembering the last time she stood here. How she had blown a kiss to the audience, scanning each face for Madame. Sorrow cut through her at the memory of that old self: so foolish, so anxious to prove her worth.

Tony took a step toward her, then held back, keeping his distance like someone who had a cold. "I waited for you out there for a while. I thought maybe you weren't coming."

"I got held up at the museum." The stage lights made her dizzy. Everything was too bright or too dark, and her eyes hurt. Why wasn't he coming forward to kiss her? She looked at the piano to steady herself. "I didn't find anything of Constantia's in the archive, but Julián called over there. The police found the metronome box."

"That's great," Tony said, the strained expression on his face briefly lifting. "Is it in one piece?"

"It's fine. I guess it was a couple of teenagers. They were hired by someone, so we still don't really know who was after it. But at least if the Dabrowskis end up having a claim on the metronome, I won't owe them any money."

Her eyes had adjusted, and she looked past him to the podium at the front of the stage, recalling how the conductor had entreated her to exit the building when the fire alarm went off. Clara had remained at the piano, disbelieving. *But is it real?* she had asked. She had been so unwilling to see the truth. *It is not our job to know 'IS IT REAL!'* the man had bellowed. *Please, follow the violins!*

"Look, Clara, I have to tell you something."

She came to attention at the note of gravity in Tony's voice.

"What is it?"

He clasped his hands behind his neck like a runner who had become winded and was trying to catch his breath. "I should have told you this morning. I should have said it last night as soon as I opened the door. I messed up, Clara. Really bad."

Alarm rippled through her body. "What happened?"

Tony dropped his arms heavily to his sides, a gesture that looked like a surrender. "When you asked me this morning what I was going to say at the museum the other day—" He paused, pressing his lips together as if he were going to be sick. "I lied. What I was going to say was that the lawsuit from the Dabrowskis is my fault. Maybe the break-in, too."

The word *lied* ricocheted through her mind, but she was too confused to do anything but stare at him. "Your fault?" Clara repeated. "How?"

His shoulders sagged. "When I came to see you in Austin back in June, and you told me you were going to sell the metronome to an antiques store, I was concerned that it would get lost, or bought up by someone who wouldn't appreciate what it was." He lifted his head to look at her, his face mournful. "So I told somebody I know at Sotheby's that Madame had a metronome and it may or may not have belonged to Starza."

Clara gasped. Tony rushed forward and grabbed her hands.

"You were saying you were going to sell it to some random dealer," he said. "I believed you were going to. I thought if I told somebody, the information would work its way into the right hands and put pressure on you to sell it to a responsible buyer. I never thought you would get sued. I never *conceived* somebody might try to break into your house to get it. I'm so sorry, Clara."

Her face felt numb. It seemed as if somewhere inside her, a version of herself had been standing on a precipice and was now falling, hurtling headlong into the dark. Her mind cycled through the events of the last three months, spinning like a carousel going round and round, the horses blurring so that only a single eye or tail stood out of the whirl: Tony showing up at The Andromeda back in June; Tony in her parents' driveway holding her hand; Tony taking her to Jess; urging her to come to Warsaw; the look of consternation on his face every time she mentioned the name Dabrowski. She couldn't somersault so quickly from the happiness of that morning to the misery of this moment, and there followed a period of seconds in which they stared at each other with the same measure of disbelief at how thoroughly he had ruined it all—an almost unifying moment of incredulity. Then it was gone. She backed away from him.

"All of this has been one big charade to get me to give you the metronome," she whispered.

"No." Tony shook his head insistently. "Everything about last night, everything I said about Brussels—it's all true. I'm so sorry, Clara. I tried to fix it. The morning you came to see me at the hotel in Austin, I called the guy and tried to walk it all back. That's why I wanted you to come here so badly. I thought if we could prove the metronome was Starza's, nobody could come after you. I wanted to tell you so many times, but I knew you wouldn't trust me after that, and I wanted to try to make it right."

That's what he had meant, she thought dimly. When he'd said that morning that he'd had more reason than the metronome to get involved. Guilt was what he had meant.

"Please, Clara." He looked at her miserably. "Please forgive me. You don't know how badly I wish I could go back and change it." He reached for her hand and held it between both of his. It seemed impossible that just hours ago, the same hands had cupped the side of her face as she kissed him goodbye.

"Please don't touch me," she said, her voice unsteady.

His face contracted, but he dropped her hand immediately.

"Clara, please."

The door to the corridor clanged open. A man in his thirties with a shock of glossy yellow hair strode in, sunglasses atop his head. Clara recognized him from the advertisements outside the building as the symphony's conductor.

"Mr. Park!" he exclaimed. "Glad to find you. And a friend, I see!"

Tony's eyes did not move from Clara's face. "Damian, allow me to introduce you to Clara Bishop." He looked at her, his expression imploring, but she turned away and began to walk toward the door. She did not stop to shake the conductor's outstretched hand, nor did she register his words of enthusiastic recognition. She heard Tony call her name a final time as she pulled open the door.

The hallway had transformed. All the white doors were now flung open. Musicians bustled between them ferrying instrument cases and garment bags, calling to one another in the excited tones of preconcert anticipation. Clara avoided eye contact with all of them, rushing toward the Exit sign at the end of the hallway. When finally she burst through the door into the quiet of a stairwell, she leaned against the concrete wall and squeezed her eyes shut. Remembering the elation that had lifted her across the hall that morning after she kissed Tony goodbye, she felt she might weep. She should have known better than to trust him. She should have known better than to think it could ever have worked at all.

She stood listening to the flurry of sounds from the hallway until she was certain she would not cry. When at last she opened her eyes, she realized with a sickening drop of her heart that she had stood in this exact place before.

There were the narrow marble steps, worn at the center from years of concert shoes. There were the black fissures in the white stone, the cracks like dead veins beneath her feet. The drywall was new, but the broad descent of the staircase was just the same. The only difference now was that a green Exit sign glowed at the bottom, casting its eerie light into the dark basement below.

The stairwell door clattered open, causing Clara to jump. Two men in concert tuxedos walked through, their undone bowties hanging loose around their necks. They had been laughing but fell silent when they saw Clara standing at the top of the steps.

The man in front had a pair of mallets tucked into his belt loop. He held a packet of cigarettes toward her. "*Chcesz zapalić?*"

Clara shook her head, and the man shrugged and tapped one from the pack and lit it. The two began to talk jovially, their smoke thickening above the landing. She looked past them toward the door, then directed her gaze down the shadowy steps. Deciding, she reached for the iron railing and began to descend.

With each step, the light from above dimmed. Her boots scuffed against the marble, echoing off the cold stone as the sound of the men's conversation grew fainter. At the bottom, she paused in the green light of the Exit sign. Upstairs, the men were grinding their cigarettes beneath their dress shoes. She heard a gush of sound as the door to the hallway opened. Then it banged shut, and all was silent. Alone, she peered into the shapeless dark.

Suddenly, a waft of cigarette smoke filled her nose. A choking feeling climbed up her throat. Coughing, she ran her hands along the wall until they connected with a light switch. White light flooded the room. Clara slumped against the wall, her breath fast and uneven. The basement had the chemical smell of a funeral home, as if bad odors had been scoured and disinfected, then masked with potpourri. The paint and the tiled floor were new. A line of dusty cellos was pushed against one wall. Music stands stood against each other in a row, their faces tilted to the ceiling like the heads of black flowers. But the long, straight hallway was just the same, the doors spaced evenly on either side like rungs of a ladder. Clara's eyes fixed past them to the end of the corridor, where another hallway slashed across this one, its lights still dark.

She forced herself to walk toward it, forgotten memories jolting her with each step. *Flowers for you, Miss Bishop! Shall I put them in your room? Powodzenia, Miss Bishop! An autograph, please?* She stopped at the mouth of the dark hall. The recollection of a leaping flame rocketed up the wall beside her. She staggered away from it, stumbling toward the door that had haunted her dreams.

It was made of new wood, the white paint thick on the edges from a slapdash job. The doorknob was cheap brass, still shiny beneath a layer of dust. Someone had cleared the smoke damage, whitewashing the past. She wondered if they had known what happened here, if they thought of her at all as they brushed on the paint. The idea of being forgotten filled her with a steadying rage. She reached out to turn the knob when a voice from behind made her jump.

"No."

Chapter 20

THE JANITOR STOOD BEHIND HER in the shadowy corridor, his hunched figure a black silhouette. He pointed to the door behind her and mimed turning the knob. "No," he said, shaking his head. "*Zamknięte.*"

Clara moved closer to the door, guarding it with her body. "My name is Clara Bishop," she said. "I was in the fire." She pointed at the ground where her body had lain on the precipice of death. *I almost died here*, she wanted to say, but the choking feeling returned to her throat, stifling the words.

The man initiated a volley of rapid Polish and marched forward, pointing at her with stringent accusation.

"Please." Clara pressed her palms together in a plea. "I just want to go in."

He was almost upon her now, and thrust out a bony arm, reaching for her wrist. Clara cried out, ready to push him away, but he did not pull her from the door. Instead, he turned over her hand.

His wrinkled forehead softened as he squinted into the cup of her palm. When he saw the scars there, he looked up into her face. "*To ty.*" He pointed to Clara, then gestured to the floor behind him. "You!" He uttered an excited string of Polish, waving his hands toward the closed door and back to the stairwell before tapping his chest. "*Znalazłem cię tutaj!*"

"Yes," Clara said, relief throbbing through her. "I was here." She pointed to the door. "I want to go inside."

Sadness passed over his face like the shadow of a cloud on a field. He held up his ring of keys. "Yes?" he asked. The keys swayed on the curve of the brass with a quiet *ting*.

Her whole body began to tremble. "Please."

He dipped his head in a grave nod, then stepped past her and slid a shiny silver key into the lock. She heard the click—so effortless—before he stepped back. She noticed for the first time the name badge embroidered on the breast of his coveralls. *Jerzy*.

"Thank you, Jerzy," she said. The words caught in her throat.

He nodded, then stepped to the side as if to give her privacy. Clara placed her palm on the cold knob.

The door opened slowly, with resistance, as if the hinges hadn't been fully flexed yet. In the instant before she flipped on the light, Clara paused on the dark threshold, remembering what the room had looked like the day of the fire: the mirror with globe makeup lights; the chaise lounge stacked with her suitcase and a new pair of black satin Manolos; a table with a bucket of ice and champagne for after the concert. Her green dress hung from the garment rack against the wall, the silk like water gliding over moss. Bouquets of flowers were crammed onto every surface, gifts from admirers of her, of Starza, of her descendancy. Built into the far wall was the steel safe, a relic of the days when opera stars had worn real jewels.

The memory vanished as soon as her finger connected with the light switch. She stood in the doorway gazing at a forgotten room. The walls were unpainted drywall. A bar of fluorescent light flickered down on rows of stacked folding chairs. Rough shelving built against one wall held boxes of paper towels. The landscape of her nightmares had become a storage room. All that remained of the old room was the safe, its steel door ajar.

So often, Clara had imagined what might have been if she had never wasted that extra minute retrieving the scores, if she had not agreed to do the lecture in the first place, if the safe had never existed at all, sparing her a few more seconds before the door banged shut. Now she walked forward and put her face level with the steel gray box, remembering a smell of sweat and old costumes. A stack of dusty programs advertising *La bohème* slumped on the lower shelf. Despite all the hours she had spent recalling the confines of this room, this building did not remember her. It would go on until the next fire burned it down or a future generation decided to demolish it. Her small tragedy would be forgotten, superseded by all the years of operas and concerts and ballets yet to come. She rose, exhaling a breath that felt as if it were expelling ten years of sorrow, then turned off the light.

Jerzy was waiting in the hallway, standing erect like a sentry at a funeral. His face softened with grandfatherly sympathy when he saw her emerge.

"*Czy wszystko w porządku?*"

Clara nodded. "I'm okay."

He smiled as if to say he understood, then stepped past her and locked the door, pointing to the Exit sign at the end of the hall. "*Pokażę ci drogę.*"

Clara followed him up a flight of stairs, her body strangely light, as if she were moving through a dream. Soon she heard the low buzz of voices, then Jerzy pushed open a door and they stepped into the blinding lights of the lobby. The box office was open; the metal grate lifted. A man in a black button-down was arranging Tony's albums on a folding table. A few older patrons were already plodding through the atrium.

"Clara!"

She turned, squinting in the bright light. Eleonora Konopnicka was walking toward her, pushing Amelia in the cumbrous silver wheelchair. Eleonora waved. "Tony told us to come early. He said he would get us seats in the front row."

The thought of Tony stung like an injury Clara knew would hurt worse later. She pushed it aside. "Eleonora, can you tell this man thank-you for me?" She put her hand on Jerzy's arm. "Tell him I'm so grateful for letting me into the room."

Jerzy became reanimated by this acknowledgment and began to speak rapidly.

"He says he recognized you when you walked in today," Eleonora said. "He recognized your face, and then he saw—" she hesitated, glancing uncomfortably at Clara. "He says he saw your scars and knew it was you. He was here, the night of the fire."

Clara felt her mouth fall open.

Jerzy nodded vigorously. He pointed to his chest and smiled, revealing three missing teeth. "I was trying to tell you downstairs," Eleonora translated. "I was in the hallway when you came out of the room. I saw you fall."

A shudder quaked through Clara's body at the memory of her arm banging against the hot floor. "You were there?" she whispered.

"Yes." Jerzy nodded. "When the fire alarm went off, I went backstage. I was trying to save the instruments. I was running to the exit with two cellos when the pianist ran up the basement steps."

Clara blinked. "The pianist?"

"The Polish one," Jerzy said. "She told me, 'Someone is trapped downstairs. The door is stuck!'"

Clara shook her head in disbelief. "You saw Zofia Mikorska?"

Jerzy pumped his head insistently. "She ran up the stairs screaming that you were stuck in the dressing room and the door would not open. I knew right away what had happened." His face contorted in a clutch of pain. "An opera singer slammed it shut the week before, and after that, the latch on the doorknob would not fully retract." Jerzy mimed jiggling a knob without getting any traction. Clara's hand clenched as she remembered how many times she had turned and pulled, turned and pulled.

Jerzy looked at the floor sorrowfully and uttered something almost inaudible. "He says he thought he fixed it," Eleonora said softly.

Clara felt the room wobble, remembering the sound of Madame's retreating footsteps. Her heart began to pulse in her ears. "Mikorska was the one who told the firemen to come downstairs?"

Jerzy lifted his head to meet Clara's eyes. "Yes. I had seen the rescue crews arriving on my last trip outside. I gave her the cellos and told her to find the firemen and tell them to hurry down to the basement. She wouldn't take the cellos. She dropped them on the floor and called me a fool. At the time I was angry, but I'm grateful now. When I got down to the basement, the fire was all through the hallway. I had an extinguisher, but it wasn't enough. The flames kept coming." He pushed up the sleeve of his coveralls, revealing a broad white scar as thick as the flat side of a knife. "I was there when you burst out of the door. Then you began to cough and fell to the ground, and I thought, 'If she is dead, it is my fault.'" His brow contracted. "We were both lucky the firemen came when they did."

Clara could barely speak. "No." She shook her head. "It was *my* fault. I should have gone outside when the alarm went off. I'm so sorry about your arm."

Jerzy dismissed this with a wave of his hand. "I have my life. You too. That is what matters." He passed a hand over his face and sighed. "When I saw you here today, I knew what you had come for. I could not go down there for three years. But eventually you must go back to the source of your pain to let it go."

At this, the sobs Clara had been damming up all day finally broke through. Hot tears began to spill down her cheeks. "You saved my life," she said.

"No," Jerzy said. "I saved some cellos. The pianist saved your life."

He put his arm around her, and Clara leaned into the rough fabric of his shirt, the gravity of the truth shuddering through her.

"She told the firefighters she went down to the basement to get her coat and then went outside with everyone else," she said. "Why didn't she tell me what she had done?"

Jerzy shrugged. "That I do not know. She *was* wearing a coat, I remember. Perhaps she did not tell you because she did not want you to feel indebted to her. Or perhaps, like me, she felt guilty that she did not do more."

The words penetrated her mind like the first drops of a cold rain.

"I thought she left me there," Clara whispered.

"Ah, no." Jerzy shook his head. "She would not have left you, of that I am certain. When they put you in the ambulance, I saw her speaking to you. She leaned over you, shouting like a mother demanding her child come to her. I believe she was insisting that you did not die." He chuckled. "And you see, you did what she asked."

He patted her hand, then gestured to the lobby, where concert-goers were now streaming through the revolving doors. "The concert will begin soon, and I have not finished my work. I am glad to see you again, Clara. It has done me good to see that you are well." He squeezed her hand one last time, then turned and walked toward a yellow trash can across the lobby. Clara watched him push it into the bathroom and disappear.

Eleonora and Amelia were staring at Clara as if they did not know whether to comfort her or give her privacy. Amelia pulled a handkerchief from her purse and passed it to Clara.

"I remember reading in the newspaper about the pianist who was injured in the fire," she said. "Now I see why you are so interested in Ms. Mikorska's past." She reached up to clasp Eleonora's forearm, then gestured to a leather messenger bag slung across the back of the wheelchair.

"She wants me to show you what we found in Nadia's journals." Eleonora produced a stack of xeroxes from the leather bag. "I translated all the entries related to Constantia and her music. They don't answer everything, but it sounds like there *was* some music Constantia left behind." She passed the pages to Clara. "It doesn't tell us where but at least it's a start."

Clara hugged the pages to her chest, this hint of Constantia's past, and Madame's, feeling even more precious. "Thank you," she said, gratitude welling up within her. "We couldn't have discovered any of this without you." She turned to Amelia. "And thank you for trusting us with your family's history. *Dziękuję pani*. I promise we will use it for good."

Amelia smiled tenderly at Clara, then pointed at her.

"She says it is up to us now to find Constantia's music, if it is really in the world as your teacher thought," Eleonora said.

The words found anchor inside her, penetrating all the murky wanderings of the past few months. For the first time in years, she felt a purpose take shape within her. "If it's out there, I will find it."

Amelia said something that made Eleonora laugh. "She says she wants to go see Tony now. He promised he would take a picture with her before the concert. After you read the journals, call me. Oh, and one more thing." Eleonora looked at Clara over her shoulder as she pushed the wheelchair toward the concert hall. "After you and Tony visited the other day, I contacted a historian I know in Kraków and asked him to do some research into Helene Pleyel. He couldn't find anything under that name, or Helene Mikorska, but he *did* find a Helene Andrysiak who died of cancer in 1928. It turns out Andrysiak is the surname of the aunt who raised her."

Clara felt a sudden torment of sadness for Helene, the daughter so beloved her father wept when he first held her. Of all those touched by Starza's death, perhaps she was the one who suffered most as a result.

"What about Madame?" Clara asked. "Did he find any record of her?"

"No, so I looked to see if there was still a St. Stephen's Orphanage in Kraków. It's called St. Stephen's Children's Home, but it's still there. The woman in charge told me they didn't have any records from before the war, but that she didn't need any records to confirm that a girl named Zofia Andrysiak lived there in the 1930s, because she remembered her. She was a child there at the same time. She was just a little girl when Zofia left, but she remembers how all the children would gather around on Saturday evenings to hear her play the piano. She told me a story about a day all the children had to wear their best clothes and shine their shoes because a famous pianist came from the Warsaw Conservatory to hear Zofia play. It made a great impression on all the children, and they talked about her for years after she left." Eleonora paused. "I thought you would also be interested to hear that this woman remembered how Zofia had a metronome that she kept on her bedside table in the dormitory. Apparently, she would wind it up for the younger children at night when they couldn't sleep."

Clara shook her head, baffled. "So it was hers after all."

"It would seem so. But none of this is the primary reason Mikorska is remembered over there. When she won the 1948 Starza Competition, she gave all her prize money to the orphanage."

"She gave it all away?" Clara asked, bewildered by this changing picture of Madame, who before had seemed so fixed and set.

Eleonora nodded. "Evidently it really helped get the place going again after the war. There's a picture of her hanging on the wall in the office."

Clara closed her eyes, trying to click the pieces of the puzzle into place. "But if her real name was Andrysiak, where did the name Mikorska come from?"

"I asked the same question. Apparently when Zofia was at the orphanage, she was particularly close to one sister—a woman by the name of Sister Elena Mikorska." Eleonora smiled. "She was the piano teacher. Whether Mikorska changed her name to disguise her past, or because she wanted to break with it, I don't think we'll ever know."

Chapter 21

CLARA WATCHED ELEONORA PUSH AMELIA across the lobby, the two of them chatting easily like mother and daughter, and felt an ache of loneliness not unlike regret. Placing the pages of Nadia's journals carefully into her backpack, she walked against the tide of people filing through the entrance and let the revolving doors spin her out into the cool breath of evening.

A cold rain had begun to fall. She clutched the backpack to her chest to shield it from the damp, maneuvering past the influx of concert-goers and their open umbrellas. Cars whooshed past on the street, water spraying from beneath their tires. Clara spotted the light of a phone booth at the end of the block and hurried toward it. She pulled open the folding doors just as the rain crescendoed to a pour.

She stood catching her breath, the glass beginning to steam as the rain drummed against the sides of the booth. Clara pulled a telephone card from her wallet. She hesitated only a moment before dialing the number.

"Clara, thank God!" Ruth exclaimed. "Are you all right? I've been trying to get in touch with you for two days!"

"I'm fine, Mom. I'm sorry I didn't call sooner. Things have been . . ." Images from the past two days pulsed through her mind, ending on Jerzy's sorrowful face. Her throat constricted. "Things have been busy."

Ruth emitted a huff of indignation. "We're all *busy*, Clara! It's not like I'm some nag tracking my adult daughter across Europe. What if something had happened to me, or to your father?"

"Did it?"

"Of course not! I'm saying *what if.* You can't just disappear!"

Clara observed that she had obviously *not* disappeared, since Ruth and Julián had been calling her at every Warsaw location Clara might have visited. But something about reading Constantia's letters had softened her to Ruth's foibles. "I'm sorry, Mom. Truly, I am. Are you and Dad all right?"

"Of course we're all right! We're not *elderly.* As it happens, I was trying, *as always,* to help *you!*"

"How are you trying to help me?"

"Well, as you know, Aunt Pauline hasn't been doing well. Her housekeeper called last week and told me Pauline had taken a spill. I went up to Madison straightaway and took her to the doctor. She's bruised up, but nothing's broken. She's a very hardy woman, you know. All the women in our family are. But I think the fall made her realize she can't live somewhere with all those steps. She wants *me* to have the house. It's been in the family for over a hundred years, you know. But I can't move to *Madison.* What would I do there? Although now that I think of it, maybe *you* should consider it. You're already used to a provincial town."

Clara turned in the phone booth to look down the street for a bus, beginning to regret this call. "Austin is the capital of Texas, Mom. And I don't need a six-bedroom Victorian. Can we talk about this when I get home? I'll be back in Chicago tomorrow night. Maybe we could get dinner or something."

"For heaven's sake, Clara, don't rush me! I didn't call about the house! We're going to put it on the market, of course. But while I was there, Pauline asked me to help her sort through some of her things. She's a terrible hoarder, you know. Really, she needs a team of professionals to clear the whole place out. It would take me a month just to—"

Ruth's voice faded as a recorded message came over the phone line. The screen beside the receiver began to flash: *Pozostało 5 minut!*

"—and in the back there was this box of my grandfather's papers!" Ruth's voice sprang to the forefront once more. "The original deed to the house, letters from my grandmother from their courtship, that kind of thing. It was fascinating, really, but I was thinking of you and this quest you told me about with Madame's metronome, and I thought you might be interested to know that Grandfather had some old letters from Marianna Starza from the year 1900. That was the year she died, you know. She had ovarian cancer, same as my mother. Grandfather was her last living relation, though they had only met a few times. It gives one pause, doesn't it, to think about what happens to one's belongings when one doesn't have close family?"

Clara gripped the phone in her hand. "What was in the letters, Mom?"

"Well. It seems Marianna was worried about some family heirlooms she had given to a friend. Well, not quite a *friend*, but *someone*. Pauline wasn't familiar with the word Marianna used to describe her. She seemed to think it was some kind of pejorative. Apparently, Marianna had given them to this person to safeguard for some missing relative of some sort, though who that could be, Pauline had no idea. She's done an extensive family history, as you know. Anyway, Marianna was writing to Grandfather because she wanted him to know that the items were with this woman—I believe her name was Nadia something or other—in case the missing relative never turned up, in which case Marianna wanted them returned to the family. Evidently Grandfather never took her up on it, since Pauline has never seen any of these objects. And honestly, I don't blame him, because it was really an odd sort of list. A toy horse, a locket—nothing of any real material value. We think he probably thought she had gone a little soft in the head. Anyway, among the items that she supposedly gave to this Nadia was . . . a metronome! Of course, she never said it was *the* metronome, but I immediately thought of you over there in Warsaw and thought you would like to know."

Clara's heart was beating fast. Here it was—the proof they had been seeking for months. This would be the letter read out at Sotheby's if the metronome ever went up for auction, the evidence she would present to the Dabrowskis proving that Marianna Starza had wanted it to stay in the family. But the news about the metronome was not what made Clara press the phone to her ear.

"Did the letter say anything else, Mom? Anything about some unpublished music, or about Constantia Pleyel?"

"No," Ruth sputtered, clearly affronted that Clara had failed to appropriately celebrate her discovery. "There was something about a painting she wanted Grandfather to have—a portrait of herself, of all things. She wanted him to come to Poland to get it. Can you imagine what it would have been, in those days, to cross the Atlantic for a painting of your cousin? She must have been a very self-important woman."

"So there wasn't anything at all about Constantia Pleyel?"

"*No*, Clara. Isn't the bit about the metronome enough?"

"Yes. It's huge! Would you mind faxing a copy to me at the hotel? There are some people I've been working with here who will want to see it."

The suggestion of involved experts seemed to mollify Ruth's pride. "I suppose I can," she said demurely. "See, I didn't *harass* you, Clara. I was calling for a reason."

"I know. And I'm sorry I didn't call sooner. I have a lot to tell you." She looked behind her at the concert hall, where the rain fell on a deserted sidewalk. "So much, actually."

"Well—" Ruth's voice became breathy the way it did when she was caught off guard. "I look forward to hearing all about it. How's Tony? Are you two having fun?"

Clara's heart sank. "Not exactly."

"Oh, Clara. What did you do?"

"What did *I* do? Why does it have to be me?"

"Oh, don't be so sensitive! I'm not making some universal proclamation about your character. I always thought he carried a flame for
you is all. I just assumed that if things aren't going well, it's because you
stopped them from progressing."

"Well, it wasn't me," Clara said, the pain of Tony's betrayal pummeling her once again. "It was him."

"I'm sorry to hear that." Ruth paused then, a hesitation so unlike her
that Clara checked the phone to determine if they'd been disconnected.

"Maybe Tony's not the one for you," Ruth finally said. "It doesn't matter to me as long as you're happy. But I don't think I'm speaking out of
turn when I say, as your mother, that you have a hard time forgiving
people for their mistakes. It's understandable, given what you've been
through." She paused again, her voice softening. "But I think it's worth
asking sometimes if maybe you hold people to such high account because
you have such a hard time forgiving yourself. You think if you had made
different choices, maybe you wouldn't have been in that fire, and things
would have turned out the way you planned. Maybe that's true, and maybe
it's not. But it's not worth spending the rest of your life wondering."

Clara was so unprepared for this moment of naked recognition
from her mother that her throat began to sting with oncoming tears.
When she felt she could speak, her words came out in a whisper.

"Sometimes I'm afraid I'm never going to figure out how to be
okay again."

"Oh, honey," Ruth said, her voice breaking a little, "there is nothing
less true in this world. Look at you. You already *are* okay."

They sniffled a moment, then Ruth cleared her throat. "Well. I don't
want you to waste your last night in Warsaw talking to me," she said
briskly. "I'll fax the letters over to the hotel. Oh, and I almost forgot!
The Austin police called here this afternoon. They couldn't find you
at home, so they contacted us. Honestly, Clara, I can't believe a home
invasion is the type of information we have to hear about from your
bartender friend!"

Clara cringed, wiping her tears with her sleeve. "Sorry. I didn't want you to worry."

"For heaven's sake! Sometimes there's reason to worry! Anyway, you'll be happy to know they made an arrest in your case."

"I know. Julián told me."

"It just goes to show you can't trust anyone. You'd think someone in the business of antiques would be accustomed to dealing with valuable artifacts without resorting to criminal activity to get them."

Clara's mind was still catapulting around the idea that it was Marianna Starza, the very person who publicly avowed she had destroyed the metronome, who had given the thing to Nadia. It took a moment for Ruth's words to penetrate. When they did, a chill bore into her chest.

"Hold on." She squeezed her eyes shut. "Julián said the cops arrested two teenagers."

"Yes, but evidently one of the hoodlums was able to identify the man who hired them. He worked in an antiques shop you took the metronome to back in the spring. He was the owner's son, I believe. Really, Clara, you should have been more circumspect. An antiques store in *Texas* with a thing like that?"

Cold tingled down to the soles of Clara's feet as she remembered the young man who had wheeled in the dolly that day at LaFleur Antiques.

"Are they sure it was him?"

"He confessed! The owner brought him to the police station himself. Apparently, the man was devastated. It just goes to show."

Clara felt something catch inside her, a pin entering a lock.

"What is it?" Ruth asked. "I thought you'd be happy."

"I am. I just—" She pictured the tortured look on Tony's face when he confessed what he had done. How he had held his head in his hands as if his own stupidity were incomprehensible. She shook the image away. "I guess I never considered it might have come from me."

The screen of the phone began to flash.

"Mom, I need to go. My calling card is almost up, and I need to find a way back to the hotel. I'll call you when I land tomorrow." She paused, struggling once more to speak. "I love you."

"Well!" The breathy quality returned to Ruth's voice. "I love you, too."

They hung up just as the bus appeared down the street. Clara watched its bleary headlights grow larger as it gained speed. Behind her, the lights of the concert hall blazed onto the sidewalk. Part of her wanted to go back inside so completely that it made her feel as if she had been split in two, and one of her was in the phone booth desperate for the bus to spirit her away to her solitary life, and another warm and dry in the back row of the auditorium waiting for the concert to begin. Just like there had been one of her who had despised Madame all those years and another who had always loved her, and one who longed to play again and another who believed it was pointless to try, and one who wanted to punish Tony and another who wanted more than anything to forgive him.

The bus pulled to the curb. Clara stood in the phone booth for one paralyzed moment, deciding which life she wanted more, then yanked open the door and sprinted back to the revolving doors of the concert hall. She burst into the lobby just as a gush of applause surged from within the theater. By the time she reached the closed doors of the hall, the first thunderous bars of the concerto had begun.

Those first chords had always been to her a warning—the threat of something terrible and wondrous coming, like a tsunami cresting out at sea. She stood transfixed, waiting for the moment when the orchestra would launch like a ship on the black tide of sound, the strings and brass and drums roiling in the thunderous froth. Then the thin, clear bell of the highest octaves of the piano rang out, one slow note at a time. There followed a terrible silence in which Clara held her breath. Then the piano blitzed ahead; the wave crashed upon the shore.

In all these months of thinking about Starza, she had never been able to bring herself to listen to the concerto. The melody had swirled in her head while she mixed drinks or sorted socks or planted flowers in the yard, but until she heard Tony playing that afternoon, she had kept it on the periphery, partitioned in the cordoned-off area of her mind where she kept Madame and the night of the fire and the years that were lost there. Now the whole coil of the past seemed to unravel with his runs up and down the keyboard, until it felt that she was going back in time to Madame's house, walking through the red door, and before that to her first days at the piano playing "Yankee Doodle," and before that to her mother doing arabesques to Tchaikovsky and her grandfather playing Starza's nocturnes on the old Baldwin spinet in the house in Madison. Back to Starza in his music room, scrawling out the notes in his head as fast as he could, hanging on for life and sanity before the end of the magic rope would be pulled up. Then suddenly next to him was Constantia Pleyel. With her injured hand, she reached down and took his pen and added something to the score. A neat flash of notes. Starza turned to look at her, the heaviness of his brow lifting, and placed his hand over her heart.

Chapter 22

Clara—

Excerpts from Nadia's journals. Note that journals from 1881–1885 are lost, presumed destroyed.

—Eleonora

15 March 1890

Today I traveled to Galicia to tell Helene her mother is dead.

I made the journey without advance announcement of my coming, hoping the gravity of my news might permit me entry where the past five years have seen me denied. It did not.

I was shown into the parlor by a maid and waited there, glad to find it clean and respectable, if too dreary for the house of a child. Presently, a woman of about sixty entered and introduced herself as Mrs. Andrysiak, the mistress of the house. I saw in her face Olivier's calculating eyes and shuddered for my niece's fate. She was polite until I revealed my name, at which point I was most abruptly asked to leave. I told her my somber news and begged to see my niece, appealing to her heart, her goodness, her Christian mercy. My entreaties only riled her anger. I was cast out with bitter words against me, Constantia, even our father and mother. That the devil lurks in our blood; that we are a cancer; that Helene is better off now my sister is dead. As I cleared the door, Mrs. Andrysiak warned that should I return, the child would suffer for it.

Oh, how my heart burst to shout the truth about the *real* demon! To tell her how her beloved nephew locked Constantia in rooms and refused food for the children and threatened to kill her if she dared leave! If ever I doubted Olivier Pleyel could harm a child, it vanished the day I visited that wretched hospital and saw the bruises circling Constantia's neck. He had squeezed all breath from her lungs, demanding to know if Helene was his, and still she had not betrayed her child. And so I, too, have held her secrets like stones lodged in my throat, that I might keep her daughter safe. For this—for Helene—I was silent.

I wept as I left that house. As I stepped into the carriage, I glimpsed at the upstairs window a pale child with dark hair. Taking in the first sight of my niece, I cried out, so much did she resemble Constantia. She was not bashful of me, but stood watchful, no doubt wondering who this weeping woman in black might be. I dared only a wave, which the child returned before running from the glass.

5 November 1899

This morning Emilia found me as I was pruning the roses in the garden and announced that a lady was waiting in the parlor. I assumed the new mistress of the Plater's house had arrived to introduce herself. Rather than the young mother I had heard news of in the village, I opened the parlor doors and discovered instead an old woman. When she lifted the netting of her mourning veil, I gasped. Miss S is much aged since I last saw her. But so then must I be. It is the burden of what our most beloved have left us to carry.

I have prayed these fourteen years for the grace to forgive her, and her brother, and Constantia too. I did not know how readily that old evil roiled within me until I saw her on my settee. She must have seen the struggle on my face.

"I have no wish to trouble you," she announced. "But my doctors expect I will not endure another winter, and I should like the child to be provided for after I am gone."

Though I saw that indeed she looked ill, I could not muster pity for this woman who wished now, on the precipice of eternal judgment, to act with honor. Fourteen years ago when I begged her to reveal the truth about her brother so that Helene might have a mother to raise her, she cast me from her house, refusing to believe the child was his. I ventured to remind her of this time, to which she said only, "What I did, I did for my brother. I cannot die by his mistakes, nor my own."

She did not tell me how she came to trust the veracity of my statements about the child. It is of no matter, as she has apprehended the truth with her own eyes. Last month, she journeyed to Galicia, obscuring her name and introducing herself as a friend of the girl's father.

Questions beat within me. Was Helene in good health? Did she seem well cared for? Had there been any love for her in that gloomy house?

Of the child's happiness, Miss S could not report. She spent three quarters of an hour with her, which was all Olivier's aunt would permit before suspicion took hold and Miss S was asked to leave. The girl was well-mannered and agreeable, though quiet. She did not appear to be ill-treated. When I asked if she resembled her mother, Miss S could not meet my gaze. "Yes," she said. "Though her eyes are her father's alone."

Understanding that to gift the child an inheritance of any kind would launch inquiries that could not withstand investigation, Miss S asked me to act as executor of the funds she has bequeathed until Helene is old enough to take possession of them. The money will be put aside with Miss S's lawyer, whose name and address were given to me, that I may pass them along when the time is right. There were in addition a few objects that Miss S wished for me to give the girl directly when and if we are reunited: a carved horse S had loved as a boy. A locket with his child's likeness inside. A lock of his hair. It was only as she set these items upon my table that I understood the depth of her anger fourteen years ago. It was not a sister's sorrow that raged against me then so much as a mother's grief. For that, finally, I can begin to forgive her.

The last object she removed from her bag, however, I could not take so willingly. When Miss S extracted it from its box, I stood from my chair and demanded to know why she had kept this object that had brought such sorrow to us all.

"It was not the object that brought us sorrow," she spat. "It was the hand that wielded it."

She thrust the box into my hands. "There is an inscription on the lid. I do not understand it."

She nodded toward it as if it both enraged and beguiled her, and I saw that this uncertainty about her brother had troubled her, the same way Constantia's many secrets have these years troubled me. Though she was too proud to ask for my help, Miss S had come here hoping I might alleviate these mysteries. Thus compelled, I lifted the lid and saw there a phrase from one of Constantia's letters. I recounted to her what Constantia wrote about the day S had comforted her about her injured hand and her absent boy.

"Perhaps your brother intended to make a gift of it to her," I said.

Miss S regarded the metronome with a look of distaste.

"And what of this?" she demanded, pointing to a small number—LXXII—etched into the metronome's winding key. "Did your sister convey anything about that?"

Of this, I confessed I knew nothing.

Looking dissatisfied with both the knowledge I had imparted and that which I had not, she rose, leaving the metronome on the table. "The child may have it if she wishes."

Seeing that now was the time to ask the question I have so longed an answer to over these fourteen years, I summoned my wits.

"Constantia wrote to me of the music she was composing. Did you find evidence of her pieces among your brother's belongings?"

A look of indignation came over Miss S's gray face—something of that old haughty lift to her chin.

"There were many scores in my brother's house. He frequently received pieces from novice composers seeking his encouragement. Whether your sister's trifles were among them, I could not say."

"But I might," I rejoined. "She sent me a few measures in her letters, and I would know her writing besides. Allow me to take a look at what was left."

"It is only a few short pieces," Miss S insisted. "None so very good, I assure you."

"If they are not so good, why not give them to me?"

Even in the pallor of her illness, I saw color rise to her cheeks. She bid me good day and walked to the door.

"Constantia sent me a nocturne she wrote," I called after her, keeping my voice strong that she might hear in it the confidence of truth. "She sent it in a parcel of linens, so her husband would not discover it. You can guess my astonishment when last year I heard the melody drifting from a window in Łódź. The young lady practicing at her piano informed me it was a work by Aleksander Starza. She called it *The Melancholy Sister*."

Miss S's thin lip curled the same way it had when she spat at me the night I prostrated myself at her feet fourteen years ago.

"Your sister was a murderer and a thief. Any music she claimed to have written was a result of my brother's influence alone."

"I have it here still," I continued. "I can prove that it was hers. There are letters, too. I know what plagued him. Surrender her music and I will not reveal it."

Miss S's gloved hand was on the doorknob, but she turned and crossed the room with such vigor I thought she might strike me.

"My brother was a genius," she hissed, "your sister a murdering whore. No one would believe you."

I did not waver. "Surrender her music and we will not test who may believe or not," I said.

Miss S's eyes blazed, but I saw her calculate the strength of my threat. "Give me the letters," she finally said. "Give me the letters and the nocturne, and after I am dead, I will have the rest of your sister's trifles sent to you."

My instinct was refusal. How could I trust her word?

"Give them to me, or I will burn it all," she spat.

Feeling my power over her gone, I went to my trunk to retrieve the nocturne and enough of Constantia's letters that Miss S might be satisfied. When I passed the pages to her, my grief rose beyond my will.

"Olivier Pleyel is dead," I pleaded. "You are dying. The child cannot be hurt by the truth. Why not tell the world they loved each other?"

"Do not dare claim that she loved him!" Miss S shouted. "I would have died before I hurt him. *That* is love!"

She rushed from the room, banging open the parlor door. Emilia heard it in the kitchen and came running. She found me stunned on the sofa. The items Miss S left were on the table. I collected them one by one, these objects that belonged to a man I wish had never lived.

9 October 1901

Helene will be sixteen today. I have sent my yearly letter to Galicia, as ever. Adam tells me to give up—that she is lost to me; that
this is for the best. But I will not relent. I promised Constantia that
her daughter should know the truth.

M—S—has been dead a year, and still there is no hint of Constantia's music. I will go to my grave cursing her name.

15 October 1908

A letter arrived today from Galicia. When I saw the address, my
heart leapt. Helene! Alas, it was not to be so. My annual letter was
returned, with a note from the new occupant of the home. Mrs.
Andrysiak is dead this past spring. Her niece, the man said, has
moved away. To where, he did not know.

20 December 1918

Christmas is upon us, and indeed it is a season to rejoice. The terrible war is over. All my sons have been spared. And now, at last,
news of Helene.

An inquiry made two years past in Kraków has yielded word.
I have learned that a family there by the name of Oginski had
in 1915 a governess by the name of Helene Andrysiak! Today I
received a note from the mistress of the house. She informed me
that Helene, who was much beloved by the lady's three children,
lived with the family until 1917, at which time she moved on to the
household of an agriculturist from Przaszysz. As the Oginskis fled
to Denmark during the war, the lady had no knowledge of Helene's
current whereabouts. She confessed she was relieved to hear from
me, as she has been burdened for some time by information she
learned months past about Helene's new employer. She would not
reveal the full of it, as the information came secondhand from her

maid, but it seems the master of the house, while masquerading as a gentleman, may be less than honorable with the young women in his employ. This information accelerated my haste.

This morning, I engaged a lawyer to search for her. Mr. Narbut had business with my dear Adam years ago, and I know him to be a trustworthy man. I left with him a portion of the money M—S— put aside for Helene and a letter instructing her to come to me, that she might gather the rest that is her due. After much deliberation, I left also with Mr. Narbut the metronome. I have kept it these many years, locked away like so much else, thinking I would give it to Helene with Constantia's letters to prove to her the truth of her parents' love. I had the injured corner repaired before I left it with Mr. Narbut, hoping it might heal the past, though when I handed it to him, I felt only sorrow. For Constantia, for *them*. The great lights, dark. Oh, Constantia, keep your daughter safe, that when I join you in heaven, I may greet you with the news that she knew the truth of your great love for her.

Clara lowered the page.

The answer to the metronome's mysteries now sat in her lap—the puzzle as solved as it would ever be. Marianna Starza had given the metronome to Nadia, who had given it to her lawyer to pass on to Helene, who then gave it to Madame. The only question remaining was how Jozef Zamoyski had gotten it—or claimed to have gotten it. Madame had known her grandmother was Constantia Pleyel all along. She had the letter Nadia had written to Helene, and perhaps had even heard the story of how Helene had gone to Nadia's home only to be turned away. What Madame could not have known was that she was also the descendant of Aleksander Starza. Helene had never reunited with Nadia to learn the full truth. The thought prompted a resurgence of sadness in Clara's heart. Madame had never known that she was the product of her grandparents' great love. Just as Helene had never known her mother had not been a madwoman, or that her real father wept when he held her in his arms. Everyone knew only part of the story. Everyone except Nadia and Marianna, who knew it all. Or at least, most of it all.

She sat alone in the back of the concert hall, the tissue she had dug from her backpack clumped in a damp clod in her fist. The auditorium was empty, but the stage lights still blazed onto the giant Steinway. Down below, Jerzy was shuffling along the rows with his yellow trash can, dumping concert programs from the seats.

She had waited for Tony for an hour after the concert, lingering outside the door to backstage until the last trombonist exited. Eventually Jerzy let her in. She ran all the way to Tony's dressing room. She was still furious with him, but her anger paled in the shadow of all the last few hours had illuminated. There was so much she wanted to tell him. Not only about Starza and Constantia Pleyel, but also Jerzy and the broken doorknob, and Marianna Starza's letter to her great-grandfather, and Madame's time at the orphanage. Ready to share all this and more, she raced down the hallway, only to discover that the door to Tony's room was wide open. She called the hotel, but he wasn't there either. The next bus wasn't due for an hour. All she could do was wait.

Jerzy called to Clara from the front row, shielding his eyes as he peered up at her. "*Idę za kulisy.*" He held up his key ring and pointed backstage.

Clara pointed to her seat. "I'll meet you here."

He wheeled away, the trash can rumbling behind him. Clara listened to it roll into a distant hallway, then recede behind a closed door.

She stood. The steps down to the front row were mauve velvet, illuminated by flag lights on either side of the walkway. She took them without hurry, thinking of Constantia's last days. For months, Clara had wondered what had caused her to forfeit her freedom rather than tell the truth. Eleonora had been right. Constantia had loved something more than music and Starza, more even than her own life. Whatever lies she had told or truths omitted, she had done it for Helene.

She stopped at the bottom of the steps and stood eye level with the stage. Then, in one fluid motion, she placed her palms on the golden wood and hoisted herself up.

The piano gleamed at her.

"Hello, old friend," she said softly.

The bench was still high, adjusted for Tony's long legs. Clara gripped the knobs on either side and lowered it, the ritual still native in her hands.

She had often wondered what it would be like to sit on a stage again. In her imagining of it, the music her body had once contained would have drained out of her, and there would be nothing in her hands to play. Sitting here now, the keys were as familiar as her own face, middle C a lighthouse shining the way. The question of what to play never made its way into her conscious mind. It was simply decided, as if another, wiser her had known all along. Her bones ached beneath her scars.

The Melancholy Sister begins with a plaintive G octave in the lowest bars of the piano. The sustained ring of that lonely sound has been described as a wail, a moan, a cry from the beyond. In the great empty hall of the Warsaw Symphony, the notes hovered over the piano, only for the first time in the twentieth century, the sound that rang into the hall, if anyone were there to hear, was not the music of Aleksander Starza. *Different metronomes*, Madame had written. She had suspected all along.

Following the great mournful cry of the opening, the melody tings forward in the upper register, like a child's laughter in the last sunlight of an autumn day. Then comes the shift to E Minor, a demi-turn to sadness. A lonesome treble trill. Clara fumbled the notes. They clanged into the hall with a terrible grating sound, and for a moment the rage and despair of ten lost years quivered in her fingers. *You see?* she thought. *I could never have come back.*

But the body does not always listen to the mind. For even as her mind was rising from the piano and closing the fallboard, railing against hope and healing, her hands were moving forward, wrists dipping and flexing with the undulating melody, a tugboat on a placid purple sea. And then she too was on the boat, sailing not into the sunset but parallel to it, the light spreading around her into sun-drenched dusk. The sound rose, gaining volume as it expanded against the giant acoustic panels above her and reached from there into the vast eaves of the hall.

But I could never be the way I was, she thought. *It is too late.*

The voice that replied was not Clara's, but the other voice, almost as familiar, that had been whispering in her ear for years.

You could. You can. SHE did. Don't you understand, you foolish, foolish, girl?

PART III

Chapter 23

1 September 1939

THE OPENING BARS OF *THE MELANCHOLY SISTER* had always reminded Zofia of a boat starting out to sea. The first low notes groaned like a ship departing dock, followed by waves of purple water, so deep. Of course, it was a sea in her mind. Zofia had never been to the ocean. Once, Sister Elena took her to the National Museum on her birthday. There she saw a painting of a ship leaving harbor, a froth of lavender foam breaking across its bow. That was all—a single ship on dark water riding into dusk, the sky the color of crushed pansies. When she played the nocturne, she felt the purple waves lap against her, pulling her out to sea.

Long before she ever heard the name Aleksander Starza or knew what he had written or how he had died, Zofia had loved the nocturne. In her very first days at St. Stephen's, Sister Elena played it in the evenings after the children went to bed. Lying on her cot in the dormitory, clutching her mother's silver-backed hairbrush, Zofia strained to hear the sound of the piano coming from the dining hall. The melody mingled with the whimpers of loneliness coming from the youngest girls and boys, all of them, and Zofia, too, aching for the same thing: the arms of a mother.

Now whenever Zofia played the nocturne, she thought of the children at St. Stephen's with an urgent desire to run to Kraków and hold them all, and, at the same time, to be held herself. If there was not to be a war with Germany, as some still hoped, or if the war was short as others promised, Zofia would perform the nocturne as her encore at the concert next month with the Warsaw Symphony. After the fire of the Third Concerto, she would break open her heart on the keys for all of motherless Poland to hear.

She paused, lifted her hands, and made a note in the score. More *doloroso* in the sixth bar. The audience must feel the pain. Then again she began. The great humped curve of the piano floated on the purple waves.

It was after midnight. Inappropriate for a woman to be alone in the conservatory, much less in the studio of Jozef Zamoyski. But there was nowhere else for her to practice.

Zamoyski had expelled her after he discovered that the conductor of the Warsaw Symphony invited her to perform. Her male colleagues, always laboring to please him, had been delighted to change the locks on all the practice rooms at his request.

"The concerto is no piece for a *woman*," Zamoyski had sneered when he dismissed her. "Even a woman as ugly as you." There was a tiny yellow stain on his front tooth, like a dribble of mustard had dried there and embedded in the grainy bone. It reminded Zofia of the indentation on the lowest G-sharp of the piano at St. Stephen's, where a boy named Dominik had fallen into the piano and broken his teeth on the ivory. "But since you are so ready to become famous," Zamoyski spat, "you no longer need my help." He thrust the paper announcing her dismissal into her arms. "You are a fly buzzing your nonsense on this piano. The world will forget you."

Zofia had lowered her head to hide the hot tears filling her eyes, but that night as she lay in bed, her hand twitched, picturing what it would feel like to pry the mustard stain up the way she had used one of Sister Alicja's sewing needles to pry dust specks from the bed of the wounded G-sharp. She imagined sliding the needle under the stain. Then she would start in on the tooth. Did he think that she did not know what it meant to fight? She, who had been wrenched, screaming, from her mother's corpse, whose father had denied her very existence, whose only living family had refused to take her in? Zamoyski had never forgiven her for her talent. She was supposed to be no one, a charity case the conservatory bestowed on the orphanage to satisfy a favor Zamoyski owed to St. Stephen's patron, Mr. Fronczak. Since the day she'd arrived at the conservatory, she had endured smacks on her neck, books hurled across the room, the ash of his cigarette in her hair. Despite it all, after her first recital, the newspaper called her "the most remarkable pianist to emerge from the conservatory this century." The next day, Zamoyski dropped his cigarette down her collar while she played the first Bach partita. The ash smarted down her back in a hot shower of sparks. She removed it and kept playing. There was no option to quit. Mr. Fronczak had died last spring, and with him the favor Zamoyski had repaid with her admittance. Sister Elena was gone, too, and the pittance the remaining Sisters scraped together for her tuition and her room at the boarding house was less each month. Her whole existence was on loan against making something of herself. And so, for weeks, she had snuck into the conservatory every evening and waited in the girls' lavatory on the third floor until the custodian turned off all the lights. Everyone knew Zamoyski kept the key to his studio on a hook beneath the coat rack in the corridor. Until the concert arrived, she would practice all night, with towels stuffed beneath the door to muffle the sound and blackout curtains over the windows in case Hitler chose tonight to send the Luftwaffe bombing.

The nocturne picked up speed, the notes blending, falling, raining beneath her hands. On the lid of the piano, her grandmother's metronome tocked back and forth: the drive of the rain, the pull of the tide.

"Where did you get this?" Zamoyski had asked that day he came to St. Stephen's to hear Zofia play.

He had picked it up from the piano to examine the back corner, where the wood was a different color. Zofia had been alarmed by the wild covetousness in his eye. Hunger, she knew from experience, was dangerous.

"It was my mother's, sir," she had said.

"It is very unusual," he said, peering at the engraving on the winding key. "I have only seen one like this before." He lifted his head to look at her, his eyes roving over her the way Sister Maria scoured the chickens in the yard before deciding which one to cull. "Where did your mother get it?"

Zofia glanced at Sister Elena, who shook her head ever so slightly. They had agreed that if she was to go to the conservatory, she must not reveal the truth of her relation to Constantia Pleyel. In this one case, Sister Elena had told her, she was permitted to lie.

"Her employer gave it to her, sir," Zofia had said, keeping her eyes locked on the black and white tiles of the floor. "He was a violinist."

Zamoyski studied her a moment longer, then set the metronome back on the piano and turned to Mother Julia.

"She is not nearly as good as Fronczak recommended, but as he is my wife's cousin and has asked for my charity, I will admit her. I understand that you are in need of help for her tuition." He tapped the top of the metronome with a long, slender finger. "You can remit this as payment for her first term."

Zofia's mouth opened to protest, and Sister Elena's, too, but Mother Julia smiled beatifically. "How generous!" she had said.

 Zofia wept for days. The metronome, the silver-backed hairbrush, and an old letter were all she had left of her mother. They had kept it on the table beside the bed they shared in their boarding house, atop a white silk handkerchief. At night, they wound it up to muffle the snores of Mrs. Papara in the next room. Now, alone on her cot, Zofia set the metronome and curled her body around it, missing her mother so badly it ached like an empty stomach.

Sister Elena had knelt before her and taken her hands the same way she had when she led her to the piano years before. "It is just a worldly object," she had said, cradling Zofia to her chest. "If you go, you will make Godlike music with your training. Honor your mother with your future, not something that reminds you of the past."

"But why does he want it?" Zofia had cried. "Why can't he get another?"

She had not understood until she overheard Zamoyski boasting of it to the violin teacher one day while she waited to be called in for her lesson.

This was his, Zamoyski had said. He pointed to the back corner where the wood was a different color and grinned. *And this is where the whore hit him with it.*

After that she had different questions. Alone in the library, she read about her grandmother, then read and reread the letter her great-aunt Nadia had written to her mother. Surely it could not be *that* metronome. Surely it could not.

The nocturne was building toward its final crescendo. Zofia lifted her hands for the concluding *sforzando* when the door banged open. Before she could even turn around, Zamoyski's fingers were in her hair.

"Trespassing *whore!*" he hissed, hauling her from the bench. She was too frightened even to scream. She fell to the ground, her shoulder knocking against the floor in a flash of pain. Zamoyski stood over her, swaying. Shaking, Zofia pushed herself up, reaching her arm out to put space between them.

"I'm sorry," she said. "I just needed a place to practice."

"I'll have you arrested!" he roared, lurching forward. Zofia shrank against the wall.

"I just used the piano," she said, trying to keep her voice strong. "I'll leave now, and I won't come back." She ventured a wary step toward the door, the way she had once crept past a pack of street dogs that skulked outside the orphanage. As soon as she moved, Zamoyski lunged at her with the full force of his drunkenness. She crumpled beneath his weight and fell to the floor. In a flash as quick as a grace note, the heel of his shoe was on her wrist.

Zofia gasped. She felt the bones of her forearm squeak together.

"Please," she said. "My arm."

Zamoyski bent down and thrust his hand into the pocket of her dress, prying out the key. "Thief!" He spit on her chest, the smell of cognac and old beef misting onto her face.

"Please," she whispered. "I promise I won't come back."

He smiled then, an evil smile she should have known better than to trust, and lifted his foot. Moaning, she rolled toward her arm, folding it into her body. She never looked up to see the shoe coming down again. All she felt was the whoosh of air it made on its descent, a faint whiff of urine and brick.

The shriek that tore from her mouth as his heel ground into the flesh of her palm was a sound of dismay as much as pain. She tried to jerk away, but he pressed harder, the heel of his shoe—his beautiful shoe, the color of brandy in candlelight—seeming to grind through her skin and bones to the planks of the floor.

"Please," she begged.

Zamoyski leaned into his heel and smiled, the yellow mustard stain a dull ochre color in the shadowed room. "You will be nothing," he said. "Just as I predicted."

The refusal that surged through her at this thought gave her strength. With her hand still pinned beneath his shoe, she lifted her leg and kicked him in the calf. She heard two uneven steps as he fought for balance, then the thud of his skull as he fell against the ledge of the piano. The room shuddered as he landed beside her, his eyes closing like a book slammed shut.

Zofia screamed in relief as the pressure left her hand. She tried to move her fingers. A spasm of hot pain traveled up the back of her arm, but nothing moved. A new cry, one that encompassed the pain of her entire life, groaned from her mouth, and she began to weep in convulsing sobs that hurt her arm with the force of their quaking. But there was no one to hear. Nowhere in the world she belonged or could heal or turn to for help. Just as there had been no one for her mother, or her grandmother before. There was no one but herself. *You must be strong,* her mother had said as she died. She had stared into Zofia's face, tears streaming down her own. *You must be your own mother now, my beautiful girl.* The memory stayed her tears. Gritting her teeth, she rolled to her injured hand, and, with the other arm, cradled it as if she were the mother and this arm her child, whispered to it the way she had whispered to the whimpering children at St. Stephen's. With her good arm, she pushed herself up.

A gurgle deep within Zamoyski's stomach made her look up. Vomit was sliding in a yellow glug from the corner of his mouth, traveling down the side of his cheek. For one electric moment, she listened as his breath drowned in the back of his throat like water glutting down a clogged drain. Then his legs and arms began to twitch.

Zofia backed away, panic jangling through her body. Zamoyski's twitching became more violent, his hand clenching in a fist. She bent to the floor and tried to roll him over. With only one arm, she might as well have tried to lift the piano. When finally, with a great straining groan she managed to tip him over, he slumped against the floor like a sack of flour and was still.

Zofia stood over him, her heart racing. She looked at the clock on the wall, realizing with terror that it was 6:15. Soon the custodian would arrive, and the first early students. She could go to the police. Or the dean of the conservatory. But what would she say? How could she explain herself? Paralyzed, she stood in the center of the room clutching her arm. On the piano, the pendulum of the metronome was suspended toward the right, pointing out the door. She reached for her coat at the exact moment the sirens began to wail.

First it was a distant cry—a single siren on the edge of the city. Then, as if a conductor had raised his baton, the others joined all at once, a symphony of warning. Fear clutched her throat. She had heard the sirens often in the drills, but never like this. And atop that, there was a new sound, far away. A drone in the distance. Planes.

Quickly, she bent to Zamoyski's body. His billfold was in the breast pocket, the leather damp from the vomit that clung to his coat. Zofia removed two of the three banknotes she found there, leaving a five złotych so as not to cause suspicion. She crumpled the others into her pocket. It was only ten zloty. Not enough for even a train ticket to Kraków. The drone of the planes grew louder. Her eyes fell on the instrument cabinet against the wall.

There was no time to make a clear decision, no plan beyond escape as she ran across the room and unlatched the iron clasp. Six violin cases lay in the semi-dark. She unlatched the case nearest her and recognized instantly Zamoyski's Guarneri. Even in shadow, the wood shone like it was coated in glass. Sensation was beginning to return to her injured hand in hot streaks of pain, and now her palm began to throb with the wild beating of her heart. She slid the body of the instrument down the front of her dress, where it warmed against her skin like a living being. Latching the case so it would not look disturbed, she opened another, removed a second violin, and stuffed it inside her coat.

Finally, she turned to look at the metronome. Her pulsing hand twitched. It was risky to take it. To whom besides the violin teacher had Zamoyski bragged of its famous owner? Who else might know where he had obtained it? It, more than anything, could implicate her.

She deliberated not even a moment before lifting it from the piano. With a tremor of joy that felt like coming home, she placed it in its box.

Chapter 24

29 December 1885

THE HOUSE WAS COLD. Colder than any December Marianna could recall. She had kept a fire blazing in every hearth, yet her hands were as cold as the frosted windowpanes. Even the wood of the desk seemed brittle, as if the boards might shatter at a touch. She shivered beneath her wool shawl, then willed herself still.

The bookshelves were dusted, the floor swept of dirt and ash, the desk cleared except for the two wooden boxes she had removed from the locked bottom drawer. Marianna had inherited her father's sense of order along with his desk. Aleksy had hated this room. When they were children, he had liked to assemble his cavalry of toy horses in the doorway, resulting in roars of protest from their father. Marianna had been the one to gather the horses and escort Aleksander away. Why must he always make a mess? *The mess is alive,* he had said, as if this were clear as sunlight. She had tidied his messes, then and always. She had flattered exasperated teachers and apologized to half-wit conductors, gone to Paris to pluck him from the brink of ruin, and later crushed an opium pipe beneath her boot to save him again. She had soothed his cries and wiped his nose without complaint. Now she had a final mess to clean.

The work was slow, done only at night after the servants had gone to bed. Every page must be scoured, compared, sorted. Aleksy had deceived her with *The Melancholy Sister*. The mistake could not be repeated. Marianna had recognized something new in the piece—something more *womanly*—but had not thought of Pleyel. She had not believed her capable. When Aleksy revealed the truth, in one of his endless pleas for Marianna to bless their disgraceful union, she had raged at him for hours. *You have debased all we have worked for. How many others has she written?*

Many more, he had said, looking at her with that new hardness in his eyes that Marianna hated. He did not need her anymore. *But none that you have seen. The nocturnes were meant to be published together. They are a complement to one another, as she and I are. I will tell Christoph when the time is right. The deception will not reflect upon you.*

This sentimental talk had infuriated her. *The world will never have faith in you again when it is made known you whored your name to that woman!*

He had regarded her placidly, the same as when she had collected the toy horses from the doorway. *One day when she is free of her husband, we will tell the world the truth. Then they will have someone else in whom to place their faith.*

On the mantel, the metronome ticked to a stop. The room felt colder in its silence. She rose and walked to it. When she had presented it to him all those years ago in Paris, the sight of it had brought the first smile to his face she had seen in months. At night, when the headaches tormented his sleep, she could hear him in the next room winding it again and again. "It paces my heart," he said once. "That it might not quit for misery." *What misery it has brought you yet, my brother,* she thought.

She had known something terrible had happened when Marek knocked on her door the night of Aleksy's death. Usually, he demanded his copecks before he issued the report of his master's doings. This time, he trembled. Marianna went instantly on foot, slipping down the streets of Warsaw in her black cloak, choked with terror. On the threshold of Aleksy's parlor, she stopped. The piano bench was upended, the desk chair in pieces. Aleksy lay on the floor, his beautiful gray eyes—so fine and deep—open like an unblinking fish. Marianna buckled, falling to her knees. For twenty years, she had lived in fear of such a moment. Now that it had come, she found she knew exactly what to do. Her nightmares had been her rehearsal.

She ordered Marek upstairs to gather the contents of the bedroom, then built up the fire. For two hours, she cleared the house of his secret—receipts from the apothecary, jars of his pills, letters from herself asking after his health, warning him to stay away from Pleyel. *She will sop up your talent like bread in fat until there is nothing left.* From that first night at Valeska Holland's house, Marianna had seen him smolder the way he did when a new melody flared in his mind. She had watched them from the next room, Aleksy's color rising, Pleyel's head so high on her chicken neck it looked as if it could tumble off with a flick of Marianna's finger. Marianna had counted on the collision of their hubris. It was the only time she had been wrong about him.

Each letter went into the fire. The paper curled, her words of warning turning orange before they capsized into flame. Next, she sorted through the desk, burning a bill from the doctor, the journal of his illness, letters from Pleyel. Never would his genius be besmirched by even a whisper of disease. The music—some in his handwriting, some in another's—she packed in a crate and took with her. The last thing she did before she left was return the fire iron to the hearth. Careful to keep her skirts from Aleksy's blood, which was warm and thin from the heat of the fire, she knelt to the ground and kissed him one last time. Then she pressed a fistful of rubles into Marek's hand and ordered him to fetch the police.

When the chief inspector returned the metronome, she had wanted to destroy it, to crush it into a thousand jagged pieces and incinerate them in a blazing fire. She had been on the precipice many times but found she could not. She did not recognize its new mahogany box. Nor could she explain its odd inscription. Had Aleksander intended to give her the metronome as some sort of peace offering?

Was it an acknowledgment of *her* pain at losing him these years, at giving up her own chance for a husband and children, any other life? Or—the thought seemed to cause the fire to darken—had he planned to give it to Pleyel? The engraving on the winding key was similarly troublesome. She recognized the seventy-two from the *Adagio* of the Third Concerto. But why have it engraved? Why this number, of all the others? Now she lifted the metronome from the mantel, forcing herself to look at the broken corner where the wood had collided with her brother's life. She slid the lion's head to seventy-two, then wound the key so tight it felt as if it would shear off like a sliver of ice. When it began to tick again, she returned to her desk and pulled the next piece of music from the crate. An impromptu, clearly *hers*. Marianna set it in the second box, where the pile was growing. What she might do with it, she had not yet determined.

Chapter 25

4 December 1885

ALREADY HER HANDS WERE GOING COLD. It was a cold more penetrating than the fireless room or the sodden sleeves of her dress. They were cold in a way that she knew would never feel warm again. Not on any instrument. Not in the hand of any man.

She looked around the room, straining for a plan. In the silence, she heard the watch in Aleksy's vest tick, tick. The watch had belonged to his mother. He had wanted to save it for Helene. The thought of the baby caused a torrent of panic to course down her arms. Tick, tick. *Think!* she urged herself.

The piano bench was upended. Manuscript paper from the piano trio they were writing littered the carpet, some notes in her hand, some in his, the pages comingling in a puddle of blood. The music stand was collapsed on the floor. She had fallen into it when she tried to wrestle the fire iron from Aleksy's grasp. He screamed when she reached for it. It was a scream not of the man she knew, a man with a soul deeper than the River Vistula, but of a deranged animal. Careening beyond her reach, he swung the iron at his head, roaring as the metal shuddered against his skull.

"Aleksy!" she had screamed. "Stop! You are hurting yourself!" But he did not hear her.

Again he brought the iron down against his head.

She lifted the desk chair and ran at him with the legs spearing outward. They collided in a terrible splintering of iron and wood. Aleksy buckled in a heap. Constantia fell into the piano in a clangorous gong of the lowest octaves she knew would sound in her mind for the remainder of her life. The fire iron clanked to a stop beneath the settee. In the wake of the noise, Aleksy looked up into her face, dismayed. For one instant she saw a flicker of his real self light his eyes. Then it was gone. He lunged for the letter opener on the desk.

The metronome, too, was on the floor. The corner was gashed, a single dark hair caught in the teeth of the raw wood. The sight of it turned her stomach.

You see, it belongs to you now, he had said when he gave it to her, showing her the *LXXII* engraved on the winding key. *Though I must warn you it is broken and cannot be fixed, like me.* He smiled, a glimmer of humor surfacing from the depth of his sadness.

You are not broken, she had insisted. *You are not.*

She could not remember picking it up. She had simply reached for whatever object was near.

Think, the voice said. *Quickly now.* Marek would be back within the hour. She must be gone before he returned. There was no explanation she might offer that would not betray them. To reveal Aleksy's illness, the music, their love would be to reveal Helene. And then— the shivering worsened. She had seen Olivier watching the child in the cradle. Once he had pressed his hand on the baby's chest, staring in her eyes while she thrashed to be free. Constantia knew what he was looking for. The child looked nothing like him. All he needed was one shred of suspicion to cast her out forever. Or—the shivering convulsed her body—worse. He had no tenderness for children. Less for girls. Oh, Helene. She moaned, remembering the first time Aleksander beheld her perfect face. *I fear she will not know me*—his voice had trembled, and he had paused a full minute before finally he lifted his head—*as I wish to be known.* The pain in his eyes had been worse than the snapping bones of her fingers all those years ago.

What if I hurt you? he had wailed last week as he battled the voices in his mind. *What if I hurt Helene?*

"You will never hurt us," she had said. "Take your mercury. You always get better, you have told me yourself. Until then, play Bach. It will order your mind."

Love is your weakness, Nadia had warned her. *Your husband will discover you. Starza's illness will worsen. There is no future there. You are a fool.*

Then so I am, Constantia had said, but had not believed it. How could the music, the love, Helene—how could it be foolish? She looked down at the metronome, askew on the floor. It was the illness that was foolish, Olivier, the unforgiving world. Not them. A sob clogged her throat.

"Forgive me, my love," she said aloud to Aleksy, and clutched his hand to her chest.

She had reached the desk first, seizing the letter opener behind her back. Without anywhere else to hide it, she ran across the room and dropped it into the depths of the open piano. It clanked to the bottom of the instrument. He roared in dismay, eyes unseeing, and barreled toward her with a shriek Dante could not have conjured. It had been involuntary, to reach for something to stop him. All those years of being ready to fight.

She saw the real Aleksander inhabit his face one last time as the metronome crashed to the floor—a blink of surprise and horror and even—she knew she had seen it, she *must not* forget—forgiveness. She caught him in her arms. He was light as a child. A pile of bones.

The blood on the floor was spreading, creeping like a storm front over the wool rug. *Go swiftly, my love,* he seemed to be saying. *Do not wait. I warned you this day may come. Take Helene and Stani. Go to London. Get away from him while you can.*

Stani. Telling him about London had been her gravest mistake. She should have lied until the moment the train was barreling them away. When Olivier returned from Paris that afternoon, Constantia had been in her bedroom nursing Helene. The milk had stopped flowing from her breast at the sound of his voice reverberating through the house. Only the maids seemed unsurprised at his arrival. Constantia had known he was paying Lucia to monitor her whereabouts. She had not known it was the rest of them, too.

All afternoon Constantia had stayed near him, feigning pleasure at his early return and delight at his performance that night for the Warsaw Benevolent Society. He would sing Donizetti's "Quanto é bella," a tender piece for a savage man. Constantia had smiled and flattered him—not too much lest she raise suspicion—all the while vigilant that Stani should not risk a word. The boy had hovered fawningly about his father, turning to look at her slyly, as if to taunt her with her secret.

He had demanded to go with Olivier to the concert hall despite her thousand protestations. She relented only after she felt Olivier listening more closely. Before the carriage left, she had whispered to him as she placed his hat on his head that he must not tell his father about their plan. "We will reveal it later, as a surprise," she said, trying to make it a great game.

"But I don't *want* to go to England," the boy said, so loud she had pressed her hand over his mouth. He smiled deviously through her fingers and looked at her with the same derision as his father. "*I'm* staying with Papa," he had announced, and ran down the hall toward the door, each clack of his shoes sickening to her heart.

The thought of leaving him made her legs quake. Nor could she risk staying to know if he had revealed her secret. Olivier would kill her if he knew the truth. She must take Helene and send for Stani later, somehow. Somehow. A scream rose in her chest, and she felt she might go mad. If only they had left yesterday as planned. They had been so close to happiness. So close.

The watch ticked louder in her ears. *Leave, leave, you must leave now.* She clutched Aleksander's hand. It was the color of ice that had thawed and frozen again in winter sun. His hands, so large and beautiful and strong.

She kissed them for the last time, then leaned over and kissed his cold lips. "Goodbye, my love," she whispered.

She rose and was horrified to see her dress was soaked to the knees. She looked around for her cloak, her eyes flitting about the ravaged room that she would never see again. She would do it all again, even knowing the end. She pulled the cloak around her shoulders, then slipped the silver watch from Aleksy's vest and placed it in her pocket with the bag of rubles he had placed in the desk for their journey. The last item she took was the metronome. Gently, she lifted it from the soaked carpet, wiped the blood with her dress, and slid it into its box. *From pain, we must make beauty.* That was the day all had changed. From thence, their future had been written.

"Do not worry, my love," she whispered. "We will get out. We will be safe. Your daughter will know you as you wish to be known."

She knelt and kissed him a last time, then tucked the box beneath her arm and stole into the night.

Chapter 26

MORNING SUN STREAMED THROUGH the windows of the Hotel Bristol. Clara blinked into the bright light, swimming to the top of a murky sleep. She had fallen asleep in her clothes. The bedside lamp was still on. The phone rested on the bed beside her. She snatched the handset from the cradle and pressed it to her ear, straining for the double beep that indicated someone had left a message. But the dial tone droned as normal. Dejected, she hung up.

Last night when she returned to the hotel, she had gone straight to Tony's room. She waited in the hallway for an hour before inquiring at the front desk, where she was informed that Tony had already checked out.

"Do you know where he went?" Clara had asked, feeling her stomach twist.

The young concierge, a friendly brunette whose nametag read *Agnes*, gave Clara a sympathetic look. "I'm sorry. He said he had a plane to catch."

Clara swung her legs off the side of the bed. Her neck hurt from the tormented angle of her sleep and her right hand was stiff and cramped, the knuckles of her ring finger swollen. But there was also within it, deep below the scars, a tingle of awakening. She looked down at this, her old enemy, and for the first time in years a seedling of hope unfurled within her.

Agnes was still working the desk when she went down to the lobby to check out. "Good morning, Miss Bishop," Agnes said cheerfully. "We have a fax waiting for you."

Clara felt her head lift an inch higher, hoping for news from Tony. But as soon as Agnes passed her the sheaf of pages, Clara saw her mother's handwriting and remembered the letter from Marianna Starza to her great-grandfather.

She leafed through the pages, flipping past Marianna's original missive to Aunt Pauline's translation. Clara scanned down to the section about the metronome.

> . . . several items of family import entrusted to Mrs. Nadia Brzezińska of Łódź, on loan for a young lady of association with our family for when she comes of age. Mrs. Brzezińska is, however, a woman of unreliable predilection. I urge you in no more than five years' time to inquire about these objects at the address below. Should the young lady in question not have claimed the items, you must insist that they are returned so that they may remain with the rest of the family keepsakes, as they hold interest for future generations interested in my brother's life and work.

"All right, Miss Bishop, I've checked you out," Agnes said. "Mr. Park paid the balance before he left. May I call you a taxi for the airport?"

A fresh tide of regret washed over Clara as she thought of Tony leaving alone. "Yes, please," she said, then thanked Agnes and rolled her suitcase toward the exit.

The rain had rinsed the sky clean, and the day was blue and fine, with a crispness to the air that portended the change of the season. Buses groaned past the hotel. Businesspeople in suits hurried by with to-go cups of coffee. Clara stood on the sidewalk and looked around at this city of past and future, old and new. She would probably never come here again. Then again, a year ago, she would have said the same thing. She rolled her suitcase to the curb, then opened Marianna's letter and read down to the end.

. . . There is in my home on Foksal Street in Warsaw a painting by the artist Jakub Rostworowski, a portrait of myself in our family home. Most of our family's belongings I have donated to the Warsaw Society of Music, cognizant as I have always been of the world's keen interest in any object my brother may have touched or beheld. The Rost- worowski painting, being of myself, holds no such value to a wider audience, and thus it is my wish that it should stay within the family for some years after my death, at least until such time that the family deem it appropriate to—

Here, Aunt Pauline had scratched out many words before deciding on the right translation.

— ~~share~~ ~~reveal~~ expose it to the world. Until then, it must be discreetly handled. I urge you to come to Warsaw to retrieve it and receive my instructions, as it is much too delicate to entrust to shipping. As my days are waning, I await your swift reply.

> Your Cousin,
> Marianna Starza

The final page of the fax featured a shorter letter, dated 22 January 1900, just a few weeks before Marianna's death. There was no transla- tion of this one. Clara peered down the street for her taxi, then, seeing none, walked back inside to Agnes at the front desk.

"Would you mind translating this letter for me?" she asked.

"It would be my pleasure." Agnes reached for the letter.

Dear Cousin,

I received your letter with great disappointment. While I am heartened to learn that you intend to take your custody of my brother's music with due gravity—and do not mistake my everlasting gratitude in this, for the music is paramount to all—there is still the matter of the Rostworowski painting that must be addressed. I understand the journey to Warsaw to be a significant inconvenience, and though I do not myself have children, I yet understand the difficulty a separation from your new baby boy must engender. Yet I must entreat you once more to come to Warsaw. As the sole descendant of our family line, you are now the protector of the great legacy of Aleksander Starza. There are matters to discuss in this regard that should not be left to the chance of letters or the interpretation of lawyers. One has only one's own reputation and integrity in this world. You must see to your own, and as my only surviving kin, I ask that you assist in preserving mine. If you are fortunate enough to live until you are an old man, you will understand that concern over whether one's affairs might be appropriately conducted after one is gone is the ghost that haunts the last days of the dying. I made a commitment that I must honor, and I entreat you to assist me in discharging it.

Your Cousin,
Marianna Starza

Agnes passed the letter back to Clara.

"Is that all it says?" Clara asked.

"Yes." Agnes nodded. "That is all."

"Okay," Clara said. "Thanks again."

The taxi was waiting at the curb. The driver, a man in his thirties with a Beatles haircut and a cigarette hanging from the corner of his mouth, jumped out.

"Airport?" he asked.

"Yes," Clara replied, and sank into the back seat.

They passed signs for Old Town and New Town, the monument to the Warsaw Ghetto. ALEKSANDER STARZA HOUSE AND MUSEUM, a sign read in English. Clara thought of the painting of Marianna in the foyer, watching each visitor enter the door, still monitoring her brother's affairs. Clara's great-grandfather had obviously concluded that a transatlantic crossing for a painting wasn't worth the trouble. *It is much too delicate to entrust to shipping.* Clara thought of the heavy wooden frame. What about it was delicate? She looked at the clock on the taxi dashboard. She had four hours before her flight departed. Maybe she would drop the fax of Marianna's letters at the museum herself. Perhaps Gregor would have an idea about why Marianna was so insistent about the painting.

"Can we make a detour to the Starza Museum?" she asked the driver. "I won't be long."

He shrugged at her in the rearview mirror. "No problem." He swerved the taxi onto the next side street, then parked at one of the entrances to New Town, where concrete pillars blocked the road to vehicles. Clara got out. "I'll just be a few minutes," she said.

The driver looked happily at the meter and turned up his radio. "I will wait."

A line of visitors was already queuing out the door of the museum. Clara maneuvered past children climbing on the Starza statue and tourists flashing cameras before joining the line behind a British family wearing matching purple T-shirts. Marianna's words swirled in her mind like a melody stuck on repeat. *It is my wish that it should stay within the family for some years after my death, at least until such time that the family deem it appropriate to expose it to the world . . . I made a commitment that I must honor.*

Clara's heart began to thrum. Ignoring the cries of protest from the people in front of her, she broke from the line and mounted the steps of the porch. The woman selling tickets behind the counter looked up sharply as Clara sped past.

"Przepraszam! Excusez-moi!"

"Get Tomasz," Clara said without stopping, and marched toward the painting.

For a moment, she stood gazing at Marianna, who sat behind the large desk, poised and young and in control, her face placid and unreadable. Then Clara's attention moved to the wooden frame, which stretched six inches from the canvas in every direction. In one fluid motion, she reached up and pulled it from the wall.

Everyone in the room gasped. The woman behind the ticket counter began to shriek. Clara tuned her out and set the portrait on the floor. The frame was a solid piece of French walnut. The painting was recessed inside, nestled into a rectangular cutout just large enough to accommodate the stretched canvas. Clara ran her fingers over the wood. The crevice between the painting and the frame was too narrow to fit more than the tip of her finger. Gently, she tested its pliability and found it immobile. She hesitated only a moment before digging in her backpack for her keys.

The ticket clerk began to scream for Tomasz. Two young men who'd been waiting in line had approached and were now shouting in Italian, first at Clara, then at each other, seemingly arguing about whether to forcibly stop her. Above them all, she heard Tomasz yelling as he ran down the steps. But already she had inserted the key to her house into the crevice beside the canvas. She began to pry the painting from the frame.

"Stop, stop, stop!" Tomasz's words rushed toward her as he approached. "Clara! What are you doing?" Just as he reached for her shoulder, she felt the frame pop loose.

Tomasz recoiled as if he'd been struck. "No!"

Clara did not even look up. As gently as she could, she slid her hand behind the painting and felt a cavity in the frame much deeper than the canvas had inhabited. Holding her breath, she stretched her long fingers into the unknown space and brushed against the rough edge of a stack of paper, bound together by a frayed piece of twine.

After a Century of Shadows, New Light on Starza's "Dark Angel"

by Tony Park

In the summer of 1881, the composer Antonín Dvořák wrote to his contemporary Aleksander Starza about his admiration for Starza's recently published Sonata in F-sharp Minor. Dvořák was so taken with Starza's piece that he composed a set of variations for string quartet on the sonata's primary theme. Starza replied with his thanks, and in the letter wrote of the sonata's genesis: "A dark angel sometimes speaks to me, not in words but in sound. She talks of the sadness beyond this world. She is unbearable to behold, but beautiful to hear. I shudder when I see her, and yet find I cannot turn away."

The identity of this "Dark Angel" has long been a point of conjecture for music scholars. Some have thought her a literal woman torturing Starza with love. Others have imagined her a personification of the depression the composer suffered his entire life. In recent years, I myself have conjectured that the Dark Angel could have been an opium-induced hallucination. Now, more than a hundred years after Starza's death, the discovery of a clandestine relationship between Starza and the pianist and composer Constantia Pleyel suggests a new identity for this mysterious ethereal being.

Starza spent the greater part of the 1860s in Paris, where he relocated to avoid political unrest in Poland. Depressed, homesick, and concerned for the fate of his home country, the Paris years were productive compositionally but personally difficult for the young composer. The only respite came for a few brief months in 1866, when the twenty-one-year-old Starza fell in love. The affair, with a woman he calls Annabelle, was intense but brief. In less than six months, Starza wrote to his sister Marianna that Annabelle had rejected his proposal of marriage and left him for another man. "I have been deluded," a heartbroken Starza wrote. "Neither her body nor her mind were true."

A few weeks later, Starza suffered the first of many episodes of severe depression he was to endure in his life. He describes to Marianna "a malaise that grips both my body and my mind, poisoning my thoughts." This description and other reports in Marianna's journals have led scholars to consider Starza's illness of 1866 to have been strictly a mental health event, albeit a serious one. This assumption is unsurprising given the emphasis in recent decades on Starza's mental health, with diagnoses as wide-ranging as manic depression and schizophrenia applied to explain the composer's volatile moods. That Starza was a sensitive and highly emotional individual from childhood, prone to bouts of "melancholy" and explosive frustration, is well documented. But a letter written from Starza to his friend, the violinist Henryk Wieniawski, depicts the illness of autumn 1866 in concretely physical terms: "A fever burns my body. My skin aches," he wrote. "My head flames with a blazing heat that silences all music, perhaps forever." He reports that he saw a doctor, and of the examination wrote, "I have seen my death foretold. It is a death of the heart, and then the mind."

In the mid-nineteenth century, syphilis was a well-known and dreaded disease. Its victims include some of the nineteenth century's greatest luminaries, from Robert Schumann and Franz Schubert to Charles Baudelaire and Édouard Manet. It was also a disease kept secret, concealed by those who suffered from it and covered up by their families—even after death—because of the heavy stigma it carried.

Early syphilis infection included symptoms such as fever, rash, and headache—many of the complaints Starza enumerates in his letter to Wieniawski. The doctor Starza consulted in Paris would have undoubtedly recognized in Starza the early symptoms of a possible syphilis infection, a disease which then had no cure. The penicillin that today can easily treat syphilis was not discovered until 1928. In Starza's time, the mercury commonly prescribed to manage the illness was itself toxic, causing a host of punishing side effects without doing much to address the underlying disease. Thus, the fate of a nineteenth-century syphilitic was largely dependent on chance.

After the symptoms of initial infection resolved, an individual with syphilis could appear to have made a full recovery. Significantly, after a time he would also no longer be contagious. But the disease would remain dormant. Some individuals could live out their days without symptoms, while for others, the disease would eventually progress to neurosyphilis. A late stage of infection, neurosyphilis causes symptoms that range from headache and dizziness to paralysis, convulsions, delusions, hallucinations, paranoia, and dementia. It is, quite literally, a slow "death of the mind."

After what most scholars believe to be a suicide attempt in October 1866, Marianna Starza joined her brother in Paris, nursed him to health, and brought him back to Warsaw to live with her in the family home. Immensely influential in her brother's lifetime, Marianna has emerged as the single most powerful force shaping the way the world has come to view his death and music. Much of what is known about the famously private Starza is from Marianna's personal journals, as well as the letters she kept between herself and her brother. Marianna knew she was writing history, and the extent to which she manipulated that historical record is yet unknown. Perhaps no greater evidence of this can be attested to than the discovery this past September of Constantia Pleyel's hidden oeuvre in, somewhat fittingly, a portrait of Marianna herself.

Discovered by the pianist Clara Bishop, a distant relation of the Starzas, after a letter from Marianna to Bishop's great-grandfather was unearthed in a family attic, the music concealed in the painting reveals Pleyel to be a composer on par with Starza himself. The collection includes seven nocturnes, a scherzo, five intermezzi, four sonatas, a berceuse for the couple's daughter, and the beginnings of a piano concerto. As has been widely reported, Pleyel has also been discovered to be the author of the famous *Melancholy Sister* Nocturne in A Minor previously attributed to Starza. The scores were concealed in the portrait to fulfill a promise Marianna made to Pleyel's sister, Nadia Brzezińska, to return Pleyel's unpublished compositions. Rightfully concerned that the publication of Pleyel's works would raise questions about the authorship of her brother's compositions, Marianna hid the scores in the painting. They were accompanied by a letter instructing her cousin, Clara Bishop's great-grandfather, to turn over the music to Pleyel's sister "only after a sufficient period of time that those who might falsely claim that Pleyel wrote any of my brother's music are deceased." Among those Marianna listed included Starza's butler, Marek Poldowski; Pleyel's husband, Olivier Pleyel; and Starza's longtime publisher, Christoph Windscheid.

Given Marianna's own stake in shaping her brother's legacy, what she knew of Starza's illness and when she became aware of it is impossible to say. Gregor Orzeszkowi, a music historian at the Starza Museum in Warsaw who was the first to speculate that Starza may have suffered from syphilis, has documented several instances in Marianna's journals that allude to a secret illness. In November 1876, Marianna describes an episode that left her "utterly astonished," in which her brother reportedly threw an inkwell at one of his pupils, a well-to-do young woman from a prominent Warsaw family. The young woman was unscathed, her ruined dress the only casualty. Nonetheless, her indignant father threatened legal action, thus igniting a stream of gossip about Starza's volatile disposition that would remain with the composer for the rest of his life. Though today Starza's famous temper is well known, prior to the 1870s, his "eruptions" as Marianna called them, were verbal only and never included violence. Moreover (and in contravention to common assumptions about the composer), Starza himself was appalled by his behavior. He immediately dismissed all his students, writing miserably to one of them that "I am a beast, unfit to be in the presence of man. My music is all I have to atone to the world for the blight I bring upon it."

The sudden rift between the Starza siblings in the spring of 1881 has mystified scholars for decades and has had the added effect of obscuring the final years of the composer's life. Marianna's journals from this time rigorously document her brother's prodigious compositional output but contain little about his personal life. What *is* known is that Starza met Pleyel in February 1881. In March, the two began a correspondence. In May, Starza moved out of the family's Foksal Street residence in what Marianna called "a repudiation of all we have worked for." That September, Pleyel began lessons at the composer's home, and though the first several months of their relationship as pupil and teacher were turbulent, it is perhaps not insignificant that Starza chose this year to withdraw from performance life and remain permanently in Warsaw. Months later, he sent his publisher a staggering collection of fourteen new works for the piano, along with a note: "Melodies have never sung so frequently in my mind as now. They flow from my hands as if I had already heard the music and was simply transcribing it from memory." Starza, who had renounced all women after Annabelle, was falling in love.

For a century, the world has believed Constantia Pleyel to be an unstable, frustrated artist who murdered Starza in a fit of jealous rage. In recent years this theory has been challenged, most notably by the Polish scholar Eleonora Konopnicka, who has revived the merits of Pleyel's self-defense claim and argued convincingly that Pleyel's husband was an abusive man who may have played a role in her incarceration at Ragin Mental Hospital. Letters recently uncovered from Pleyel to her sister reveal a startling new dimension to these theories. In the three years of Starza and Pleyel's romantic relationship, the two served as each other's muses, composing incredible works for the piano. They also had a child, Helene, who went on to become the mother of one of the greatest pianists of the twentieth century, Zofia Mikorska.

In the weeks leading to December 4, 1885, Constantia Pleyel wrote to her sister that Starza was ill: "He warned me this day would come, but I did not realize how terrible it would be. He begs me to leave him, and wounds me with the most terrible insults to spur me to go. But I know it is the fever in his mind that speaks. I would no more abandon him than I would you."

Pleyel took the truth of what happened on the night of December 4, 1885, to her grave. Nevertheless, it seems that at least some of the details of that fateful evening were revealed to her sister, who, in a 1919 letter to Starza and Constantia's daughter, wrote, "What the world believes about that night is untrue." In her journals, she alludes to an illness, saying, "I know what plagued him."

The beginning of the end for many untreated syphilitics is commonly an intense psychotic episode, after which death from general paresis usually comes within a few excruciating years. Whatever happened on the night of December 4, it is reasonable to presume that the composer was not in his right mind. Did Pleyel kill him in an act of self-defense, as Eleonora Konopnicka has always believed? Or was his death a terrible accident, as Pleyel told the police during her initial interrogation? Like so much else about Starza, we will never truly know.

When I first learned of the relationship between Pleyel and Starza, I believed that perhaps the Dark Angel was Pleyel herself. But after reading Pleyel's final letters, a new theory emerges. Perhaps Starza's Dark Angel was something far more insidious: a hallucination borne from a mind tragically aware of its own withering.

Since the days of its first discovery, the composer's death has been thought of as a theft from the world of music. It is possible instead that 1885 was the beginning of the end of both the man and the artist Aleksander Starza. Robert Schumann, another famous, tortured syphilitic, spent the final years of his life in an asylum, believing he was being persecuted by demons and desperately clinging to a mind riddled with dementia. Whatever her role in Starza's death, Constantia Pleyel may have granted an act of love she did not know she was bestowing: the opportunity for Starza to end his life as the man he was and wanted to be, the music in his mind still playing.

Chapter 27

CLARA STIRRED A VIEUX CARRÉ behind the bar. Up, light on the vermouth. She strained the liquor into two glasses, then, with expert fingers, dropped a cherry into each one.

The Andromeda was decorated for Christmas. A tree glowed in the corner. Twinkle lights hung from the whiskey shelf. On the piano, Jerry was cycling between Christmas carols and a greatest-hits list of farewell songs. He caught her eye as he began the opening bars of "Goodbye, Yellow Brick Road," adding a Baroque flourish to show her he'd been practicing his trills. Clara gave him a thumbs-up. She'd been teaching him lessons every Friday before the bar opened. He had always wanted, he said, to play Bach.

Julián set a tray of empties on the counter. "The couple at table three is asking for a Brown Derby. Do you know what that is?"

"Whiskey with grapefruit juice and honey." She passed him the second Vieux Carré, and they clinked glasses. "I'll make you a cheat sheet before I go."

Julián groaned, the pom-pom of his Santa hat flopping over his shoulder. "I almost didn't hire you, you know. I had a feeling you wouldn't stick around."

Clara pulled the honey jar off the shelf, afraid if she looked at him, she might cry. "You do realize I've worked here for six years."

Julián made a sound of disapproval, but lingered close while she mixed the drinks. For weeks, he'd been trailing her like a lost kid. Clara didn't mind. Of everything about The Andromeda, she would miss him the most. When she passed him the cocktails, he enveloped her in a tight hug.

"You have a job here whenever you want. You know, if being famous doesn't work out for you." He kissed her on the cheek, then walked the drinks to table three.

The bar was busy for a Wednesday. She suspected Julián had padded attendance with the promise of free drinks. John and Colette LaFleur had been the first to arrive, with a fresh apology for their son, who had avoided jail time as a result of Clara's testimony. Everyone, she had come to believe, deserved a second chance. The LaFleurs stood in the corner drinking French 75's with her parents, who were staying at the Driskill Hotel for a few days before the three of them flew to Wisconsin to visit Aunt Pauline. Jerome and his boss from the library, Jeff, were on the stools next to Barb and Lisa, Jerome gesturing wildly with his glass of Pepsi, seeming to mime the blow of a blunt object to the head.

The only person who had declined to attend her going-away party was Tony. She hadn't expected him to come but had allowed herself to hope anyway. The morning Clara tore apart Marianna Starza's portrait at the Starza Museum, he was already on a plane back to Chicago. The one loss that day was that he hadn't been there to witness it. Clara told him about the triumphant recovery of Constantia's music over the phone later that night, after which had come a difficult conversation about where things stood between them. She had hoped they might rekindle the romance of their night at the Bristol Hotel, but Tony had kept his distance. "You've always been that person for me," he said. "The one I always wondered about—what might have been. But I've messed things up with you twice now, and I want you in my life. Maybe it's safer to just be friends."

In the months since, his series of articles, *No Mere Starling: The Love and Music of Constantia Pleyel and Aleksander Starza*, had catapulted him back to fame. He had invited Clara to join him on the lecture circuit and coauthor his forthcoming book. She had been tempted, mostly because she was so glad to hear from him. Ultimately, she declined. The spotlight, she realized, had never really been for her.

Ruth sauntered up to the bar, adjusting her red silk scarf. "I'll have another of these French 75's, Clara," she said, passing over her empty glass. "I must say, I'm beginning to see why you like it here." She looked around the room appraisingly. "I think with a fresh coat of paint and maybe some more modern lighting, it could really be quite charming."

"Thanks, Mom."

"Though I don't understand why this address is any better than sending mail to your house. It's not as if you live in some crime-riddled neighborhood. Where did your mail go all those years?"

"Who knows?" Clara said and passed her mother the drink.

"I guess I'll have to start sending it to your office at the university. Or perhaps to Julián. A PO box?" Ruth looked at her pointedly. "Or maybe it's been worked out by now?"

Clara felt her shoulders creeping toward her ears. "Maybe it has," she said.

"I'm so glad to hear it," Ruth said, then smiled primly and walked away.

Tony had been right that Clara had a career's worth of knowledge to share. News about her involvement in the discovery of Constantia's music had resulted in a profusion of job offers from universities around the country. The one that quickened her pulse was from UT, right down the street. She wasn't ready to leave Texas. She would teach Constantia's music to her students, and if she ever chose to perform again, as her new hand therapist was promising she would, it would be of Constantia and Starza's works, and how they echoed and informed each other like bells ringing from two separate towers, playing in harmony, apart. She knew if she ever returned to the stage, she would not play the way she used to. It would be different by necessity, and totally new.

Down the bar, Julián was laughing with starry eyes as Jeff the librarian tried on the Santa hat. When he came to the tap to pour Jerome another Pepsi, Clara leaned against the bar next to him.

"Somebody's got an apple in his eye."

Julián lifted his chin. "I don't know what you're talking about."

"Hmmm," Clara said. "Maybe I should give him your number."

Julián cut his eyes at her. "Don't even think about it."

"What is it you like to say? 'Somebody has to move things along'?"

Julián turned to face her. "Listen, Professor. You can complain all you want, but we both know if it weren't for me, none of this"—he waved his hand at the party—"would be happening. Your piano teacher lady is lucky it turned out the way she wanted. If it weren't for my nagging, you would have stuck that metronome in a drawer and never looked at it again."

"Maybe. I think she knew me better than that."

Had Madame really wanted Clara to go on a quest to discover Constantia's music, or did she simply believe that the metronome belonged to Clara as Starza's descendant? She had come to accept that she would never really know. But Madame had known that Clara would be able to investigate the metronome's past in ways Madame herself had never been able to. Clara was Starza's heir, both in music and by blood. No one would question her authority to have it. Madame had figured out that the metronome was Starza's long ago, back when she was making her metronome calculations in the score of the *Fire Concerto*. But she didn't understand how Nadia had obtained it because she never knew that Starza was her grandfather. Perhaps more importantly, she could never have proven that the metronome was rightfully hers without implicating herself in Jozef Zamoyski's death, or in the theft of the two violins.

Had Madame been the one the janitor heard playing the piano in Zamoyski's studio in the early-morning hours of September 1, 1939? Or had she slipped in during the chaos of the invasion to take the metronome and violins? It was impossible to say. But after learning about Zamoyski's treatment of Madame and the specious grounds on which he expelled her from the Conservatory, Clara had been anxious to prove that at least one of the items Madame was alleged to have taken from him was hers all along. Before leaving Poland, she and Eleonora had gone to Kraków to visit the orphanage at St. Stephen's. An afternoon of sorting papers in the musty basement had yielded an old ledger from 1937. It showed that Madame's first-term tuition at the Conservatory was waived "in exchange for Zofia's metronome, which Mr. Zamoyski was quite taken with." This, along with copies of Nadia's journals and the letter from Nadia to Helene, had convinced the Dabrowskis to drop their threat to sue Clara. Whatever disappointment they might have suffered was overshadowed when Clara revealed that Zamoyski's missing 1738 Guarneri violin, now worth nearly two million dollars, was safely in the possession of Alan Feldman.

Somewhat fittingly, it turned out that it was Feldman himself—not Tony's friend at Sotheby's—who had inadvertently alerted the Dabrowskis that the metronome had resurfaced. Three days after the beneficiaries were called to Madame's house, he gave a private performance with the Guarneri in New York, regaling the audience with the tale of the bizarre gathering at Madame's home and the disbursement of her instrument collection. A guest at the concert had been an associate of the Dabrowskis' eldest son, who related the anecdote to his friend, prompting Mr. Dabrowski to anonymously call Mr. Borthram's office and inquire about the metronome. Feldman had agreed to surrender the Guarneri with no contest. The second violin—the Amati Madame sold to the Rademakkers—was still missing, presumed hidden somewhere in the corners of the former Third Reich. Jess was still searching.

"I still don't have any ideas about what the seventy-two is all about, though," Clara said. "I don't think I'll ever figure that one out."

She thought of the metronome, housed now at the Warsaw Conservatory pending the opening of the Constantia Pleyel Museum that

Eleonora had begun planning. Its presence had been a draw for music historians across the world, who continued to argue about the significance of the number seventy-two. So far, no one had put forth a convincing theory.

Julián shrugged. "There's some romance in that. Maybe not all their secrets need to be revealed."

Clara smiled. "I think you're right."

"Speaking of romance—" Julián looked at her sternly. "Are you still mooning over Tony?"

Clara made a face. "I don't *moon*."

"Right." Julián rolled his eyes, then put his arm around her. "Well, next time somebody falls in love with you, Clarita, maybe you'll be ready." He squeezed her tightly. "In the meantime, I know you said no presents, but I have a surprise for you in my car. No arguments!" he said, seeing Clara begin to object. "I'm parked down the block. You go ahead. I'll see if anybody needs another round, then meet you out there."

She grabbed her coat from the rack near the door, then walked out into the chilly night. The stars were bright overhead, the air crisp. Fourth Street was quiet, the stoplights green into the distance. A group of people coming back from a holiday party walked past her, huddled together against the cold. Clara smiled at them. Seven months ago, she had thought this would be her path forever: working at The Andromeda, biking home from the bar each night looking forward to Bingo and a drink and a shower. She would miss her unremarkable life and its solitary pleasures. But Madame had been right: *Find a way to play again, whatever you must do. Otherwise, your life will be a waste.* Finally, Clara understood.

She spotted Julián's Jetta beneath a magnolia tree down the block. She was almost to it when she saw him.

Leaning against the trunk of the tree, shadowed by the evergreen branches, was a tall figure in a dark suit. He straightened when he saw her coming, shoving his hands into his pockets as if suddenly unsure.

"My flight came in too late to make it on time."

Clara's heart fluttered, a quiet, bright trill.

He looked at her over the expanse of sidewalk, as if afraid to come any closer. "Am I too late?"

She knew what he was asking. She shook her head. "Not too late," she said, and hurried forward to meet him.

It was after two when Tony kissed her good-night at her door with a promise to pick her up in the morning. "I don't believe in starting over anymore," he had said. "So how about we pick up where we left off, and I take you to breakfast?"

She was sorry not to invite him to stay the night, but they both knew there was something waiting for her inside that she had to face alone.

Bingo licked her hand when she unlocked the door. The great beast was there, in the dining room, as her parents had promised. It had been their Christmas gift to her, at her request. Even with the legs off, the movers had barely been able to clear the door. It filled the entire room, the butt of the instrument sticking out into the hall. Bingo stood with her, staring at it skeptically. The black finish gleamed in the moonlight.

"What do you think?" she asked him.

He tilted his head to the side in disapproval, and she laughed. She walked forward, running her hand over the great, smooth curve.

"Welcome home," she said, then sat at the piano and began to play.

Epilogue

January 1885

THE FIRE WAS HIGH AND BRIGHT in the hearth. Neither was comfortable in darkness, though for different reasons. He feared the specters that visited him on the worst nights, faceless angels that hovered in every shadow. For her, darkness meant hiding behind locked doors. When they were together, the lamps were always lit, the fire large. There was nothing they wished to hide. All they might have concealed had been exposed the first time they passed the manuscript paper back and forth. What was any nakedness—a bare chest, a leg, a breast—after that? Besides, there was not time to waste. His illness stalked always behind them. Her husband waited at home, sniffing her hair each time she returned. One would catch them. They must move swiftly. There was so much to share. So much to write.

Tonight, though, is a special night. The Third Concerto is finally complete, but for the tempo of the second movement, on which they do not agree. They lay curled on the scarlet rug, their bodies like sixteenth notes pressed together.

"You want it too slow," she said. "It plods, like a cart through mud. It should glide." She made a dart of her hand like the silhouette of a bird, her crooked fourth finger an injured wing.

He stroked the black coarseness of her hair. "You are wrong. It is meant to be melancholy. Any faster and it would seem to frolic."

She made a sound of disagreement but said nothing. The concerto belonged to him, aside from a lament in the second movement she had written for low brass. When he first showed it to her, shoving the score through the carriage window that day she returned from France, he had enclosed a note that she destroyed alone in her bedroom. *The weight of being away from you, now and always.* She had understood. Some absences stretch beyond the present to include the irretrievable past.

He rested his hand on her heart, feeling the life pulse so steadily there, as if it would beat forever and could carry him on its strength. After a time, he stood. Plucking the metronome from the mantel, he wound the key and set the pendulum ticking. For a moment he listened, his face rapt, then set it on the floor beside her.

"That is it," he said, decisive. "Seventy-two."

She shook her head. "Too slow!"

"No," he said. "Listen."

He took her hand in his and placed it on her chest. The pendulum rocked. She felt the pulse of her heart beneath her hand, and his hand on top of that, until the two sounds dissolved into each other, beating on, and on, into the cold night.

Historical Note

The Truth Behind Aleksander Starza and The Fire Concerto

Aleksander Starza never lived or breathed except between the pages of this book, but his story was not created from nothing. Like so many fictional lives before him, his is drawn from those of real people—composers of the Romantic period who could themselves have been characters in a novel.

Frédéric Chopin was a Polish nationalist who lived most of his life away from the political tumult of his occupied country. His longing for home imbued his music with a yearning that has moved listeners for two hundred years. The musical genius Robert Schumann died in an asylum at age forty-six of what was thought to be general paresis of the insane—complications of late-stage syphilis. Johannes Brahms, plagued by insecurity about his talent, sometimes threw his musical drafts into a fire in despair. These composers and more found their way into the character of Aleksander Starza.

In similar fashion, the historical record provided the inspiration for Starza's faulty metronome, which is based on scholarly conjecture about the real, famously inaccurate metronome of Ludwig van Beethoven. The specific theory about Starza's metronome being too fast at one end and too slow at the other is drawn from the fascinating paper "Was Something Wrong with Beethoven's Metronome?" by Sture Forsén, Harry B. Gray, L.K. Olof Lindgren, and Shirley B. Gray, which posits a theoretical explanation for the great composer's inconsistent metronome markings.

And then of course there is Constantia Baranowska Pleyel. Like many of the characters in this book, her name is an homage to real female musicians of the nineteenth century whose contributions to music are now footnotes at best: the Polish soprano Constantia Gładkowska, who attended the Warsaw Conservatory at the same time as Chopin and is remembered primarily for being briefly engaged to him; the Polish composer Tekla Bądarzewska-Baranowska, who enjoyed popular success of her piano pieces but who, despite her talent, was never considered a serious composer; and the virtuosa pianist Marie Moke Pleyel, to whom Chopin dedicated his op. 9 Nocturnes.

More than these nominal tributes, it is Constantia Pleyel's struggle to be a woman artist that is real. Many music enthusiasts have heard of Clara Schumann, the nineteenth-century pianist and composer whose musical achievements are beyond mythic when we consider what she was up against: pervasive sexism, money troubles, the death of multiple children, an insane husband. Yet for every Clara Schumann whose name has endured into the twenty-first century, there are a thousand Tekla Bądarzewska-Baranowskas. This tragic omission illustrates one of the greatest vulnerabilities of making art. There is always the risk of obscurity—of no one reading that novel, or hearing that piece, of the brilliant painting collecting dust in an attic trunk.

This, as much as any divine inspiration, is the artist's contract: There are no guarantees. The ultimate truth behind Aleksander Starza and Constantia Pleyel, as well as Frédéric Chopin and Robert and Clara Schumann, is their struggle to create, and to do so despite self-doubt, financial duress, loss of patronage, illness, and grief. It is a struggle to find meaning in life's challenges—to take our pain and make from it beauty, as Starza would say, and to persevere despite obstacles. That is the life art teaches us to live.

Creative expression is born from a desire to express in tangible form this wild human experience in a way someone else might understand. The creative act has power to provoke transformation and joy—sometimes for the artist alone, and that in itself is enough to make it worthwhile— but sometimes, too, for the reader, viewer, or listener miles or centuries away who finds, for a brief time, that same transformation and joy tunneling, perhaps just barely perceptibly, into their heart.

Acknowledgments

This book is the product of many generosities. Special thanks to Henry Dunow, a brilliant reader, outstanding agent, and steadfast support. I feel privileged to know you.

To my editor, Claire Wachtel, thank you for your insightful criticism and for seeing all this book could become. To the rest of my team at Union Square & Co., especially Juliana Nador and Barbara Berger, thank you for your enthusiasm and for your devotion to the details. Jared Oriel, I love the jacket of this book.

Endless thanks to Sarah Jarboe, who read every scrap and draft of this novel and the unpublished one before it. You've been making me a better writer for twenty years.

Thank you, Małgorzata Stegenka, for patiently correcting my Polish.

To the many people who lent their professional knowledge, personal insight, and lived experiences to the technical and historical information in this book, I hope I did you justice. Thanks to Rebecca Hartsell Samson; Haley Jennings, RN, BSN; Laura Landenwich, Esq.; Agnes Jackman; Sue Landenwich; Professor Mary Ann Grim; Whitney Ensor, DPT; Adam Portelli; Anna Moore; David Toner; Kathi West; Gina Portelli; Phil Stosberg; Rebecca Metcalf; Bob Dixon; Alison Heustis; Kathleen Coughlin; and Jill Clateman. If I've made any errors from the wealth of information you provided, it is entirely my own fault.

The Fire Concerto would not have been possible without the academic and historical works of dozens of writers whose research helped me create the world of this novel. I read widely to write this book, but feel especially indebted to the following works: *God's Playground: A History of Poland* by Norman Davies; *A Romantic Century in Polish Music*, edited by Maja Trochimczyk; *Pox: Genius, Madness, and the Mysteries of Syphilis* by Deborah Hayden; "Was Something Wrong with Beethoven's

Metronome?" by Sture Forsén, Harry B. Gray, L.K. Olof Lindgren, and Shirley B. Gray; the *Chicago Tribune* series "The Great Violin Chase: How Nazis Targeted the World's Finest Violins" by Howard Reich and William Gaines; *The Life and Works of Frédéric Chopin* by Jeremy Siepmann; *Music in Chopin's Warsaw* by Halina Goldberg; "Diagnosing Unnatural Motherhood: Nineteenth-Century Physicians and 'Puerperal Insanity'" by Nancy Theriot; "Witnessing for the Defense: The Adversarial Court and Narratives of Criminal Behavior in Nineteenth-Century Russia" by Louise McReynolds; "A Fallen, Abominable, Wicked Girl" (about Clara Schumann) from the podcast *Decomposed*, hosted by Jade Simmons; *The Mask of Warriors: The Siege of Warsaw, September 1939* by Marta Korwin-Rhodes; and *The Pianist* by Wladyslaw Szpilman.

Speaking of research, thank you, Denver Public Library, for procuring every obscure interlibrary loan I requested and cheerfully walking it to my car during COVID.

To the early readers whose enthusiasm and criticism helped shape this book into what it is, I am forever grateful: Jay Wilson, Michael Barber, Gillian Stern, Kathleen Coughlin, Mary Frances Landenwich, Ralph Landenwich, Greta Landenwich, Laura Landenwich, Jenna Barnes, Andrei Moldoveanu, Niles Barnes, Rebecca Metcalf, Bob Dixon, Gina Portelli, Kristin Bellucci, and Fred Smock.

I would be remiss to bookend a novel about a teacher and student without mentioning the teachers who got me here: Paul Griner, who taught me for one year and mentored me for fifteen more; Rebecca Hartsell Samson, who talked to me for countless hours about music, grammar, violins, and life; and the late Fred Smock, who was that person for me—the one who said, at the exact right time, *You should be a writer*.

Finally, to my husband, Jay Wilson, my greatest champion in art and in life—thank you. I love you.

Discussion Questions for
The Fire Concerto

1. Clara's scars make her trauma visible to the world. She is very conscious of her appearance, and many people she encounters remark upon it. How has her physical appearance shaped her personality? How does physical appearance shape personality in general? What do you think about the ways Clara deals with the attention and comments she attracts because of her scars?

2. Madame had a profound influence on both Clara and Tony, though in different ways. Was she a good teacher? How do you think Madame felt toward her students, especially Clara?

3. Both Clara and Tony, as well as Starza and Constantia, were child prodigies. All had complicated relationships with their parents. What responsibilities do parents have toward children with exceptional talent? Is it fair for Clara to resent her parents? In what ways does her attitude toward them change by the end of the book?

4. Mothers are hugely important in this book, even though, as in real life, they are often not featured in the prime action. Ruth, Constantia, Helene, and Starza's mother all had significant impacts on their children. All faced difficult and sometimes devastating choices regarding their children. How did you feel about each mother in the book? To whom did you most relate? Were there elements of them you found yourself judging or disapproving? If so, why?

5. The women in this novel struggle against great obstacles to pursue their artistic dreams. Are there women in your own life or family history who attempted to pursue a dream despite societal pressure or forces to do otherwise? How did it go for them? How are they remembered?

6. The early working title for this novel was *Descendant* to reflect the theme of what is passed down from one generation to the next, both from family member to family member and from teacher to student. To what extent is Clara's life shaped by events that occurred before she was born? To what extent are these types of generational forces active in your life, or the lives of those to whom you're close? How does Clara attempt to break free from them? Is she successful?

7. How did Madame's life experiences shape her personality and her teaching? Do you understand her? Sympathize with her? Why didn't Madame tell Clara her version of what happened the night of the fire?

8. At the end of the book, Constantia says that she would do it all again, even knowing the outcome. Do you agree with her that her relationship with Starza was worth the cost? Was she foolish to fall in love with him? Was Starza selfish to admit his love for Constantia, knowing his own circumstances, and hers?

9. An important theme in this novel is the way that physical limitations such as illness and injury impact our ability to pursue the life we want. How did the characters respond differently to their physical limitations? Has an injury or medical condition ever derailed your life plans? If so, how did it affect you, in both the short and long term?

About the Author

Sarah Landenwich is a writer and writing educator. Also a classically trained pianist, her debut novel, *The Fire Concerto*, was inspired by her love of music of the Romantic period. She lives in Louisville, Kentucky, with her husband and daughter.